ARGYLES
and
ARSENIC

Also available from Pegasus Crime:

Plaid and Plagiarism
Scones and Scoundrels
Thistles and Thieves
Heather and Homicide

BOOKS ONE, TWO, THREE, AND FOUR OF
THE HIGHLAND BOOKSHOP MYSTERY SERIES

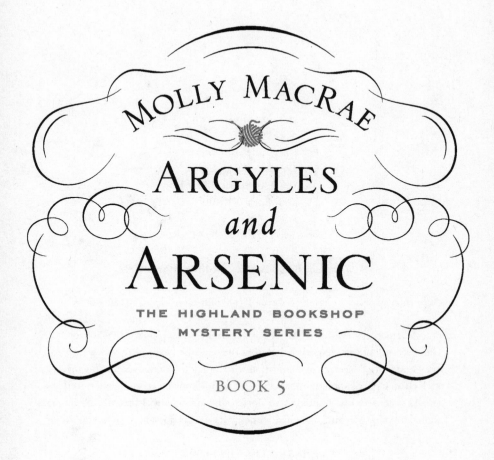

MOLLY MACRAE

ARGYLES

and

ARSENIC

THE HIGHLAND BOOKSHOP MYSTERY SERIES

BOOK 5

PEGASUS CRIME

NEW YORK LONDON

ARGYLES AND ARSENIC

Pegasus Crime is an imprint of
Pegasus Books, Ltd.
148 West 37th Street, 13th Floor
New York, NY 10018

First Pegasus Books hardcover edition March 2022

Interior series design by Sabrina Plomitallo-González, Pegasus Books

ISBN: 978-1-64313-889-3

10 9 8 7 6 5 4 3 2 1

Printed in the United States of America
Distributed by Simon & Schuster
www.pegasusbooks.com

For Juj, with xoxoxox ad infinitum

Argyles
and
Arsenic

1

Diary, day one

    I trace a circle around the last entry in the scrapbook. With my finger, not a writing implement. Carefully so I don't disturb the yellowed edges or the glue, which might be brittle after all these decades. The elegance of the penmanship touches me, and the endearing placement of the note—pasted in the center of the page, but ever so slightly askew. And the poetic impact of those scant lines, unintended, no doubt, is as warming as a good secret.

    Methods of administering arsenic:

broth and barley, bread and cheese

porridge, cocoa, coffee

tea and scones

unknown

    I love that last line, stuck on like a signature. <u>Is</u> it a signature? That warrants more study. But study at my leisure, not according to the whims of the keeper of this mausoleum where I visit the book. It's an unhealthy place, in truth if not in reality—a monument to the dead or soon to be.

    Surely my eyes just popped wide, because when was the last time I made such a momentous decision? I can't remember, but now here are three of them. One: I need unrestricted time with the scrapbook. Two: the scrapbook needs to be cared for in a better environment.

Three: I can answer both needs by giving the scrapbook a new home. Ideally, a home away from so much dreich here in Inversgail. From so much dreich everywhere in the Highlands, but that won't be happening. Not any time soon.

But how can I remove the scrapbook without being seen? And do it safely—it should be treated like any other antique. Like a dear old person and not an unwanted stepchild shunted into a corner.

A messenger bag could work, if I wrap the scrapbook in something, and if I had a messenger bag. I had a rucksack, once upon a time. Where do they go—rucksacks, school ties, and scarves? Carelessly shed. Lost in the clutter of an expanding life.

I'll do my shopping before coming in next time and bring my clutter of carrier bags with me. No one will notice an extra carrier bag on the way out. Another good decision. I wonder, when the decision was finally made—to add arsenic—is this how poisoners in the golden days of yore felt? I think it must be.

And now I have a name for my dear diary, too.

∿

Inversgail, late November

The bell over the door at Yon Bonnie Books jingled, catching Janet Marsh with a warm scone halfway to her mouth. Janet put the scone back on its plate, and smiled at the young woman blowing in with a hint of fish from the cold gust off the harbor.

"Good morning." The woman's greeting and outstretched hand coordinated well with her smart coat. The bounce in her step went better with her windblown hair. Before Janet could shake the outstretched hand, it changed course for the hair, where it patted to little effect. The woman seemed to realize that and laughed. "Hello, I'm Isobel Ritchie, from down the High Street. I'm the curator at the Inversgail Heritage Museum." She stuck out her hand again.

"How nice to meet you. I'm Janet Marsh and here comes my daughter Tallie Marsh."

"The new American owners," Isobel said.

"Two of them," said Janet. "In total, we're three Americans and one expat Scot back home from the prairies of Illinois where we met thirty-plus years ago."

"Curious question from the curator, then," Isobel said, "how did you all land here? In Inversgail, but also at Yon Bonnie Books?"

"Equal parts luck, planning, and the need for change," Tallie said. "Inversgail because we love it. Christine—she's our expat—invited our family to visit one summer when I might not even have been in school yet."

"Just a *wean*," Isobel said.

"A darling wean, both of the children," Janet said. "We bought a house here and came back every summer we could."

"Our businesses are part retirement scheme, part change of career," Tallie said. "Plus, my brother Allen married an Inversgail woman. Do you know Maida Fairlie?"

"Oh yes."

"Allen married Maida's daughter Nicola," Janet said. "They live in Edinburgh, and moving here is my way of making sure I see enough of them and the grandboys." She didn't see the need to add the more personal details of Christine's recent widowhood or her return to Inversgail to look after her aging parents. Nor her own divorce from her husband, formerly known as Curtis, now *formally* known as Curtis the rat.

"Yon Bonnie Books came up for sale at the right time, then," Isobel said.

"Our amazing good luck," Tallie said. "So, although we aren't *new* new to Inversgail, we're new permanent residents since spring, and that makes us new for at least the next two hundred years to the curator of the history museum."

"New and very welcome," Isobel said.

"Thank you," said Janet. "Tallie and I are the bookshop half of the partnership. Christine Robertson and Summer Jacobs are through the communicating door in our tearoom, Cakes and Tales."

"With the lovely smells." Isobel pointed at Janet's scone. "I've a weakness for scones and shortbread."

"Oh yes," Janet said. "My downfall. One of them, anyway. Another is that I haven't been in the museum since we arrived."

"Summer and I were there for the opening of the St. Kilda exhibit," Tallie said. "Even on a *dreich* day there's great light in the gallery along the harbor."

"*Isn't* there." Isobel's eyes seemed to carry that light with them.

In the quiet that followed Isobel's glowing remark, Janet wondered what she'd come to ask them. As charming as she found Isobel's bounce and disheveled hair, she knew the original outstretched hand and direct gaze were there for business purposes. The brightness fading from Isobel's eyes now convinced Janet she was right; here fidgeted a young woman unused to making cold calls.

Maybe to further avoid her mission, Isobel turned to gaze around the shop. Her survey stopped at the fireplace area, with its inviting chairs, and Janet saw her eyes relight. "What a lovely wee nook. Not so wee, though. Do you allow groups to meet here?"

"A writers' group meets there," Janet said. "We've started calling that the Inversgail Writers' Inglenook."

The bell at the door jingled again. Tallie went to greet the customers, and Isobel took herself for a walk around the inglenook. When Tallie returned to the sales counter, so did Isobel.

"They're happy having a wander on their own," Tallie reported, "but they think we're lovely and cozy."

"Think how cozy your shop would look with a group of knitters by your fireplace," Isobel said.

"We had a resident knitter for a while," Janet said. "Unofficial. And she wasn't really a resident. It just felt that way."

"But we liked her," Tallie said.

"We did," said Janet. "She looked right at home."

"Brilliant. Then let me tell you why I'm here." And Isobel described an exhibit of traditional and regional knitting patterns they were mounting at the museum. "The spotlight will be on ganseys. Do you have them in America?"

"Not in central Illinois," Janet said. "What are they?"

"Jumpers." Isobel waved her hands up and down her front. "Sweaters. A type traditionally worn by coastal fishermen. And not just our coast. All over the UK and parts of Scandinavia. They're known for their intricate patterns, and often you can tell where a gansey's from by the pattern. Wendy wants to show—do you know Wendy? Wendy Erskine, she's the museum's director. She wants to show how our local patterns developed over the years."

"Cool," Tallie said.

"And she's letting me do the same for Inversgail stockings." Isobel raised her eyebrows. Janet's and Tallie's rose, too, inviting another explanation. "Long socks," Isobel said. "Knitted in a particular argyle pattern that's found only in the Inversgail area. Have you ever seen them?"

"Long socks, yes," Tallie said. "In the states we call them knee socks."

"Inversgail stockings, no," Janet said. "But I love the idea of them."

"Sadly, I've found that not many know about them these days."

"All the more reason for your exhibit," Janet said. "It's a shame when local crafts die out and traditions get lost."

"Yes!" Isobel said. "I told Wendy that what goes for ganseys goes for stockings, which helped convince her. Mind, she took a bit of the pep from my step when she asked if anyone will care enough about socks to stop and look at my part of the exhibit."

"If they're looking at old sweaters, what would they have against old socks?" Tallie asked.

"Right?" Isobel said. "But the stockings will have to be in a separate room, and more exhibits mean more work, more expense, and we're aye pinching pennies, so I *ken* why she's reluctant. But that's when I had my

flash of inspiration, and where I hope you and your lovely inglenook will
come in. We're going to have a 'Rocking the Stocking' knitting competition with a public component. Groups of knitters will madly work away
at Inversgail stockings in businesses all up and down the High Street and
beyond. At the knitting shop, obviously, but can't you picture knitters
going at it in the library, the bank, and Sea View Kayak? Several of the
pubs have signed on, as well, and of course we'll have knitters in our own
light-filled gallery."

"And our inglenook?" Janet asked. "I love it. Please count us in."

"Thank you," Isobel said. "Won't it be grand? With the right publicity,
people will come for the museum exhibits and stay for the knitting and
the shops. Or vice versa, and with the added benefit of rekindling interest
in local traditions, history, our ganseys, and our stockings."

Janet took out her phone and looked at the calendar. "When does the
competition start and end?"

"The exhibit opens the week after Hogmanay." Isobel's eyebrows rose
again.

"We know that one." Tallie raised her arms in triumph. "New Year's Eve."

"Aye, we'll give folks something to do after the parties die down and
they're over their sore heads. It will be a good time to sit and knit. We'll
get the exact dates to you soon."

"But sometime after the first week in January." Janet added a note to
the calendar. "How does the competition work? Are we expected to, I
don't know, referee in some way?"

"Only in the event of open combat with drawn knitting needles,"
Isobel said.

Janet blinked.

"I'm having you on. All we ask is use of your inglenook and we'll take
care of the rest. I've found a very generous donor, so we're able to offer
a raft of prizes, and we've dreamed up a massive range of categories for
awarding them—for age, speed, accuracy, creative interpretation. We'll
have a day when, essentially, anyone who shows up at the museum with

yarn and a pair of needles gets a prize. But the serious knitters, the ones you'll be hosting, will be registered for the real test. They'll have two months. They can work at home all they like, but they'll be required to take part in the public knitting once a week. They must complete at least one pair of stockings, but may knit as many as they like beyond that. They'll be judged on accuracy and skill. We *dinnae* have all the fine details worked out, as yet, but we picture small groups of knitters moving from venue to venue, stopping at each one for several hours of action."

"It's a terrific idea," Tallie said. "We should let you know, though, that one of the chairs by the fireplace is spoken for on a sporadic but semi-permanent basis, so we can only let you have three of them."

"Two or three knitters per participating space is perfect," Isobel said. "They won't take up too much room and having more groups around town will spread the joy."

∽

Inversgail, mid-January

Janet tapped VIDEO on her phone then panned it slowly around the inglenook at Yon Bonnie Books. She moved as she filmed so that she captured each member of the trio knitting in the chairs arranged around the gas fireplace. One of the knitters raised a needle in greeting, smiling shyly. Janet zoomed in for a closeup of flashing needles and an emerging sock. The needles didn't glint, but to Janet's eyes they moved lightning fast. Fast enough to hypnotize several customers who'd stopped to watch. And with Peter Maxwell Davies's solemn, unfussy piano piece "Farewell to Stromness" playing in the background, they seemed even faster.

Judging from this excellent start on its first day, Isobel's "Rocking the Stocking" knitting competition was going to be a winner. Janet felt sure the combination of blazing needles and rapt customers would light up Isobel's eyes. She finished filming the knitters in the inglenook and took the phone back to the sales counter to show Tallie.

"Knitters have a hard time looking competitive, don't they?" Tallie watched the short video again. "This is perfect. Warm and inviting, like an ad for coffee or tea—"

"Or a bookshop and tearoom," Janet said.

The first team of knitters had arrived on the dot at ten for the first day of competition. Each contestant wore an official "Rocking the Stocking" badge—a swatch of argyle pinned on the left shoulder. Isobel had sent a registration list. Tallie had duly checked off the names, and the knitters had settled themselves into the inglenook chairs for a two-hour stint of intense needlework.

"Good video, Mom." Tallie handed the phone back. "If the whole competition goes this smoothly, Isobel's project should be a success for the museum. Maybe it'll attract business in the cold dark of winter, too."

"It's hard to imagine what could go wrong," Janet said. "The knitters look just the way I pictured when Isobel presented the idea."

"This is just the morning group." Tallie scanned the registration list. "Knitters have come out of the woodwork for the competition—that's a nasty image, isn't it? Anyway, we'll have another group this afternoon, two completely different groups tomorrow, and more on Monday."

"Coming out of the woodwork only sounds nasty if you take it literally," Janet said. "But there could be a nasty knitter among them somewhere."

"When the photographer from the *Inversgail Guardian* comes around, maybe they'll get feisty and brandish their needles at each other," Tallie said.

"Or accidentally on purpose spill tea in each other's knitting bags. But let's not go too far down this path," Janet said. "It sounds rocky and we want smooth. I'll post the video online with a note about the sale on knitting books and the new Knitter's Nutmeg Scones in the tearoom."

"We should find out about specials at the other shops and include them," Tallie said.

"And politely ask them to reciprocate. You're every bit as brill as Isobel. I'll text them right now." Janet planted herself on the high stool behind the counter and set her fingers to work.

A woman approached the counter, a stack of paperbacks in one hand, a white bag from the tearoom in the other. Tallie gave an appreciative sniff as she took the books. "A nutmeg scone?" She asked.

"Two," the woman said, "because I'd be daft to go home without one for my husband."

"Or if you bought just one, you could eat it on the way home and he'd never know," Tallie said.

"I like the way you think. Mind, I already ate one in the tearoom and I can only live with so much guilt. Does your sale on knitting books apply to mysteries with knitting in them as well?"

"Absolutely," Tallie said, with a quick look at Janet who gave her a thumbs-up.

"That's all right, then," the woman said, "because this is as close as I get to knitting. I *would* be a dafty if I let myself anywhere near real yarn and needles. Know your limits, my da said, and get on with your life."

"And you can go beyond your limits through reading." Tallie tucked a bookmark into one of the books before handing the stack back to her. "All the adventure you want, without leaving the comfort of home or your favorite chair, with a cup of tea and a fresh-baked scone."

"Or two, if I'm lucky and my man's away when I return. Cheery-bye."

Janet waited for the door to close behind the woman, then said, "Good move with the discount, dear. But how were we that slow? Knitting fiction is an obvious addition to the sale."

"Never mind. We're including it now and I'll go add some of the mysteries to the window display. Goldenbaum's Seaside Knitters series is perfect, considering the harbor out our front window, and the Haunted Yarn Shop series because Geneva is a ghost I'd like to know."

"A few picture books, too," Janet called after her. "*Extra Yarn* by Barnett and *Love from Woolly* by Michaels are a good start."

"And my favorite—*Ned the Knitting Pirate.*" Tallie waved over her shoulder and disappeared down an aisle flanked by the tallest of their handsome, antique (though mismatched) bookshelves.

Janet finished sending texts to the other businesses hosting knitters during the competition. Almost immediately she had a smiling emoji response from the couple who owned Sea View Kayak.

Tallie came back and set an armful of books on the counter. "Hand me three or four book easels, will you? Make it twice that. I'll see how many of the mass markets I can squeeze in front of the register."

"For anyone who isn't daft enough to pass up a good impulse buy when they see one?" Janet took half a dozen of the display easels from under the counter and handed them to her daughter.

"Speaking of daft," Tallie said. "Are you going to Violet MacAskill's party tonight?"

"Is it daft? The idea behind the party, I mean." Janet took a small, cream-colored envelope from a pocket of her blazer. "Isobel says Violet is still pretty sharp. Of course, she might be biased because Violet's her grandmother. Certainly, the envelope and invitation are lovely, if that has any bearing on the party."

"It's very posh," Tallie said. "You let me hold it when it arrived. And now you're stroking it."

"Because it's good quality paper, which I love, but also because envelopes like this, and what they contain, can be just as magical as the pages in books." Janet slipped the stiff card with its embossed border from the envelope and read aloud its spidery, handwritten invitation. "The pleasure of your company is requested for an evening of Decanting and Decluttering, 14 January, 7 P.M., Fairy Flax Hall, Inversgail." She propped it against the cash register so she could admire it. "See? There's a story behind an invitation like this. And if you put the envelope, the invitation, and the rich paper all together, you have possibilities."

"Like the adventures beyond limits our customer is looking forward to with her mysteries and a scone or two," Tallie said.

"That's it, yes. On the other hand, if Violet only invited a select group to this shindig, as Isobel said, then inviting me, whom she's never met, doesn't make a lot of sense. That's a good enough definition of daft."

"That and the elephant in the lovely prose of that invitation—a decanting and decluttering?" Tallie, a former lawyer and law professor, let her glasses slip down her nose. "Have you ever heard of anyone inviting people over to drink, browse their possessions, and take whatever they want home with them?""

"It's certainly unusual."

"But none of that will keep you from going?"

"You know me better than that," Janet said.

"I do. I'm sure that hint of daft is the very thing that's convinced you to go."

Janet couldn't help grinning. "Does that worry you?"

"Let me think." With an exaggerated look of contemplation, Tallie crossed her arms and stared at the ceiling, then back at her mother. She shook her head. "Not enough for you to worry about. Just a bit—to counterbalance the hint of daft."

"Good. I value your sensible way of approaching things. So does Christine."

"Ah. Christine. For the most part I value *her* sensible way of approaching things, but somehow when it comes to a decanting and decluttering? She might be one who helps put the D in daft."

"Christine is eminently sensible." Janet emphasized their partner's eminence by tapping the counter with the edge of the envelope. Janet and Christine had each followed their professor husbands to the University of Illinois and met when Janet thrilled her son's classroom by demonstrating her state fair, prizewinning pig call. Christine, a school social worker, had walked past the classroom at the moment of Janet's reverberating *sooey*. They told their husbands they'd bonded over Janet's pig call and cemented the friendship with Christine's recipe for shortbread. "We'll go, have a lovely time," Janet said, "and I won't bring home anything outlandish or anything I can't carry."

"And Christine?"

"She'll be busy keeping an eye on her mum," Janet said. "Helen and Violet MacAskill are apparently old friends. But you know Christine's mum; Helen is half-doddery and half-deaf. From what I hear, Violet's neither deaf nor doddery, but she's somewhat fragile. They're a couple of wee old ladies. They won't be sliding down bannisters or swinging from chandeliers."

"Neither will you. I know that much."

Janet shuddered. She had a horror of heights and edges. "And you don't need to worry about Christine. She won't abandon Helen to lark about." Janet stroked the envelope again and a thought struck her. "Tallie, are you jealous? That we're invited but you and Summer aren't?"

"What? No. Not at all."

"Because I'm pretty sure I would be."

"But we do go places separately, and you'll tell me all about it in perfect detail. So no, I'm not, and this way I don't have to worry about what to wear."

"Then, honestly dear, what do you think is likely to go wrong?"

"Nothing, really," Tallie said. "To even say I have a 'hint of worry' is probably an exaggeration."

"Good."

"And yet the phrase 'beyond limits' keeps running through my head. Let's call it disquiet."

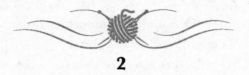

2

Tallie added the knitting mysteries and picture books to the window display and then stepped outside. Janet watched as she checked her handiwork from a passerby's perspective. She knew that the simple act of useful puttering would let Tallie work through her worries about that evening's unusual party. Whatever she wanted to call them—the worries *or* the party.

Janet waved when Tallie looked up, then composed a text for Summer in the tearoom. Summer rounded out their four-woman business partnership, taking on the role of baker extraordinaire. Like all of them, she'd reinvented herself when they bought the business, packed up their Midwestern lives, and moved to Inversgail. She and Tallie had been college roommates, Tallie in pre-law and Summer in journalism. She'd prospered in her career as a newspaperwoman, but she'd seen the writing on the masthead when print journalism began to die. Still, she kept her hand in the writing game. In addition to working in the tearoom and managing Bedtime Stories, their B&B upstairs, she wrote a weekly agony aunt column for the *Inversgail Guardian*. The correspondents *she* answered were real, but Janet, Tallie, and Christine enjoyed dreaming up answers to imaginary letters and sharing them with Summer.

"Here's advice for someone calling themselves 'Bundle of Nerves,'" Janet texted to Summer. "*The simple act of useful puttering slays more dragons than Saint George with his sword ever dreamt. Try organizing the linens or dusting."* Tallie came back in and Janet immediately doubted the wisdom of her advice to Bundle of Nerves. The crease between Tallie's eyebrows told her that puttering hadn't saved the day. Or perhaps something else had happened. "What's up?" she asked.

"We might have another knitter." Tallie found the registration sheet. "Nope, we aren't expecting a fourth this morning."

"Maybe he's scoping out the competition," Janet said. "Or he's early for this afternoon."

"Maybe. Or maybe he's just odd. He was hesitating out there, so I said hi, and when I asked if I could help, he turned his back on me and started fussing with his carrier bags. If he's got yarn in them, he's got enough for a dozen pairs of Inversgail stockings plus one or two blankets. He *is* wearing a competition badge, but it's on the wrong shoulder."

"He sounds confused about where both he and the badge should be. Thank goodness we aren't responsible for policing badge placement."

The bell above the door jingled. And although there was nothing difficult about how their door opened, the man coming through it with bulging carrier bags somehow gave the impression he battled it and a strong headwind, or perhaps a throng of shoppers, equally laden, trying to get past him on the way out. Tallie rushed to help. He looked at her, either with alarm or surprise, dipped a shallow bow, and dropped two of the bags. He retrieved one and put his foot on the other, holding it in place just as Tallie tried to pick it up. She apologized and retreated behind the sales counter, looking alarmed *and* surprised.

"Good morning," Janet said, only just able to stop herself from shouting to be heard over the tumult he seemed to carry with him. "Would you like to put your bags on the counter?"

He preferred to put all of them on the floor at his feet. "I'm Kyle Byrne," he said when he straightened.

"Yes?"

"It's an easy name to remember. Because it's two bodies of water."

"So it is, strait and stream. Nice to meet you, Kyle. I'm Janet and this is Tallie. Welcome to Yon Bonnie Books."

"It's easy to jeer at, as well."

"We try never to jeer at Yon Bonnie. So then, Kyle, how can we help?" Out of the corner of her eye, Janet saw Tallie check the registration list, again, and give a minimal headshake.

Kyle performed the new customer ritual of turning to look over the shop. As he did, Janet noticed a darned spot on his scarf. That she could see the spot made her think the darning must be a fairly inexpert job. She also saw how wrong she'd been about his age. When he'd battled his way into the shop, she thought he might be near her own—mid-sixties—and somewhat less competent or agile. His rather lumpy overcoat and poorly darned scarf would be right at home on a scrimping pensioner. But the creaseless skin on the back of his neck put him nearer to Tallie and Summer's late thirties. When he turned back to the counter, Janet recalculated again. His smooth, pink cheeks hadn't seen a year beyond thirty. Kyle smiled at them, expanded the smile, expanded his chest with a deep breath, and slapped his hands to his abdomen.

First, he was a pensioner, Janet thought. Now he's acting the part of a bluff country squire out for a bracing constitutional. Or a young army officer, newly commissioned and about to burst his brass buttons. Even his coat and scarf are suddenly nattier. And, he was apparently interested in local knitting traditions and Inversgail stockings. She decided she liked this young man.

"They told me to stop here before jumping in with my yarn and needles." Kyle looked toward the inglenook. "I'm running a wee bit late and it wouldn't do to get too far behind the others. So, I'll just take myself over and get started, shall I?"

Now that she liked him, Janet didn't want to disappoint him. "We weren't expecting another knitter this morning," she said, "but let's see what we can do."

"I see an empty chair," Kyle said. "That will do me nicely."

"It's actually taken," Tallie said.

As if on cue, the background music segued from a somber orchestral piece that Janet couldn't name and didn't care to hear again, into Percy Grainger's sprightly "Country Gardens." Much better for keeping the mood bright and perfectly suited to the small dog trotting toward them from the tearoom.

The sandy-haired Cairn terrier, who carried a folded tea towel in his mouth, added a jaunty click-clicking of claws to Grainger's piano. The dog's companion, Rab MacGregor, followed more sedately with quieter footfalls. Dog and man kept an intermittent work schedule in the bookshop and tearoom. Rab as staff in either shop, as needed, and Ranger as picturesque local color who didn't mind photo ops with customers and put up with endless pats from children.

"Morning, Ranger," Tallie said. "Morning, Rab."

Janet fluttered her fingers. She wasn't a flutterer by nature but found she couldn't help herself around Ranger.

Rab and Ranger acknowledged the women's greetings with nods. Then Ranger continued past the counter to the inglenook. The knitters paused as he studied each of them and sniffed each knitting bag. They watched as he jumped into the fourth chair, dropped the tea towel, arranged it to his satisfaction, and sat. The knitter who'd earlier raised a needle to Janet, raised it to Ranger. He opened his mouth and let his tongue hang over his bottom teeth in a grin. Then he settled into the business of his first morning nap. Rab took a duster from behind the counter and set about tidying shelves.

Kyle pointed at Ranger. "Is that allowed?"

"A beloved bookshop tradition," Tallie said.

"I think I'd like to speak to management," said Kyle.

"You are." Janet tried a finger flutter on him.

Kyle ignored her overture, picked up his bags, and marched to the inglenook. He had no problem with his bags or spurious headwinds now. He dropped his bags next to Ranger's chair and stared back at the counter, arms crossed. Ranger picked his head up, grinned briefly at the knitters, then turned interested eyes to the sales counter.

Kyle jerked his head toward Ranger. "What are you going to do about this?"

"We'll find a way to make everything work," Janet said. "It won't be a problem." To Tallie she said softly, "A chance to prove our good customer service." She looked at Ranger, then Kyle. Ranger blinked and yawned, appearing the more reasonable of the two. Definitely more portable if it came to that. But why should it? "Will you call him, Rab?" Hearing no response, she looked around. "Rab?"

No answer, no Rab. Not unusual for Rab and his *easy-oasy* ways, but not always convenient.

"Hang on Kyle," Tallie said. "We'll have you knitting in no time. I'll bring a chair from the tearoom."

"Not necessary." Rab reappeared—also not unusual behavior. "We've another competition venue in Cakes and Tales."

"We have?" Janet asked.

"A late addition to the schedule," Rab said. "As well, we've another knitter ready and waiting with her needles."

"Good man." Kyle stooped to gather his bags. In doing so, he missed the look that came and went from Rab's usually pleasant face. A look, like a sudden blatter of rain, surprising and intense.

Janet and Tallie caught the look, though, and when Rab had escorted Kyle to the tearoom, they exchanged looks of their own.

∽

"'Knitters Gnash Their Needles in Bookshop Inglenook.'" Christine framed the words with her hands. "What do you think of that for a headline? Or this—'Cutthroat Competition and a Cuppa at Area Tearoom'?"

"I think you're enjoying yourself," Janet said. "I am, too, but stop waving your hands and keep your voice down." She'd taken advantage of a quiet spell in the bookshop and gone to see their unexpected second competition venue in the tearoom for herself. Also, to sample one of their new nutmeg scones. "Is it kosher for Bethia to keep taking Kyle's needles to fix his mistakes?"

"He hasn't a hope of winning, so why not?" Christine handed Janet a napkin. "Crumb on your cheek."

Janet felt for the crumb and popped it in her mouth. "Too good to waste. Summer, the nutmeg scones are perfection," she called.

Summer stopped clearing a table to take a bow. The women at another table applauded.

"Christine, what are you and your mum wearing to Violet MacAskill's tonight?" Janet asked. "More importantly, what should *I* wear?"

"Never mind that," Christine said. "Did *you* know Nana Bethia is one of the stocking judges?"

"Is she? Why doesn't that surprise me? But no, I didn't know. How did that happen? Not that it matters. It's good to have her back. Is she staying with Norman?"

"I haven't had a chance to ask."

Bethia Ferguson was the woman Janet had told Isobel about—the one they'd called their resident knitter. She'd spent the better part of a week drinking tea and knitting in the bookshop, in the spring, shortly after they'd taken over from the previous owners. She'd bought several pattern books over the week and happily accepted samples of Summer's scones (which she'd wrapped and taken away in her handbag), but she'd never said a word. At the time, they'd guessed she might not speak English or wasn't comfortable with it. Later, they learned she'd taken the scones away with her, and hadn't spoken, because she was embarrassed. She'd had a denture catastrophe, the replacement set hadn't yet arrived, and she'd been reluctant to reveal her toothless plight. They'd also learned her relationship to Constable

Norman Hobbs; she was his maternal grandmother and kept him well-supplied with handknitted jumpers. They'd seen her infrequently since her week of knitting, as she now lived in a care home some distance from Inversgail.

"We also didn't know about the tearoom becoming a competition venue," Janet said. "How did that happen?"

"I've no idea. It was news to me and news to Summer," Christine said. "We were all in the dark, but Rab knew." Christine said.

"Did he? How did *that* happen?"

"You sound like your own echo. And I see that look in your eye, Janet. Don't ask me how *that* happened. Your penchant for echoes is no doubt an intractable result of the social dynamics of your upbringing on a Central Illinois pig farm. And I hope you know that reference to the pig farm is part of my observation, not an insult."

"And I didn't take it as one."

The two stood amicably side by side—Christine tall and spare, Janet shorter and better upholstered. They watched Bethia take the knitting from Kyle again.

"What *does* one wear to a decanting and decluttering?" Janet asked as Kyle took the needles back and dropped his ball of wool on the floor.

"It's anybody's guess. Did you know I'm not actually invited?"

"What?"

"Violet sent the invitation to Mum and Dad." Christine started gathering the plates from a vacated table. "I've never known Dad to turn down an invitation to an evening where something is going to be decanted, and rarely have I known him to dislike anyone. This party and Violet MacAskill are the exceptions. Her house, too. I'm sure you'll love it, but he says it's like a mausoleum."

"That sounds ominous and unpleasant. Is it a mausoleum?"

"I'll be right with you," Christine called over the top of Janet's head to a table of women raising their empty teapot. To Janet she said, "Dad's refused to go to Violet's, and that's upset Mum, so I told her I shall be her date for the evening."

"Do *you* like Violet?" Janet asked.

"I've not set eyes on her since I was a *wean*."

"What does your dad know about her that we don't?"

"Ah." Christine leaned in close. "Let's just go and find out, shall we?"

3

Arsenic Diary, day two

The wind off the harbor comes at me cold as a slap. I blow on my hands and tip my head back to catch the last of the day's sun. Tepid, and about as satisfying as weak tea. I open my eyes and I'm looking straight up the bronze nostrils of Robert Louis Stevenson. There's not a shred of historical evidence that Stevenson spent time in Inversgail. Not even on a flying visit whilst his father built the lighthouse on the headland. He's here now, though, and a nice addition to our waterfront. He stares across the harbor at the lighthouse. People say he's brooding, but I don't agree. I've seen that look on my own face in family photos. We're a melancholy pair. He, because he's leaving Scotland, and I, because I'm not. He's also had a premonition that he hasn't long to live. I've no idea if that's true, but it suits my mood.

I turn my collar up and wish I had that scarf some twit has wrapped round Stevenson's neck. I don't fancy the colors, or scaling up to snatch it, but he wears the thing with flair. What each of us needs is a pair of the stockings that people are madly knitting all over town. They're a lovely argyle in blues and greens.

I pat Stevenson's calf in chilly commiseration, dredging my memory for a quotation of his I learnt in school. Despite his sunny garden of verses, he didn't much care for Scottish weather, either. The dredging is successful. I find his words where they've kept *warm under heaps of other childhood memories. "One of the vilest climates under heaven," he said. "The weather is raw and boisterous in winter, shifty and ungenial in summer, and a downright meteorological purgatory in the spring." I wonder how many statues there are of the poor fellow, rooting him forever to his native soil to suffer the misery of our elements?*

A shiver takes me by the shoulders. Delicious. Nothing to do with our dreary elements and everything to do with my element—atomic number 33. Arsenic.

Christine and Summer came through from the tearoom as Janet and Tallie finished closing out the cash register for the day.

"Is that new?" Janet asked about Christine's dark blue duffle coat.

"Vintage," Christine said as she did up the toggles. "It's the very coat I took away with me to university. Violet's decluttering gave Dad ideas about our attic. Except that his method created *more* clutter with no clear idea of what should go back in the attic and what in the dust bin. Mum and I objected when it seemed to be getting too far out of hand. We prevailed. Dad thanked us for returning him to his right mind, comfortable chair, and newspaper."

Summer unclipped the barrette at the back of her head, letting her blond hair fall around her shoulders. "Your coat's a classic," she said, zipping up her own jacket. "Will the clutter tonight include clothes?"

"If it does, do you want us to look for something?" Janet asked.

"No, no, no." Summer shook her head, her hair flying with her protests. "One woman's clutter is *another* woman's clutter."

"Unless you find something Downton Abbey-ish," Tallie said. "She'd like that."

"Oh, yeah, I really would." Summer sounded apologetic but looked hopeful.

"A duffle would be more practical." Christine said.

"But an evening of decanting and decluttering whispers 'hunt for treasure,'" Tallie said. "And a vintage gown answers with so much more pleasure." She flipped her brown braid onto the top of her head and pulled a watch cap down over her ears. "Ready?" she asked Summer.

Christine squinted at Tallie. "You're oddly poetic. Where are you two off to this evening?"

"Poetry and knitting slam at the pub next to the bank," Summer said. "James can't cover it so I said I would. He claims a subsequent engagement. And yes, he does mean something better's come up."

"She was feeling kind and said she doesn't mind." Tallie closed her eyes and held the bridge of her nose. "I want you to know how painful that rhyme was for me, too, Christine. I'm trying to immunize my brain so it doesn't freak out when I start reading our McGonagall entries. I know the contest was my idea, but we haven't advertised it yet, so maybe—"

"No," Christine said. "The contest must go forward. No second thoughts."

During his lifetime, nineteenth-century Scottish poet William Topaz McGonagall delighted and appalled audiences with his labored rhymes, awkward scansion, melodramatic subject matter, and general butchery of the art form. Christine adored him. Tallie found him fascinating in the way videos of avoidable disasters fascinated others.

Janet agreed with both of them. Shortly after she and Curtis the rat had bought the house in Inversgail, she'd embroidered the last two lines of McGonagall's "The Tay Bridge Disaster" onto an antique linen tea towel. The words, "For the stronger we our houses do build; The less chance we have of being killed," suited the sturdy, granite house, and she'd hung the framed needlework above their front door. She still loved the embroidery, but was sad her marriage hadn't been stronger.

"Christine's right about going forward with the contest," Janet said. "If for no other reason than it might warn a whole new generation of parents against saddling some poor kid with the middle name Topaz."

"Or wake them up to the glorious possibility." Christine ushered the other three out the shop door and locked it behind them. "As your pub is on our way, Janet and I will see you safely there. For the longer we, our friends, do keep whole, the greater chance we have of reaching our McGonagall goal." Christine's only regret about holding a McGonagall write-alike contest was that, as one of the business owners, she couldn't enter.

Water lapped at the harbor wall, that liquid sound joining the murmur of voices from a boat riding at anchor. The boat's lights reflected like stars on the water's black surface. Tallie and Summer waved goodbye when they reached the pub. Janet and Christine turned at the next corner, leaving the business district and its bustle, such as it was, behind.

"Nice to have a clear night for a change," Janet said.

"Though the murk is always gathering somewhere. My lungs, for instance." Christine puffed a bit beside her as they went uphill. "Perhaps I should declare this the first day of a new regimen of exercise and fresh air."

"You chose an interesting day to start. You usually drive, and I thought you didn't want to be late for the party."

"I didn't want *you* to be late and miss out on the crème de la crème of clutter. But Dad needed the car for a suddenly remembered dentist appointment. As I left the house, he was telling Mum he'd insist on having a root canal before he'd ever go to Violet's party or willingly spend time with Edward or Teresa. Edward and Teresa being Violet's son and daughter. Teresa is Isobel's mother."

"If you ask me, the evening is sounding more and more iffy," Janet said. "What do you and your mum think of Edward and Teresa?"

"I've no opinion. They're enough older that we traveled in different circles. Mum has much the same feeling as Dad, but she'll put up with them because she's quite fond of Violet. Violet's Dundee cake and black bun, as well. I'm under strict orders from Dad to bring home nothing but Dundee cake, although I'm sure the black bun wouldn't go amiss either. But absolutely nothing resembling clutter, or he *will* start on the attic again. We'll have to keep an eye on Mum to see that she doesn't put anything but the cake in her handbag. Don't look so worried, Janet. You'll have a lovely evening picking through Violet's oddments with the rest of the vultures."

"Being called a vulture makes me feel so much better," Janet said.

They turned the next corner, passing the kirk and kirkyard with its gravestones, some lichen-covered, some so new they seemed to be marking raw wounds. It occurred to Janet that the oldest markers looked almost as ancient and resilient as standing stones. Thoughts of standing stones and grave markers jogged a memory and a question for Christine. "What makes you think I like surrounding myself with dead things?"

"Who says you do?"

"I just told you. You do."

"If I did, that doesn't make it true. Either you saying I said it, or me saying it in the first place, which I don't remember doing." Christine stopped and put a hand on Janet's arm, bringing her to a stop, too. "Be honest with me, Janet. Have I forgot that I said it? Am I getting like Mum?"

Janet admired the calm in Christine's voice, but she felt the worry in that hand now clutching her arm. Helen, Christine's mum, was more often away with the fairies since Christine had returned to Inversgail. Janet put her own hand on top of Christine's. "*Dinnae fash.* Your memory runs rings around mine."

"Good, then what's all this fuss about dead things?" Christine started walking again. "And come along, Janet. If you'll stop dawdling, we'll hardly be late at all."

"You described Violet MacAskill's house as a mausoleum and said I'd love it, implying that I like being surrounded by dead things."

"Ah. I see the problem," Christine said. "You added words to my implication, and then read meaning into your words."

"I examined *your* words for meaning and the meaning seemed fairly obvious."

"Because I didn't finish what I was saying. I was distracted by that table of women who wanted another pot of tea. Dad calls Violet's house a mausoleum. Mum swats him for it. She says there's nothing dusty, fusty, or dead about the MacAskill's bit of rubble. I'm sure I can find people who might say that your lifelong obsession with books is the same thing as doting on dead things—"

"Who?"

"No one of consequence. Forget them. Philistines. We won't go looking for them. Anyone who knows you knows that you care very much for the living. That you have a passion for solving their problems. Hold up a moment. I'll text Dad and let him know we're imminent so he can get Mum into her coat."

Janet rubbed away the chill that had crept into her hands. "I don't know if it's a passion," she said when they were walking again, "but I do like helping people."

"We both do. We've a flair for it. Inborn, I should think."

Christine stumbled on a section of uneven pavement. Janet steadied her, and they linked arms for the rest of the way.

"There now," Christine said when they turned the corner into Westray Wynd. "Dad has my ancient wee problem waiting for us at the door. I'll back the car out. You go see if the old dear remembers who you are today. And Janet, she's become a tyrant about sitting up front. She won't let us hear the end of it if you beat her to it. So, if you'll hop in the back, that's one more problem you've solved on our way toward world peace and the MacAskill bit of rubble."

Once settled in the car, and after reminding Christine's mother where they were going, they followed one of the roads that wound through the hills surrounding Inversgail. Janet guessed they were roughly following the Sgail, a small river that flowed peacefully into town and calmly met the harbor, the town seemingly having a civilizing influence. Here in the hills, the river leapt and tumbled with abandon through the wild and deeply wooded Glen Sgail.

When Christine slowed and made a turn into a narrower lane, the headlights showed tall trees crowding in on either side. The stars disappeared as branches met overhead, and Janet knew she'd been right about their route. As the lane climbed another hill, the trees gave way to a bare hillside, a lone house standing at the top. Backed by the rising moon, with its façade lit by invisible spotlights, the house appeared to be an asymmetrical assemblage of turrets and towers suggesting medieval knights and dragons more than warmth and comfortable beds.

"*That's* the MacAskill bit of rubble?" Janet asked.

4

F ondly known as," Christine said. "The official name is Fairy Flax Hall. It's a fine example of Scottish Baronial architecture. Dad calls it a fine example of fairytale foolishness."

"Humbug," Christine's mother piped up from the front passenger seat.

"Did you just call David a humbug, Helen?" Janet asked.

"Humbug built Fairy Flax Hall," Helen said.

"She means Horatio MacAskill, fondly known as Humbug," Christine said. "MacAskills fondly refer to any number of relatives and possessions by alternate names."

"Humbug because he kept sweeties in his pocket and pulled them out for the *bairns*," Helen said.

"It's like a movie set," Janet said. "Do they always light up the front? It's like one of those historic sites with a sound and light show after dark. *Is* it a historic house?"

"Nothing more historic than Victorian excess," Christine said. "And the lights must be contemporary excess. They're new since I was last here, thirty or forty years ago anyway."

"Speaking of excess, look how many cars are already here," Janet said. At least twenty cars lined either side of a circular drive. Another car now followed their own slow progress up the lane. "What kind of clutter do they have? Spare armor?"

"Possibly but unlikely," Christine said. "The house is rather like a reverse Tardis from *Doctor Who*. This has more frills on the outside than actual relics or living space on the inside."

"Still, it's mind-boggling."

"Nay, lass. It's Scots Baronial," Helen said.

"Dad calls it Scots maniacal," Christine said with a snort.

Helen snorted, too, then chortled until she had a coughing fit.

Christine slowed further. "All right there, Mum?"

"Here? Aye, I've always enjoyed coming here," Helen said. "It's a nice wee bit of land. Room for sheep. Fat ponies, as well."

"Mum was one of the bairns Humbug gave candy to," Christine said. "He made his pile of money then built this pile, complete with a bit of faux rubble at the base of the corner tower on the right."

The driver following them honked then pulled around, spitting gravel that pinged off the Vauxhall.

"*Glaikit* numpty," Christine growled. "If I'd caught the number plate, I'd leave a note on the windscreen. I didn't get a proper look at it. Too busy keeping us on the road. Was it a van?"

"Pickup," Helen said.

"Was it, Mum?" Christine asked.

"It was," Janet said.

"Aye," said Helen. "With room for sheep or a fine fat pony."

A car pulled away from directly in front of the broad front stairs of the house as they approached. Christine maneuvered into that prime parking space and Janet heard her muttering about impatient numpties being served right if they had to park in a mire at the far end. She and Christine got out and Janet witnessed a transformation.

Christine shrugged off her sensible-Scotswoman-dressed-in-trousers-and-duffel persona and became an irritated Queen Elizabeth II. Janet had never seen this regal side of Christine during their years of friendship in Illinois. The queen had only been making her appearance since they'd arrived in Inversgail. Janet had recently asked Christine if she was aware of her alter ego. Christine, turning royally affronted eyes on Janet, had replied "havers." Now the queen turned her eyes to the other parked vehicles, no doubt searching for the offending pickup.

"Bollocks," Christine said, reverting to herself and going around to help Helen out. "There are half a dozen pickups and no telling which one zipped past us."

"Unless you find one with a hood that's still warm," Janet said.

"Oh, that's very good. Nip off and run your hand over their bonnets, will you?"

"No! I didn't think you'd take me seriously and because we don't want to create ill will," Janet said. "It won't be good for business if we leave a note for that glaikit numpty."

The queen flashed in Christine's eyes. "The note will be anonymous. If you won't nip off, I will. Mum, here's Janet to take you into Violet's party. I'll be right behind you."

"We'll have a grand time," Helen said as Janet took her arm. "Violet serves lovely sherry."

"Wonderful," Janet said. "I do like a glass of sherry in the evening."

"What's that? Merry, did you say?" Helen cackled. "David and I are often merry in the evening. Keeps us young."

The MacAskill's immense front door was wide enough for several sheep and a brace of fat ponies to enter abreast. With its rounded top, bolts, and reinforcing bands of wrought iron, it looked to Janet as though it could be barred on the inside with half a tree—and at odds with a man named Humbug who kept candy in his pockets for children. Janet pictured the door swinging open with a groan of timbers and a moan of hinges in need of bear grease. As she helped Helen up the broad stone stairs, an almost invisible normal-sized door, set into the corner of the larger door, opened without a murmur.

"A mousehole in the wainscoting" Janet said to Helen.

"And here's our wee mousie in his waistcoat," Helen said, startling the man coming out. Her laughter startled him further and he stopped short.

"Hello, Kyle," Janet said.

She almost didn't recognize their unexpected knitter from that morning, without his carrier bags, and wearing waistcoat and tailcoat. He wore a more pedestrian pair of trousers and had a sweater draped over his arm, the way a wine steward might carry a white linen serviette. Neither the waistcoat nor the tailcoat quite fit around his middle, but his eyes and pink cheeks shone with the pleasure of them. Kyle's lips parted as though he might say something. Instead, he looked back over his shoulder into the house, then bounded down the stairs and away down the drive.

"Violet's sherry put the roses in *his* cheeks all right," Helen said.

"Are we about to be embarrassed, or was he overdressed?" Janet asked.

"Who?" Helen asked.

"Never mind. He's left the door open. Let's go in."

Before they reached the door, a voice called from the stairs behind them. "Helen Maclean, is that you? It is! And look who I found."

Helen, still holding Janet's arm, performed an unsteady pivot, bringing Janet around with her. "Chrissie!" Helen said with warm pleasure. "You came after all."

Christine came up the stairs with an expression Janet couldn't read and a balding man Janet didn't know. The spotlights shining on the front of the house turned the fringe of hair above his ears silver. His corduroy trousers and waterproof jacket seemed more appropriate for a decluttering than Kyle's tailcoat.

"So good to see you, Helen." The man kissed her cheek. "I teased David about your venerable Vauxhall earlier today. He pretended to take offense, said he wouldn't come tonight. I didn't think he meant it. But then who should I find traipsing amongst the other cars, as though dreaming of trading up, but your Chrissie. Or—you weren't looking for David out there were you, Christine? Has he taken to wandering off?" The man looked toward the parked cars with concern.

Christine drew herself up. "No, Edward. He hasn't. I wouldn't have let him drive this morning if that were the case. He's home, and like the

Vauxhall, running smoothly. Let's get Mum out of the cold, though, shall we?"

Christine took Helen's arm from Janet. They proceeded through the door into a walnut-paneled entrance hall. Although close to Janet's living room in size, the space felt neither cavernous nor intimidating, and proportionally more in keeping with the mousehole door they'd entered than the ironbound portal. Janet turned around to see the effect the Goliath door had on the room—only to find a fourth walnut-paneled wall where the larger door should be, and the man—Edward—standing closer behind her than *he* should be. Janet stepped back and gestured toward the wall.

"A lovely bit of fakery, isn't it?" Edward said. "But I'm being a poor host—I don't believe we've met. I'm Edward MacAskill, aged son of the house."

"Janet Marsh, in business with Christine at Yon Bonnie Books." Janet took the hand he held out and appreciated that he didn't hold hers for any longer than necessary.

"Where were our manners, Edward?" Christine said. "Janet, I'm sorry. I should have introduced you immediately."

"Not a problem," Janet said. "It's nice to meet you, Edward. Thank you for having me."

"All thanks go to Mother," Edward said. "I'm merely an able body this evening. Along with my sister and niece. One of them is meant to be here at the door."

Three arched doorways, one in each wall, led to other parts of the house. Edward glanced toward them as though Isobel or Teresa might be waiting to pop out and surprise them. They heard faint noises that Janet interpreted as happy bursts of decluttering—murmured oohs, laughter, and a solid thump that sounded exactly like a stack of heavy books dropped on a table. Edward turned back to them with a vague shake of his head, seemingly at a loss for how to conjure his sister or niece.

"Let's start with where to put our coats," Christine said. "Mum's anxious to see Violet and Janet is dying for a good declutter."

"Yes. Right. Why don't *I* take them, then?" Edward helped Helen out of hers, and after taking Christine's and Janet's, nodded toward an antique desk. "There's a guestbook on the secretary. My contribution to the evening. Ever the record keeper. Can't seem to stop myself. So then, after you've signed, have a look round and carry off clutter to your heart's content. Anything that isn't behind locked doors or marked with a big red dot like the one on the secretary is fair game. And do come have a glass of sherry with Mother in her sitting room. She'll be happy to see you." He looked at the coats in his arms, looked around the entry hall again, and left.

"He is definitely iffy," Janet whispered to Christine.

"One man's 'iffy' is an entire family's eccentricity. This house is a monument to that. What do you think of this desk, Mum?" Christine led Helen to the secretary. "Is it a genuine Mackintosh?" She signed the guestbook then handed the pen to her mother.

"Charles Rennie Mackintosh and Humbug MacAskill sat side by side on the *braes* of Inversgail painting the bonny wee fairy flax flowers," Helen said. "I wonder if that's true or if the flax fairies have been blathering in my ears." She signed her name, then peered at the other names on the page. "Has David signed? Is he meeting us here?"

"Dad's having a quiet evening at home," Christine said. "And I know it's not the same, but Janet and I are here."

"That's fine then. Let's go find the sherry and my old friend, the violet fairy." Helen gave the pen to Janet and without hesitation set off through one of the archways so that Christine had to skip to catch up. Janet scribbled her name in the guestbook and hurried after.

Helen's memory of Fairy Flax Hall proved unerring. She led them through a chandelier-lit dining room where a trio of guests packed dishes, silverware, and linens into boxes; the adjacent room, where a quartet of declutters eyed tools, small appliances, and a variety of containers displayed on folding tables set up for the occasion; and through the next doorway, where they found Violet and Edward.

"Helen!" Violet said. "Come *ben*, come in. Edward, sherry for our guests, please. Helen, sit next to me." Violet, looking as delicate as a porcelain flower, patted the sofa beside her. Helen plumped herself down and the two old friends clasped hands. "It's your birthday soon. I haven't forgot. Does David still take you for lunch at the Argyle Trout?"

"It's where we first laid eyes on each other. Reservations always for that exact time—quarter past twelve."

"You two never fail to delight. Isn't that right, Christine? So good to see you home again. And who have we here?"

"Janet Marsh, Mrs. MacAskill," Janet said. "Christine and I are in business together at Yon Bonnie Books. Thank you for inviting me this evening."

"Edward." A woman near Edward's age, but with an enviable head of hair to his balding pate, appeared in the doorway. She fussed into the room with the harassed air of a stage manager on opening night, the curls in her hair on the alert for anything amiss. "Where have you been?"

"Ah, Teresa." Edward smiled at his sister. "There you are." He presented sherry glasses to their mother and Helen, then to Christine and Janet.

Christine raised her glass to the bristling woman. "Lovely to see you, Teresa. Do you know my business partner Janet? A bit of lark, this. We've never been to a decluttering."

"That makes all of us, I should think," Teresa said. "I told mother she could have a sale."

"And I told you I could not," Violet said.

Edward had moved beside the sofa and put his hand on his mother's shoulder. "Mother's parties are legendary. This decluttering do will be as brilliant as any of them."

"Darling Edward," Violet said. "The idea came to me after watching a show about hoarders. Also, the movie *You Can't Take It With You*. And that

Bible verse about a rich man and the eye of a camel. But this evening is Teresa's brilliance. Despite her misgivings, she took care of everything. Thank you, Teresa."

"Under your eye, Mother," Teresa said. "Always under your eye."

"Pie?" Helen piped up. "Och aye. A wee slice will be grand. What kind?"

Janet leaned close to Christine. "Have fun. I'll go rummaging."

Sipping her sherry, Janet wended her way back through the drawing and dining rooms. She didn't need dishware or appliances but—did she spy tartanware napkin rings? Too late. Another woman reached the antique beauties first. With a conspiratorial gleam in her eye, she told Janet she'd already filled the boot of her car. Janet drew her own hand back with a smile, her competitive spirit unleashed. Hearing the call of clutter in rooms yet unexplored, she went to see what else Violet was so happy to be giving away. More guests circulated now, none of whom she knew, but as she passed back through the entry hall, she heard her name.

"Sorry I missed you coming in." Isobel, bubbly and rosy, waved at her. "Isn't this grand? Are you finding your way round?"

"I found the sherry," Janet said. "That's a good start. Oh, I've been asked to look for vintage evening gowns."

"Sorry, no. No clothes at all. Books galore, though. Through there." Isobel pointed at one of the archways then rushed to open the front door for a couple laden with boxes and bags.

The archway led to a short hall, and the hall to a lamplit room. The scene before her led Janet to put a hand to her heart and one to her mouth. Four walls of floor-to-ceiling books! Declutterers rooting through them like happy swine and leaving utter shambles! Janet didn't know whether to scold them with her librarian's voice or jump in and wallow, too. Her phone buzzed, saving her from a decision.

Look whose poems are slamming it out of the park, Tallie said in a text from the poetry and knitting slam. A photo arrived showing Maida Fairlie, prim mother-in-law to Janet's son, standing before the audience, microphone in hand, handbag on her arm.

Go, Maida! Janet sent back. Then she muttered to herself, "Good advice. Save yourself, Janet. Go." She shuddered at the book bedlam surrounding her and picked her way across the room to another door. It opened into a sunroom at the back of the house. She saw a scattering of wicker chairs with red dots, meaning they weren't for the taking, and a smaller number of people making idle chat or admiring their treasures. One of the latter was a good friend.

"Hello, James," Janet said.

"Evening, Janet." James Haviland, editor of the *Inversgail Guardian*, cradled an elegant antique typewriter in the crook of each arm.

"Congratulations, it's mechanical twins," Janet said. "They have your eyes. What are you calling them?"

Her question tapped the right key, launching James into a loving description of each machine. As he sang a hymn to the glory of ornate copper typebar shields, she became aware of a commotion muffled by a door behind him. A woman carrying a watering can and punch bowl heard it, too. Janet watched her move closer to the door and tip her head to listen. The woman awkwardly shifted the watering can, freeing a hand, and listened again. Her free hand hovered near the doorknob. Thinking she should help the woman with the door (and escape James), Janet shifted her weight.

At that moment, the woman glanced around. She saw Janet watching her and came over to say quietly, "Something's amiss. I'd best fetch Teresa."

James, now caroling the wonders of rubber platens, hadn't noticed the exchange or the commotion. He snapped to attention when Janet tapped SOS on one of his spacebars. She nodded him toward the door.

"One of the locked doors," he said. "Off limits."

"Something's going on in there, though. A woman's gone to get Teresa." Janet put her ear to the door. "Arguing," she whispered. "Indistinct. I wish I knew what—"

"Easy enough to find out, then. If they got in, so can we. Open the door."

"*Wheesht*," Janet shushed. "We don't know who that is or what they're up to. But we *do* know Violet's giving away carloads of valuable things, so can you imagine the tempting stuff locked away in there?"

"Wheesht yourself." James had his own ear to the door. "Did I hear the word ambulance?"

"If you did, I missed it, trying to talk sense to you. *Oh.*" Janet pulled back. "They're coming toward the door."

"At a creep," James said. "Why so slow?"

They looked at each other and backed away from the door. As they did, one of the voices grew steadily louder. Louder, more querulous, and recognizably Helen.

"I know what Violet's like, Chrissie. She's pernickety, with good reason, and she'll not be pleased that we've left a dead body cluttering up her Fairy Flax Hall."

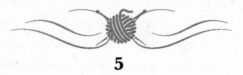

5

Arsenic Diary, day two and a half

I quite like the stilted language in old newspapers. Did reporters learn the style at the knees of their editors, or did this kind of speech naturally fall out of people's mouths?

"HOST AND GUEST DIE. POISONED BY A SUPPER.
3 February 1911, Dalkeith, Scotland
14 guests, 2 dead
Further light has been thrown on the Dalkeith murders, by a statement of the police. John Hutchison, who poisoned his father and a guest, was in desperate financial straits. His chief creditors were among his father's guests during a midnight supper after the play of several tables of whist at the elder Hutchison's house. It is believed that John Hutchison planned to utilize the supper for the purpose of killing his creditors and also his parents, Mr. and Mrs. Charles Hutchison, whose lives were jointly insured for £4,000.

Charles Hutchison and one of his guests, Mr. Alexander Clapperton from Musselburgh, died from the effects of arsenical poisoning, supposed to have been administered by John Hutchison in the coffee served at the supper. The latter was a chemist, and suspicion fell on him because a bottle of arsenic was

38

missing from the shop where he was employed, and also because on the night of the tragedy, he carried the coffee from the kitchen to the drawing room. Mr. Hutchison and Mr. Clapperton were dead by morning. Charles Hutchison was a highly regarded figure throughout Midlothian and Edinburgh. A further 12 guests were violently and seriously ill, including Mrs. Hutchison, the accused man's mother."

There's something about my mouth. People look at it and feel they need to tell me there's no need, or I've no reason, to be so unhappy. This happens frequently at parties. Perhaps, in an earlier life, I attended a supper party where I fell violently and seriously ill, and the memory lingers, to this day, in the corners of my lips.

∽

Janet grabbed the knob and swung the door open, surprising Christine and Helen to a standstill.

"Ambulance, Janet," Christine said.

"Nay, Chrissie," said Helen gently. "It's too late for that."

Christine, pale and with her arm around her mother, nodded. Having come to a standstill in the doorway, they made no further effort to move.

"Not a good sign, if it's too late for an ambulance," James said quietly as Janet pressed 9-9-9 on her phone. "Even less so when you and your pals are around."

"We don't go out of our way to stumble over dead bodies," Janet snapped.

"Of course not, not meaning any offense."

"I'm reporting a fatality," Janet said when the dispatcher answered, speaking softly and turning her back on James. "I'm calling from Fairy Flax Hall. My name is Janet Marsh. I'm a guest here. I—" Janet stopped and looked at Christine. "I actually don't have details. Can you hold a moment? I'll put someone on who does." Janet held the phone to her chest and asked Christine if she felt up to answering the dispatcher's questions.

As Christine nodded and reached for the phone, Janet felt a tap on her shoulder—James. "Teresa approaching," he whispered. "*Rampant guardant.*"

Janet turned to see what James couldn't just say in plain English. Or maybe he had. Teresa, with her enviable mane, strode toward them looking ready for heraldic combat.

"9-9-9 is on the line," Janet said, bringing Teresa to a halt. "We should—"

"Thank you," Teresa said. "You should let me handle this."

"You might want to let Christine answer—"

Teresa intercepted the phone Janet held out to Christine. "Teresa MacAskill, here," she told the dispatcher, "I've already spoken to Constable Norman Hobbs. He's on the scene and will communicate our situation as needed. Thank you." She ended the call and handed the phone back to Janet. "Now then, Christine, Helen, this door was locked and these rooms are off limits. Do come along and we'll quickly sort this."

Christine, less pale and more rampant herself, opened her mouth, but Helen spoke first. "Norman, did you say? He's a good lad. Best leave it to him. We'll sit by those ferns and wait. The *polis* always have questions."

Helen, holding Christine's arm, crossed to a set of ratan chairs and a sofa grouped near a lush fern taller than she. Janet and James followed. The women sat together on the sofa, Helen between her daughter and Janet. The furniture looked more comfortable than it was, Janet thought, but the comfort of closeness made up for it. They watched as Teresa locked the now closed door, shooed a few curious guests, closed the two doors to the sunroom, then strode back to the locked door and took up a position in front of it.

"The people she chased off were curious about what's going on," Christine said. "One of Norman's questions should be why she isn't."

"Sudden and unexpected death at a party isn't the sort of thing anyone imagines, though," Janet said, "and I don't think she knows that's what's happened."

"She imagined *something,* or she wouldn't have brought Norman into it," Christine said. "Who brought *her* into it? From the dirty looks she's shooting this way she isn't imagining anymore at all; she's convinced she caught us looting in the forbidden zone."

"A woman went off to find Teresa," Janet said. "Did you know her, James?"

"Sorry, I only had eyes for my two beauties." James gazed fondly at the typewriters he still cradled.

"I don't think Teresa is happy about the decluttering in the first place," Janet said.

"Probably not," James said. "I wonder what's taking Norman so long. He'd a stuffed badger under his arm and was eyeing a toaster in the dining room last time I saw him."

"I didn't see him at all," said Janet.

"I doubt Teresa went looking for him," Christine said. "She must have phoned him, thinking it would be faster. Otherwise she wouldn't have arrived without him."

"No," James said. "Not even Norman would dare say, 'Hold on a mo. Be with you by and by.' Not to Teresa. So, Christine, who have we got in there?"

"Mum called her Wendy."

"That's right," Helen said. "David recognized her right off."

"Dad's not here, Mum."

"But he knows her well enough. Wendy from the museum."

"Och well." James handed one of the typewriters off to Janet with a "Do you mind?" He set the other on the floor at his feet, took hers back and set it down, too. Then his phone came out and his newspaper-man's fingers went to work. "Wendy Erskine, director of the Inversgail Heritage Museum. Isobel's boss. Edward does something there, too. I'm not sure what. *Blethering,* at a guess. Any details from beyond the door to share?"

"Get the details from Norman, will you?" Christine tipped her head toward Helen.

"If you're worried about your mum, I think she's fallen asleep," Janet said.

Helen had drifted sideways, her head on Janet's shoulder, face peaceful.

"The dragon at the gate might be wondering what we're talking about," Christine said. "But all right."

"Recording's faster than my thumbs, if you don't mind. What rooms are beyond the dragon?"

"Sitting room, bedroom, bathroom. The old housekeeper's quarters, Mum said. She, Wendy, is in the far room, the bedroom. She appears to have been taken ill before she died. Quite violently. *Won awa*, as Mum said. Suffered as she died."

"The poor thing," Janet murmured. "Why didn't she call for help?"

"Perhaps she did," James said. "But with her back there we might not have heard."

"But her phone?"

"That's for Norman to wonder. Speaking of, where is he? The house isn't that big. I wonder if we should call him ourselves." James looked toward Teresa and the closed door. Janet saw a smile quirk his mouth and disappear. "I'll tell you what else I wonder," he said, noticeably louder. "Did Wendy suffer a bout of food poisoning? There's been a rash of it. Unconfirmed, but attributed to the new food truck—Mr. Potato Chef. Also called the tatty tattie truck, because of its shabby appearance. Rust spots and a dinged bonnet. Unsightly, I'll give you that, but I've no problem with a lovely tattie. Could be that Wendy hadn't either. Oh, hello, Teresa. Had enough of guarding a locked door?"

"What's this about Wendy and that dreadful food truck?" Teresa asked. "I doubt she eats street food. I don't know why anyone would. So, what are you havering on about?"

"Ah, well, here's Norman," James said. "I'll tell you both at once. Save us all time."

Constable Norman Hobbs marched toward them. His brush of salt and pepper hair, as always, standing at attention, his trousers crisp, and regulation boots resounding. Indeed, everything from the constable's neck up and from his waist down, appeared to be Police Scotland issue. In between waist and neck, a lilac-colored sweater rode in glory. The climate between Hobbs and the women of Yon Bonnie Books was generally favorable, with long periods of amicable respect disrupted by only brief spates of suspicion. They'd developed an arrangement of mutual aid while solving several recent crimes in Inversgail. Hobbs and the women each felt that they put up with a lot from the other. Christine had known him since she'd babysat for him as a small boy.

"Mrs. Robertson," Hobbs said, after a nod to Teresa, "may I ask that you and your mother stay a wee while longer. I'll be as quick as I can and then I may have questions for you. Will your mum be all right waiting?"

"We'll be fine," Christine said. "Thank you, Norman."

Now then, Mrs. Ritchie," Hobbs said to Teresa, "I've spoken with the police call dispatcher. Where will I find the body?"

Teresa's mouth opened and closed without sound. Neither Christine nor James came to her aid. When she tried again, she managed a single word, strangled by disbelief, *"Body?"*

Janet took pity on her.

"Behind the door, there, Norman. In the back bedroom. Teresa has the key."

"Thank you, Mrs. Marsh. Are you fine to stay as well?"

"I am."

"Mrs. Ritchie?" Hobbs said. "If you'll be so kind."

Janet, Christine, James, and Helen—who'd waked at the strangled noise that finally came from Teresa's throat—watched Teresa clumsily try to unlock the door. Hobbs took the key from her, opened the door, and put the key in his breast pocket. Teresa made a plea to accompany him, which he denied, closing the door. She stayed facing it, head bowed.

"I feel rather as though we're a group of fates watching this play out as we sit here," James said.

"Do you think the jumper is Nana Bethia's handiwork?" Christine asked.

"Unusual color for Norman and a wee bit snug," James said. "Fetching, though."

"Are you fetching?" Helen asked. "I'd like a sherry, ta very much."

"Would tea be more suitable, do you think?" James asked Christine. "Sherry."

"Teresa?" James called to her back. "Can I bring you a sherry?"

No answer. No indication she'd heard.

"Bring one for her anyway," Janet said.

"Aye then. Be right back."

James returned as Hobbs came out of the suite and relocked the door. He spoke quietly to Teresa. She nodded, took a breath visible to the four fates sipping their sherry by the potted fern, nodded again and strode from the sunroom. Hobbs joined the fates. James handed him the fifth sherry.

"On duty?" Christine asked. "Have the regulations changed?"

"A bad business in there," Hobbs said.

"You're right. You should probably have another, too," Christine said. "Ask your questions and we'll let you get back to it."

"I've only a few and then you can be away home. But first, a quick question for Mrs. Marsh."

"I called 9-9-9," Janet said.

"Aye, I know."

"I didn't go in the room at all."

"My question is of a different nature. A favor. May I ask you to take my grandmother home with you for the few hours I'll be tied up here?"

"I didn't know Nana Bethia was here," Janet said. She didn't know she'd be put on the spot like this either. She didn't answer Hobbs immediately, hoping he'd mistake her silence as rapt interest in his description of Bethia's joy when she found a cache of knitting needles and wool in the clutter. Her wariness stemmed from the last time Bethia had stayed at her house.

"She'll take the lot back to the care home when she returns," Hobbs said, "for the knitting circle."

Janet knew that Hobbs would be wary of her wariness. He'd created it by housing Bethia in her house, without her knowledge. This had happened after a mishap, involving vandalism of the house, before she and Tallie had been able to move in when they arrived in Inversgail. Hobbs had made matters worse by spinning stories of a rat infestation to prolong their displacement. Janet and Christine occasionally held the "Nana Bethia Incident" over his head when they needed an advantage.

"I shan't be too long in coming to collect her," Hobbs said.

That was all Janet needed to hear. "No worries, Norman. I'll be happy to take her with me. She can stay as long as she likes, or as long as you need her to." She smiled to let him know she meant it. And she did, because she liked Bethia, and wouldn't actually be bothered by having her as a houseguest, as long as she knew she had one.

"Thank you. Now then, Mrs. Robertson, Mrs. McLean," Hobbs said. "Can you tell me how you came to be in the suite this evening."

"Are you needing the toilet?" Helen asked. "It's just through door, there. Run along, Norman. Be a good lad. You know what happens when you wait too long."

Christine answered the rest of Hobbs's few questions, while he took notes and James recorded the brief interview. Christine told them she and Helen had gone into the suite looking for the toilet Helen remembered being there. Helen used the facilities, and while Christine took her turn, Helen had wandered to the bedroom and found Wendy. "Mum recognized her," Christine said. "I didn't know her. Could it have been food poisoning, like James said?"

"Any particular reason you thought of that?" Hobbs asked James.

"Not really. Food poisoning's been on people's lips, so to speak."

"I hope you won't mention your unfounded suggestion in *The Guardian*," Hobbs said.

"I won't," James said. "You know how people talk, though. The rumors are a bit hard on Euan Markwell, who owns Mr. Potato Chef."

"I've heard," Hobbs said. "To answer your question, Mrs. Robertson, we'll know more after autopsy."

"Is Teresa sending everyone home?" Janet asked.

"No need for that," Hobbs said. "The suite is locked, and I asked Teresa to mark this room off limits. I'll go bring Mrs. MacAskill up to speed, but I see no reason to curtail her decluttering. Her guests are doing her a favor. Going about it quickly and quietly. No, the death of Ms. Erskine is unfortunate, but I see no reason to send the guests home."

Hobbs looked at his empty sherry glass and stood. Janet wondered how many glasses he'd had earlier. They might have something to do with his unusually chatty answer.

"We'll come with you to see Violet, Norman." Christine helped Helen to her feet. "Mum wants to say goodbye to Violet, and our pocketbooks are there. We won't stay. Janet's riding with us, so where will we find Nana Bethia?"

"I left her with Mrs. MacAskill."

"I'll just tag along," James said. "Pay my respects."

"No nosy questions," Hobbs said.

"Wouldn't dream of it." James hefted the typewriters back into his arms with Janet's help.

In the sitting room, Violet held out her hands to Helen. The two said their goodbyes, Violet's role as gracious host subdued from earlier in the evening. She didn't mention the death. Helen might have already forgotten. Janet thanked Violet, and quietly asked if Isobel was holding up.

"She is," Violet said after briefly closing her eyes. "But I'd expect no less."

James and Hobbs had settled into a pair of wingchairs with more sherry. With nods to the men, Janet and Christine tucked their respective elderly women's arms in their own, collected their coats, and departed. Janet didn't see Edward or Isobel on the way out. Teresa opened the front door for them, and, although the four women each said goodnight, Teresa closed the door behind them without a word.

∽

Tallie opened the door when Christine dropped Janet and Bethia off at the house on Argyll Terrace. She brought them inside with greetings and promises of hot tea and biscuits—dark chocolate Digestives. Smirr and Butter, the big gray tom and the yellow kitten, hadn't yet met Bethia, and went to work fixing that.

"How lovely," Bethia said, standing still while the cats twined their introductions around her ankles.

"Come along, lads," Tallie called to them. "Crunchy, fishy things in the kitchen for good cats who don't trip guests."

Janet put Bethia in the most comfortable chair in the living room and went to help Tallie with the tea.

"You're home early." Janet took cream from the refrigerator. "And you were expecting us." She scratched each cat on the head. "You boys can't really be expecting cream, can you?"

"Summer got a text from James."

"How detailed? Enough that you weren't worried, I hope."

"Enough for that, but maybe not all the details?" Tallie took a third teacup and saucer from the cupboard and held them up—a silent question about how long Bethia might be staying.

"Norman might be a while yet."

"That's not much of a detail either," Tallie whispered.

"Hours," Janet whispered back, "not days."

Janet carried the tea tray to the living room. Bethia, with a cat on either side, smiled at her from the sofa.

"They convinced me we needed more room," she said, accepting a cup and saucer from Tallie. "Now Janet, I hope I can convince you to tell me what went on this evening. Norman only said he thought it best if I came home with you and that he'll be along later. I didn't like to ask him what 'later' means to a policeman."

Janet put her teacup down. "Violet didn't say anything?"

"An incident of some sort, but she didn't like to go into detail."

"Did you meet Wendy Erskine at the museum?" Janet asked.

"Oh, yes."

"She took ill at the decluttering this evening. She, uh—" Janet took a moment before continuing. "Sadly, she passed away."

"Peacefully?" Bethia said. "Did she *slippit awa?*"

"If *slippit awa* means peacefully, then no. Christine said she'd been violently ill."

"How very sad." Bethia moved the sleeping yellow kitten to her lap.

"I'm sorry, Bethia," Janet said. "This is an unhappy way to end the evening. Not a nice conversation over tea and biscuits."

"It's what we do, though, isn't it," Bethia said. "Talk it over. Ask why and how a tragedy could happen. If we can find the answers, we might do better under similar circumstances. Or avoid it altogether. It's our way of holding back the end for a wee bit longer."

"There but for the grace of God, go I," Tallie said.

Bethia nodded. "Could no one help her? Where was she? The house isn't that large, and with so many people walking around."

"Large enough though," Janet described the location of the suite and the bedroom. "The area wasn't part of the decluttering and the door should have been locked. I wonder why she didn't phone for help."

"No time, maybe," Tallie said. "It could have been her heart."

"True," Janet said. "Or a stroke. They can be very fast. James wondered about food poisoning. He said there's a rash of it. Heart attack or stroke sound more likely. That leaves the question of why she was back there and how she got in, but Christine said the door wasn't locked when she and her mum went looking for the loo."

"That's probably what Wendy was doing, too," Tallie said.

"Norman will sort it," Bethia said. "I don't know why he had me come here, though. I *couldhae* just gone to my rooms. Two rooms, with an en suite. Terribly posh."

Janet wondered if her living room had just been dissed. Norman's, too, because Bethia's posh en suite accommodations didn't describe his rooms behind the police station at all.

"To be quite honest, though," Bethia said as Smirr nudged the kitten so there'd be room on her lap for him, too, "I'm far more comfortable in a room such as this. Would you mind handing me my knitting bag? I wouldn't like to wake the cats."

Tallie passed the bag to her. "What did you mean when you said you could have just gone to your rooms?"

"Isobel made the arrangements when she asked me to judge the knitting competition. I'm staying at Fairy Flax Hall." Bethia took her knitting from the bag. "No Inversgail stockings tonight. I'm knitting my second pair of those but save working on them for the knitting venues around town. This is for one of my great-granddaughters." She held up lace so fine Janet thought she could be knitting it using a selkie's whiskers for needles.

Hobbs arrived not long after and stopped only long enough to pick up Bethia and thank Janet and Tallie. At the door, he agreed that, apart from the unfortunate incident, the decluttering had gone well.

"James said he saw you with a stuffed badger," Janet said.

"Aye, he's a lovely chap," Hobbs said. "James can be, too, when he likes. Mind, I did think I might see fins a time or two. Sharks, aye? Circling and going after the clutter like chum."

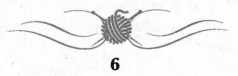

6

Arsenic Diary, day three

Brilliantly executed. My plan to liberate the scrapbook, that is, not the demise of Ms. Erskine. Imagine dying that way, surrounded by celebratory sherry sippers, yet all alone and unremarked behind a closed door. I bow my head and vow I'll no longer think of her as the harridan of the museum. Also, that I will not weigh the likelihood of roasting in perpetuity as opposed to resting in peace.

But delivering the scrapbook into my own safe keeping. A pure rush of adrenaline, that was! Hand on heart (and head no longer bowed because life goes on), I did not know I had it in me. And now here I am—here we are—my new ward and I, my old girl. I had no sherry this evening. I needed a clear head for Operation Liberation, but now I feel quite drunk on the power of subterfuge and secrecy.

The scrapbook is a gey secret thing as well. An inspiration, this was, using the pages of one book as the tabula not-quite rasa for another book that's so much more interesting. Not every page, mind. My scrapbook artist used stealth there, as well, slicing some of the pages out all together so that the whole thing did not swell beyond its leather binding as she pasted in her own additions. Her clippings and notes—her drops of arsenical wisdom and lore—are sprinkled through the remaining pages, turning a dusty tome of arcane tedium into a living, evolving document. With the possibility

50

of further evolution; quite a few of the original pages are still waiting to be used.

A book like this was never meant to sit in the corner of a shelf, half-finished, clouded by dust, beginning to moulder. I have done it a favour. I've done several favours lately. I shan't enumerate or pat myself on the back, though, as pride goeth, etc. But we are both heroes, the scrapbook artist and I. I, for bringing her masterpiece away with me. She, for grappling with the original—A Monograph of the British Nudibranchiate Mollusca: with figures of all the species, volume one—liberating it from its own dreadful mundanity. Mundanity—I lick my lips as though the word is a last scrap of pudding.

Funny how I've come to think of her as female. Not just the artist but also the book. And not because arsenic, or poison in general, is traditionally a woman's weapon. Let it not be said that I prostrate myself at the feet of tradition. No, this old girl strikes me as the pastime of someone whose spirit was thwarted. Every step of the way? That I cannot say, but this I will hazard—thwarted though she might have been, by custom, society, or tradition, the creator of this masterpiece did not allow her spirit to be destroyed.

Arsenic cannot be destroyed, either. It can only change form or become attached to or separated from other particles. As well, rats have a way of escaping complete destruction.

Romantics say they will always have Paris.

I say, the world will always have rats.

And arsenic.

∽

Inversgail, though a year-round tourist town, did experience quiet winter days when a dog could safely nap in the High Street—if it didn't mind the weather having turned to rubbish. The morning after the decluttering dawned such a day. A brief appearance by the pallid sun from its bed of clouds, around ten o'clock, caused a spasm of people in and out of the shops. The sun and the spasm disappeared again without adding much to anyone's enjoyment.

On their way to Yon Bonnie Books, Rab MacGregor and his dog, Ranger, stopped to sniff a buffet of wind off the harbor. Ranger stopped again in the middle of the High Street to sniff a chip dropped by a seagull. At a whistle from Rab, Ranger left the chip. Sleeping on a cold, hard street no more crossed his mind than it ever would Rab's.

"Morning, Rab. Morning, Ranger," Janet said when they entered the shop. Rab took Ranger's tea towel from a pocket of his jacket and handed it to him. Ranger carried the towel to the inglenook and hopped into his favorite chair. He arranged the towel, arranged himself, and started the first nap of the day. As the day grew steadily colder and damper, Ranger abandoned his favorite chair for one closer to the fireplace, sprawled with his belly fully exposed to the heat.

"You look like you might want to join him," Tallie said to her mother. "Rough night?"

"Nah." Janet sat on the stool near the cash register, an elbow propped on the counter, her cheek resting on her fist. "How about you?"

"I slept all right. Do you want to go home early? Rab and I can handle things here."

"I think I want to take a walk."

"Brrr."

"The museum's open," Janet said. "I wasn't sure it would be."

"They have tours scheduled, I guess, and the knitting in public. Calling the competition Rocking the Stocking seems kind of flip at this point. Life goes on. That sounds flip, too."

"I thought I'd go over there and express our condolences to Isobel."

"Wear your scarf and mittens and pull your hat over your ears, and take some scones."

Janet stopped in the tearoom to tell Christine and Summer where she was going. Summer packed six scones in a bakery bag then took off her apron, saying to Christine, "It's quiet enough, mind if I go with her?" Then to Janet, "All right with you?"

"Sure," Janet said.

"Rab's here if I need him," said Christine.

And there came Rab, putting on an apron and waving them out the door.

Small waves lapped at the harbor wall, lightening the mood of the seal-gray water. Janet and Summer walked on the shop side of the street for the small amount of protection the buildings gave from the wind. As they passed Sea View Kayak, they waved at a group knitting in the front window.

"Life and knitters do go on," Janet said.

"Life, knitters, and knitted outfits for the statue. What's he wearing today?" Summer asked. But they weren't close enough yet to see his embellishments clearly. "Oh, hey, here's a new business opportunity for someone. Make scale models of the statue and sell little outfits to go with it."

"New outfits for every season, plus fancy wear for holidays," Janet said. "And for children, an R.L.S. paper doll. I wonder if the museum would want to do that."

"Forget I said 'someone.' *We* could do that. I bet Rab could anyway." They crossed the street and looked up at the statue.

"Knitted aviator goggles," Summer said. "And don't they look fine."

The Stevenson statue stood in front of the new home of the Inversgail History Museum, a two-story shipping warehouse dating from the early nineteenth century and long retired from its original purpose. Janet's last visit to the building had been years ago when the Inversgail library was still crowded into a windowless space on the ground floor. Except for the musty smell, the building had given the library a wonderful vault-like atmosphere. Tallie and Allen had spent many rainy summer afternoons there, calling it "The Dungeon of Lost Legends." Thanks to successful fundraising and timely grants, the library had since relocated to a new building with stunning views and was more elegantly called the Inversgail Library and Archives.

"This is different." Janet said as they pushed open the warehouse office door. She remembered the door opening directly into the library, inviting the day's weather in with every patron. Now they stood in a quiet, fresh-smelling entryway with one sign welcoming them to the museum and another inviting them to visit the exhibits and gallery on the first floor. An ornate arrow pointed to stairs and an elevator off to the right. "Nothing to see down here?" Janet asked, pointing to the left.

"Storage and behind the scenes stuff, I think. Elevator or stairs?"

"Stairs," Janet said. "Unless the elevator's some antique clanking thing big enough to haul a load of—what did they ship out of Inversgail?"

"Beats me, but that elevator doesn't look like it's hiding any clanks. When Tallie and I were here in the summer we took the stairs."

"And the stairs are a nicely dramatic entrance. Look at the balcony at the top. I'm not sure I want to look down from up there, but I love looking up—so much space. So let's go, and maybe we'll become better educated about shipping."

The stairs weren't antique or clanking either. The women climbed wide, noiseless treads, with a railing on the left, and rising past the exposed stonework of the outside wall on the right. At the top, they stepped into a wide corridor filled with light from windows along the same outside wall. All along the wall to their left, enlarged photographs showed the life of Inversgail from decades, scores, and centuries past. They walked to the reception desk, fifteen or twenty feet along the photographic wall, with no one in sight.

Or earshot. It was so quiet, Janet wondered if she'd hear whispers from the sepia-toned, solemn-faced people in the photomural—men with boats at the harbor, women with baskets, waulking wool, or gazing back at her. The thought made her wish she *would* hear them, and then made her scalp prickle. She turned from the photographs to the view out the windows, where Summer was taking a picture toward the headland. "UV filters on these windows, I bet," Janet said, using practicality to banish ghosts. "Or on the pictures."

"Both," a voice said behind them.

Janet spun around.

"We have all the mod cons." Isobel smiled at them from a doorway, having opened an unobtrusive panel in the photomural behind the reception desk. "Including an alert that pings us when someone's come in down below so we can greet them up here. Sorry, though, I'm running behind. It's nice to see you." She came through the door, followed by her uncle Edward in a dark gray wool overcoat.

"No need to be sorry. It's nice to see you, too." Janet hoped the loss of joy in Isobel's smile and voice were temporary. "We came to offer our condolences. Christine and her mum and I were sorry not to see you to express them before we left last night."

Edward put an arm around Isobel, and she leaned into him.

Niece and uncle, standing side by side, didn't look much alike. Except for their eyes—deep-set and blue. But the spark of curiosity Janet had seen in each the evening before had dimmed. Edward's overcoat hung a bit on him, helping to give the impression that he drooped, as though weighed down by cares or old wool, or that he intended to look at something interesting more closely.

"We brought scones from the tearoom," Summer said.

"Oh, for goodness' sake, yes." Janet handed the bakery bag to Isobel. "Do you both know Summer? She's the fourth member of our small business enterprise. More importantly, she's the main baker."

Edward took the bag from Isobel. "A valuable member of the team, then. How lovely. And how unique. Two mother and daughter teams in business together. I can't quite see Teresa coming on board here."

"Uncle Edward."

"Be honest, Isobel. Can *you*?"

Isobel didn't answer. Janet thought she might be controlling the urge to roll her eyes.

"Anyway," Summer said, "it's one mother daughter team and one team of women frequently *mistaken* for mother and daughter. But it doesn't bother Christine *or* me when people think we're related. We can both be prickly, so it's only natural."

"Jolly good," Edward said, opening the bakery bag and looking inside. "Perhaps I shouldn't leave just yet. Or had I just arrived?"

Isobel's lips quirked as she took the bag back from him. "In the staff room, Uncle Edward. Not out here." Then to Janet and Summer, "This is very kind. Thank you. We're all devastated about Wendy." She stopped and held a fist to her lips before continuing. "Grandmother more than anyone."

"Mm," Edward said, then as if realizing more might be required, "Yes, quite."

"I'd been afraid the evening might be sad," Isobel said. "Watching things I'd been surrounded by since I was a wean walk out the door. Gran knew what she was doing, though. It was definitely a party. People loved it. Until it was terrible . . ."

Edward filled in when Isobel faded out. "I hope that up until our unexpected tragedy you enjoyed yourself, Janet."

"I did. I loved looking around and being tempted, but I mostly enjoyed knowing that I didn't want a thing."

"Really? Not even one wee bauble?" Isobel asked.

"Well, maybe the tartanware napkin rings. But someone else got to them first, and that's fine."

"Just as well more of the guests didn't arrive with your attitude," Edward said. "With all those lovely soup tureens and bookends and what not Mother wanted rid of. Free for the taking, Janet. How could you resist?"

"And for the carrying, and for finding a place to put, and, eventually, for dusting," Janet said. "I probably should have looked at bookends, though. There were so many beautiful things I'd be happy to see again. Visiting privileges would be nice."

"Then you *should* go visit. Gran would love the company," Isobel said.

"Is she happy with how much did go out the door?" Summer asked. "Or will she have another decluttering?"

"Teresa wouldn't be keen on that," said Edward. "Over her dead body, I should think."

"Uncle Edward. Wheesht."

"Sorry. I'm incorrigible, though Teresa is more likely to say unbearable."

Janet recognized the smirk of sibling rivalry and she couldn't help smiling.

"Now," Edward said, "have you also come to see the exhibit? It's been terribly quiet so far this morning."

"We have time, don't you think?" Janet looked at Summer.

"Good with me. Isobel, I'm also part-time at the *Guardian*. If *you* have time, I'd like to get background material for an article I'm working on about the exhibit."

"The *Guardian* ran one just before the exhibit opened. Not that I wouldn't love another."

"Kind of what we thought. The first one was more of a rah-rah piece to let people know the exhibit's open and worth seeing. I'm interested in the stories behind the family gansey patterns. The reality and the myths. Personal interest stuff." Summer's enthusiasm proved infectious.

"That's brilliant," Isobel said. "My kind of article exactly. Hang on a mo." She handed the bakery bag back to Edward and ducked behind the reception desk. With two hands and a practiced heft, she brought out what looked like a large and very heavy cow bell and set it beside the desk. "Medieval Christian handbell made of lead, coated with bronze. A replica," she said. "Similar to the one stolen from St. Finan's Isle in Loch Shiel a few years back. Great fun for visitors. Ringing the bell, I mean." She set a sign on the desk that read PLEASE RING OUR WEE BELL

AND WE'LL BE RIGHT WITH YOU. "Uncle Edward, did you want to take those to the staff room?"

"No, no," he said, hurriedly closing the bakery bag. "I'm on this tour with you. Lead on."

"Good. Come see the rest of the gallery," Isobel said, "then we'll go through the exhibit."

"People must love the old photographs," Janet said, falling in beside Isobel.

"People love giving us their old photos, too. We've a catalog of all the identifiable people in them. Houses, shops, streets, boats, dogs, horses—"

"Pictures of Yon Bonnie Books?" Janet asked.

"Quite a few. If you hunt, you'll find several round the corner. The gallery extends along three sides of the building and the mural with it. Anyone or anything with a name or an address is searchable. We've an online album, as well, and look at this."

Isobel stopped at the corner where the last antique photograph had been enlarged to life size. In it, a boy and girl of nine or ten stood in front of a shop window. The boy appeared uncertain. The girl, her hand on his shoulder, looked willing to smile. A label beside the picture identified the children as Ian and Ann McNab, photographed in front of the chemist in the High Street in 1903.

"Children and families love taking selfies with Ian and Ann," Isobel said. "Then some go down the street, and if the chemist isn't rushed off her feet, they take one with her. Do you know Kathleen? She's Ann's granddaughter."

"Do people share the selfies with you?" Summer asked. She had her phone out. "And do you mind if I take voice notes as we go?"

Isobel laughed. "Hashtag: See me in 1903 Scotland. We've a lively Instagram account. And no, go right ahead with your notes."

They left Summer taking her own selfie and went around the corner. The gallery widened and brightened, the windows now floor to ceiling. Janet went right up to the glass.

"Nose and handprints are a constant battle," Isobel said.

"I don't doubt it," Janet said. "And I thought the views from the library couldn't be topped. But every view in Scotland is like that, isn't it? Each one is the best, until the next one opens up before you. I see pretty much this same view from the shop every day, and when I walk down the High Street, and from my own back garden, but—" She didn't finish, just spread her arms.

"We're unimpeded from this vantage," Edward said, joining her at the windows. "We're at one with water and air. No harbor wall. No cars, coaches, lorries, rooftops. Standing here, we're part of the atmosphere."

"The view is our history, too," Isobel said. "Every bit as much as the hills, the town, the harbor, and the events that happened there. This section of the gallery might be my favorite part of the museum. We've our photographic history on one side and our elemental history on the other. In between, visitors can listen to a program or just sit back and be stupefied. Or knit. This is where our knitters work, as well. We've a couple of the groups due in this afternoon."

Janet turned to look at the chairs—easily three dozen of them grouped randomly down the length of the gallery. A random assortment, too. Comfy chairs, straight backs, wingbacks, rocking chairs, several recliners, three sofas, at least four beanbag chairs, and an assortment of child-size chairs.

"A motley assemblage," Edward said. "Eclectic chic, they call it."

"Also called *saving money*," said Isobel. "We put out a request for gently used castoffs. Now people proudly bring in relatives and friends to show off the museum 'artifact' from their own home."

"I should interview some of those people," Summer said. "Do a series called 'Little Chair Stories.'"

"Oh, please do," Isobel said. "Let me know when you're ready to start. I'll line up the interviews."

"Deal."

"I'm blown away by this," Janet said. "What a difference from the last time I was in this building. I'm embarrassed to say that my first thought, right through the front door, was where did you hide the smell of rising damp?"

"When were you last here?" Edward asked. "During the Roman Age? And why have you not been in since you arrived in town?"

Janet, tempted to ask why he hadn't been in the bookshop, thanked years of customer service for a veneer of politeness. "Mea culpa, though not quite that long. I haven't visited the museum since our last summer here, at least five years ago, and haven't been in this building since the library's Musty Book Age."

"You *are* behind times," Isobel said. "We've moved twice since then. Once to get away from roof leaks in the house where you last saw us. We dubbed that derelict beast 'The Hovel' when we shut its door for the last time. We decamped, as Uncle Edward likes to say, and took the collections to a temporary shelter while this lovely old place was renovated from top to bottom. We spent an interesting two years in the not *quite* derelict former cinema on Harbor View."

"Oh, fun." Summer walked her fingers down an imaginary slope. "How did the floor work out for you?"

"A laugh a minute. We held marble races for the kids on Saturday afternoons. But now we're content. We've everything we want—plenty of storage on the ground floor, flexible exhibit space in the central area and the gallery on the first, a sound roof over our heads, and temperature and humidity control."

"And plans for a gift shop," Edward said.

"Down the road, Uncle Edward."

"Ah." Edward nodded. "The constraint of a proper mourning period. To everything there is a season."

"Among other things." While Isobel gave her uncle a look that he avoided by studying a freckle on the back of his hand, a deep bonging arose from around the corner.

"Visitors!" They went to the corner to see a dozen or so pensioners taking turns with the bell. "Unexpected day-trippers," Isobel said between bongs. "They usually call ahead, but I'll take whatever we can get on a day as dreich as this. Sorry to cut out on you, ladies, but Uncle Edward can show you to the exhibit. It's self-guided. Uncle Edward, take some of the scones home with you. *Some*, mind, not all."

"Righty-o."

Janet and Summer called their thanks to Isobel's retreating back.

"Cheery-bye!" Edward added, as he watched Isobel greet the leader of the group. "I rather thought our surprise visitors might be the police come to start their enquiries." He looked over his shoulder at Janet and Summer. "Didn't you?"

Did Edward know this trick of the light, Janet wondered, that suddenly made his eyes glint sharp as scalpels? The gray light out the windows changed, altering the atmosphere as well. Outside and in. And with his next blink, the glint disappeared.

"Righty-o," Edward said, "let's go see the drowned sailors and toxic socks."

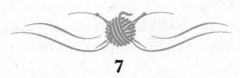

7

W e've taken up so much of your time already, Edward," Janet said, trying not to be obvious about backing away. "Don't let us keep you from the rest of your day. I'm sure we can find our own way to the exhibit. Don't you think so, Summer?" She realized she was prattling. Also, that it wasn't possible to back away inconspicuously. "Or you can point us in the right direction."

"Nonsense," Edward said. "Volunteer MacAskill at your service. It's not my usual day to contribute an hour or two to the museum, but this is the least I can do for dear Isobel. Time of crisis, and all that. We'll steal a march on those day-trippers and go in the back way. Follow me."

Edward, if not prattling, at least submerged their protests, and waved them along to the far end of the gallery. They shrugged and followed.

"Doing my bit, don't you know, so Isobel needn't close the museum after the tragic loss. She'll close on the day of the funeral, of course. Goes without saying." He led them around the corner and started down the last leg of the gallery. "If there is a funeral, because that's not a given, and *that* goes without saying. If that strikes the wrong tone, my apologies. One never knows how people will choose to shuffle off this mortal coil in these modern times."

That might not have had the right tone, either, Janet thought. *For that matter, neither did his remark about over Teresa's dead body.*

At the far end of the third side of the gallery they stopped, and Edward opened a panel as unobtrusive as the one behind the reception desk. "Exit only. Come ben," he said. "Always was a rule-breaker according to Teresa."

A small part of Janet's mind expected a stone stairway, dank and possibly dripping, spiraling down, down into the dark. Instead they entered another well-lit space, this one carpeted in a pleasant grayish-blue.

"Like walking on water," Janet said.

And, as if from across an expanse of water, they heard Isobel's voice and murmurs from the day-trippers.

"This is where the St. Kilda exhibit finished up," Summer said.

"Aye, tail end," Edward said. "Do you mind working backward?"

"As long as it won't make the labels confusing," Janet said.

"That's your advantage in having me along," Edward said. "No need for labels. I'm a natural at guiding tours. Now, let me tell you about ganseys and gansey patterns. Have you got your voice memo recorder going?"

Summer held her phone up and Edward took up a position beside a display case mounted on the wall.

"Today, some might call this knitted artifact a jumper, or, if you're American, a sweater," he said, "but this vital article of clothing, seamless and tightly knit, is properly called a gansey. The example before you was knitted here in Inversgail by Jennie Brockie, in 1941, and worn by her husband Bill. It's all one color, the traditional navy blue, and you can see the intricate pattern Jennie knitted across the chest and on the sleeves. The photograph in the background, taken in late summer 1933, shows a group of fishermen in front of their boat. Tell me, what are they all wearing?"

"Ganseys," Janet said.

"And flat caps," said Summer.

"The cap was the fashion of the day," Edward said. "But the gansey was the fishermen's uniform. Ganseys were a source of pride for the women who knitted them and the men who wore them. The patterns were handed down from generation to generation, in families and communities. Not just along our coast, either, but in fishing villages all around the UK, the islands, and the Netherlands, too. Because of the regional nature of the patterns, some call ganseys the tartan of the sea."

Next to the case with Bill Brockie's gansey was another photograph enlarged to life size. In it, a trio of young women sat on a doorstep and smiled for the camera as they knitted.

"Is Jennie Brockie in this picture?" Janet asked.

"Ah, let me see, you might be right." Edward peered at the faces. "Yes, there's Jennie," he said, pointing to the woman on the right. "Now, step over here and let me tell you why family patterns were so important."

Janet hung back for a moment when she spotted the photograph's label—and felt a ping of disappointment—none of the women were identified and the picture had been taken in 1894.

"Gansey patterns, being family patterns, were designed with one special use in mind," Edward said. "This pattern, for instance." He pointed to a faded and many-times-mended gansey in the next display case. "This pattern is an ID. A fingerprint. So that, should the worst happen, and a fisherman was lost at sea—as happened all too frequently—if his body washed up, he would be recognized by the pattern his wife or mother so lovingly knitted into his gansey."

"Wow. There's practicality for you. And heartbreak enough to take my breath away." Janet shivered at the memory of drifting in a sabotaged rowboat on a fogbound night. She leaned close enough to the display case that she bumped her nose. She straightened and polished her nose print from the glass with her sleeve. "Imagine how awful, if you couldn't recognize your husband's, or son's, or brother's face, but you could identify him and lay him to rest through the miracle of your knitting needles. But—" She scanned the label in the case again and then looked back toward the others she'd read. "Why isn't that in any of these labels? It's such a poignant part of the story."

Edward lowered his voice. "Wendy's influence, I'm afraid. Isobel leaves some of the best details out of her labels." He smiled and went on to the next case.

Before following, Summer stopped to read a label Edward had been standing in front of. "Hey, here it is," she called. "The label you wanted, Janet, about identifying sailors by the stitches in their sweaters. Oh. Bummer."

Janet and Edward backtracked.

"There aren't any documented cases of that actually happening," Summer said. "Gansey experts say it falls into the category of knitting myths."

"Wendy again," Edward said. "She had a very literal interpretation of history."

"Is there another kind of interpretation?" Summer asked, but Edward was already moving on.

"It's called *interprétation avec un grain de sel*," Janet said with an exaggerated French accent. "Let's look at the stockings and then skedaddle."

As they made their way through the exhibit, albeit backward, Janet tried to imagine a bird's eye view of the whole space. A square room, she decided, with a wending pathway created by the exhibit cases and moveable panels. She heard Isobel's tour more clearly, now, and a few renegade day-trippers passed them. She and Summer took the next jog in the path and found Edward waiting for them. He looked disappointed when they told him they'd like to skip ahead to the stocking exhibit.

"Only because our co-workers might be getting jealous of our holiday," Janet said. "But we'll be back, and we'll bring our co-workers with us."

"Over and over," Summer said. "I'll need to immerse myself to get the article just right."

"I'll hold you to it," Edward said. "And in that case, come this way and be prepared for 'Shocking Stockings.'"

He led them past a wooden rowboat draped in fishnets, past the interior of a croft house kitchen, and more ganseys. At a corner he stopped in an open doorway. A sign over the door let them know they'd arrived at "Shocking Stockings." A graphic beside the door quoted a *London Times* article from 1869: "What manufactured article in these days of high-pressure civilization can possibly be trusted if socks may be dangerous?"

"Ours is one of the largest exhibits of ganseys in recent years, in all of Scotland," Edward said rather loudly. "With over—"

"I can believe it," Janet said. "Truly astonishing. Are the stockings in here?" And why are you still standing in front of the door, she wondered. She looked for help from Summer in moving things along, and that's when they saw that Edward's audience had grown with the addition of four day-trippers. "Sorry Edward. I didn't mean to interrupt."

"Quite all right, my dear," he said, lowering his voice again. "We should move inside before the room fills with old dears and duffers, anyway." Nodding toward a whole gaggle of day-trippers tottering their way, he took Janet's elbow.

Janet took her elbow back, tucked it closer to her side, and took herself into the exhibit. She felt slightly ashamed of her reaction. Edward's manners were simply those of someone raised in a place like "the MacAskill bit of rubble." They were probably automatic. But her reaction was just as automatic. She'd never liked what she considered "little lady" treatment. Also automatic was feeling ashamed for bristling at anyone else's manners. But Edward hadn't seemed to notice the bristle. Or maybe that was his manners kicking in again. Anyway, he looked happy enough as he and Summer exclaimed together over a pair of orange and green striped socks.

Looking around, she wondered if the *stockings* were happy. The space given to "Shocking Stockings"—a corner sequestered from the larger exhibit space—wasn't much bigger than the interior of the croft house kitchen. Janet's immediate impressions were *closet* and *claustrophobic*. The walls were formed by upright display cases, and the cases were crowded with stockings and their associated labels.

A riot of stockings, Janet saw, as she turned in a circle to take them all in. There were dozens of examples of Inversgail stockings in various color combinations—mostly blues, greens, and grays—but many other styles of socks, long and short, in much brighter colors and patterns and made of less bulky yarns.

"Oops, sorry." As she'd turned, Janet had backed into Summer. "This is sort of an out of the way cul-de-sac for a major part of the exhibit, isn't it? And small?"

"It is somewhat hidden," Edward agreed, "and a room of rather mean proportions. That's why I wanted us to slip in ahead of the crowd. My tours in this room are wildly popular. The stockings, too, of course."

"I'm surprised Wendy had to be convinced they would be," Janet said.

"She was damnably rude about my tours." Immediately, Edward held up a hand. "That was completely uncalled for. Please excuse me."

"It's my fault. I should have been clearer," Janet said. "I wasn't referring to your tours, Edward. I heard from Isobel that Wendy didn't want to include stockings in the exhibit when Isobel suggested the idea. Or, as Isobel put it, Wendy took the pep from her step."

"Quite possibly," Edward said. "Isobel isn't one to complain, though, and she's always found a way to get things done."

"It does seem like there's room to spare out there with the ganseys," Summer said. "Maybe it has something to do with exhibit philosophy."

"Or turf?" Janet asked.

"Also possible," Edward said. "Not to say that is the case, but it so often can be when personalities are involved. And, quite frankly, when are they not? Now, step this way. Close quarters. But look at this wonderful pair knitted by a local lass." He pointed to a pair of stockings in the traditional Inversgail pattern using blue and gray wool.

"It might shock you to learn," Edward said, "that although the knitter appears to have followed our local argyle pattern, she included a clever alteration with a secret meaning. I see I've caught your attention. Whilst I have it, let me first point out the shape of the stockings. Isn't it lovely how they're knitted in the shape of a leg, with ankles and calves, rather than today's generic tube? So then, can you find where the pattern has been altered?"

Janet and Summer moved in closer to study the socks, but soon looked back at Edward, shaking their heads.

"I gave you a clue when I spoke of the calves. Look again at the diamonds in the widest part of the calf on each sock.

"There's a row that looks different," Janet said. "But not in any major way."

"Do the stitches in that row remind you of something?" Edward asked. "Fish, perhaps?"

"How fun! Yes, I can see them," Janet said. "But couldn't that be a mistake the knitter made in the first sock and repeated in the second for the sake of symmetry?"

"I'd totally do that," Summer said. "If I knew how to knit. What's the secret meaning of the fish?"

"Here's another clue. Our lass knitted these stockings during the Second World War."

"A code?" Summer said.

Edward tapped the side of his nose. Janet covered *hers* to stifle a snort.

"Cool," Summer said. "I've read about knitters doing that during the war. Getting information past enemy lines. Passing messages to the front."

"I passed information about the codes to some of our competition knitters," Edward said. "I'd jolly well love it if at least one of them includes a coded message in their entry."

"I smell another article rising in the proofing bowl of my mind," Summer said.

"I'll be happy to do my bit for the cause by answering any questions you have," Edward said.

"I have one." Janet had stared at the line of fish stitches in the stockings until she felt her eyes might cross. "The message—what is it? I thought I was good at codes, but I'm not getting anywhere with this one."

"Ah, no, my dear. It is not my place to divulge the secret. The enigma, the conundrum, the mystery—they are the beauty of a good code."

"Well, darn," Janet said. "A little sock humor to cover my disappointment. Are you going to tell us about toxic socks?"

But Edward scrolled, unhearing, through something on his phone. She turned her attention to a display case full of bright, unlikely color combinations that she'd never have associated with historic footwear. A large warning label across the top of the case read DANGER: SOCKS. Smaller warning labels peppered the rest of the display.

"YOUR BRIGHTLY COLORED FASHION STATEMENT IS HAZARDOUS TO YOUR HEALTH."

"VICTORIAN YARN DYES OFTEN CONTAINED TOXIC CHEMICALS."

"VICTORIANS KNEW THEIR DYES WERE TOXIC. THEY USED THEM—AND WORE THE RESULTS—ANYWAY."

"ANILINE IS SLIGHTLY SOLUBLE IN WATER—BEWARE HOW YOU LAUNDER."

"ANILINE DYES ARE TOXIC BY SKIN ABSORPTION AND INHALATION."

"WARNING: STOCKINGS ARE MORE DANGEROUS THAN GOWNS OR WAISTCOATS BECAUSE STOCKINGS HUG YOUR CALVES AND YOUR POTENTIALLY SWEATY FEET."

"VICTORIANS HAD A DIFFERENT IDEA OF HYGIENE. THEY MIGHT WEAR THEIR STOCKINGS FOR DAYS IN A ROW. ANILINE DYES MADE THIS PRACTICE HAZARDOUS—LEAVING PEOPLE WITH SORES ON THEIR LEGS IN THE SAME FASHIONABLE PATTERNS AS THEIR STOCKINGS."

"Good Lord," Janet murmured and moved to the next case. The large heading over this one read, BRILLIANT GREEN! SENSATIONAL GREEN! MIRACULOUS GREEN! BROUGHT TO YOU BY: ARSENIC!

"Quite intense," Edward said, startling Janet as he slipped in beside her. "Arsenical green, I mean. The brainchild of Karl Scheele, a Swede and a chemist, in 1778. Must have been an amazing fellow. The process revolutionized the dye industry. The color bears his name—Scheele's Green. Marvelous stuff."

"But arsenic," Janet said.

"Different priorities back then," Summer said. "Imagine the workers who handled the dyes, the paints, the inks, the cloth."

"The shop clerks who had to sell the toxic socks," Janet said.

"Reminds me of an interesting story about a member of Parliament and socks," Edward said. "Poor fellow suffered from painful eruptions on his feet. He was confined to his sofa for months."

"Do we really want to hear the details?" Janet asked.

"Point taken. Suffice to say the chap made a full recovery when he abandoned the practice of wearing fashionable socks. Of course, you Americans like to do things bigger and better, and several California miners were not so lucky. They lined their boots with bright flannel dyed with Scheele's green. Warm and cozy and fetching to the eye, I've no doubt, but in that event, not survivable. Although it is possible that they did not line their boots themselves. That someone else did it—shall we say *to* them. Ah, the nefarious deeds that went on in the mine fields of yore."

Isobel had silently appeared behind Edward. As his story unfolded, her nose wrinkled, and she shook her head at Janet and Summer. Janet thought she might have to cover another snort.

"All still smiling, I see." Isobel put her hand on Edward's shoulder. "Thanks to Uncle Edward's expert guidance, I'm sure. What do you think of our dangerous darlings?"

"Absolutely shocking," Janet said.

"Can you imagine the *bowff* in a room full of people wearing their socks for a week or more?" Isobel said.

"If bowff means horrible smell, I'm using that in my article," Summer said. "But I refuse to imagine that room."

"Smart," Isobel said. "And if a museum of historic smells is ever invented, I will not be visiting it."

"But *arsenic*," Janet said. "Is there arsenic in the green socks on display?"

"Oh, not just green," Isobel said. "They used arsenic in other colors, as well. Yellow, blue, mauve."

"Delightful," Janet said faintly.

"To answer your question, though, we aren't one hundred percent certain. That's one of the reasons Wendy hesitated mentioning arsenic."

"You won out," Edward said.

"In the end—" Isobel made a face. "That sounded wrong. Sorry. The information in the labels about arsenic-dyed textiles is accurate, and there are plenty of examples of arsenical artifacts in collections elsewhere in the UK. It's true, as well, that some of our greens, and possibly some of the other colors, are suspect. We'd like to have them analyzed, but, as we've not done that yet, we handle them with, well, not with kid gloves, but definitely with gloves."

"This is mind-blowing," Summer said. "I don't remember reading much about the stockings in the museum press release you sent out. They sure didn't show up in their full toxic glory in the first *Guardian* article."

"Wendy wanted the emphasis on the ganseys. That's the more serious display. She had a point, and you recognized it," Isobel said. "The ganseys have the power of personal stories and family history."

Edward made a noise in his throat.

"Uncle Edward? All right?"

"Just chewing over an old slight. Not the day to do it, I realize, but there should be room for more than one story about the local museum in the local newspaper."

"Who says there isn't?" Summer asked. "I've never heard—did *James* set that limit?"

"Haviland? No, he's a fine chap," Edward said. "The limit is something Wendy imposed. The limit was in her attitude. I know I've been negative about her and speaking ill isn't the done thing. But the truth is that Wendy had her shortcomings; being shortsighted was one of them."

"I'm sorry about her attitude, but glad to hear it wasn't James," Summer said. "I can easily see two or three articles coming out of this visit. I'm sure he'll agree. Isobel, do you mind if I take pictures of the labels? If I use direct quotes, I'll give proper credit."

"Sounds good." Isobel cocked her head, and they all heard the slow bong of the handbell. "I'll try to catch you on your way out," she said, jogging away. "Cheers."

With new respect, Janet looked at the stockings in the cases surrounding them. "Mind-blowing," she said, echoing Summer. Then she told Summer to take her time getting her pictures, and she would meet her at the reception desk. But first, she wanted to take a quick look for something and say goodbye to Isobel. "Edward, thanks for the tour. Come see us at Yon Bonnie Books. And if you touch any of these socks, wash your hands."

She left Edward chuckling and opening the bag of scones. On her way toward the beginning of the gansey exhibit, she scanned the displays for photos of women knitting. By the time she reached the starting point, she felt vaguely cheated. She hadn't found Jennie Brockie among them.

The door to the exhibit let Janet back out into the gallery not far from the reception desk. There, she saw Isobel opening the panel door behind the desk. Isobel saw her, too, and waved her over.

"Come on in and have a quick look round the staff area," Isobel said. "It's small, but the floor is level, and the roof is sound."

"What more can you ask for?"

They stepped into an open-plan office. "And here you have it," Isobel said. "Efficiency at its best. You get the whole tour in three seconds with a one-hundred-eighty-degree turn of your head. More or less. My own wee space and Wendy's on the left. We like to call them offices. Makes us feel more important. And on the right—the worktables, sink, and cupboards—are grandly referred to as the staff room. We can spread out a bit and do final prep or minor repairs on exhibits there. A proper workshop is below us on the ground floor."

"Do you do the actual construction yourself?"

"Minor work, only." Isobel bent to look under the worktables. "Anything complicated goes to a local carpenter." She opened and closed the larger cupboards. "I thought I left my programming basket here. Hmm, I also thought Uncle Edward left the scones here."

Janet decided not to tell Isobel that Edward might be enjoying a scone picnic with the toxic socks. She did tell her she saw a large basket on Wendy's desk. "It's gorgeous."

"Aha! The very one I'm looking for. Isn't it a beauty? Willow. Handwoven locally."

While Isobel sorted through the contents of the basket, Janet asked what had begun to pray on her mind. "Will you continue with the knitting competition?"

"Hm?" Isobel looked up, puzzled. "Sorry, I thought I had a pair of stockings here with the rest. What's that about the competition?"

"Will it continue?"

"Yes. Why? Oh—has someone suggested it shouldn't?"

"No! Not that I've heard, anyway. I hope you do go ahead with it. We love having the knitters in the shop and tearoom. But you need to consider your time and energy. It won't do the museum any good if you work yourself into—" *Into the ground*, she'd been going to say. "Just don't run yourself ragged, Isobel. That's all I'm saying."

"The competition will continue." Isobel looked through the basket again. Sent darting glances around Wendy's area and her own. Then zeroed in on Janet. "It has to continue. We've lost Wendy. We can't lose the knitting, too. And I know they're not the same—a human life and people knitting socks—but it's programs like the competition that keep us from becoming a dead circus."

Janet raised her eyebrows and didn't know whether to hug Isobel or to creep quietly away.

Isobel took a shuddering breath. "That sounded completely daft. I know it did. *Dead circus*—it's what a small boy told his mum he'd seen after his class went to a museum. True story, but you can understand it from the lad's point of view. That description has become a warning to curators. Don't let your exhibits become graveyards of stuffed animals, bones, stones, and dusty, inanimate objects belonging to long dead people. A place where we come to stare and walk away unmoved."

"Wow."

"I get worked up. I know. It's just that I think there's room for *life* in a history museum. So, yes, the knitting competition will go on."

"You'll get no argument from me.

"And I wonder what I did with those stockings?"

"Can I help?"

Isobel made a noncommittal noise and went to search around her desk. Janet glanced around Wendy's, and something in a waste bin caught her eye—food wrappers from Mr. Potato Chef with the name *Teresa* scrawled on them.

"Does your mum drop by the museum often?"

"Not really. She's one of these people who's busier since she retired. Mind, she works from home, now. That might be one of the reasons Uncle Edward spends so much time here."

Janet laughed. "They can't avoid each other in a place the size of Fairy Flax Hall?"

"If they lived there, yes. He's kipping at Mum's. Hence the problem."

Hence his discussion of friction when personalities are involved, Janet thought.

"Family issues," Isobel said. "I shouldn't force them on an unwary audience."

"Not a problem. Give your mum my best. I'm sure last night was a terrible shock for her, and she'll miss Wendy, too."

"I don't think she knew Wendy all that well."

"Oh. I thought they might." Janet pointed at the wrappers.

Isobel came to look. "Good Lord."

"People mentioned Mr. Potato Chef last night and rumors about food poisoning."

"If any of that's true, then Mum must not have had what Wendy did, because she didn't get sick."

"Did Wendy have any food allergies?"

"She never mentioned any." Isobel scrubbed her hands over her face. "I'd best let Constable Hobbs know."

∽

On the way back to the bookshop, Summer bubbled over with the information she'd gathered for her newspaper articles. "The poison angle! What a trip! I wonder if it's a good idea, though, considering Wendy's unexpected death. Nah, James will be fine with it. There's no connection and he'll fall back on his favorite cliché—no such thing as bad publicity. Isobel will love it, too. Speaking of which, I have an idea for a new bookmark for the shop." She didn't bubble over so far as to share the idea, but Janet knew they'd be seeing a prototype soon.

Up ahead, parked in front of Sea View Kayaks, Janet saw the Mr. Potato Chef food truck. She told Summer about the wrappers in Wendy's waste bin. "I'm tempted to buy something from the truck," she said.

"I'm going to say *ugh* to that," said Summer. "If this has nothing to do with the truck, then I feel sorry for Mr. Potato, but nope. Not that I'm squeamish, but I won't eat anything from them until they're in the clear. And I *do* feel sorry for the guy, because that's probably how a lot of people feel."

"Oh, I agree," Janet said. "I wouldn't eat anything either. I'm only tempted to buy something to give it to Norman, but I'm sure he has things well in hand and doesn't need me to collect evidence for him."

"Are you going to leave it to Isobel to call him about the wrappers?"

"I'm sure she will call him." Janet thought about that and nodded. "I'm sure she will. But I will, too."

They stepped into an odd atmosphere when they arrived back at Yon Bonnie Books. Summer rushed on through to the tearoom, so Janet couldn't be sure she noticed. She couldn't put her finger on the oddity, at first. It wasn't in the music floating down from the overhead sound system—the rich tones of a marimba concerto. Nothing amiss with Tallie—she and a customer conferred quietly near the poetry books. Not Rab behind the sales counter—but yes, that was it. Rab, so naturally easy-oasy, had unnaturally flushed cheeks. And Ranger? Janet glanced at the chairs near the fireplace—no Ranger. Ranger, she saw, was behind the counter with Rab—not quite cowering. Ranger probably didn't have it in him to cower. But he was sitting on Rab's feet.

Janet greeted Rab and Ranger as though she'd noticed nothing out of the ordinary. She put her jacket and purse away in the office behind the counter. When she came back out, Rab and Ranger were gone.

"What is it?" Janet asked when Tallie joined her. "What's happened?"

"I'm not entirely sure," Tallie said. "But in reverse order it seemed to go like this. Kyle the knitter said something that riled Ranger. Some of the other knitters said something that riled Kyle. Someone else started it by saying something that riled the other knitters."

"Who started it?"

"I'll tell you, but only on the condition of anonymity."

"Tell me."

"Christine."

Janet sent a text to Summer, trying to sound casual: *How's Christine?*

Summer sent one back, sounding suspicious: *Unusually docile. Keeps muttering "But it is cheaper to buy them."*

8

Arsenic diary, day four

A ditty I've been working on runs through my head these days:

Like regimental soldiers,
Standing at attention.
Always smart and crisp,
in atomic number order.
It's purely elemental,
it's the periodic table!

There, I feel rather like a pipe major standing before the assembled corps with my regimental mace. Someone should hire me to write ad copy for the periodic table. Or perhaps not. Still, what I lack in poetic art I make up for with exuberance and excellent posture.

Periodic. Apparently that's how I keep a diary. I'm not bothered. I have a life, even though it might not be the one others would choose.

My lovely arsenic lives forever as atomic number 33. My statuesque friend Stevenson dies of a cerebral hemorrhage at 44. Wendy Erskine, neither lovely, statuesque, nor my friend, dies at 55. Is that cosmic synchronicity? While I wonder about Wendy's place in the cosmos, other people wonder about her death.

Let them.

❧

Summer unveiled her design for a new bookmark Monday morning. The four women met most mornings in the doorway between the bookshop and the tearoom before opening their front doors. *Our meeting of minds between our tea cozies and bookends,* as Christine liked to say, although she changed what she liked to say fairly often. The partners used the time to start the day on a positive note, catch each other up on sales and promotions in their two businesses, share good news and concerns, and to sample the day's special tea and scones.

"Two-sided, advertising Rocking the Stocking on one side and Shocking Stockings on the other." Summer handed them each a sample of the bookmark, tucking Christine's in the front pocket of her bib apron when she didn't hold out her hand. "Tearoom and bookshop names prominent, too."

"Is this a bottle of poison tipped over on a tea table?" Tallie asked.

"Too gruesome?"

"No, make it a little bigger so it's easier to see."

"But will people get the connection to the exhibit?" Janet asked. "With the rumors of food poisoning circulating, do we want to suggest poison in the tearoom?"

"It's probably okay. The text explains it," Tallie said.

"So it does. I like it," Janet said. She looked at Christine, who'd been subdued since the riling of the knitters on Saturday, remaining uncommunicative about the cause. "Christine? What do you think?"

"That Norman looks thirsty. He's at your door."

Tallie went to let the constable in. He made occasional appearances at their morning meetings to pick up information or pass along some of his own. He'd never questioned their practice of standing in the doorway rather than make themselves comfortable at a tea table or by the fireplace.

"Here for a scone, Norman?" Christine asked.

"I'm here concerning the incident Friday night at Fairy Flax Hall," he said with a hopeful or possibly wistful sniff of the air.

"First a question to satisfy mum," Christine said. "She's like a broken record about it. Did your grandmother knit the jumper you wore Friday night, and if so, was lilac her choice of color or yours?"

"Nana Bethia asked me to try it on for sleeve length. She's knitting it for my sister. We've similar builds."

"I'll tell Mum, but she'll be disappointed. It brings out the color of your eyes."

"It's a lovely color, Norman," Janet said.

"Thank you, Mrs. Marsh. And for telling me about the Mr. Potato Chef wrappers you found at the museum."

"Did Isobel call you about them, too?"

"I did hear from another person, though for privacy's sake, I'll not divulge the name."

"Could they have been planted, Norman? To make people believe Wendy died of food poisoning?"

"She might well have died of food poisoning, Mrs. Marsh. And very likely the wrappers would have gone out with the rubbish, if not for you."

Janet heard an accusatory emphasis on the words *if not for you.* "I wasn't snooping, Norman. I just happened to glance down and see the wrappers."

"A hazard of the curious mind, I've no doubt. You might like to know that Wendy Erskine was a frequent customer at the tattie truck."

"Was she? Teresa didn't think she was. She said she didn't know why anyone would eat there."

"Did you speak to Mrs. Ritchie about the wrappers?"

"No. She said that Friday night. While we waited for you. So don't you think it's odd the wrappers were in Wendy's bin and had Teresa's name on them?"

"Or might it be that Mrs. Ritchie joined Ms. Erskine at the museum for lunch on Friday and, at Ms. Erskine's suggestion, stopped by Mr. Potato

Chef to pick up the food. Mrs. Ritchie is not shy about expressing her opinions—" here he glanced at Christine, "so if she didn't enjoy the food, it's not surprising she expressed that opinion Friday evening."

"She couldn't have hated it all that much," Janet said. "She ate all of it. Or someone did. Maybe someone wrote her name on the wrappers and planted them to implicate her."

"Implicate her in what, Mrs. Marsh?"

"Food poisoning?"

"Sounds over-complicated. And iffy," Hobbs said.

"He's right." Christine gave Janet a sympathetic look. "It's good you pointed that out to her, Norman. Janet's not keen on 'iffy.' But tell us, have there been credible reports of food poisoning concerning Mr. Potato Chef?"

"I've heard talk," Hobbs said. His tone hedged and his look skated toward suspicion.

"Heard talk, Norman? Nothing more than that?" Christine asked. "We expect better from you. Surely there's a food crime division to your outfit. Why don't you ring them up?"

"The Scottish Food Crime and Incidents Unit is meant for industrial-size crimes, Mrs. Robertson. Consumers wishing to report an incident are to contact their local authority. I am not that authority."

"You say that in a rehearsed manner, Norman."

"I have said it before."

"Presumably to consumers wishing to report incidents," Christine said. "Meaning you are aware of such incidents. How many people have you referred on to the local authority?"

"Related to Mr. Potato Chef, none at all."

"Then where did the rumors come from?"

Hobbs's look now combined suspicion and longsuffering.

"It's not a daft question, Norman," Christine said. "You might have some idea."

"From the very air, perhaps." As if demonstrating, he sniffed the air toward the tearoom again.

Summer, hiding a smile, excused herself and disappeared in that direction herself.

"The rubbish weather this time of year breeds all manner of discontent," Hobbs continued. "Overindulgence at Hogmanay as well."

"You've a *pawkie* sense of humor, Norman."

"Don't fuss at him, Christine. He's doing the best he can." Janet guessed, from Hobbs's sigh, that he didn't take her words as the positive statement she'd intended. She hurried on to a happier topic. "Where is Bethia staying now, Norman?"

"I've found comfortable accommodations for her."

"Because she could stay with us or upstairs in the B&B."

"The current situation works well for all concerned," he said.

Summer returned with tea and a scone for Hobbs. "Almond scones, this morning, and Highland breakfast tea. Cream, no sugar."

"Ta very much." He took a grateful sip and then a bite. "Brilliant."

"*Did* you come by just for the scone?" Christine asked.

Hobbs took another sip before answering. "I came to let you know that Mrs. MacAskill is devasted by Wendy Erskine's death."

"So we've heard," Janet said.

"Do you doubt it?" Hobbs asked.

"What? No, not at all and I'm sorry if it sounded that way. Being devastated is hardly police business, though."

"Mrs. MacAskill is also concerned about an item she's not been able to locate since Friday evening. She asked me to make enquiries on her behalf."

"You buried your lede then, Norman," Christine said. "Is this something that went out with clutter?"

"It was not meant to."

"Aye, well, this will sound insensitive, but would Violet know the difference between missing and misplaced?"

"It's a relevant question and I did raise it," Hobbs said. "Mrs. MacAskill is certain it's missing."

"Is she accusing either of us of taking this item?" Janet asked.

"I can't believe she would accuse Mum of taking it," Christine said. "She didn't, did she? Because I can assure you Mum took nothing home, *including* Dundee cake. She did have a slice of pie, but she ate every crumb."

"There was pie?" Hobbs looked momentarily stricken. "Mrs. MacAskill isn't accusing anyone of taking the item, but because some of the doors that were meant to be locked were not *actually* locked, she reckons someone took it home."

"Is anything else missing?" Summer asked.

"Not that's been noticed."

"Is she embarrassed by this 'item'?" Tallie asked. "Otherwise, why are we dancing around naming it? What's missing?"

Hobbs, or at least his pursed lips, considered her question. If his eyebrows had anything to say about it, they might be debating the wisdom of identifying the item, or the wisdom of speaking to the women in the first place. Considerations and debates didn't take long. "Mrs. Robertson, Mrs. Marsh, did either of you see a container of Rodine?"

"Never heard of it," Christine said. "If you want us to be helpful, Norman, then *you* need to be helpful. Ending in *ine* like that makes it sound medicinal. What is it?"

Hobbs didn't answer her, instead saying, "Mrs. Marsh?"

"I'm with Christine. Without knowing what it is or what it looks like, I have no idea if I saw it."

With a brief look at the ceiling, less like an eye roll and more like a quick prayer, Hobbs said, "A square pasteboard box, red and white, containing a flat tin, not so different from a tin of Dubbin."

"Which is?" Summer asked.

"Waterproofing for leather boots or shoes," Hobbs said.

"Like a can of shoe polish," Christine said. "Are you telling me we're getting ourselves into a lather over shoe polish, Norman?"

"No, Mrs. Robertson. Before the decluttering, Mrs. MacAskill set a number of items aside as a donation for the museum. The wee box of Rodine was among them—for a new exhibit planned for the spring. Rodine is rodenticide, not shoe polish."

"Whoa, whoa," Janet said. "I grew up on a farm. I know what rodenticide is." She turned to the others. "Violet's looking for rat poison."

"Rat pois—shouldn't missing rat poison ring bigger alarm bells?" Summer asked.

"It's decades old and no longer dangerous," Hobbs said. "World War II era and covered in dust, if Mrs. MacAskill is to be believed."

"Do you believe her?" Summer asked.

"I've no reason to doubt her."

Tallie took out her phone. "How do you spell it?"

"R-o-d-i-n-e," Hobbs said.

"When did she last see it?" Summer asked.

"Sometime before Friday evening," said Hobbs.

"That's not terribly specific, and I sense further dancing," Christine said. "When did she discover it missing?"

"Yesterday. Mrs. MacAskill spent the day looking for it. She called me this morning."

"Did *you* see it at the decluttering, Norman?" Janet asked.

"No."

"You showed up here early," Christine said, "so she called you *awfully* early."

"She said she'd not slept well for the worry."

"Worry that the presence of a tin of no-longer-lethal rat poison will make or break a museum exhibit?" Christine asked.

"Worry over not delivering completely on her promise to the museum. The promise she made to Ms. Erskine, who's death she is taking quite hard."

"Of *course* she is," Janet said.

"Bigger alarm bells," Tallie said, staring at her phone. "Loud, clanging alarm bells. Rodine contains phosphorous. Phosphorous poisoning can look a lot like acute gastroenteritis—food poisoning. It doesn't have a shelf life." She looked up from the phone. "The stuff is still lethal. Have you reported it missing, because we need to find it."

With a disappointed look at Tallie, Hobbs drained his teacup. He put the last corner of scone in his mouth, put his hat on, and walked to the tearoom door without another word. Summer let him out.

"He should have known I meant *he* needs to find it," Tallie said.

"Your remark got him out of our hair, though," Christine said. "That and asking him if he's reported the missing poison. After all, we have a business to run."

"I wasn't trying to get him out of our hair," Tallie said. "I wanted to hear the answers."

"I wonder where in that amazing house we would start looking?" Janet mused. At a look from Tallie, "I meant that purely in a throw-my-hands-in-the-air kind of way. Of *course* Norman should be the one to track it down. In that house it would be like looking for a knitting needle in a yarn shop. Although, come to think of it, that wouldn't be all that difficult."

"It might be like catching a rat that thinks it's safe in its rat nest," Christine said. She also received a look from Tallie. "What?" Christine asked. "That's what we're all thinking. Come along, Summer. Our teapots are whistling for us." Christine twirled imaginary rat whiskers and went to greet the tearoom's first customers of the day.

"She's up to something in that head of hers," Tallie said.

⟡

That afternoon, Summer alerted them to a police statement in the online, breaking news edition of the *Guardian*. Tallie opened the app on her phone. Janet read over her shoulder.

> The body of Wendy Erskine, 55, was found at Fairy Flax Hall, home of Violet MacAskill, near the Argyll and Bute town of Inversgail on 14 January. A postmortem examination will take

place in due course to establish the exact cause of death, however we are treating the death as suspicious in the meantime.
Enquiries are ongoing.

"This doesn't clear up the question of acute food poisoning. From
Mr. Potato Chef or some other place," Tallie said, "her own kitchen, even."

"There still might be something funny about those food wrappers,
too," Janet said. "I don't think Norman liked the idea that I might have
asked Teresa about them."

"He might not like that on general principle. He might see it as
bothering her. Or meddling."

"Which your mother didn't do." Christine emerged from the aisle
of bookshelves that created a direct pathway between the tearoom
and the bookshop sales counter. "Your mother is the soul of propriety and
non-meddling unless it's for a good cause."

"I know. Sorry, Mom. I wasn't accusing you. Just seeing it from Norman's point of view. Here's another example of seeing it from his point
of view: If Wendy didn't die from food poisoning, maybe they *should*
suspect rat poison."

9

Arsenic diary, day four and a half

Arsenic. I write it in looping letters as though I'm a schoolgirl testing out the surname of the boy making calf eyes at me from across the room. A r s e n i c.

Once so easy to obtain, easy to use, easy to mistake! Good Lord, what were the Victorians thinking? Selling it to children in half-penny, unmarked bags when their mums wanted rid of rats. Keeping it in unmarked containers on pantry shelves—a white powder—as though it might not be mistaken for sugar and dolloped into the morning coffee. Using it in the bloody blancmange. Not literally bloody. Not red at all. Green. Poisonously green because the bloody eejits used arsenic as food coloring. Used it and knew the dangers. But even more evil than poison in the pudding, more unscrupulous and unworthy, was adding arsenic to the ale. People had something to say about that, I can assure you.

I turn to the scrapbook's last page. I haven't read the book through yet, but I always flip ahead and read the last page of a book. Some call that a cheat. I call it giving myself every advantage to which I'm entitled, and I'm never disappointed. This last page is one of my favorites. Another note is stuck here at the end, with the same elegant penmanship of her first endearing note, the one pasted slightly askew at the beginning of the book.

Oh, fugitive additive, you are
disruptive,
destructive,
vindictive,
extinctive.
Though once impossible to trace,
with consequences harsh,
you led police a merry chase,
until
along came the investigative Marsh.

It boggles the mind, really, what people used to get away with. Then along came James Marsh with his chemistry sets and definitive tests. He sounds quite a bore. And now another Marsh is on the scene. Here! What are the odds?

And so, I end this entry with a sigh for days gone by. Dear white arsenic, once not dear at all in shops. Used by women to lighten their complexions and kill rats. All kinds of rats.

✍

It had become the women's habit to spend Monday evenings at Nev's, a pub they considered their local. This Monday evening, with a cold rain bucketing down, Christine offered to drive them. "The Vauxhall is round the back. Thank goodness I haven't made the commitment to an exercise regime yet," she said. "'Yet' is an excellent word, don't you think?"

They left by the back door, Janet locking it behind them, and all dripped past their rubbish bins and into the Vauxhall. The narrow lane that ran behind the High Street businesses allowed snug parking for a few cars.

"What about your mum and dad?" Tallie asked as Christine nosed the car out of the lane. "Will you drop us and go back for them?"

"They've opted for a quiet evening in front of the telly. Dad's more rattled than I would have thought by Wendy's death. He's got it in his head that Mum could have been in danger."

"The poor dears," Janet said. "Do you think she was in danger? Or any of us?"

"I suppose it's crossed my mind, since Norman so casually dropped the case of the missing Rodine into our laps. I don't *think* any of us were in danger. Then again, I don't really have any way of knowing, do I?"

"I think you're more worried than you realize," Janet said. "You turned the wrong way back there. And that turn isn't going to fix it. We should stop discussing it until we're at Nev's, so you can concentrate. You do realize you're headed out of town, at this point, don't you? Would you like to pull over and I'll drive?"

Christine didn't answer. She didn't change course, either.

"Ahem from the back seat," Tallie said. "Where are we going?"

"She's not answering," Summer said. "You're not answering," she called to the front seat. "Are we going to Nev's or what?"

"Oh ye of suspicious faith. Of course we're going to Nev's. With a stop first."

"We've been kidnapped," Tallie said. "By our own business partner."

"Where are we stopping?" Summer asked.

"Fairy Flax Hall. Violet MacAskill asked us to help her look for the Rodine," Christine said. "I told her we'd pop round this evening and have a go at it."

"Really?" Janet said. "When did she ask?"

"After I offered our assistance."

"Oh for . . . what if we refuse to get out of the car?" Tallie asked.

"You might be sitting in it for a while, then," Janet said. "Four sets of hands will be faster."

"Listen to your mother," Christine said. "And to me. You know I'm almost like a mother. The sooner we find the Rodine, the sooner we get to Nev's. And the better Violet will sleep. A deed well done by all."

"You'll get to see the house, too," Janet said. "The MacAskill 'bit of rubble' is built with built-in rubble—a wing sticking out on one end. Like a folly. The place isn't enormous, but it gives that effect. It isn't like any building I've seen outside a book of fairytales."

"You were there in the dark," Tallie groused. "How much of it could you see in the dark? It's dark now. And pouring."

"They have spotlights lighting up the front of the house," Janet said. "Now that I think about it, though, the spots made it look three parts enchanting, one part spooky. Anyway, I'm glad we're going back. I didn't see enough of it inside or out. I'm surprised we haven't ever heard of it before, though. You'd think a house like that would be a topic of conversation. The spotlights made me wonder if it's ever been a tour stop for coaches out of Fort William or Oban. Day-trippers would fall all over themselves getting pictures."

Christine turned onto the tree-lined drive to Fairy Flax Hall while Janet carried on her one-sided conversation. The trees, sodden with pouring rain, bowed close on either side of the Vauxhall. Christine took the lane slowly. Janet hushed, then leaned forward, expecting the spotlights to break through the drenched dark around every next bend.

Summer's voice made the others jump. "I wonder if Violet's told anyone besides Norman that this stuff is missing?"

"Huh," Tallie said. "And back to a couple of things from this morning. Norman said, 'If Violet is to be believed.' And Christine wondered if Violet would really know if it *is* missing. So how *is* her memory? *Should* she be believed? I'm just whining for a friend who thought she'd be eating a warm supper over a half pint by now."

"Norman was talking about the Rodine being covered in dust," Janet said.

"Was he?"

"I thought so at the time, anyway. As for Violet's memory, I certainly don't know. You don't either, do you Christine?"

"No, else I'd not have asked. Although here's a possible indicator. She seems to have forgot to put the outside lights on for us. At least the rain's no longer a sump. It's only blattering now."

"What's the difference between a sump and blattering?" Summer asked.

"Not much."

"The back window on this side is starting to leak," Tallie said.

"All the more reason to come inside. Umbrellas out and open, lasses."

Edward opened the door to Christine's robust use of the heavy knocker and hurried them in out of the rain, telling them not to worry about drips from their umbrellas.

"I can't imagine what *isn't* dripping on a night like this," he said. "I feel as though I'm dripping just from looking at you. Now then, to what do we owe the pleasure?"

Edward stood in front of them, smiling at each woman in turn. Smiling pleasantly, Janet thought, except that she couldn't help feeling like they were sheep faced with a border collie determined not to let them pass.

Christine made Edward blink first. She shrugged out of her dripping coat and handed it to him. "Violet is expecting us. In the sitting room, is she?"

Violet was in the sitting room. And looked as though she'd rather stay there with the television program her eyes kept drifting back to while Christine introduced Summer and Tallie.

"We're glad we can help," Janet said. "Norman tells us you're quite worried about finding the Rodine."

"I'm not sure what you think you can do," Violet said. She might have been speaking to the hapless policeman in her program.

"More hands to help, more eyes to winkle it out from wherever it's hiding," Christine said.

"What are we winkling?" Edward asked, catching up to them after dealing with the wet coats.

"Now, you see," Violet sighed, "this is what I wanted to avoid. Edward, I didn't want to disappoint you and Isobel, but the Rodine I promised to the museum is missing."

"Possibly just misplaced," Janet said. "We've come to give your mother a hand finding it."

"But that's wonderful," Edward said. "Mother, you've worried far too much. Leave this to us. Come along, ladies. You can start your winkling in the most likely spot."

"Thank you, all of you," Violet said. Before they left the room, she'd turned back to her program.

Christine walked beside Edward, her always excellent posture looking, Janet thought, even more excellent. This gave Christine at least an extra quarter of an inch, so that she topped Edward by at *least* two inches, a fact she obviously enjoyed. Janet saw Christine give the top of Edward's head a side-eye with a smirk.

"Where did your mother store the museum donations?" Janet asked. He'd led them on a rather roundabout way and to the small library. When Janet had seen the room on Friday night, she'd shuddered at the chaos of book lust. Now, the almost denuded shelves looked indecent.

"There's nothing here," Christine said.

"Well, no." He sighed.

"What are you playing at?"

Edward scratched his ear. "Nothing, but it's dawned on me why Mother is fretting about looking for that silly tin of Rodine, and why this might be upsetting to you, as well, Christine."

"We don't have to do this tonight," Tallie said, her lawyer's antennae twitching.

"I'm muddling it," Edward said. "Looking for it isn't the problem. It's where we need to look for it." He crossed the room, stepped into the sunroom, and pointed at the door behind which

Christine and Helen had found Wendy. "Mother has the museum donations in there."

"Edward, you mean well," Christine said, "but none of us is squeamish."

"Especially not Christine," Tallie said. "May I?" She moved past Edward, opened the door, and found a light switch. "Neatly piled on whatever furniture is handy. Some of it boxed. That helps. Has anything been taken to the museum yet?"

Edward shook his head.

"Then let's get started. If we each take part of the room and work systematically, this shouldn't take too long."

Christine gave Tallie a thump on the back and a thumbs-up. She started picking through a box of antique hand tools on the right side of the room. Janet took the left side where piles of clothes hid two chairs. Tallie knelt to sort through a collection of glass and tinware under a table. Summer sat on the floor, near the door, and pulled a box of household ledgers toward her. Edward leaned against the doorjamb, hands in his pockets, and watched.

"What kind of exhibit will be improved by rat poison?" Summer asked. "I'm sensing an interesting theme developing in the museum's exhibits."

"Land Girls and Lumber Jills. Have you heard of them?"

"Never."

"Ah. British Women's Land Army. Set up during the First World War, 1917. Reformed in 1939 at the start of World War II. Fascinating stories. There should be a Land Girl's uniform here somewhere," Edward said, making no move to look for it.

Janet chuckled to herself as she felt through the pockets of an army uniform. Edward's share of the work would be to entertain them. Not such a bad deal.

"As for the stories," Edward continued. "You're in for a treat."

Janet heard footsteps and a voice she'd heard Friday night.

"What treat are you talking about, Edward?" His sister's voice. "What's going on here?"

"It's all right, Teresa. I've got this."

"*I've* got this, Edward."

"Righty-o. I defer to your brilliance."

Teresa came into the room, hands on her hips, and surveyed the four women. Edward followed Teresa but stayed out of her line of sight. Catching Janet's eye, he widened his own eyes in a look of mock horror, adding the humorously twisted lips of a younger—though he was approaching elderly—brother bent on mischief.

"Are you looking for something?" Teresa asked.

"Yes, something was possibly mislaid," Christine said. "We're taking a quick look to make certain, to put your mum's mind at ease."

"Then I'll explain to you what I explained, again, to Mother. The decluttering was confined to the ground floor. Off limit rooms on the ground floor and rooms upstairs were locked."

"Or were meant to be?" Janet asked.

"*Were* period," Teresa said. "Are you acting on behalf of the museum?"

"So it would appear," Edward said.

"I didn't ask you. Where is Isobel?"

No one took a chance on answering out of turn.

"Well then, except for Isobel, it's unlikely anything is missing."

"We agree," Tallie said. "Constable Hobbs told us about a missing tin of Rodine this morning, and, as Christine said, we're here to put your mother's mind at ease."

"Oh, have you seen our missing Rodine?" Edward sang in a surprisingly mellow baritone.

"I don't know anything about a tin of Rodine," Teresa said. "Why is Norman Hobbs concerned? Is he suggesting someone poisoned Wendy?"

"No," Tallie said.

"Are *you*?"

"No one's said anything like that, Teresa," Edward said. "I'll be happy to start, though. See what you think of this. Can we ever live it down?

Whatever shall we do? Our guest has swallowed poison and she's died inside our loo."

"That's inaccurate and completely distasteful," Teresa snapped.

"Being inaccurate makes it less distasteful," Edward said. "You didn't know Wendy as well as I did. She might have been shortsighted, but she would not have been bothered at all by my distasteful inaccuracies. In fact, that wee verse might be just the thing to start my entry for the Yon Bonnie McGonagall contest. Tell me, Janet, are you the genius behind that?"

"I didn't know word had spread yet," Janet said. "We haven't finalized details. But no, it wasn't my idea. That's all Tallie."

"Brava, Tallie."

"Thank you. We look forward to reading your entry at some future date, Edward."

"My question remains," Teresa said. "Are you people suggesting that someone poisoned Wendy?"

"No, Teresa, as Tallie and your brother *both* did say. As Tallie and *I* both said, we're doing your mother a favor." Christine crossed her arms, and Janet caught sight of Queen Elizabeth tapping her toe with growing impatience.

"I don't know whether to be insulted or appalled," Teresa said. "What have you told Norman Hobbs? Does he know what you're up to here? Have you told him what you so clearly *do* seem to think happened?"

It was clear to Janet that Teresa wasn't listening to them, or that she heard them but didn't believe anything they said. She tried another approach. "There's no reason to believe Wendy was deliberately poisoned, Teresa. There are those rumors going around about food poisoning from the food truck, and Wendy did eat at Mr. Potato Chef."

"How do you know that?"

"I found the wrappers in her bin at the museum."

"*Found* them?"

"Saw them," Janet said. "I wasn't looking for them."

"And now you're here. Contaminating a possible crime scene," Teresa said. "You obviously did not think of *that*, did you?"

Tallie, at five three, couldn't use height to her advantage the way Christine did. Instead, she used her well-honed law professor's voice. "Considering the number of people in and out of the house Friday night," she said, adjusting her glasses, "and considering the amount of time with an unknown number of people moving freely through this room and the rest of the house *since* Friday night, it's unlikely the police will take issue with our presence now."

"If you're trying to be clever—"

"We're not," Summer said. "We're really only here for your mom."

"My *mother*."

"Right," Summer said. "Mom, mother, mum, whatever. We aren't clever."

Teresa looked them over. "No, I suppose not. Otherwise it *would* have occurred to you. Or perhaps it did, and you don't feel it's your place to question any conclusions Norman Hobbs might have reached. Fortunately, questioning the constable does not bother me one bit so I shall come right out and say it: Rather than food poisoning, this Rodine *might* have killed Wendy Erskine. More to the point, someone might have *used* the Rodine to kill her. That is a horrible thought and worse accusation."

"Which we have not made," Christine ground out between her teeth.

"As well you haven't, because neither I nor anyone else in this house did any such thing. I knew the decluttering was a mistake from the moment the idea flitted into Mother's head. I should like you to know that I am a personal friend of the Assistant Chief Constable and I find it highly suspicious that you are here disturbing evidence. You should leave. Now."

The four women and Edward filed out of the room. Teresa turned a key in the lock.

"As you might have gathered," Edward said as he helped them into their coats at the front door, "Teresa is best suited for living alone. But here's a bright side for the evening—the rain's nearly stopped."

Janet hadn't said anything since telling Teresa about the food wrappers. She'd simmered, and then steamed. In the car, and as Christine started back down the tree-shrouded lane, Janet finally boiled over. "She's a self-satisfied, aggravating, irritating, supercilious, patronizing, condescending, bi—" She lopped off the rest and sank into her seat, stewing.

"*Mom,*" Tallie said in tones of aghast admiration. "Were you about to call Teresa a bi—"

"*Beetroot!*" Christine pounded the steering wheel. "Your mother is exactly right. Teresa is a bloody, *hoaching,* numpty, nyaff of a bloody beetroot. And I'm hungry and crabbit and *now* we'll go to Nev's."

"Good," Summer said. "Because now both your back windows are leaking."

"*Beetroot,*" Christine snarled, and pounded the steering wheel again.

10

Nev's, their local, wasted little energy on curb appeal. On a street less attractive to tourists than the High Street, and a bit of a hike uphill from the harbor, the pub sandwiched itself between the *Inversgail Guardian*'s building and Smith's Funerals. People unfamiliar with Nev's, stopping on the pavement out front and not quite able to see through the only window, tended to think twice before opening the door. If, beyond good reason, they took an optimistic step back to look for the pub's sign, missing for at least a decade, many were disappointed and trailed back down the hill toward the shinier establishments nearer the harbor. When Janet, Christine, Tallie, and Summer opened Nev's door that Monday night, the barman, Danny Macquarrie, and the smells of good ale and fried food waved them in. The women hung their damp coats on hooks near the door and felt comfortably at home.

"A round of the Selkie's?" Danny called. "Halfs?"

"At least," Janet said, "but that'll be a good start."

Over steaming bowls of Scotch broth and a plate of cheese, Christine was willing to admit she might have insisted they be allowed to help when she'd phoned Violet. "But I didn't strong-arm her. That's hardly my style."

The other three took judicious swallows of their ale.

"Even so," Christine said, "something changed between phoning her and our arrival. Violet definitely was not keen on having us looking round. On having us there at all."

"She's not the one who sent us away with our tails between our legs," Janet said. "That was Teresa the—"

Tallie quickly handed a wedge of Isle of Mull Cheddar to her mother. Janet accepted the distraction.

"Violet probably just had second thoughts about strangers traipsing around," Summer said.

"The woman who gaily invited people to traipse round her house and help themselves to her possessions?" Christine asked.

"But look how that turned out." Summer handed a wedge of the cheese to Christine. "Our feelings are hurt. We'll get over it. Violet hasn't been sleeping, according to Norman, and we just saw how worried Teresa is."

"Thank you, Summer," Christine said. "For old cheese and clear thinking. You, in the younger generation, have wise heads."

"Unlike some, who are old enough to know better," Janet said. "Like Teresa Ritchie—"

"Teresa, is it?" Danny arrived with a basket of fried mushrooms. "You missed out on these once before, and I don't like to see my favorite customers go without." He glanced at the bar, then pulled out the empty chair next to Christine and joined them. An empty chair next to Christine had become their unspoken habit.

"We developed a strong opinion about Teresa this evening," Christine said.

"Not surprised," Danny said. "Four strong women meet another?"

"What do you know about her?" Janet asked.

"She's a chartered accountant. That *accounts* for a lot. Her abrasiveness for starters."

"Abrasiveness is a nice euphemism," Janet said.

"It's not a euphemism." Tallie handed Janet another piece of cheese. "She *is* abrasive.

"Proud, as well," Danny said. "Of her profession, at any rate. Chartered accountants claim to be the first accounting group to form a professional body."

The women looked at him.

"Aye, well. It happened here. 1854."

"In Inversgail?" Tallie asked.

Danny waved an arm. "In Scotland. It's part of our history."

"You're an odd font of information about chartered accountants," Christine said.

"Rab would know it. Basant. Anyone who's anybody who claims to be Scottish. In truth, I heard it from Teresa. Her specialty is small businesses." He stood and rested a hand on Christine's shoulder. "Another round of Selkies?"

"I think we deserve it tonight," Christine said.

"On its way."

Janet raised her nearly empty glass to the others. "I'm over it," she said, and drained the last of the ale. "Over my snit. Back in my right mind."

"Your mind that's ever curious?" Tallie asked.

"That one. Yes."

"Good. So, I'm curious; if Teresa specializes in small businesses, why didn't we go with her when we were looking for an accountant?"

"We went with David's recommendation," Janet said.

"And Dad has an antipathy toward Teresa."

"I'd call it more of a loathing, wouldn't you, Chrissie?" Danny handed the fresh glasses around and collected the empties.

"Danny, what do you know about the Mr. Potato Chef food truck?" Janet asked.

"What do you know *and* what have you heard?" Christine added.

"Euan Markwell—he's the chef in question—did some cooking for me a few years back. Lost his footing somewhere along the way. He's getting his feet back under him with the new business. I wish him luck. He doesn't deserve the rumors. He does deserve a better van. Anything else?"

They shook their heads. Summer passed the mushrooms.

"May I suggest we resume our discussion of this morning?" Christine said.

"Which part of it?" Tallie asked.

"Rewind to when Norman told us Violet was worried. Was she worried that the tin is missing? That Isobel and Edward are going to be disappointed if it isn't found? Or is she worried that someone used it to poison Wendy? We worried about that, and Teresa's nimble mind jumped to it immediately."

"Is *Norman* worried?" Janet asked. "He must be. And I'm beginning to feel guilty about reacting to Teresa the way I did."

"I don't think you have to go that far," Tallie said. "How many people wandered into that suite of rooms?"

"That's probably impossible to know," Janet said. "Teresa's right. The door was supposed to be locked, and it might have been most of the time, but there's no telling how long it wasn't. Violet invited people to wander around taking things, and that's what they did."

"You can include me and Mum in your count of wanderers. We didn't wander *into* the suite; we went straight in and Mum headed for the loo. But then Mum wandered whilst *I* was in the loo. That's how she found Wendy in the bedroom."

"What about the smell? You said Wendy was quite sick, didn't you?" Janet asked. "Didn't you notice anything when you went in?"

"I did, but Mum didn't seem to, and I didn't want to distract her. Expediency was necessary. But that's a good point, Janet. If other people had wandered in, they would have smelled it, too. And if Violet's right, that nothing else is missing, then it sounds like no one else did wander about in there. People were complete scavengers in the designated decluttering areas."

"Bethia." Janet set her glass down. "Bethia could have been back there. She was staying at Fairy Flax Hall. She could have been in the suite any time before Friday night. *That's* why Norman came to see us."

"I knew there was another reason," Tallie said. "Not just to dance around the facts of Rodine. He didn't believe Violet's assurance that the Rodine was safe after all these years and despite a coat of dust."

"He got her out of the house pretty quickly," Christine said. "Sent her home with you."

"She could have just gone up to bed at Fairy Flax Hall," Janet said. "She said so herself. She also told me about clutter that I didn't see. I thought I missed more than one room. She must have been looking through the museum donations."

"Why is that a problem?" Summer asked.

"He's worried she saw something or left fingerprints somewhere," Janet said.

"What if she saw someone," Christine said. "What if she saw the someone who poisoned Wendy, either by accident or on purpose, and now she's in danger, or she herself could be accused of something. Norman isn't up to this kind of pressure. No wonder he came to us."

"Okay, two things," Summer said. "First—I ate the rest of the mushrooms. Sorry. Second—why didn't Norman come right out and say all of that? I like Tallie's description of him—dancing. Norman's a straightforward guy. Either he knows something, or he doesn't. Either he has facts he can share, or he doesn't. Why the dance?"

"He wants our help," Tallie said.

"That coming from you?" Summer asked. "You're our careful counselor. Our voice of reason and caution. Our resident skeptic."

Janet and Christine murmured agreement. Christine found a crumb of breading on the mushroom plate and ate it. All three women looked at Tallie.

"He trusts us," Tallie said. "That's why he told us as much as he did. And until he knows more, he doesn't know who else to trust."

The other three nodded.

"I just hope we haven't broken that trust by meddling at Fairy Flax Hall," Tallie added. "On the other hand, everything I said might be the other half of the Selkies speaking. Fancy a game, Summer?"

The two younger women took themselves off to the darts room. Janet and Christine relaxed into the sounds of neighbors and acquaintances enjoying the pub. Christine, seeing some of Helen and David's friends, waved and went to tell them her parents would be in next Monday, if not sooner.

Janet checked the back corner and saw the weekly meeting of Pub Scrawl in progress. Though the gatherings were difficult to identify as such; the members never discussed anything and rarely exchanged more than nods of hello and goodnight. Their purpose at the table in the corner was to write. They were an odd trio—James Haviland, Rab MacGregor, and Maida Fairlie. Maida, whom Tallie had sent a picture of from the poetry slam, gave the immediate impression of dour respectability without a softening edge of humor or playfulness. After getting to know her, that impression generally solidified. It was arguably her presence that made the trio most odd. She never drank and might never have been in a pub until she came up with the idea for Pub Scrawl. That she wrote poetry with obvious passion made Janet love her.

Maida glanced up from her writing and saw Janet looking her way. Janet waved. Maida closed her notebook, gathered her belongings, and nodded to James, Rab, and someone under the table—presumably Ranger. She came toward Janet, carrying her handbag before her like a shield. Janet wondered if she'd learned that from watching Joan Hickson when she'd played Miss Marple. Maida, sometimes referred to as "Mousie Maida," had once used a frying pan like a battle axe to good effect. Janet was sure Joan Hickson would have approved. Tallie arrived back at the table as Maida sat down.

"Evening, Maida," Janet said, then turned to Tallie. "Game over so soon?"

"Summer's got the competition crying for their grannies. I remain hopeless. Good writing this evening, Maida?"

"Aye. There's something you might like to know." She set her handbag on the table in front of her. "I'll just wait for Christine." She'd raised her voice just enough, so that Christine heard.

Christine came to reclaim her seat. "Nice to see you, Maida." She raised her eyebrows. "Something to tell us?"

"I spent the day at Fairy Flax Hall. MacAskills are one of our accounts." Maida managed the local office of a cleaning company based in Fort William. "I thought you'd like to know that the police were *not* crawling all over the place."

"Oh aye?" Christine said. "And why would we think they might be?"

"You seem to hear things of that nature," Maida said.

"What would we have heard?" Tallie asked.

"That Norman Hobbs crawled all over the place, at Violet's direction. A policeman, aye, but not official police business." Maida sat back with a rare look of satisfaction.

"Huh," Janet said, and she read clearly on Tallie and Christine's faces, *No one at Fairy Flax Hall said a word about that.*

"Were you at the decluttering, Maida?" Christine asked.

"Violet invited me to help myself earlier in the day."

"What did you take?" Christine asked.

"Not much."

"Did you help arrange the clutter?" Janet asked.

"Teresa did that."

"With any help?" Tallie asked.

"On her own. Best that way."

"For her?" Christine asked.

"And everyone else."

"Did she put aside the stuff for the museum donation, too?" Janet asked.

"I've heard nought about that." Maida folded her hands on her handbag, apparently having nothing more to say about Fairy Flax Hall, either.

"Maida blew everyone away at the poetry and knitting slam Friday night," Tallie said. "I've got a picture." She passed her phone to Maida.

Maida passed it back. "Send it to me?"

"Sure." Tallie sent the picture, then passed the phone to Christine.

Christine made complementary noises and passed the phone along to Janet. Janet had seen the picture Friday night, but looked at it again, and then she looked more closely. She enlarged it. Off to the side, to the left of the low stage where Maida stood, she was certain she saw the back of a tailcoat. "Did you see Kyle at the slam?" she asked Tallie.

"Knitter Kyle? No."

"Oddball question for you, Maida. Did you see someone in a tailcoat at the slam?"

"Kyle Byrne. Aye. The only person I know named after two bodies of water. That's one of the first things he tells people when he meets them. It's a badge he seems to hate and can't seem to shake. So why bring it up?"

"Did he do that when he first came to knit?" Janet asked. "I don't remember."

"You might have intimidated him," Maida said. "You have that way about you."

"You do, Janet," Christine said. "Dinnae fash yersel. I'll work with you on it."

Janet tried to find Christine's ankle under the table, with her own foot, to give the ankle a kick. She gave up when she couldn't reach it.

"How do you know Kyle, Maida?" Tallie asked.

"He works for the cleaning company. He's not particularly good at the job, mind, but he has an ear for poetry. He came to cheer me on at the slam."

"He was at the decluttering, too," Janet said. "Wearing the tailcoat. That's how I recognized him in the picture. Helen and I saw him leaving as we went up the steps. Leaving in a hurry. Heading for the slam, I guess. He did hesitate for a split second, and I thought he wanted to say something, but then dashed off. Did you see if he was knitting at the slam, Maida?"

"Not that I saw. Bethia, now, she's the one for knitting. Knits every evening whilst we watch the telly."

"Is Bethia staying with you?" Janet asked. "How nice."

"Och, well, nice enough. She likes it. Says Fairy Flax Hall was lovely, but she felt isolated. Easier for her to get around now she's in town. As well, between my company and judging the knitting contest, she says she feels like a real part of the community. And I've no stairs in my wee house."

"I hadn't thought of the stairs," Janet said.

"I thought you probably hadn't. I'd best be away. Bethia and I like a cup of cocoa before bedtime." Maida stood to go. "I'll be in touch if I hear anything else you might like to know."

"Thanks, Maida," Tallie said.

"Cocoa before bedtime," Janet said, watching Maida go. "That's a very sweet picture in my head."

"Bethia safely at Maida's makes things less complicated for us, too," Christine said. "Norman will be able to keep a clear head and his mind on the task at hand. Working with us."

"Do you think Maida sees herself as Miss Marple?" Janet asked.

"Doubtful," Christine said. "An avenging angel maybe."

"No, not an avenging angel," Janet said. "Our better angel."

11

Arsenic Diary, day five

My last entry started with my ditty. Now I shall get down to the nitty-gritty. Definitely the gritty. Arsenic, unheated, has no smell or taste but is gritty in the mouth. As a cup of coffee or tea cools, the arsenic precipitates out and can be found in the bottom of the cup. Or a bowl of cooled oatmeal. Maybe combine it with the sugar? Which one—demerara or turbinado? If this is going to be a problem, then an obvious solution is to encourage drinking up or, in the case of oatmeal, eating up. Who really enjoys tepid tea or cold porridge?

I pass by Mr. Potato Chef. The truck could use a refurb. People call it the tatty tattie truck. So unkind. Not everyone shines.

When heated, by bright sunlight or in a test tube, arsenic passes directly from its solid state to a gas and smells like garlic.

✐

The Tuesday online edition of the *Inversgail Guardian* reported that health inspectors had found no health code violations in the Mr. Potato Chef operation. Summer read the report to the other women during their morning meeting between the book covers and teabags, as Christine had renamed it.

"There's no credible evidence of food poisoning associated with the truck. This is great news." Summer looked up from her phone. "He serves food, but we aren't really competitors. No more than we compete with Nev's. So, the clean bill of health feels like a victory for all small food vendors." She looked back at the article. "Oh, beetroot."

"What is it?" Tallie asked.

"The last line. 'Health inspectors did not rule out the possibility that contamination of the food occurred in some manner after leaving the truck.'"

"That means exactly nothing," Tallie said. "Any food can be contaminated after leaving a restaurant or kitchen or any place at all. That shouldn't stop people from eating at the food truck. Not logically, anyway."

"I'm surprised you don't already now know this, Tallie," Christine said. "People are rarely logical."

The stair rods followed by blatters of rain the evening before had washed any hint of gray from the sky. People stepped out into a day of sunshine and a sky that some felt should be worshipped. Shops and pubs did a good business, Yon Bonnie Books and the tearoom included. When Janet finally had a chance to look out the front window, shortly before noon, she saw a line of people waiting to buy lunch at Mr. Potato Chef. Rab and Ranger among them.

"Tallie, come look at this."

"Nice," Tallie said. "Shall I go tell Christine people are more logical than she thinks?

"Why don't you tell her we'll buy her lunch, instead. Summer, too. If you don't mind watching the shop, I'll go stand in line."

"On my way."

Christine, buttoning up her duffle coat, came back with Tallie. "Text from Danny," she said. "He's already there. Come along, Janet. The line is growing."

By the time they got in line, they'd spotted enough friends that it felt like a party. "Maida and Bethia. And Kyle's with them," Janet said, nudging Christine with her elbow. "What are we going to have on our potatoes? Smell the garlic! Heavenly."

"Garlic, yes," Christine said. "Butter, broccoli, cheese, more cheese, maybe even more garlic. Look, Isobel and Edward are at the window."

"No Teresa in sight."

"Her loss," Christine said. "*Here's* Danny. And Basant. Hello, you two. How have we all managed to abandon our shops at once?"

"For a good cause," Basant said, getting in line behind them.

"For a good lunch." Danny already had his. "Haggis tattie," he said. "Excellent. Sorry to gulp and go, but I left them short at the pub. Worth every second I'm away, though, if it counteracts the arses—" He stopped and put a large forkful of baked potato and haggis in his mouth. After chewing and swallowing, he smiled. "Needed a moment to collect my thoughts, aye? What I meant to say, before I interrupted myself, is that it might behoove Norman to mind those braying loudest."

"Your thoughts might not be as neatly collected as you thought," Christine said. "What braying are you talking about?"

"Euan's truck is in the clear," Danny said, "but some are still waving pitchforks at his tatties."

"Who's waving them?" Christine looked up and down the line as though she'd missed a pitchfork and planned to go after it.

"And why?" Janet demanded. "Because someone might have contaminated the food after they left the truck? How is that his fault?"

"You'll find no pitchfork waving from anyone queueing up here," Danny said. "But it might be interesting to know who's braying and why. And why keep it up after the clean bill from the health inspector?"

"It is perhaps someone who does not follow the news as carefully as we do," Basant said. Basant Paudel, a Nepali native, owned and operated one of Janet's favorite shops. Paudel's News Agent, Post Office, and Convenience carried a little of everything she needed and indulgences she rarely needed but always enjoyed anyway. Basant, who'd arrived in Inversgail a decade or so earlier, was a good source of local information.

"You could be right, Basant." Danny eyed the line as he finished his potato. "Or it could be personal. Some of his mates were right *neds* when he cooked for me."

"Then it is good that he has exchanged unsavory friends for his savory potatoes," Basant said. "I hear he is so relieved by the health inspector's report, after the recent stress of unfounded rumors, that he has had to take time to recuperate. Hence this long wait. Mr. Potato Chef is absent and his tattie truck short-staffed."

"Sleeping it off after celebrating, more like," Danny said. "Takes time for moggies to change their stripes. He'll make it, though."

"He's not even here to appreciate this outpouring of support?" Christine asked. "Who's serving the potatoes?"

"His best supporter. His mum." Danny crumpled his trash into a ball and tossed it into the nearest bin. "See ya."

Basant looked at the time on his phone, then, worriedly, at how many people were still ahead of them. "I am happy for Euan and his mum, but I had not thought I'd be waiting this long."

"Basant, I never thought this day would come," Christine said. "You frequently help your customers by offering wise counsel. Let me now offer you advice. We lose out on too many opportunities in life by waiting. Don't wait. Tell me what kind of potato you want, and I'll order it when I order ours. Janet won't mind running your tattie over to your shop on her way back to ours."

"You would be so kind?"

"Of course," Christine said.

"Of course," Janet echoed, wondering how either Christine or Basant imagined his shop, two blocks beyond the food truck, could be on her way back to the bookshop. But the blue sky and the almost warm sunshine argued against quibbling.

"In that case, I will have the excellent haggis tattie, and if there is extra garlic available, some of that on top." Basant took an expansive sniff of the smells coming from the truck. "I cannot resist when it smells so good. And as the day is dry, and only slightly too cold, I will wait five more minutes."

"Speaking of waiting," Janet said, pulling a slender paperback from her jacket pocket as they moved forward two steps. "You remember Heather and her brother, Calum?" It wasn't really a question. Neither of them would have forgotten the sad details surrounding Heather and Calum's deaths. Heather had come to Inversgail posing as a true-crime writer. She'd been looking for the truth behind Calum's death and lost her own life in the process. "I've been dipping into his book, *On Waiting: Short Meditations on a Lengthy Subject.* It isn't the kind of thing you read straight through, but I'm enjoying it. I read a piece and my mind wanders off to rethink one of my own experiences. You might like it, Basant."

"It is the brother's work, then?" Christine asked. "Not Heather writing as Calum?"

"Jury's still out," Janet said. "I'm not sure I'll ever know."

"Does it matter?" Basant asked.

"Probably not. But waiting sometimes does. Suppose someone decides not to wait. Suppose they rush into a project before they're ready or the time is right, and by rushing, they get it wrong?"

"Ducks roaming at will can rarely be trusted," Basant said. "Although it takes more time, it is better to queue them up. And now I will take you up on your kind offer to wait on this queue for me. Thank you."

Janet and Christine moved forward another two feet as Basant walked quickly back to his shop. Janet watched Christine's eyes and lips puzzling over something, until Christine finally asked, "What were you getting at with your talk of waiting and ducks messing about? What experience are you rethinking?"

Janet looked to see who might overhear. The line was nicely strung out and people were busy with their own conversations. "Haste makes waste, Christine. What if someone did plan to use the Rodine, but not to poison Wendy? What if this person rushed, to take advantage of the coming and going during the decluttering, and got it wrong?"

"Had someone else in mind?" Christine asked.

"And plans to try again. To get it right."

∾

Constable Hobbs stopped in the bookshop shortly after lunch, while Tallie restocked the displays and Janet helped a customer find a picture book about pirates. Janet saw Hobbs peering at them from around the end of the next row of bookshelves. Her young customer saw him, too, and decided he wanted his mummy. Janet took his hand, and they went to find her. Upon finding her, he burst into tears. Janet explained what had happened. The boy's mummy wiped his nose and took him to the tearoom for a treat.

Hobbs came to the sales counter a few minutes later. He rather sheepishly set a copy of *Wee Granny's Magic Bag and the Pirates* on the counter. "For the wee boy. My great-niece says it's brilliant."

"That's kind of you, Norman." Janet rang it up and took his money. "I'm sure you didn't mean to have that effect on him."

"Just be glad you don't have that effect on us." Christine came to stand behind the counter beside Janet. "You put a two-shortbread scare into the lad."

"That's helpful for the bottom line," Janet said. "So thank you, Norman. And as long as you've chased off our customers for the moment, tell us what you think is going on with the missing Rodine. With poor Wendy. With the food truck. Please."

"I came to let you know that I've been told to have no further official connection with the case."

"Good Lord." Christine sat down on the high stool.

"How much of what I just asked you is part of the case?" Janet asked. "For instance, when Violet called you about the Rodine, was she worried it was missing or that someone used it?"

Hobbs gave that some thought, looking toward the ceiling, nodding almost in time to the nocturne floating down from the sound system. "I spoke with her before being dismissed from the case. So, this is a clarification of information I gave you in that earlier time frame."

"Nicely rationalized," Christine said. "What put the bee in Violet's bonnet?"

"Mrs. MacAskill only mentioned worry over the missing Rodine. I did not get the impression she worried about anyone having used it."

"Yet, there you were, crawling all over Fairy Flax Hall yesterday at her direction," Christine said. Then, at a look from him, "Our ears are always to the ground, Norman."

Janet took pity on him. "Maida told us."

"Who told you to step away from the case?" Tallie asked. She left the window display and joined her mother and Christine behind the counter. "*Why* did they?"

"An omission on my part. I didn't immediately relay information about the missing Rodine to the ME."

"Really?" Janet said. "Why would you? You weren't sure it was missing, and there was no obvious connection to Wendy's death. Did they expect you to report it immediately without finding out more first?"

"Possibly."

"Is your equivocal answer to that question part of the problem?" Christine asked.

"It might well be."

"Would you like to discuss the situation?" she asked.

Hobbs did not answer that question. Instead, he said, "Mrs. MacAskill is worried that her daughter, Teresa, feels guilty about Wendy Erskine's death, and that in feeling guilty she will appear so."

"Hanging up on the 9-9-9 dispatcher, the way she did, couldn't have helped," Janet said.

"*Is* she guilty?" Christine asked.

Hobbs didn't answer that question, either. "Mrs. MacAskill would like you to talk to Teresa, to clear her name. As SCONES."

It was the women's turn for silence. SCONES—the Shadow Constabulary of Nosy, Eavesdropping Snoops—had started as a joke, an insult. A visiting author in Inversgail had hatched the name and pinned it on them. They'd decided they liked it and had continued to use it the few times they'd helped solve local crimes. But they'd tried to keep the name private.

"From what I understand, Maida mentioned your—" He cleared his throat. "Your organization."

"So many questions, Norman," Tallie said, tapping the counter with a pencil eraser. "For starters, has there been an accusation?"

"And how do *you* feel about Violet's request?" Janet asked. As SCONES, they'd worked well with him, happy to let him take the credit. Being called upon, *as* SCONES, with him on the outside of an investigation, added an interesting wrinkle.

"I am merely the messenger," Hobbs said.

"*Why* are you the messenger?" Christine asked. "Why didn't Violet ask us herself? We've noticed friction between various MacAskills, but is there a problem that keeps her from talking to us directly? Is she afraid of something?"

"That's an interesting question," he said.

"Christine asked four," Tallie said. "They were all interesting. So was mine about an accusation against Teresa."

"The only one I can answer is Mrs. Robertson's first. I told Mrs. MacAskill, when she asked, that as SCONES you are discreet and effective. I offered to ask you on her behalf. In part because of the friction Mrs. Robertson mentioned." He studied the ceiling again, briefly, then shook his head. "I don't know if fear has anything to do with that."

"You asked us *in part* because of the friction. What's the other part?" Janet asked.

"I would like help from the SCONES in this matter as well."

"But that's a connection to the case, isn't it?" Janet asked.

"Inspector Reddick only said I'm to have no further *official* connection to the case."

"Norman Hobbs, you *skellum*," Christine said. "Inspector Reddick, is it? Our other favorite Norman."

Norman Reddick was also their favorite inspector with Police Scotland's Major Investigation Teams. As an MIT inspector, he might be called up to work a major crime in any part of Scotland. The women felt lucky any time a case brought him to their part of Scotland. Reddick and Hobbs worked well together. Reddick's dog, Quantum, got on with all of them, too. When the women had found out the inspector's given name was also Norman, Christine had declared they only had room in their lives for one Norman. Reddick had since remained Reddick.

"What kind of help do you want from us?" Tallie asked.

"Eyes and ears for the most part. You can go places I should not, at this point. Fairy Flax Hall, for instance."

"Our usual arrangement?" Janet asked. "We'll share what we learn. You pass along information and answer questions as you're able?"

Hobbs nodded. "Though my ability to answer questions and share information might be curtailed."

"First question," Tallie said. "Will the autopsy look for phosphate?"

"First curtailment. I do not have full details."

They heard a small boy replete with shortbread coming toward them. Hobbs headed for the door. Janet followed him. "Norman, do you believe Teresa is guilty?"

"Not enough information, Mrs. Marsh. Let me know when you've spoken to her, will you?"

When Janet returned to the counter, Tallie had delighted the boy by handing him *Wee Granny*. Christine had gone back to the tearoom.

"Norman *should* have contacted the ME sooner," Tallie said when the boy and his mother had waved and gone out the door. "For obvious professional reasons and for several personal reasons."

"Bethia." Janet took out her phone.

"Yes. Even so—" Tallie waited.

"Hm?" Janet looked up from her phone. "I was listening. I'm just looking at our previous shared documents. If we're going to clear Teresa, it'll help if we find someone else who looks guiltier. There. A new 'Suspects' document created and I let the others know. What were you going to say?"

"I wonder if Norman is really off the case. Even officially."

Janet went back to her phone. "New 'Questions' document created." After more tapping she put the phone away. "Lots of interesting questions already. Including yours about Norman and the case and a new one of mine. Why hasn't he mentioned worries about Bethia?"

"Too close to home?"

"That could certainly be. He must be worried sick, although I don't for a minute believe she had anything to do with Wendy's death."

"We need to clear her as well," Tallie said.

"Yes. Absolutely. Here's another question. Can Rab tell us when Kyle arrived at the poetry slam? He's into poetry and he seems to have antennae for knowing when Kyle's around. Did you see Rab there?"

"No, but he might have been wearing his cloak of invisibility. Knitters will be in tomorrow morning, won't they? Then Rab and Ranger probably will be, too, and you can ask him."

"Next question," Janet said. "When do we contact Teresa and set up an interview?"

"Do we dare wait a day or two? See what transpires?"

"I like the word *transpires*," Janet said. "It gives your weaseling request to delay the unpalatable a day or two the right sort of gravitas. So much so, that let's give ourselves two or *three* days."

∞

Hobbs stopped by mid-morning the next day with an update on Teresa. Janet thought his visit might be an excuse to surreptitiously check on Bethia in the tearoom. Christine thought it might be an excuse for a cup of tea and shortbread after hearing about the small boy's treat the day before.

"You're right," Janet said. She and Christine stood in the doorway between the shops watching Hobbs, Bethia, and Kyle at the table in the window. "There's nothing surreptitious about watching your tea grow cold and someone else filching your shortbread while your grandmother uses your hands for winding wool. Don't let him get away without giving us that update on Teresa. If we're lucky, it'll mean we don't need to talk to her at all."

"Or ever again. A lovely thought." Christine waved and went to refresh a teapot.

True to Tallie's prediction, Rab and Ranger had come to work. But when Janet asked him, Rab said he hadn't gone to the poetry slam.

"Not to support Maida?" she asked.

Rab nodded at Ranger, asleep in his chair while a knitter perched on the arm. "Best not to. The lad is sensitive to tortured rhyme schemes."

Hobbs came into the bookshop from the tearoom a short time later, and almost right behind him, Summer. "I saw Kyle filch your short-bread while you couldn't defend it," she said, and handed him a white bakery bag.

Janet thought she heard a low growl from Ranger. He still slept in his chair, though, and the knitter didn't look the least disturbed. But here came Kyle from the tearoom, stopping to browse in the knitting books. Tallie gave her a nudge and nodded at Rab standing behind the cash register. Rab didn't take his eyes off Kyle, and Janet suddenly wondered if the growl had been his.

"You have an update, Norman?" Tallie asked.

"I'll watch here," Rab said. "More privacy in the office."

"Thank you, Rab," Janet said.

Summer, Tallie, and Hobbs went into the office, and before Janet closed the door, she looked back at Rab. Still alert, still focused on Kyle. Odd behavior from Rab, but she trusted his instincts.

"Mrs. Ritchie was arrested," Hobbs said, "but she was not cautioned or charged, making her an NOA, a Not Officially Accused person, and she has been released."

"Arrested, not accused, released," Janet said, then pointed at herself. "Confused."

"The investigation remains live. You might say active. She remains a suspect, but this allows for inquiries to continue and Mrs. Ritchie to be released on Investigative Liberation."

"It sounds kind of like our bail system," Tallie said. "Except different."

"And with much cooler jargon," Summer said. "So, Norman, if we're going to meet with her, is there anything we should know ahead of time? Like, is it safe?"

He briefly thought that over then shrugged. "If you stick together, I reckon you'll be fine."

"Has this information been released to the public?" Tallie asked.

"Possibly not."

He left the three of them looking at each other.

"That wasn't the ringing *yes* for our safety that I wanted to hear," Summer said.

"And I wonder, again, if he's even officially off the case," Tallie said. "Are you in the cloud putting that question in bold italics, Mom?"

"No. Leaving a message. For Teresa. Asking her when she'd like to meet."

⁓

Waiting to hear back from Teresa put a damper on their spirits. Summer tried to counteract the gloom by putting out the new bookmarks and telling Rab about her idea for Stevenson statue reproductions and paper dolls. He immediately whistled for Ranger, and the two went to take pictures of the statue from various angles. Kyle had gone by then. Bethia stopped in the bookshop after the knitters left.

"You and Norman looked very sweet together this morning," Janet said.

"He's a good lad, and worried because of that poor woman at Violet's party."

"Has he told you he's worried?" Janet asked.

"Och no. He's so serious about not letting me see his concern. Plays his cloak and dagger game. But I didn't like to let on that I ken perfectly well what he's about. He's easily embarrassed."

When Janet hadn't heard back from Teresa by Thursday morning, the women dared hope she wanted nothing to do with them. By lunch time, Christine declared their lives a Teresa-free zone, and went out to buy them all lunch from Mr. Potato Chef to celebrate. When she returned with the smells of garlic and shrimp, she saw defeat on Tallie and Summer's faces. Janet, phone to her ear, stood with her eyes closed, her face screwed up in silent pain.

"Let me check with my partners. I'll be right back." Janet held the phone against her chest and whispered, "She wants to meet with us."

"Is that suspicious?" Christine whispered.

"At one of our houses," Janet whispered. "Tonight."

"Is *that* suspicious?" Summer whispered.

"Tonight's fine," Tallie said at normal volume. "But tell her the meeting is here."

The others nodded. Janet relayed the message, nodded at the others in return, and rang off. "Right," she said. "That was easier than I expected."

"And now we need to prepare," Tallie said. "We need to have questions ready. Why does she feel guilty? What were her movements that night? What did she see? What does she know about Wendy?"

"We need to know a lot more about Wendy, too," Summer said. "How she ran the museum. Her personal life. Any issues or friction."

"Two new documents just created." Janet held her phone up. "Labeled 'Teresa' and 'Wendy.'"

"Another question of logistics," Christine said. "Shall we serve anything tonight?"

"No," Janet said. "And if she brings anything, don't eat it."

12

Teresa didn't make it easy or pleasant for the SCONES that evening. They escorted her to the inglenook, offering a chair close to the fireplace. She chose another. She agreed they could record the meeting, and then made a show of putting her own phone on the arm of her chair and hitting record. When they offered commiseration for the situation in which she'd found herself, she told them not to gush.

"I am *free* thanks to my friendship with the Assistant Chief Constable. I don't call this a *situation*. I call it a shambles that someone will soon regret, and I am in it because my mother insisted on going through with her *decluttering*." She didn't make air quotes, but her emphasis carved them as clearly as claw marks.

"Was there any question she would go through with the decluttering?" Janet asked.

"None in my mind. I knew the idea was a mistake from her first mention of it."

"It sounded like an ingenious way to downsize," Summer said. Then, at a look from Teresa, "But kind of eccentric, I guess."

Teresa switched her gaze to Janet. "Did you know my mother before she invited you?"

"No."

"And what did you take home with you?"

"I—"

"She invited strangers to walk through her house and told them to help themselves. Like corbies after carrion."

"Crows makes it sound almost as unpleasant as sharks after chum," Janet said. "That's how Norman Hobbs described it." At Teresa's sneer, she flinched, feeling like chum herself. She rallied and tried to soften the image. "It made your mother happy, though, and the guests looked happy. I thought of it more like a scene from the picture book *Blueberries for Sal*, with Sal and her mother and the mother bear and baby bear all wandering and helping themselves."

"Is that an American habit?" Teresa asked. "Judging events through picture books?"

"A habit of librarians and readers the world over," Janet said. "Describing, not judging."

"She said judgmentally."

"Guilty." Janet enjoyed her bullseye. Then she regretted reacting to Teresa's snooty remark. Her superiority. Her—Janet patted her hair to smooth her hackles, and sat back thankfully when Christine redirected the conversation.

"Your mother told us that you and the rest of the family had already taken what you wanted," Christine said. "Is that not true?"

"The point is," Teresa said, embedding the point into the arm of her chair with a manicured finger, "if she so desperately wanted to clear the place out, it would have been better to have valuers in and sell the lot. The tartanware and Govencroft pottery alone would have made whatever commission they asked for worth it."

"Was there anything so valuable that someone would kill to get it before or away from someone else?" Summer asked.

Teresa appeared to think that over, though she stared at Summer while she did. Janet thought she might squirm in Summer's place.

"It would be an extreme way to react," Teresa said, "but avid collectors aren't known for their absolute sanity. James Haviland practically driveled over the typewriters he took. But you're grasping. The murder you're describing would be unhinged and unplanned."

"Does your mother need the money?" Tallie asked.

"Not at all. Far from it. She has more than she needs and she's left a substantial amount to the museum in her will. She could have added any money from a sale to that. She could have sent a check to each of the people she invited, for that matter." Teresa raised her eyebrows. "There's an idea I should have had earlier. She may have gone for that."

"Also eccentric," Tallie said, "but it might have saved you this trouble."

"I wonder if you would so blithely call it *trouble* if it were you who'd been arrested and your own reputation damaged. Och well, my *trouble* is here and too late to stop it." Teresa picked up one of the new bookmarks from the small table next to her chair. She scanned the side promoting the museum exhibit, and then the reverse promoting the knitting competition, flipping the bookmark back and forth as though evaluating a rasher of bacon for even crisping. "I'd not seen these."

"I made them. With Isobel's permission," Summer said. "A little cross-promotion between the museum and our business. We thought it was kind of fun to capitalize on the shock value of the poisonous stockings." She winced when she said poisonous.

"Capitalizing—another American trait," Teresa said. "This is smart, though. Isobel's public knitting idea, too. *And* your idea to look for another suspect." She tapped the edge of the bookmark on the tabletop. "Bethia Ferguson is knee deep in the knitting contest. There you go; your new bookmark promoted a new idea, and that brings us to the reason for this meeting. You needn't look far or hard for another suspect. Find out what Bethia was up to Friday night."

Janet hoped Teresa couldn't read minds. Faces, either. Christine, Tallie, and Summer appeared admirably unflapped, but she felt so flapped she couldn't catch her breath. If Teresa had the ear of the Assistant Chief Constable, what was she telling him, and would that convince him Bethia should be the prime suspect?

"Why Bethia?" Tallie asked.

"Several reasons. I saw her hand a cup of tea to Wendy that evening. The obvious questions about that are what was *in* the teacup and where *is* that cup? Then you have the fact that Bethia was staying at the house, as arranged by Isobel. Unnecessary, as far as I can see, but a perk for Bethia I suppose. As she was a guest, Mother presumably gave her a key. Though why she would need to lock her door, I can't imagine. To safeguard her knitting needles?"

"Bethia had a key to that door?" Christine asked. "Was she staying in the suite where you put the museum donations?"

"I?"

"You arranged the clutter," Christine said.

"If I'd also put aside the museum donations, they'd have been boxed and labeled."

"Bethia had a room upstairs," Janet said. "Why would she have a key to the suite?"

"They're skeleton keys. Completely false security. I've been telling Mother for years she should have new locks installed. Half the time the skeleton keys are unnecessary."

"Then why bother telling people that anything behind locked doors is not fair game?" Christine asked.

"Who told you that?" Teresa asked.

"Edward."

"Moving on," she said, "if you're taking my advice and suspecting Bethia, then by extension you should also suspect Norman Hobbs. Don't you think it's suspicious that he didn't ask these questions? Isn't it likely that he's covering up for his grandmother? And tell me this, if he was in the house, why did it take him so long to respond when I called?"

"That's a good question," Tallie said. "What did you tell him when you called?"

"Are you saying it's my fault?"

"Is it? In retrospect, I mean. Stress does funny things. Makes us stutter. Messes with our memories." Tallie's voice and face remained open and neutral. Almost friendly. Janet felt like giving her a fist bump for each of the zingers.

Teresa gave Tallie a narrow-eyed look. "I gave him clear instructions. Ask him."

"So, Teresa." Christine sat forward, her elbows on the arms of the chair and her hands clasped. "Your mother says you feel guilty. Why is that?"

"Mother told you that?"

"Norman did."

"Then, please. Consider the source."

"Norman does a fine job," Janet said. "He's well-respected by members of the Major Investigation Team."

"If that's what you want to believe. Keep in mind he's no longer a part of this investigation. As for your clue in Wendy's waste bin, I will reiterate that I know nothing about the wrappers. I'm proud of Isobel's work at the museum, but unlike Edward, I haven't hours of free time on my hands to drop in for lunch or for any other reason. I have never been in Wendy's office. The food wrappers, that you say had my name on them, were obviously meant to frame me. And you obviously snoop, so snoop into that. Now—" Teresa mimicked Christine's posture, though with fingers steepled rather than hands clasped. "I see this meeting as a job interview. First question. How do you—*scunners*, do you call yourselves? How do you scunners conduct an investigation?"

"Not scunners, no," Christine said. "And we try *not* to irritate people."

"We conduct investigations with the utmost discretion," Janet said.

"If you're running your investigations from here, how discreet can you be? Or effective? Unless your shop doesn't attract many customers. Next question. What's your standard operating procedure? Your SOP?"

"To put it succinctly, we ask questions and gather information," Tallie said.

"Looking for discrepancies and connections," Summer added.

"Examples of questions," Teresa said.

"Who arranged the museum donations?" Janet asked.

"Continue."

"Do you know who did?"

"I want to hear your questions."

"Part of our SOP is to obtain answers," Christine said.

Teresa's steepled fingertips separated and re-met several times as her lips appeared to think that over.

"It helps us," Summer said. "And we'd like to help you."

"Thank you, but I might not want your help."

"Fair enough," Janet said. She'd opened their shared document on her phone and read from it. "Here are more examples of questions. What were your movements that night? What did you see? What do know about Wendy? Who helped with the party that evening? What exactly were the logistics of the decluttering? How many people were invited? How long were they expected to stay? Were guests required to take items home with them that night? Did they have to provide their own boxes and transportation?" Janet put her phone down. "Your mother's clutter and the whole evening were beautifully organized, but obviously more went into that success than the guests saw or were aware of. Wendy died there, in the room with the museum donations. It makes sense to know as much as we can about the evening."

Teresa gave a flick of a shrug.

"Who do you think is guilty?" Tallie asked.

"I can only speak for myself."

Janet glanced at Christine. Recognizing the look of quiet fuming on her face, she braced herself in case of eruption and rushed to contribute another step of their procedure. "We keep in touch with Constable Hobbs and turn our findings over to him."

Teresa looked at the nails of her right hand, scraped at something on her thumbnail, then swept them with the look of a disappointed school principal. "You, who are shopkeepers, and Norman Hobbs, who is no longer part of the investigation? No, I'm sorry. I feel quite certain there's nothing you can do for me that the police specialists aren't already doing and doing better. I'm also certain they'll be doing it legally. They'll finish their inquiries and reach the only possible conclusion." She stood.

Christine also stood. In a voice low and molten, she asked "We've failed your interview process then?"

"Let me put it this way. You were either negligent or just plain foolish when you destroyed whatever evidence there was by traipsing around looking for Mother's possibly imaginary tin of Rodine."

"Is it imaginary?" Christine asked.

"How will we ever know?" Teresa countered. "To continue, you told me about looking in Wendy's bin, and what did you find there? Only what anyone would expect—rubbish." She laughed. "An apt metaphor, I think, for your amateur detective theatrics."

Teresa put on her coat and walked to the door. Finding it locked, she waited, her back to them, until Tallie came to open it. Tallie wished her goodnight. Teresa didn't return the wish. She hadn't said another word after her comment about amateur theatrics. Tallie did, though, addressing the door after relocking it. "You weren't prepared to listen to us, but my mother did ask you inciteful, intelligent, entirely legal detective-type questions, and if you'd deigned to answer *any* of them we were prepared to ask lots more." Tallie growled, sounding like either Ranger or Rab, then rejoined the others and dumped herself into her chair. What *are* we going to do?"

"I've already made a 'Bethia' document," Summer said. "Tonight I'll listen back through the recording and make notes in the Teresa file."

"We need to let Norman know we have a hostile witness," Janet said. "He might be able to give us some direction."

"I wonder if he can get us into Wendy's house?" Christine asked.

"Let's keep in mind 'legal,'" Tallie said.

"Easier to get into her office at the museum anyway."

"I will not grind my teeth," Tallie said. "No, maybe I will. I wanted to ask that . . . beetroot what the police think they know about her."

"She might not know," Summer said. "Or she might not have told us the truth."

"But we could've compared her answers to anything Norman knows."

"I made a mistake when I told her about the wrappers," Janet said. "But planting them makes no sense, anyway, because Wendy didn't have food poisoning from the truck. So, either Teresa is lying about them, or there's some other reason for them being there."

"To buy time?" Summer asked.

"Time for what?" Janet asked.

"I don't know," Summer said. "To dispose of the real evidence? To come up with a better story? To muddy the waters with a red herring?"

"Do red herrings live in muddy water?" Tallie asked.

"It's probably their natural habitat," Christine said. "But if the wrappers were planted, for whatever reason, that proves intent. Of something."

"Of covering up a crime, being scared, being stupid." Summer ticked the possibilities off on her fingers.

"Where are the wrappers?" Tallie asked.

"Probably long gone," Janet said.

"Well, rats."

"It's easy to think of Teresa as a rat." Christine said. "Compared to the other MacAskills, especially. Humbug handed out sweeties. Violet handed out possessions. Isobel's a delight."

"Edward's a hoot," Summer said.

"To each her own MacAskill," Christine said. "But Teresa is the odd woman out. She isn't sweet, delightful, or a hoot. She's the definition of a scunner and I think she's afraid."

"She *is* kind of a rat, though," Tallie groused.

"She is," Janet said. "And that fits what Christine just said. Cornered animals are afraid, and they lash out in fear, right? What if Teresa's putting up a front because she's afraid?"

"We've each experienced people who do that in our professional lives," Christine said. "Inside the bully at school is a child being abused at home. Inside the tough guy awaiting trial is someone terrified of prison. Summer's seen it as a reporter, no question. Janet made whole phalanxes of grown men cry by demanding they pay their library fines."

"We stopped collecting fines just for that reason," Janet said. "Here's a horrible thought, though. What if she isn't afraid for her herself, but for someone else? I found the food wrappers in the staff area. It's open plan. Wendy's 'office' is completely accessible to Isobel or Edward."

"Ugh," Summer said. "I like this better. Teresa is guilty. She's blustering to throw us off, because she knows incriminating information is out there and she's afraid the SCONES *are* going to find it."

"She's a sneak, a scunner, *and* a rat," Tallie said. "I like it."

∞

Janet had hopes of a meat pie for supper. Flaky crust, savory filling, more palatable than their encounter with Teresa.

"Basant's?" Tallie asked.

"Yes."

They walked together in the dark, along with a smattering of rain that came and went, urging them toward the convenience shop and then home. Basant greeted them warmly when they pushed open his door, then disappointed them with the sad news that meat pies were done for the day.

"But close your eyes and listen," he said. "Cauliflower, potatoes, tomatoes, onion, and peas. Cumin, garlic, ginger, turmeric, coriander, red pepper, ghee, and, last of all, cilantro. Nepalese curry—tarkari—as my mother made it."

"Yes, please," they said, and warmed their hands with containers of curry and flatbreads the rest of the way home.

"I still think Teresa is afraid," Janet said. They had wiped their bowls clean with the last of the bread, and pushed back from their kitchen table, satisfied and each with a cat on their lap.

"But?" Tallie asked.

"But we blustered, too, after she left. She rejected us. That hurt our feelings. We shouldn't let that cloud our thinking."

"Let's not let the warm fuzzies from eating excellent curry cloud our thinking, either."

Janet lay in bed that night, regretting her second helping of tarkari, listening to the cats purring to drown out the wind, and the wind trying to scour the roof from the house. She played the evening over in her head and came back around to believing Teresa might be afraid of what they'd find if she agreed to let them look. But what had they said or done that convinced Teresa they could be her undoing? And as she drifted off to sleep, she wondered if she'd imagined it, or if Teresa's laugh had sounded like a bray.

13

Arsenic diary, day six

Here is another decision before me: Shall I, too, play amateur sleuth? The women at the bookshop and tearoom handle the challenge well. As a pastime, it seems to put a cheerful skip in their steps. But if I play along, where shall I start? Research!

I open the scrapbook—my secret search engine—and skip from page to page. I am more than cheerful. I am tickled. I am in awe at all the names by which my darling arsenic is known. King of Poisons. Gift of the Borgias. People's Choice. I close my eyes, breathing in the power of finding exactly the right name, then put my finger on one. Aha. Inheritor's Powder. Apropos?

Imagine all those years of ease, before the Marsh perfection of detection, when one simply stirred arsenic into the morning coffee, sat back, and waited to collect from a loved one's burial society account. But how does that help me now?

More newspaper clippings on more pages. Flip, flip, flip. An advertisement for Fowler's Solution, sold in pharmacies as a health tonic, boasting a one-percent solution of potassium arsenite. <u>Not</u> boasting the side effects of cirrhosis and various cancers. But that is my own aside. The scrapbook offers no commentary or editorializing. An appropriate mindset, no doubt. A sleuth cannot afford a prejudiced mind. Hard facts only. Like hard muscle from a hard-nosed drill sergeant. Hut! Hut! Hut! Hut!

Arsenic lies between phosphorous and antimony in group 15, the so-called nitrogen group of the periodic table, _sir!_

Arsenical pesticides leave harmful particulate residues, which can be inhaled or ingested, _sir!_

Coming into contact with arsenic can cause myriad health problems, _sir!_

Ingestion is not necessary, _sir!_

Symptoms of arsenic poisoning include: diarrhea, vomiting, fatigue, confusion, vision problems, loss of taste, loss of smell, skin discoloration, skin eruptions, skin abscesses, and cancer, _sir!_

Breathless. Exhausted. If only in my imagination. Still, I put my head between my knees.

Recovered, I skip to another page and read an excerpt. A page torn from an unattributed article. "Take enough or give enough and you cause a quick and painful death with gastrointestinal symptoms you might recognize from those of cholera." Not I. I have no interest in cholera, and now I find I've lost interest in descriptions of symptoms and effects. Suffice to say they are varied and unpleasant. I close the scrapbook.

Decision time. Shall I play along? To what end? If I do, what information will I divulge? What sort of conduit will I be? What does that last question even mean?

I sigh. Asking questions like a numpty will get me nowhere. I sigh again. There is more to learn about this detecting wheeze.

I try to focus.

∞

Edward surprised Janet by stopping in the bookshop Friday morning. He charmed the knitters near the fireplace, chatting, and taking videos of work in progress with his phone. He spoke to each knitter and put his hand out to Ranger, who sniffed it suspiciously then turned his back. Edward then went to the tearoom to repeat his charm and chat with the knitters there. Ranger followed. They both returned from the tearoom half an hour later, Edward carrying a white bakery bag, Ranger at a distance.

"You have a shadow," Tallie said. "That's unusual. Ranger usually takes his work as resident napper too seriously to socialize."

"I'm a coincidental traveling companion," Edward said. "He went to confer with Rab and Bethia, and counted dropped stitches for the young fellow, Kyle. Unless Ranger's attention caused the dropped stitches. Kyle seems to be a nervous knitter. That would make a jolly good title, don't you think? 'The Case of the Nervous Knitter.'" He leaned across the counter and lowered his voice. "I am also here on a covert mission. Isobel tells me that a pair of the historic stockings have gone missing."

"You're looking for them here?" Janet asked.

"My theory," he said, one elbow now leaning on the counter, forcing Tallie to move a customer around to the other side of the cash register, "is that one of the competition knitters borrowed the stockings for a *leg up*, as it were."

Knowing he'd appreciate a roll of the eyes, Janet obliged.

"As I visited among the knitters and made my video, I tried to get a look in their knitting bags. No luck, here, but I'll do the same at the other venues."

"What will you do if you find them?"

"I'm not terribly brave, so that might depend on who has them. Speaking of, thank you for coming to Teresa's aid. Please thank your colleagues, as well. You're brave to do so."

"I'm sorry?" Janet said.

"Are you?" Edward asked.

Janet felt like rolling her eyes again, for her own benefit. "Why did you say we're brave?"

"Because it wouldn't surprise me if people stay well away from Teresa for the foreseeable future. If she's guilty, she might be dangerous, aye? Not that I believe for a single moment that she is. She had a wicked bite as a two-year-old, mind."

Janet didn't like hearing their worries about Teresa echoed by her own brother. But Edward was right; anyone might feel leery of her, and not without reason. But hadn't Teresa told him she'd turned down their help? Maybe not. The way she'd bristled at him during the decluttering and when they'd searched for the Rodine might be typical of their relationship. Typical of her SOP.

"Teresa decided—" Janet started to say, but over Edward's head she saw Tallie, and then Christine and Rab standing at the end of a book aisle, close enough to hear the conversation, but out of Edward's sight. Tallie shook her head at her. Janet changed course. "Actually, encouraged is a better word," she said. "Teresa encouraged us in our independent research."

"Research, is it?" Edward made one of his younger brother faces. "Well, as I said, thank you. I firmly believe the truth will out and justice will be served. To quote your countryman:

> Though the mills of God grind slowly;
> Yet they grind exceeding small;
> Though with patience He stands waiting,
> With exactness grinds He all.

Cheery-bye the *noo*, I must be off to complete my mission."

Tallie came behind the counter. Christine tried Edward's pose of leaning on one elbow.

"Did you hear what he said about mills?" Janet asked. "Was that supposed to be comforting? *My* countryman? Who said that?'

Christine's height didn't lend itself to leaning on the counter and she gave up. "I've always thought some Roman spewer of philosophy said it, or that it came from the Bible."

"I read some version of it in an Agatha Christie," Tallie said.

"'Retribution,'" said Rab.

"That's going rather dark," Janet said.

"I was right, then," Christine said. "Biblical."

"Henry Wadsworth Longfellow," Rab said. "'Retribution' is the name of the poem."

"Longfellow *looked* Biblical," Tallie said to a scowling Christine.

Janet gestured at the other three. "Has something happened? Did you think something was *going* to happen? You guys had a watchdog vibe going there."

"Coincidental," Rab said, then he looked at Christine and Tallie. "Unless?"

"Coincidental's good with me," Tallie said.

"I'm suddenly enamored with coincidental retribution," Christine said. "But I'll go with honesty and admit I'm nosy and that I don't entirely trust Edward. That might be Dad and Ranger rubbing off on me. Did you learn anything useful from him beyond Teresa being a biter?"

"A pair of the historical stockings is missing from the museum. He thinks a knitter 'borrowed' them. He was being charming to their faces while he snooped around their bags. That's what he meant by his mission. He's off to check at the other venues."

"And I'd best go check my teapots."

Janet waved, then turned to ask Rab a question, but man and dog had slipped away.

"You look mopey," Tallie said.

"I'm not really. I was going to ask Rab about Ranger's beef with Edward and his own with Kyle. A whole lot of beefs going on. And now Teresa has one with us and if she crabs at Violet about us, then maybe Violet will have a beef with us, too. It's depressing."

Tallie handed her a dust cloth. "Go, be at one with your books. Let them soothe you. I'll get the customers."

Janet spent an hour dusting, straightening, reading back covers and fly leaves, and occasionally sneezing. As she swiped the last of the dust from a bottom shelf in the cookery section, Summer bounced in from the tearoom.

"I've been reading about Land Girls and Lumber Jills. I want to go back in time and be a Lumber Jill for a couple of months, but first let me tell you what I've learned about Land Girls, rats, and Rodine."

They went to the counter so Tallie could hear, too. Tallie finished ringing up a sale and sat on the stool. "Okay, spill."

"The Land Girls wouldn't have used a little bitty tin like Violet's," Summer said. "They were rat-catching queens. I mean hundreds and hundreds of rats. Thousands. You should see the pictures. Anyway, they used industrial quantities of rat poison. Gas, too. So, if we find the tin, it might be interesting in a Land Girls exhibit, but it won't be accurate."

"So once again, we can't put Violet's mind at ease," Janet said. "The stuff is still lethal, still missing, and now it's not even the right stuff."

"We keep talking about putting her at ease," Summer said. "Why?"

"Why not?" Janet asked. "She's a little old lady whose lovely party fell apart because a horrible thing happened, and whose daughter was arrested for doing the horrible thing."

"Think of it more like changing a recipe, then, instead of disappointing her," Summer said. "Stirring in a new ingredient to see what happens. You might learn something new. You might make everyone happy. Or not and the guinea pigs you try the recipe out on will want to throw the food back at you."

"I want to take this opportunity to remind you," Tallie said quietly, "that we've been asked to clear someone as a suspect in an as-yet-unexplained death, which might be murder, and we've decided to do that by finding other suspects, who might be killers. Quiet, crafty killers. So, we might not want to experiment with stirring up those suspects. Agreed?"

"Is Violet a suspect?" Summer asked.

Janet nodded. "She has to be."

"Cool. I'll go add her to the 'Suspects' document," Summer said, and bounced back to the tearoom.

"Now *you* look mopey," Janet said.

"Thank you for noticing," a voice behind her said. "I am."

"I think she was talking to me, Ian," Tallie said. "But you do look incredibly mopish. It's not your best look. Have you seen anyone about it?"

"I can't even laugh at your jokes, which I usually love." Ian Atkinson, bestselling, and fairly annoying, mystery author, came to prop himself against the nearest bookshelf. He'd forgone his usual writer's garb of jacket with elbow patches and corduroy trousers for solid black.

"What's got you moping, Ian?" Janet asked. She had acres of patience for most people but very little for him. It was a failing that disappointed her, so she tried to use the disappointment to grow as a person. She only seemed to be growing more impatient with him, though, and worried it might become a vicious circle.

Heavy sigh from Ian. "A scrapbook I've been ogling for some weeks is missing from Fairy Flax Hall."

Janet, experiencing a flashback to the bedlam in the library during the decluttering, closed her eyes and shuddered.

"Janet! Are you all right?"

Touched by what sounded like genuine concern, Janet assured him she was fine. "But if your scrapbook was in the library, it probably went in the decluttering Violet had Friday night."

"A *tragedy*." It was Ian's turn to close his eyes, but only briefly. He came to the counter and launched into an animated description of the scrapbook. "It dates from the late nineteenth century. Filled with clippings about the murder trials of poisoners and information about their poisons, primarily arsenic. Fascinating! For research purposes, only, of course. More of a curiosity, really. Authoritative information is so easy to find these days, but the Victorians were so delightfully macabre." He toyed with a stack of the new bookmarks by the cash register, tapping one edge of the stack on the counter and then another.

Tallie took the stack away from him. "Sounds cool, Ian. It fits right in with the exhibit at the museum. Isobel probably has your book."

"I asked."

"And?"

"She claims she's never seen or heard of it. I say, do you know what I'm just now wondering?" He picked up a pen and flipped it between his fingers. "Given its subject matter, and Wendy Erskine's unfortunate and gruesome death, do you suppose the scrapbook's existence is significant? Or more specifically, its absence? Food for thought, yes? Though not any food *I'm* tempted to consume."

Ian wandered toward the door, with an air of rumination, still flipping the pen—one of Janet's favorites. They didn't interrupt his departure by saying goodbye, but Tallie went to the window to make sure he'd really gone.

"That is an actual, bona fide saunter he's doing down the street," she reported.

"Disingenuous, sauntering twit."

"My eyes are throwing daggers at the twit's back."

Janet pulled out her phone. "I'm texting Norman."

"I'll let you know if he ignores it," Tallie said. "He and Reddick are at Mr. Potato Chef. The truck's parked on the corner. The twit's saunter has turned into a near-lope as he appears to be avoiding the Normans. *They* appear to be getting lunch. Unofficially."

"Two Normans lunching, unofficially. What are they up to?"

"Our Norman is looking at his phone," Tallie said. "Now he's looking toward the shop. Now Reddick is looking at *his* phone. The two are conferring. Reddick is heading for his car. At an official-looking trot. Our Norman is heading this way."

"You could have a successful career calling horse races," Janet said.

"Our Norman is closing in fast, looking grim."

When the bell at their door jingled, Janet and Tallie stood shoulder to shoulder behind the sales counter. Hobbs entered, removed his cap, and tucked it smartly under his arm. Stopping first to survey the area, he marched forward and turned to face them.

"Not yet public knowledge," he said, voice grave and low. "There's been a second death."

14

Arsenic diary, day six and a half

How can such a frail scrap even exist? Caught and pinned like a brimstone from a long ago garden, forever on display in this scrapbook of arsenical wonders. Where did this scrapbook artist find you? Perhaps in some earlier collection of ephemera and impermanence. Are you evidence of genetics at work? A family tic devoted to reports of the macabre?

I stroke your paper wings. Your foxed and crumbling corners mark you as a moth, not a butterfly, but a marvel in either case. Clipped and pasted from <u>The Glasgow Morning Journal</u>, 13 November 1858. A marvel you exist at all.

ACCIDENTS AND OFFENSES.
THE POISONINGS BY ARSENIC AT BRADFORD.

"On Friday, the magisterial inquiry into the extensive poisoning by peppermint lozenges, in the making of which arsenic had been used in mistake for plaster of Paris, was resumed at the Bradford Courthouse. Two hundred sickened, twenty-one dead, and among them the particular death which was the subject of this inquiry, that of Elizabeth Mary Midgley, a child seven years of age, who—"

I won't read more. A child's death by poison, even amongst so many others and accidental, is too much. Turn the page.

∞

"This is too much." Janet groped for the stool, then pushed it away and clutched the edge of the counter. "Who? How?"

Hobbs would only tell them to expect a visit from Inspector Reddick. He did not know when. He didn't ask about the scrapbook. They forgot to bring it up. His boots rang with somber purpose as he marched out the door, and Tallie went to tell Christine and Summer in the tearoom. For the rest of the afternoon, the four women jumped every time their doors jingled.

Shortly before closing, the jingle announced James Haviland. "You'll have heard the news, I assume?"

"About a second body? Sadly, yes," Janet said.

"Aye, I'd be surprised if you hadn't. To echo my remarks from the other night," he said, "it's not a good sign, when it's too late for an ambulance, and less so when you lot are involved. And again, not meaning any offense."

"Offense taken anyway," Janet said. "We are not and never have been involved in a homicide."

"Forgive me. Of course not. Mind, since you arrived, the *Guardian*'s circulation is up."

"You're rude bordering on nasty today," Janet said. "What's wrong with you?"

"Might be a bit of indigestion." James stifled a belch. "I'm the official taste tester for the new menu at Nev's."

"Oh dear," Janet said. "That bad?"

"No. It's excellent, but I ate more than I should." He covered another belch. "Sorry. Getting back to rude and nasty, was anything I said untrue?"

"Not really," Tallie said.

"But we don't know anything about this except that another poor soul has died. And that the two deaths might be connected." Janet clucked her tongue. "Maybe more than just *might be* from the way Norman looked and talked. What do you know about it, James?"

"Bare minimum. Spotted by a farmer in a layby. Too late for an ambulance."

"Norman didn't give that much away," Tallie said.

"And I've not heard beyond that, so don't ask," James said. "We'll know more after next of kin are notified."

⁓

They hadn't heard from Reddick by the time they locked their shop doors. Police had released a basic report of the second death, but no details. Summer toasted cheese sandwiches. They sat by the fire, still on edge, and nibbled at the sandwiches in case Reddick came by.

"He might yet chap at the door," Christine said. "Do you get the impression that Norman is avoiding us?"

"No, not really," Janet said. "Sometimes I think he keeps a more regular schedule here than Rab."

"Ranger's schedule is more regular than Rab's. But Norman could have saved our nerves and told us more about this second victim by now. I'm calling him." Christine pulled out her phone and dialed. "Norman? Christine Robertson, here. I feel this investigation is becoming a one-way street. What's happened to our arrangement?" Christine took the phone away from her ear and gaped at it. "He said he's not able to talk and hung up."

"He's told us what he can, in the past," Summer said. "We can't ask him to do more than that, and we can't ask him to jeopardize the investigation, or his standing with the department. He wouldn't, anyway."

"There might not be much to know," Tallie said. "We haven't passed much along to him, either. It's early in the investigation."

"He's still a policeman and more of a skellum than I knew." Christine took a triangle of sandwich from Janet's plate. "Are you feeling well, Janet? You're as white as I imagine Norman's thighs must be."

"Leave Norman's thighs out of it. I don't need that image burned into my retinas. I've been wondering about the victim. Worrying about who it is. Violet? Edward? Isobel? Bethia? I have no reason to think it's any of them, but—"

"But we shouldn't jump to any big conclusions," Summer said. "Big or small. We don't know if the second death is even connected to the first."

"I haven't concluded anything," Janet said. "Worry is a process."

"One of her superpowers," Tallie said.

"What did you see in Norman's face?" Christine asked, wiping her fingers after eating Janet's last triangle. "You would have known from his face if it was Bethia. In fact, he wouldn't have come here at all. He'd have followed Reddick."

"Reddick wouldn't have let Norman drive on his own after news like that," Tallie said. "Let's count Bethia as safe."

"You didn't include Teresa in your worries," Summer said.

"Because there's so much more to worry about with Teresa," Janet said. "Like, is she the killer?"

"Double killer," Christine said. "And did Reddick bollocks it up by not locking her up after the first murder?"

"Or," Janet said, "is she the victim?"

"And again, did Reddick bollocks it up by not having her safe under lock and key?" Christine shook her phone. "Bloody Norman for not giving us the victim's name."

"If Teresa killed Wendy, why would she take a chance on killing again?" Summer asked. "Silly question. She'd kill a person if they could be a witness against her."

"And if she's the victim?" Tallie asked.

"Same reason," Summer said. "She might not realize she knew something, saw something, or heard something, and the killer wouldn't take a chance she'd turn star witness."

"Those are the same reasons Norman's worried about Bethia," Tallie said.

"He hasn't said that, though. We came up with those worries," Janet said. "Okay, *I* came up with them. But he hasn't stopped her from taking her competition duties seriously and knitting from one end of town to the other."

"He might now," Tallie said.

"She'll hate that." Janet looked at her plate, surprised. "Well that goes to show how worry can distract. I didn't even know I was eating. Oh! Talk about being distracted. Norman never got back to me about Ian's scrapbook, and we haven't told you two."

"Ian passed through the tearoom late this morning," Christine said. "That's how you know he's trying to be sneaky. He treats the tearoom like a back door then scuttles in here, so you don't know he's coming. Scrapbooking doesn't sound like him, but it hardly seems worth reporting to Norman."

"Unless he's into pasting naughty pictures," Summer said. "Did he come in here and flash something full frontal at you?"

"He probably has two naughty scrapbooks," Tallie said. "One on the pillow bedside him and the other in his messenger bag."

"For emergencies." Summer and Tallie high-fived. Ian didn't always act like a twit. Sometimes he acted like a louche twit.

Janet repeated Ian's description of the missing scrapbook. Tallie described his faux realization that its presence and absence from Fairy Flax Hall might interest the police.

"He's a twit, but I feel his pain," Summer said. "I love things like that."

"You're still looking pale, Janet. Are you sure you're feeling well?" Christine asked. "Would you like Summer to toast another sandwich for you?"

Janet waved Summer back into her seat. "It's just another worry eating away at my peace of mind. One of those late-night things that doesn't seem so bad in broad daylight." She glanced at the front windows and their view of the harbor—only black, no lights from boats bobbing at anchor. "If Teresa blew us off last night because she saw or heard something that convinced her we're a threat, what was it? What are we being blind to?"

"It might not be anything we said or did," Tallie said. "Bright as we are. It might be something she's afraid she'll give away if she spends too much time with us."

"That's a nice spin," Janet said.

"Or," Tallie said, "she might be afraid we'll be biased in our investigation."

"Never," Janet said.

"Of course not. But she's keen on pointing her finger at Bethia and Norman, whom we like very much. Teresa might be afraid we'll work to prove *them* innocent instead of her."

"*That* I can see running through her mind." Janet sighed. "Shall we call it a night, then? Reddick won't expect to find us here much later."

"Not just yet," Christine said. "Something's been running around in my head ever since Norman told us he's off the investigation, and I think I've finally grabbed it by the arm and wrestled it to the ground."

"That's an interesting tactic," Tallie said.

"This concerns both Normans. I wonder if they're in cahoots. If they've devised a ruse."

"Why would they do that?" Tallie asked. "Cahoots I can see, but a ruse? Why?"

"To give Violet and the other MacAskills a false impression," Christine said. "So they let their guards down. So they see Norman as someone more attuned to traffic violations than trace evidence. To lull them."

"Or make them think he's incompetent?"

"That's more or less the same thing, isn't it?" Christine said.

"No, it's not," Janet said. "If they're lulled, they're being lazy in their thinking. To make them think he's incompetent is willful and inaccurate. I don't think you're being fair to Norman. Ours, I mean."

"I'm not finished yet."

"But Christine, do *you* believe Norman—Norman Hobbs—is incompetent?" Tallie asked.

"Not exactly, but he did say the Rodine wasn't dangerous."

"So, because he doesn't know everything there is to know about bygone rat poisons, he's incompetent?" Tallie asked.

"I didn't say that," Christine said.

"*If* knowing about the Rodine even makes a difference," Summer said. "We still don't know the cause of death."

"Anyone else, or may I continue?" Christine pinned them each in turn with a look down her nose. "Let's look at this like a MacAskill, that's all I'm saying. To them, Norman's seeming lack of familiarity *with* and lax attitude *toward* the Rodine are merely the underpinnings of incompetence. His true ineptitude reared its glaikit head when he didn't alert his superiors to the missing poison in a timely manner, delaying a murder case during its crucial early hours and days."

"You sound like a police review board," Summer said.

Christine looked to the ceiling. "I am not Norman's nemesis. I am trying to sound like a MacAskill who's fallen for the Normans' ruse.

"May I?" Tallie raised her hand. "I'm confused. Reddick arrested Teresa. How does that lull the MacAskills?"

"Maybe the arrest is part of their ruse," Janet said.

"Do you really see by-the-book Reddick and our stodgy Norman putting their heads together and dreaming up a *clever* ruse, though? Christine asked.

"You're the one who brought it up," Janet said, trying not to sound exasperated.

"Their ruse, yes, but a *clever* ruse is more up our alley."

"This is a lot to digest," Summer said.

"It's nearing indigestible," said Tallie.

"We *are* clever, Christine," Janet said, "but we're actually more methodical and insightful than prone to clever ruses."

Christine pulled a paper from her pocket and made a note.

"What's that?" Tallie asked.

"I regret our lack of clever ruses." Christine folded the paper and returned it to her pocket. "That's a reminder to look for ripe opportunities."

"*This* is a ripe opportunity," Janet said. "Right this minute." She pulled her phone from her pocket. "I'm calling Teresa. If she answers, at least we'll know she isn't the second victim. Hello, Teresa? Janet Marsh, here. Hello? Hell—well, of all the . . . she hung up on me. I heard her breathing."

"Scunner," Christine said.

"Do we know it was her?" Tallie asked. "Is she a heavy breather?"

Janet looked at her phone as though it might bite. When it rang, she almost dropped it. Then she saw the caller's name. "It's Inspector Reddick."

15

David bustled around when Christine and Janet arrived. He fed Janet a nice piece of leftover salmon, for which she was grateful, put on his best cardigan, and set glasses and a bottle of single malt on a side table. When the doorbell rang, he insisted on answering it himself. He brought the inspector into the living room.

"A pleasure to see you, Mrs. MacLean. Thank you for letting me barge in like this and monopolize your evening."

He sounded tired and smudges under his eyes showed his long hours. The Normans were both upright in their posture and approach to policing. If the two were birds, Janet saw Hobbs as a stork, steady of eye and careful with each long-legged step: Reddick had the quicker movements, though just as cunning, of a merlin or kestrel. He was more compact than Hobbs, with the build of a gymnast, and younger by a decade or so. Of the two, Reddick was more likely to spring into action than sit down for a cup of tea, but he enjoyed one now and then, or a tipple. Now he accepted a glass of single malt from David, with thanks, and sat in the chair across from the sofa Helen, Christine, and Janet sat on.

"Mrs. MacLean, Mrs. Robertson, Mrs. Marsh," Reddick toasted them. "Thank you for indulging me this evening. What I'd like you to do is think back over the evening of Violet MacAskill's party and then take me through it. Is that all right?"

The women agreed, though Christine asked him to tread carefully with Helen's memories.

"Of course," Reddick said. "Call me off at any point."

"I don't mind things as well as I used to," Helen said.

"We forget where we leave our heads, sometimes, don't we, love?" David said. He turned to Reddick. "She's been having nightmares since the party."

"I mind that night, but it's more than that," Helen said. "Now my mum and dad come and hold out their hands to me. It's a sign, but David and I aren't ready to stop our dancing yet, are we, love?"

Janet was touched to see Christine take her mother's hand and hold it in both of hers. She knew Christine didn't believe in signs and omens, but Helen seemed to believe in them more and more. Christine, who fiercely battled for reason over emotion, would just as fiercely protect her mother from whatever Helen thought the signs and omens meant.

"Where should we start?" Christine asked.

"Let's start when you arrived. A general outline is fine. I'll ask questions when you're done. So, what did you do and what and who did you see?"

"That pickup truck," Helen said.

Christine told him about the impatient driver spewing gravel as it sped around them.

"I never did ask," Janet said. "Did you find your warm pickup when you went looking?"

Christine thought for a moment. "No," she said. "I didn't. I was interrupted mid-pursuit. And I must say, Janet, that asking if someone scored a warm pickup is an off-color question in polite company."

"So was the answer."

"What interrupted you?" Reddick asked.

"Edward MacAskill."

"He walked us in," Janet said. "But there was no one at the door checking names against a guest list. He seemed to think Isobel or Teresa should be there. We stood around for several minutes, talking, and then signed the guestbook, and neither of them ever showed up. Anyone could have come in. Or gone out with something they shouldn't have. Someone came out the door as Helen and I walked up the stairs. A young man named Kyle Byrne."

The women walked him through the rest of the evening, taking turns as they remembered details, ending with them sitting by the potted fern in the sunroom, waiting for Hobbs. Reddick made occasional notes, but otherwise listened intently.

"Very thorough," he said when they'd finished. "Before I ask my questions, I'd like to hear yours. Because I'm certain you do have questions." He toasted them with his glass before continuing. "The caveat is that I'll listen to your questions. I won't necessarily answer them. Hearing them helps me see the case from other angles. And I always appreciate the angles you discover in these unfortunate situations."

"Does Edward drive a pickup?" Christine asked. "I'm not bent on revenge, if he was the gravel-spitter, but Teresa lit into him when she saw him in the sitting room. She asked where he was, as though she'd been looking for him. He didn't answer. Maybe he'd been AWOL and didn't want to say."

"He didn't ask her why she wasn't greeting people at the door, though," Janet said. "Interesting dynamics between those two."

"He drives an eight-year-old Isuzu," David said. They all looked at him. "Bit of a snob about it." He took a sip of his whisky.

"I've another question," Christine said. "Two, actually. Are the deaths connected, and are they connected to the decluttering?

"No answer just yet."

"Teresa told us she saw Bethia give Wendy a teacup," Janet said. "She also thinks Bethia could have let Wendy into the suite of rooms with a skeleton key."

"She told us that as well," Reddick said. "We've found no teacup that was not thoroughly washed and put away. Not to say there wasn't one with Wendy's fingerprints at some point.

"Or dregs of whatever," Christine said.

"As you say."

"I have more of an observation than a question," Janet said. "I'm surprised you hadn't heard there was a guestbook."

"And what makes you think that?" Reddick asked. "It happens to be true, but how do you know, and what do you know about the book?"

"You have a tell. I can see you're skeptical, but there—you're doing it now. You breathe evenly until something particularly interests you, then you seem to hold your breath. Edward said the guestbook was his idea."

"Calls himself a record keeper," Christine said. At a disbelieving noise from David, she added, "Dad's right. It's not likely to be a complete record."

"Not everyone signs them, do they," Reddick said. "Still, it might be useful. Your observation, as well, Mrs. Marsh. I will make an effort to breathe steadily from now on. None of you mentioned seeing Wendy that evening before the incident in the suite. Did you see her?"

They shook their heads.

"Mrs. Marsh, tell me about the woman you saw near the door. What she did before she went to get Teresa."

"I wasn't aware of her until she moved closer to the door. That was right after I heard voices on the other side of it. She must have heard them first. Her arms were full—she had a watering can and a punch bowl. She looked ready to open the door but stopped and looked around when I moved away from James. That's when she said she'd go tell Teresa."

"Did she touch the door?"

"No. Not while I watched. James wanted to touch it. I wouldn't let him. But then I opened it. Did I screw up fingerprints?"

"Yours and Mrs. Robertson's were the only fingerprints."

"Well, that doesn't seem right—oh. It isn't, is it? Someone wiped the knob clean before Christine turned it to go in?"

"You don't know the woman with the watering can?" Reddick asked.

Janet shook her head. "And I don't think James saw her at all. He only had eyes for his typewriters."

"I'll check with him."

"Teresa doesn't know her?"

"Teresa said she didn't see her. She said a man told her she was needed, and she doesn't know who he was. The punch bowl and watering can, though. Those details might help. The guestbook, too, so thank you. One of the other MacAskills or another guest might have seen your watering can woman and know who she is. Now, Mrs. MacLean, how are you holding up? Do you mind answering questions about the suite?"

"You ask all the questions you like. My sweet is sitting right there next to you."

"Wonderful. How long do you think you were in the suite?"

"What do you think, Mum?" Christine asked. "Mum had a bit of a nostalgia tour after the loo. She and Violet used to visit the housekeeper there when they were girls. We were there maybe ten minutes? I can't be sure."

"Time behaves oddly in such situations," Reddick said.

"Not much less than ten minutes," Janet said. "James was in the sunroom when I got there, and I'm sure he would have seen you going in. He and I might've talked for five minutes."

Reddick made a note and nodded. "Mrs. Robertson, you told Hobbs you noticed a smell?"

"From the wee bedroom," Helen said. "The door *wasnae* quite shut. But the smell, and the poor woman. I'm a district nurse—ah, no. I mind now. We retired some months back, didn't we, David?"

"Many months back, love. We're pensioners and proud of it."

"It's not so easy for me to get down on the floor as it used to be, so I had Chrissie try to wake the poor woman."

"I did," Christine said. "Then I checked for a pulse."

"Why did you not call 9-9-9 yourself?"

"We'd left our pocketbooks in the sitting room with Violet."

"Did Wendy try to call out for help?" Janet asked. "Did she try to phone someone?"

"No one at Fairy Flax Hall claims to have heard her," Reddick said. "Her cell records show no calls made or received during that time. Well." He looked at each of them. "I think that's me, then. I know the questions become repetitive, but every iteration helps. Fairy Flax Hall remains a conundrum I'd like to decipher. But you made it through this whole rehashing of your ordeal, Mrs. MacLean. Thank you very much for that." He raised his glass to David then drank the last of his whisky. "You didn't go along Friday night, not even for the decanting?"

"Dad's allergic to Fairy Flax," Christine said.

∽

When Janet and a swirl of mist blew in through the back door of their house on Argyll Terrace, she found Tallie and the cats waiting with patient anticipation. She obliged all three. To the cats she gave the fishy tidbits they craved that also cleaned their teeth. Tallie heard the results of Janet's invigorating walk home.

"Reddick offered me a lift," she said, "but I wanted time alone to process."

"Would you like something to warm you up? Sherry? Tea?"

"Hm? No, I'm fine. I walked fast." She paced now, not quite as fast, the cats watching from the sofa as they licked their whiskers. "Christine said she'd write up the gist while it's fresh and send a copy to Norman. Reddick learned at least a few things from us. He didn't know there was a guest book, for instance."

"An interesting omission."

"Isn't it?"

"Does Norman know about it?" Tallie asked.

"We'll ask him. He might've arrived before Edward put it out. We learned a few things, too. Like Edward drives a pickup; Reddick didn't tell us that. David did. That's interesting, too. David's dislike of the MacAskills."

"He's such a sweetheart." Tallie said. "It's hard to imagine him not liking someone or anyone not liking him."

"He's kind of like Ranger in his feelings for Edward. The big news is that we have a new suspect. The woman with the watering can. The woman who didn't knock."

"You're bouncing back and forth like a ping pong ball, making the cats dizzy. You might be kind of wound up."

"I know. But this woman is definitely a person of interest. I'm sure Reddick thinks so, too. Ask yourself: Why didn't she knock or open the door? If she thought something was going on in there, and it was worth going to tell Teresa about, why not interrupt it and find out *what* was going on?"

"You have an answer?"

"Yes. For the same reason I stopped James—fingerprints. Maybe she'd already cleaned hers off the doorknob."

"Or she's not as brave as you so she went to get Teresa, the battling beetroot."

"But she *didn't* go get Teresa. She handed that off to someone else and beetled out of there."

"Huh."

"Yeah. Not damning, but here's what I wish I knew. Did she pull back from the door and then see me watching her? Or did she see me and then pull back?"

"Makes a difference," Tallie said.

"It does. So then think about what she had with her. A punch bowl and a watering can. Watering cans are gardening tools. Gardening tools are kept in garden sheds. Rat poison might be found in a garden shed, and it might be picked up along with gardening tools."

"That seems like a bit of a stretch. If she gave Wendy rat poison, she did it earlier, because Wendy was already dead when Helen and

Christine found her, right? So why was she there at the door when you saw her?"

"Returning to the scene of the crime?" Janet said. "Listening for signs of life?"

"With her hands full of clutter?"

"Sure. It was a good opportunity to pick up a beautiful punch bowl and watering can. Besides, that way she didn't look out of place. I probably looked strange because I *wasn't* carrying anything. She blended right in."

Tallie nodded. "You could be onto something. Clutter as camouflage."

16

The headline Christine attached to the gist she wrote up prompted comments from her partners the next morning. Not all of them favorable.

"You didn't tell me Reddick gave us an assignment." Tallie looked accusingly at her mother.

"That's because I don't remember that happening," Janet said. "Christine?"

"This is why I waited to share the document until just before our meeting between the flyleaves and tea leaves," Christine said. "One or two of you are apt to stew." She looked at Tallie. "If I'd shared the document last night, you might not be so bright-eyed and bushy-tailed this morning."

"Is the assignment real or perceived?" Tallie asked. "I'm not against going to Fairy Flax Hall again. I'd just like to be clear. So that I don't upset the customers by stewing among the flyleaves."

"Reddick did call the place a conundrum," Janet said. "And he said he wished he could decipher it. I wouldn't mind seeing Violet again. In fact, Isobel said Violet would love to see us."

"We actually have a reason to go," Tallie said. "Violet's the one who asked us to help Teresa. We can give her an update. Tell her about the new suspect. That might put her at ease."

"We can tell her that Wendy's symptoms don't quite match phosphorous poisoning, too," Summer said. "You didn't see anything smoking or glowing when you found her, did you, Christine?

"Good Lord no."

"So then that's not *definitive* proof," Summer said, "but apparently whatever the poisoned person ejects, one way or another, often smokes and or glows because of the phosphorous."

"If we're trying to ease minds or soothe, maybe we shouldn't go into that level of detail," Tallie said. "But I do want to go see Fairy Flax Hall again."

"I think we need to," Janet said. "Preferably without the dragon at the door. Or Edward. Christine, can you or your mum finagle us an invitation? For as soon as tomorrow?"

"Mum had nightmares again last night."

"Oh, I'm so sorry," Janet said.

"She falls back asleep easily enough, but Dad's not been sleeping well as a result. It's taking a toll on him. He hasn't been himself since the party, neither of them have been. So, I'd just as soon skip—"

"Of course you would," Janet said. "If anything comes of another visit, we'll let you know."

"Not skip the visit," Christine said. "You're right, we need to see the place inside and out. But I'll skip revisiting the wee back bedroom so I don't start having nightmares, too."

"Fair enough," Janet said.

"I *do* want to see the bedroom," Summer said.

"Seconded," said Tallie. "We need the full picture. Speaking of which, the second body hasn't been identified yet. Do you want to try calling Teresa again, Mom?"

"No."

∞

Christine came through from the tearoom before their usual Saturday rush for elevenses. She brought a teapot and cups with her and the news that Violet would be delighted to see them the next morning. Rab poured the tea.

"That's great, Christine. Thanks, Rab." Janet took a cup from him. "I'll be glad to finally see the house in the light of day. I'd love to see it from top to bottom. I've toured plenty of grand-scale stately homes. Castles, too. Biltmore, in North Carolina, outdoes a lot of them in the grandiose category. But they're so big they're unrelatable. Fairy Flax is a fairytale castle on a nice, homey scale."

"Fairy flax," Rab said. "Also called purging flax. The plant, not the house."

"Okay, that makes it less homey," Janet said.

"Do people use fairy flax for purging?" Tallie asked.

"I reckon there are modern options," Rab said.

"Fondly known as," Janet murmured, remembering the MacAskill penchant for using other names. "Do any of the MacAskills call the house Purging Flax Hall?"

"Not that I've heard," Christine said. "But if the younger generation does, I might *not* have heard. That's one of my only regrets about spending so many years in the states—huge gaps in my local knowledge base. Have you heard anything like that, Rab?"

"That local knowledge base just walked past the window," Tallie said. "He left a note. He'll be back around two."

Janet shot a surprised glance over to the fireplace chairs. No napping dog in sight. "How?" she asked. "The dog was just there. The man was just here. Do they evaporate? Phooey. Now I've lost my train of thought, and I think I had a point."

"You were telling us that personal-sized castles are homey and relatable," Tallie said.

"That doesn't sound nearly as intelligent as I meant it to." Janet thought, then shook her head. "Nope. Between disappearing dogs and the thought of purging, whatever came into my head after that slipped away like Rab and Ranger."

Her phone buzzed with a text. She looked at it with trepidation.

"Teresa?" Tallie asked.

"Norman. He wants you and me to meet him, Christine. Half-two at Sea View Kayaks. All right with you, Tallie?"

"You'd almost think he knew when Rab plans to be back."

∽

Sea View Kayaks, down the High Street from Yon Bonnie Books, occupied a granite building similar to the bookshop and tearoom. Kayaks and assorted outdoor gear were newer to the High Street than the books by nine decades, but proving to be longer-lived than some of the building's earlier tenants. Janet remembered an ice cream shop and then a video store.

"I bought a pair of platform shoes here before going off to university," Christine said. "Between the shoes and my duffle, I looked frightfully smart."

Bethia and three other women sat knitting in the front window beside a sky-blue kayak draped in myriad pairs of argyle socks. Janet and Christine waved and went in to find Hobbs.

"In the back corner," the young woman behind the sales counter said when they asked. "Behind the pop-up tent." She pushed a teacup and saucer across the counter to each of them. "Our treat. Special on days the knitters are in."

Hobbs stood when he saw them and offered them each a camping chair. Janet sat, marveling at how comfortable it was. Christine bypassed the camp chair for a battered but more comfortable-looking easy chair. When she sat, she sank so deep her knees rose to her armpits, sloshing tea on the floor.

"You might have warned her," Janet tsked at Hobbs.

"I'm perfectly fine," Christine said.

Hobbs took a camp chair. Their corner, behind the tent, gave them a bit of privacy, while the tent and a row of sleeping bags made it quiet and almost cozy.

"Why are we meeting you here, Norman, rather than more conveniently at our place of business?" Christine asked.

"I've been in and out of the shop a fair amount lately. I didn't want to attract more attention than necessary."

"Said the uniformed, beanpole policeman to the women being laughed at by an entire troop of cherubs." Three small children, holding new wetsuits on hangers, chortled gleefully at the odd trio, ignoring their mother's *wheesht*. Christine put her thumbs in her ears, wagged her hands, and scrunched up her face at them. They shrieked and ran off. "Tell Norman about glowing and smoking Rodine, Janet."

Hobbs took out his notebook and Janet told him why they'd decided finding the Rodine was no longer a priority. He made a few quick notes then tucked the notebook away in his breast pocket. Any comments he might have had were tucked away, too.

"Rats," Christine said. "Amazing how often we've come round to rats in our conversations, Norman, since taking up our lives in Inversgail. And speaking of them, is Teresa still the prime suspect?"

Hobbs nodded.

"Because we've found another—the woman who didn't knock. Did you read the notes I sent?"

He nodded.

"Good," Christine said. "She seems a decent prospect, though I'd much rather suspect Isobel. Or Bethia."

"That's a horrible thing to say. When did you decide that?" Janet asked.

"I've felt that way since the beginning. Isobel and Bethia are easier to rally round because *they* are likeable."

"But we don't want to let those thoughts loose in the universe," Janet said.

"Superstitious havers."

"It's not," Janet said. "If you say it often enough, and if people hear you, then for some of those people it becomes a possibility. For some a reality."

"You're not talking about the universe, then," Christine said, "because the universe isn't full of havering absurdities."

"Saying that you'd rather suspect either of them suggests there's a possibility they *should* be suspects. Even if it's a miniscule possibility."

"You don't believe that," Christine said. "Putting the suggestion out there could just as easily do the opposite—reveal it for the absurdity it is. The universe has an operating manual. It's called the law of physics. Or astrophysics. Either way, it's the law."

"A law more effective than I am," Hobbs said.

"Did you hear that, Christine?" Janet clattered her teacup into its saucer. "Did you hear the utter dejection in his voice? And look. Plain as day, you can see what's going on in Norman's head. If he ever thought Bethia is the guilty one, it obviously didn't worry him too much. But now that he's heard that evil thought that you let out of the Pandora's box you call a mind, he's sinking into a sea of despond before our very eyes."

"You're confused, Janet. The phrase is Slough of Despond. It's from *The Pilgrim's Progress*. Although Norman is more likely sinking into the tea of despond," Christine said. "This stuff is dreadful. And tepid." She handed her cup and saucer to Janet and attempted to rise from the engulfing chair. After two tries, she boosted herself free of it.

If Janet hadn't had tea in both hands, she would have applauded. Hobbs, sighing at the dregs of his own tea, missed the feat. He looked up when Christine went to loom over him, her shadow like an eclipse of the shop's lighting.

"Look at you, wallowing in melodrama, Norman Hobbs," Christine said. "Snap out of it. No one seriously suspects Bethia and talking doesn't make it so. What even put that notion in your head?"

"She's been known to add a bit of this and that to her tea. Sugar, of course. But also her own version of homeopathic remedies. As well, she's generous. She's happy to share."

Christine sank back into her chair. "Did she put something in Wendy's tea?"

"Chamomile. Unless it was coltsfoot," Hobbs said. "Or both. I told Reddick it was an accident. Either she put the herbs in the wrong cup or Ms. Erskine mistook Nana Bethia's cup for her own."

"You told him?"

"And it broke his heart to do it," Janet said.

"Of course it did," Christine said. "But not mine, because we know she's innocent and this invigorates our investigation. And with Norman off the case, he'll have time on his hands, so he can be at our beck and call."

"I've not been relieved of duty entirely," Hobbs said stiffly.

"But Norman," Janet said. "Our usual arrangement will only work if you're more forthcoming. About what you want from us, and about giving *us* information. And no more secret worries."

His phone buzzed and he looked at it. "I'm required elsewhere now. I'll be in touch."

"That was probably his sandwich order ready at Mr. Potato Chef, not a real call at all," Christine said when he'd gone. "Now, where shall we start?"

"So many suspects, so little time," Janet said. But it was obvious that Christine didn't catch her sarcasm. That was one of the things she liked about Christine, her ability to focus and ignore sarcasm.

"Why did Norman not tell us about Bethia doctoring Wendy's tea sooner?" Christine asked. "Was he afraid we would focus on her?"

"Ask yourself the question we asked about Teresa—is he afraid we'll find out the truth?"

"That Bethia's a stone-cold killer? No, I like this rat connection. This theme," Christine said. "Arsenic was a rodenticide, once upon a time, wasn't it? Ian's missing scrapbook mentioned arsenic, you said. Your ex, Curtis, was and always will be a Grade-A rat. And remember how we first met the sainted Nana Bethia—when Norman kept you from moving into your house with tales of entire villages of rats in residence there, all so he had a place to keep her free of charge. Rats, Janet, can't be trusted."

"Bethia wasn't to blame, though, and she really is a dear."

"Agreed. But I stand by my statement: Rats cannot be trusted."

The competition knitters had packed up and gone by the time Janet and Christine returned their teacups to the counter. Bethia still knitted beside the blue kayak, though. Without interrupting her stitches, she gestured to the empty chairs beside her.

"Was Norman up to his cloak and dagger tricks today?" Janet asked.

"He tipped his hat to me before he took it off and went to wait for you," Bethia said.

"Nothing gets by you, does it?" Christine said with a laugh. "You look right at home knitting next to this kayak, too. Mind, I think you'd look just as comfortable knitting in the kayak out in the harbor. Do you get along as well with the knitters as the knitting?"

"Och aye. I get along with most people, and if I don't, then I ignore them."

"My mum and dad are much the same," Christine said.

"Then I'm certain I'd enjoy their company."

"Maybe at Nev's some evening," Christine said. "Get Maida to bring you and your knitting along."

"What do you think about while you knit?" Janet asked.

"Sometimes nothing at all. This morning I've been thinking about the words *ponder* and *wonder.* I like that they are so much alike and so different. Norman pointed that out to me when he was a wean."

"Did Norman have a nickname when he was a little boy?" Janet asked.

"He's always been Norman."

"It suits him."

"None better." Bethia switched from gray to blue wool. "Now I've moved on to pondering unhappiness. I'm not unhappy, mind, but unhappiness interests me. Fenella, a woman I know in the care home, talks an awful lot about people who complain of their circumstances and blame others *and* the circumstances for their unhappiness. *She* complains about *them*." Bethia's sweet smile came and went as she switched back to the blue wool. "Fenella believes these blamers don't want to take responsibility for their own lives and happiness. Because, she says, that would mean they're responsible for their unhappiness as well. Blaming external factors and other people makes them feel better."

"What do *you* think?" Christine asked.

"It's more that I wonder. If Fenella is right, might all that unhappiness and blame become a motive for murder?"

"Something to ponder," Janet said.

"Do *you* ever complain?" Christine asked.

"Only when Fenella complains too loudly," Bethia said with a sweet primness, belied by a sweetly wicked chuckle.

"Bethia, the night of the decluttering, did you see a woman with a watering can and a punch bowl?" Janet asked.

"I've never owned a punch bowl, and never felt as though I'd missed out, but that was a fine-looking watering can."

"So you *did*. Do you know who she is?"

"No. Did you want that bonny watering can? I don't know who she is, but I often see her on my way between knitting venues. She helps out at the tattie truck."

17

Arsenic Diary, day seven

I shake myself. Try to dispel this feeling creeping over me the past few days. As though a lowering, glowering sky presses on my spirit, compresses it. I am aimless. Distracted. My usual je ne sais quoi is gone to rubbish.

The scrapbook is to blame. Taking that dark turn toward killing bairns, as it did. I give it a thump. And immediately hug the poor thing. The book is not responsible for my gloomy frame of mind. The book is passive. It offers information. I choose how to react. For proof, I open to a random page, and choose not to be disappointed that nothing is pasted here—but wait. Nothing pasted, but six lines scribbled next to a drawing labeled "Doris aspera." Sounds like someone with whom I might have been at school, but it's a type of sea slug. Come to think of it, I might have been at school with a sea slug or two. Doris looks rather made up, frankly. Polka dots, feathery appendages, multiple feelers, and the whole thing shaped like an odd loaf of bread. Honestly, who is interested? But my darling's scribbled lines—

> Karl Scheele, that crafty Swede,
> Produced a green as sly as greed.
> Poison in your wallpaper,

Poison in your paint,
Poison in your evening gown,
But ye dinnae make complaint.

This, this is the kind of joy I need. The joy I choose.

∽

"Is there more than one woman helping out on the food truck?" Christine asked on their way back to Yon Bonnie Books.

"There certainly could be," Janet said. "If not, that makes our watering can woman Euan's mum. And that makes his mum a sus—"

"Don't say it," Christine cut in. "Not here on the street, anyway. And Bethia could be wrong. Or watering can woman could be his auntie."

"His mum's sister. I suppose it's possible," Janet said. She sent Bethia's information about the watering can woman to Reddick and Hobbs—separately, to keep up the appearance that Hobbs was not involved in the investigation. Her phone buzzed with an incoming text almost immediately. Janet stopped walking when she read it. When Christine noticed, she backtracked and peered at her old friend.

"Norman," Janet said.

Christine gently took the phone from her hand and read the text. "Second victim is Euan Markwell from Mr. Potato Chef."

"Let's keep walking," Christine said. "Let's get to the shop. It's as good as home, aye? We can fall apart there if we need or want to. Come on."

"He didn't say it's not for public knowledge," Janet said.

"Then word will spread, and it won't take long."

Word spread faster than Janet and Christine could walk. Janet saw it on Tallie and Rab's faces. Christine saw it on Summer's. The sunny faces of tourists remained unaware, though, and so the women and Rab focused on them. They wrapped themselves in the routine of books, pots of tea, and warm scones. In between customers, Janet created two new documents—"Questions about Victims" and "Theories"—and sent a text to let the others know, reminding them to add their initials to their entries.

"You remember you already made a 'Questions' document, right?" Tallie said as they passed each other in the fiction aisle.

"The first one's general. The new one's specific."

"Okey doke."

When Janet had a free minute, she opened the "Questions about Victims" document and saw that Tallie and Summer had already jumped in.

TM: What connections are there between Euan and Wendy?

SJ: Connected by their deaths? Do we know that? Do the police?

Janet added her own.

JM: Connected by watering can woman?

JM: By the business—Mr. Potato Chef?

JM: Is watering can woman Euan's mum? Where does that take us?

She didn't want to think about the answer to that question. She put the phone on the counter to ring up a sale and tell the customer how to find the cheese shop. When she finished, Rab handed the phone to her.

"Ranger ran someone off from the food truck the other night. We were passing by."

"When?"

"One or two. The lad likes to fill his lungs when the tide's out."

"That's morning, not night." Tallie scootched between them to ring up her own customer.

"He likes the quiet at that time," Rab said.

Janet motioned Rab to the end of the counter, farther from customer ears. "I meant was this before or after Euan's death?"

"After. I didn't think much of it at the time. I'll tell Norman now that we know."

"What do you know about Euan, Rab?"

"He had a hard row. He had his problems with drugs. But those were his own demons. He was a gentle soul."

"Who in town knew that?"

"He wasn't shy about it. Spoke to schools and church groups."

"Any idea who Ranger ran off?"

"Kids most like."

Janet went to straighten the inglenook. Tallie found her there, sitting with Ranger, a few minutes later.

"Not really enough room for both of us in one chair," Janet said. "Ranger's being kind enough to share." She gave him a kiss between his ears and got up. "I'm going to nip into the office and call Teresa with a progress report."

"She fired us."

"Yes, but we have new information. We have the watering can woman. This will be my own clever ruse. If Teresa's the killer, and I tell her we have a different prime suspect, she won't feel as threatened by us and then we won't feel so threatened by her."

"Such a quiet retirement you're having," Tallie said. She kissed her mother, just as her mother had kissed Ranger, and went to tend customers.

Janet shut the office door and tapped out Teresa's number. "Hello—"

"I knew I had no need of your help," Teresa interrupted. "This latest crime fully exonerates me. I would never eat at a food truck and have never gone near one."

"Euan Markwell didn't die in his food truck," Janet said. She heard silence from the other end—and she guessed seething. "But what you say is good to hear," she rushed to add, "because it bolsters what I called to tell you." Continued silence on the other end. "Teresa?"

"Please do tell me." Teresa's sarcasm wasn't an improvement over her silence.

"We've developed a very strong suspect," Janet said. "A person associated with the food truck. That association seems like too much of a coincidence, don't you think?"

"'A person associated with the food truck.' The fact of the association isn't nearly as odd as the way you phrase it. As though you've taken a course in Police Officialese. And too much of a coincidence, you ask? Is there an agreed upon standard for an appropriate amount of coincidence? If this person is the killer, then I think you will find there's no coincidence at all. He or she most likely started the rumor of food poisoning, thus making the tatty tattie truck a decoy."

Janet pretended she'd disconnected before Teresa. She said *beetroot*, quietly but with vehemence, and logged into the office computer. She opened the "Teresa" file and added notes about the irritating conversation. Then she opened the "Theories" document and read the only entry.

We don't know enough to have theories.

No initials prefaced the entry. Janet said *beetroot* again, less vehemently, and made her own entries.

JM: Who says we don't have theories?

JM: We can bandy theories with the best of them.

JM: We need to keep track of them.

JM: Initial your entries.

She logged off, breathed deeply, and left the office feeling ready to do her fair share of their real business.

"Feeling a little irate there, Mom?" Tallie held up her phone, open to the newly amended "Theories" document.

"Not anymore. Breathing normal. Mind calm. Everything copacetic. Got it out of my system with heartfelt beetroots and friendly suggestions. Now I'll go help that lovely couple looking lost in the Gaelic section. *Mar sin leat.*"

"Bye."

"Her accent's improving," Rab said.

The couple in the Gaelic section turned out to be more curious than interested in shopping. Browsers didn't bother Janet, sometimes they turned into the best customers. The next jingle of the door brought in Isobel.

"Came to check on the knitters," she said with a wave.

Janet followed her to the inglenook where Isobel stopped and gave her a look at first blank and then panicked.

"They didn't show up?"

"We're not on the schedule this afternoon." Janet said. "Maybe at the library? Isobel, honey, sit down."

Isobel slumped into the nearest chair and shook her head as though to clear it. "I forgot my cell. Left it at the museum. Thought I'd remembered the schedule." She blew out her cheeks, looking pale and sleepless.

Janet pulled the footstool closer and sat there. "You've got a lot going on. You should give yourself a break."

"From everything? I reckon there's a lot of everything going on. I heard from Gran that you're helping Mum. Thank you."

"Your mum's actually not that happy with us." Janet told herself she wasn't fishing for information. Then told herself to get real. Give Isobel a hook and she might drop a useful line.

"Gran's grateful." Isobel had her gran's smile. "It doesn't matter now, though. I've just come from Euan's mum and dad. I'm glad my mum's in the clear. I knew she was. But I never would have wished for it to turn out like this. You've heard, aye? About Euan? Suicide. I can't believe it. Don't want to."

"Suicide? Are you sure, Isobel? I haven't heard anything about that." And why not? What happened to Norman's forthcomingness?

"They found a note. It said why he did it—Wendy was an accident and he couldn't live with himself. His mum and dad are gutted. He's their only son. All they've got."

"Like you and your mum."

"His dad's paralyzed. Drunk driving accident. His poor mum. Euan's put himself, and them, through a lot. She's willing to believe the suicide. But not Wendy. She can't believe he killed her."

"I can't imagine what they're going through. Does his mum think the note's fake?"

"I didn't ask."

"Isobel, I'm so sorry. This on top of Wendy. And your mum. And the missing stockings." Janet flapped the thought of stockings away with her hand. "The least of your worries."

"With doing Wendy's job as well as my own, the stockings are one more thing I've no time to worry over."

"Can your board members give you a hand in the short term?" Janet asked. "Is it that kind of board?"

"Most of them are retired. Those who aren't are busy with their own jobs. Oh, but that changed recently. Now there's only James Haviland who's working. The rest are great. They're fully into supporting the museum. But having them around would be like having more Uncle Edwards to keep track of."

Janet stifled a laugh.

"I didn't mean that the way it sounds. Wait, yes I did." Isobel stifled her own laugh. "He's terribly smart and a dear. He means well."

"But he has a lively imagination?"

"Aye. A lovely way to put it. He's a conservative in the true sense of the word, but his 'conservations' aren't always accurate."

"Does *he* believe his stories are true?" Janet asked. "For instance, I've read articles about people knitting codes into socks during World War Two, but is there a pair like that in the exhibit?"

"Has he told you he can't reveal the secret?"

"He did."

"Then I'll not spoil his fun. Thank you, Janet. I'll come check on the knitters another day. Maybe on a day when they're here."

Janet moved from the footstool to the chair Isobel had vacated and took out her phone. She'd forgotten to make a "Euan" document and was glad to see that Summer had. She added the information about the suicide and Euan's note claiming he'd killed Wendy, then opened the general "Questions" document and noted they hadn't heard about the suicide or a note from Hobbs or Reddick. She added three question marks to the note, even though it wasn't a question. Then she sent texts to both policemen asking for details on Euan's death. She waited a few minutes, staring at the phone's display, willing an answer or two to buzz in her hand. None did.

"Isobel isn't much like Teresa, is she," Tallie said when Janet slipped back behind the sales counter.

"A plus for us. Summer made a 'Euan' document." Janet handed her phone to Tallie. "Take a look."

Tallie read Janet's brief entry, her reaction a succinct, "Yeesh." She passed the phone to Rab who'd returned from showing a customer to the DIY section.

"I sent texts to both Normans. No answers. So many things missing. Rodine, stockings, scrapbook, suspects, motives, completely cooperative constables and their colleagues."

"We can't expect *completely*," Tallie said. "Cooperative and timely would be good. But speaking of scraps and books, look who's padding silently in from the tearoom. Hello Ian. I looked up just in time to see you before you saw us and were able to eavesdrop."

"I'll go watch the tearoom." Rab handed Janet's phone back to her. He took a tent-fold sign from under the counter and set it next to the cash register, then sidestepped Ian and disappeared toward the tearoom.

"That's a new sign," Tallie said. She plucked it from the counter and read it aloud. "'Kindly pay for your purchases in the tearoom.' Nice to have a resident problem solver."

Christine and Summer soon emerged from the tearoom. Christine said, at full volume, "What's this about someone craving a bigger audience? Oh, hello Ian. Rab must have meant you. You look nice, all togged out in author couture. What's the occasion?"

"Spoke to a book club. Went rather well. Enjoyed by all. Wonderful refreshments."

"Good, then you won't be wanting tea," Christine said.

"Have you found your scrapbook?" Summer asked.

"No, and I'm actually becoming concerned."

"That's interesting," Tallie said. "You actually do sound and look concerned. Tell us."

"I think it was you, Janet, who asked if the scrapbook disappeared in the decluttering. I've thought back to when I last saw it, and I'm sure that it disappeared before the decluttering. I do wish I'd known that was happening. I would have loved to plunder Fairy Flax Hall."

"Plundering wouldn't have really been the right attitude," Janet said.

"I suppose my invitation went missing in the post. That happens more often than you'd think."

"You think the scrapbook is significant, though?" Summer asked. "That it has some bearing on the—" she lowered her voice "—on the murders?"

"I do, and I'll tell you why. I came across it whilst doing a spot of preliminary research at Fairy Flax. I'm toying with the idea of writing a historical mystery, and wouldn't that be a frightfully good setting?"

"Oh, frightfully," said Tallie, tapping a pencil on the counter. "As frightful as it is for the current real-life mystery going on there."

"Come to think of it, yes."

"What about the scrapbook, Ian?"

"A *stealth* scrapbook. Well-disguised. That's part of the fun, and also part of my concern. If you were looking for such a thing, with a casual perusal of the shelves, you'd never find it. Particularly because of where I found it. Top shelf, in fact, and being stuck up there made it unlikely that anyone had taken it down in recent memory. You'd simply see another mid-eighteenth-century scientific monograph, yawn, and move on. But what this fellow did is both ingenious and evil. He sliced out every other page and used the remaining pages for the scrapbook. He ruined the book but created an amazing repository of newspaper clippings with a focus on arsenic, arsenic poisonings, and then branching out in the later pages to poisonings in general."

"The book's been grangerized," Janet said. "Crudely, anyway. Grangerizing was a hobby in the eighteenth and nineteenth centuries. People took pages of illustrations and information out of other books—*mutilating them*—and then added them to another book to augment it. They're also called extra-illustrated books. People didn't usually slice out pages to make room, though. They rebound the books, as necessary, to accommodate the extra material. I'm glad you think slicing the pages out was evil, Ian."

"Appalling," he said. "Apart from the location of the book, the dust on that shelf and on the books made me think that none of them had been taken down in decades. I think it's possible that none of the MacAskill's knows the scrapbook exists. Make that past tense—existed—if it's never located. I found another gem up there, as well."

"Describe it better," Christine said. "What's the title?"

"*A Monograph of British Graptolites* by Gertrude L. Elles and Ethel M.R. Wood, published in 1908. In my toying with the historical mystery I've got as far as murdering a nineteenth-century geologist. Don't you love the idea of killer cliffs and homicidal hammers? And those very severe women geologists—I can't decide whether to kill one of them or make one the detective."

"Detective," Tallie said immediately.

"Or one of each? Detective and victim?" Ian fished a small notebook from a pocket.

"No, better make the victim male," Tallie said.

"A snoopy, sneaking-type male," Summer said. "That kind of personality suggests so many motives."

Ian nodded as he scribbled notes.

"Sounds fascinating, Ian," Christine said. "Your mystery and the book that's been sliced, diced, and pasted into a repository for all things arsenic. But you've wandered. Get to the significance of the scrapbook, please."

"What's that?" Ian looked up from his scribbling. "Oh, I see. No. The mad scrapbooker didn't use Gertrude's graptolite book. No, he mangled the next book along the shelf with the delightfully dull title of *A Monograph of the British Nudibranchiate Mollusca: with figures of all the species, volume one.* Written by Joshua Alder and the unlikely-sounding Albany Hancock. The figures were beautiful, what you could see of them between the blasted pasted-in scraps."

"Trust you to find a book of nudes, Ian," Christine said.

"Not nudes. Nudibranchiates. They're a type of mollusk. The book was a lovely thing. Leather spine and marbled cover with psychedelic swirls, published in 1845. I wonder what he did with the pages he sliced out?"

"Book butchery," Janet said.

"Whodunnit?" Christine asked.

"I feared, very much, it was a woman. So trite it almost hurt, but people often assume poison is a woman's weapon. To that I say 'Humbug.'" Ian paused. "Horatio 'Humbug' MacAskill, that is."

"The one with sweeties in his pockets?" Janet asked.

"The very one. Whilst at university in Edinburgh, he read old newspaper accounts of a confectioner in Bradford, England, who accidentally added arsenic to a batch of humbugs and killed close to two dozen of his customers. Sickened hundreds more. Thus, began Humbug's lifelong fascination with arsenic and humbugs."

"How could you know that?" Summer asked.

"I found out all this through my own bit of sleuthing. I, uh, I didn't want to ask any of the MacAskills about the scrapbook. As I told you, it seemed unlikely that anyone had touched it in decades. I was afraid that if I asked, they would decide it was too precious and whisk it away. But then, after I told you about it, I mustered the courage. My original thought was correct. They knew the book was there on the top shelf, but only in a vague way. 'Oh yes, one of Humbug's rather boring sets of monographs.' That sort of thing. They didn't know its true nature."

"Good Lord," Christine said. "You don't suppose Humbug carried one or two poisoned candies in his pockets mixed with the rest?"

"Playing humbug roulette? I wonder if I have room for a character like that in my historical?" Ian reached for his notebook. "Or a second book in the series."

"Ahem," Janet enunciated clearly.

Ian set the notebook aside with a fond pat. "So, then, *is* the scrapbook important? I can't say that it is. I can only tell you that since I spoke to you about it, someone nicked my messenger bag. I'd slung it over the back of a chair at the library and, at some point, left it to run down a book in the stacks. Careless in retrospect, but it's the *library*."

"I feel your pain," Janet said, "but it *is* a public place in a tourist town, Ian."

"Understood. I blame myself. I'm usually more careful. But the point is, someone took the bag, rifled through it, and then tossed it behind the shrubbery. Taking nothing. Including my wallet, anything in it, or my mobile."

"It could have been random," Summer said.

"Easily," Ian said.

"But the timing," Janet said.

"Exactly."

18

Rab returned from the tearoom with a pot of tea and plate of scones, which he took to the inglenook. Bethia and Ranger, one of them knitting and the other snoring, occupied neighboring chairs.

"Like old times," Janet said. "Except now we know who Bethia is, and she's not embarrassed to talk to us. In fact—"

"Go have yourself a wee chat," Tallie said.

Bethia offered Janet one of the scones. Janet sneaked a peek toward the counter and accepted.

"Thank you for taking one," Bethia said. "Norman is taking me out for a meal but I didn't like to say no to Rab." She told Janet that Norman didn't want her walking home to Maida's by herself. "That isn't what he told me, mind. He came up with the idea for a meal and then said your shop is a more convenient place to pick me up."

"More cloak and dagger?" Janet said, planning to get some answers out of Norman when he showed up.

"I think I'd be quite good at cloak and dagger myself," Bethia said.

"You'd be perfect. Like Miss Marple. So how else are you filling your time while you're in Inversgail?"

"Eating far too much. Maida's a wonderful cook."

"I didn't know that."

"Aye, as long as you like tatties, oats, and fish."

"I'll ask her for her recipes."

Bethia smiled. "I toured the museum exhibit again this afternoon before coming here. I love the ganseys." She held up her knitting. "For Norman's birthday."

"He'll love it."

"Edward took me round the exhibit, and I noticed that the tour script has changed. He mentioned the two recent deaths. He called them the Inversgail stalkings. I'm not sure what to think of that, and wonder what the tourists think. He mentioned a scrapbook, as well. Have you heard of it?"

"Did you hear Ian at the counter?"

"Aye. So it is the same book. Edward said there's a clue to the murders in it. He sounded quite convinced, but I wonder. I also wonder what will happen if the killer hears Edward's story."

"No kidding. Thank you, Bethia."

"You might pass that along to Norman. I would, but I don't like to worry him."

"He worries with good reason, Bethia. This person has killed twice."

"The deaths are definitely connected?"

"We actually don't know that."

"Inquiries ongoing, aye? Och well, Norman needn't worry. There's nothing much safer than sitting and knitting and stopping by for a chat with friends."

"Is this your subtle way of offering to be ears and eyes for us?"

Bethia looked pleased. "These are all public places, not the dark wynds or closes of a city like Glasgow or Edinburgh. And I feel very safe at Maida's. *She* is a force to be reckoned with."

"Amen," Janet said. "You're sure though?"

"I'm not Norman's granny for nothing."

"In that case, what's your opinion of the MacAskills?"

"I've pondered that whilst I knit. Isobel is the wool—lovely to work with, surprisingly strong and resilient. Teresa is the needles—straight and to the point. Edward is the pattern handed down through the family—possibly not accurate but not hopeless either."

"And Violet?"

"She doesn't fit into my knitting world view. I wonder if she does needlework? That's neither here nor there. I ken what she is. She's the old family recipe someone gives you that's missing a key ingredient."

"The cardamom missing from Beverly Hinman's orange cake," Janet said darkly.

"So annoying," Bethia said.

"Is Norman picking you up at closing?"

"Aye."

"Will you tell him I'd like a quick word?"

Bethia said she would.

Janet knew her request was a mistake when she saw Bethia getting into Norman's car out front. Sure enough. They drove off. Norman hadn't answered her text and he hadn't listened to his nana.

∽

"You're a glum chum." Christine sat on the stool behind the sales counter, having offered to help Janet close out the cash register. Tallie had gone to help Summer.

"Thank you," Janet said. "Now I'll have to count again."

"You should take up knitting. Bethia's never short-tempered or snappish. I'm sure it's the knitting."

"How miraculous. Even your suggestion calmed me. Counting again, now, but without the snapping."

"Bethia isn't sarcastic either," Christine said. "She's the ultimate granny. Adding the tearoom as a knitting venue has worked well for just that reason. Small children don't whimper when she's around. She could charm the socks off a snake."

"Snakes don't wear socks."

"But if they did, she could do it. And if she lived locally, we could hire her to actually be our resident knitter."

"We could advertise for a knitter."

"It wouldn't be the same."

"It wouldn't."

"What wouldn't be the same?" Summer asked as she and Tallie came in from the tearoom.

"Hiring some random knitter to add the charm Bethia does," Janet said. "There. Finished. And, with your invaluable help, I only had to start over twice." She smiled with all her teeth at Christine. "In other Bethia news, she's offered to spy for us."

"What's her going rate?" Christine asked.

"Christine!" Tallie's shoulders rose along with her voice and eyebrows. "Norman would never forgive us if we let Nana Bethia get mixed up with a murderer."

The others, eyes wide, stared at her.

"Too loud," Tallie said. "Sorry."

"She's already mixed up in this anyway," Janet told them why Bethia had been knitting in the inglenook late that afternoon and what she'd said about Edward and the scrapbook.

"He's an old bampot if there ever was one," Christine said.

"What exactly was her offer?" Summer asked.

"Sitting, knitting, listening, and stopping by to chat," Janet said.

"And Norman told her to come here and wait for him this afternoon?" Tallie drummed thoughtful fingertips on her lips then said to her mother, "You told her yes, as long as she's careful, didn't you."

"I did, and she's already doing it anyway. She doesn't need our say-so. She's a grown granny. Now, let me tell you how she describes the MacAskills."

When Janet finished, Summer asked, "If Violet's a recipe, what's the key ingredient she's missing?"

"Let's add that to our growing list of missing things," Tallie said. "Maybe our visit tomorrow can help us figure that out. What about Ian's scrapbook? How does it fit in now that bampot Edward is spreading tales about it?"

"Do we know they're tales?" Summer asked.

"If they aren't, then Edward leaps ahead of any other suspect," Christine said, "because how does he know there are clues in the blasted thing unless he put them there?"

"He might leap ahead, anyway," Janet said, "depending on why he's spreading the tales. He might be indulging his hobby of enhancing local history. But if someone orchestrated the food poisoning rumors, maybe that was him."

"Not enough verifiable information," Tallie said. "Our constant bugaboo. Here's what we do know. Ian's right that current information about poison is easily available. *Poison* is easily available. Go online and look. Yikes. We also know he's careful with his messenger bag. He likes to be seen with it. It's part of his author costume. People who know him know his bag."

"Norman's never gotten back to me about the scrapbook," Janet said. "That might or might not mean anything, considering how stingy he's being about sharing information these days. I don't think we need to go looking for the scrapbook, but I do think the Normans should talk to Edward. Anything else before we call it a night?"

"Baloney," Christine said.

"*What's* baloney?" Janet asked.

"Baloney is my *anything else* you asked for. The Normans talking to Edward isn't baloney, and I agree we nix looking for the scrapbook. Although, that might be interesting, especially if it requires clandestine snooping. What I meant is that we should watch for baloney. Guard against it. Particularly if it comes from Ian or Edward."

"I'd say that's a given, but it isn't," Tallie said. "Baloney monitors on."

"And one more thing," Christine said. "Let me see that text you sent the Normans asking about the suicide note."

Janet found the message and handed her phone to Christine.

"Too soft." Christine returned the phone and took out her own. "I'll have a go." If the strength of her message matched the jabbing of her thumbs, it was hard-hitting. "Let's see them ignore *that*."

They waited. Nothing happened.

Janet's phone buzzed. "It's Norman. Nothing about suicide, but the woman with the watering can has been identified. Elaine Markwell. Euan's mother."

∽

Janet and Tallie stopped at Basant's on the way home to pick up flowers. They'd decided not to go empty-handed to Fairy Flax Hall the next day. Basant, an avid reader, marked his place and set his current book aside.

"What are you reading these days, Basant?" Tallie asked.

"*Primitive: The Art and Life of Horace H. Pippin*, by Janice N. Harrington. It combines two of my interests—World War I and modern poetry. As so often happens with a good book, I have found myself gaining a different perspective and following a fascinating bylane."

"Different perspectives are important," Janet said. "Bylanes can be, too."

"Also distracting," Basant said. "As I have distracted you from your reason for stopping in this evening."

"Flowers," Tallie said. "I found them."

"What is the current perspective on your second murder? Forgive me, neither murder is yours. Is there any news you can share?"

"What have you heard?" Janet asked.

"Only that we are all sad to hear that the second victim is Euan, who was coming into his own with baked potatoes."

"We mostly have questions," Janet said.

Basant gestured at the empty store, inviting them to spend some time. But without official word on suicide or a suicide note, Janet didn't feel right sharing that piece of information, even with Basant. "Lots of questions, but short on time," she said.

"Do you have humbugs? Tallie asked.

"I do. I also have fish pie."

"A quarter pound of humbugs, then, and pie for two, please."

He dished up the pie, then took a jar of brown and white striped oblong sweeties from the shelves behind his counter. "When you buy a quarter pound of humbugs," he said as he handed over their purchases, "they are essentially already eaten."

"In that case, you know we'll be back," Tallie said.

"I will count on it."

They walked the rest of the way home in a flurry of snow. The cats supervised the supper of fish pie and were rewarded with dishes to lick clean. They then spent the evening in a flurry of naps, and the women, with their laptops open and a handful of humbugs, in a flurry of reading notes and adding their own to the shared documents.

"Did you see the one from Summer in the 'Questions about Victims' doc?" Tallie asked. "She asked if watering can woman slash Euan's mother is still our best suspect."

"Being his mother doesn't explain her behavior at the decluttering," Janet said. "Given his troubles with drugs and his father's paralysis from the accident, my mind has no trouble piecing together a scenario where his mother could see his death as a first step out of a downward spiral. As horrible as that is to think or say out loud."

"Put it in the doc," Tallie said. "But how does Wendy's death fit into that horrible scenario?"

"Misdirection? Practice?"

"If it wasn't his mother, we're back to the reason Norman is worried about Bethia. Euan knew, saw, or heard something that threatened the killer. Here's an entry from Christine. 'Isobel has already been to see Euan's parents. Seems quick. Does it suggest prior knowledge of victim's name?' Oh, and under that one from you. 'If the suicide note's fake, so is the suicide.'"

"We've seen that before," Janet said.

"Doesn't mean it isn't true. They say there are only so many stories in the world. There might be more ways to cover up a murder, but if you're just beginning a career in killing you might be kind of a bumbler."

They worked for a while in silence except for the occasional purr from a well-petted cat. Tallie called it quits first and wished the cats and her mother goodnight. "Don't stay up late," she said. "Sleuth work is addictive."

"I'll be along soon," Janet said. "I'll just look through the docs one more time." They seemed to be getting their entries muddled between documents, but Janet decided it didn't matter. At least for the time being. In the "Theories" document she read:

CR: Do we take Edward's baloney about clues in the scrapbook seriously?
JM: Until we know enough to separate fact from baloney, yes. Include any theory, rumor, or bit of baloney about any suspect.
SJ: Agreed. Any theory might spark an idea that gets us somewhere. Even baloney can catch fire.

They were short on theories, but Janet knew they'd come. Theories in their past investigations had developed from their questions, and some of the entries in the "Questions about Victims" document were leaning that way.

SJ: Mr. Potato Chef was cleared. Did that somehow seal Euan's fate?
JM: If wrappers could be planted, poison could be, too.
TM: Do we know if food from the truck was poisoned after it left?
CR: Norman H or Norman R might. *We* don't.
CR: Planting wrappers would be easier than planting poisoned food in the truck.

TM: Would it?

JM: Ranger and Rab ran someone off from the food truck. 1 A.M. Could have been random. Could have been someone trying to plant evidence.

TM: Big if.

CR: Agreed. Also, a wee bit after the fact.

TM: We aren't dealing with a professional. We aren't professionals, either, but in our own bumbling, amateur way we're dangerous to murderers.

Janet gave herself the satisfaction of typing the last entry in that document. The last she'd see that night, anyway, because then she'd close the laptop and take two sleepy cats to bed.

JM: Do you know what they call a bumbling, amateur killer? A killer.

19

Christine called in the morning to let Janet know the Vauxhall needed a day of rest. Janet said not to worry, that it must be her turn to drive anyway. Tallie rejoiced at the change in plans as the snow had turned to either a sump or a blatter and the Vauxhall still had a leak. She hopped in the back seat with the flowers when they picked up Christine. When they stopped for Summer, she dove in the back seat with a bag of fresh scones.

"Nice," Janet said. "Scones and flowers might not ease Violet's mind, but how can they not be soothing? They might even lessen the chance of riling."

"Too bad," Christine said, "I'm in the mood for a bit of riling. Mum woke three times last night."

"She's the one who needs soothing," Tallie said. "Is there anything we can do?"

"Find who did this," Janet said.

"It might not help." Christine fell silent, and might have slept, while the others talked around her.

"It seems like we need a better reason than sight-seeing for this visit," Summer said. "So, what's the plan?"

"Solving Reddick's conundrum is pretty vague," Tallie said, "but getting a better idea of the floorplan might be useful. Do we still bring up the Rodine?"

"If nothing else, it gives us a place to start," Janet said. "We can tell her not to worry about it. Maybe it'll get her talking."

"There are lots of options for that," Summer said. "Ask her about the scrapbook, about Humbug, if she knows Euan's mother, ask her about Teresa and Edward."

"Who lives there, who's in and out a lot," Janet said. "Ask her why Edward's living with Teresa if they don't get along."

"Without getting carried away," Tallie said. "We need to be careful *how* we ask questions. Try not to ask them like inquisitors. Or prosecutors. That's more of a note to self. *I* need to be careful."

"She knows we ask questions, though," Janet said. "But you're right. My note to self—don't be too nosy. Just nosy enough. But we'll keep in mind to keep *her* mind at ease."

"Snore," Christine said, startling the others.

"Dinnae fash. You haven't been snoring," Janet said kindly.

"Of course I haven't. I haven't been asleep. I've been listening. And agreeing with everything you've said, including the need for a gentle touch. I still think there's merit in riling, but I also think we're enough in the murk about what's going on that we need to be careful. We want to keep our suspects somnolent. Hence, SNORE—Soothing, No Overt Riling Evident."

"Love it," Summer said.

"I do, too," Tallie said. "One for all and all for SNORE."

"It's perfect, Christine," Janet said. "Let's just be sure we don't slip up and poke a sleeping bear."

"Or a nest of vipers," Christine said. "Our turn's just ahead. Take a left."

"Vipers," Janet said. "Lovely."

∽

Violet started talking as soon as she opened the door. "Och, you're *droochit*. Like drowned rats. Come ben, come ben. Don't mind the drips. This floor's seen far worse than a bit of rain. Come ben and shake yourselves off."

Tallie and Summer presented the flowers and scones. Violet thanked them and gave them directions on where to hang up their coats before turning to Christine and asking about her dear friend Helen. Janet considered the marked difference in Violet's liveliness between this visit and their last. Why the change, she wondered? *They'd* been hoping to avoid Teresa and Edward. Maybe Violet felt a sense of relief when her spatting children stayed away, too.

"We'll sit in the sunroom," Violet said, herding them ahead of her like a flock of chickens. "We can sit with ferns and pretend it's a beach in Portugal. I've never been but Teresa and Isobel tell me it's lovely. I'm not drinking caffeine these days, and I can't abide herbal drinks that call themselves tea. But I can make some for you. Shall I?"

"Och no," Christine said. "We don't want to be a bother."

"That's fine then." Violet sat and beamed at them. "I've a confession. I prattle. It's because I get a wee bit lonely here by myself. There now. Good for the soul. Only a few come to visit, and most of them are more interested in the house or something in it, than the old lady who lives in the shoe. Now I'm being silly and sorry for myself."

"Who comes to visit the house and not you?" Tallie asked. "What nonsense is that?"

"The writer chappy. Ian. I don't like his type of books. I prefer romance. Wendy visits. It's possible she prefers the house to the old lady—" Violet held up her hand for a moment. "I forget the tragedy that she's gone."

"It must have been nice to have Bethia here," Summer said.

"Delightful. Isobel arranged it, though I do understand about it being easier for her to get about in town. I want to thank you all for taking on Teresa's case. Do you call it a case?"

"Among ourselves, anyway," Janet said.

"I did hear that you are very quiet about your work, so I've not spread it around and warned Teresa not to as well. I worried when she told me she had no intention of talking to you again, but now there's no need, so I suppose that's all right." Her voice sank. "Isobel told me about the suicide and the note. A terrible heartbreak and a burden his mother will carry to her own grave."

"Unimaginable," Christine said. "Janet saw his mother at the decluttering."

Violet nodded.

"I'm glad she enjoyed herself that night," Christine said, "because none of us ever knows what's coming around the next corner. It's nice to think back on the early part of that lovely evening and remember all the happy faces. Isn't it, Janet?"

"Absolutely. I didn't know most of the—" Janet wished they'd practiced this. "But James Haviland. He was there and had a great time. And . . . Kyle. I saw Kyle Byrne."

"The young man who works for Maida Fairlie's cleaners," Violet said. "He isn't much of a cleaner. He has a tendency to sit and read rather than work. I found him knitting one time. But I'm glad he came."

"So many interesting people," Christine said. "Did all of you work together on the guest list? You, Isobel, Teresa, and Edward?"

"No, I asked them to leave it to me."

"Then, will you solve a mystery for me?" Janet asked. "I had a great time at the decluttering, but you'd never met me. How did I get on your list?"

"I let Isobel whisper a few suggestions," Violet said with a twinkle. "Don't tell Teresa and Edward, because I did not let them."

"Is that why Euan's mother was invited?" Tallie asked.

"Aye.

"I think the decluttering was a cool idea," Summer said.

"So well-planned, too," Janet said. "Who organized the clutter so beautifully?"

"Teresa. Her forte," Violet said. "Such a mind for details."

"Did she set the museum donation aside, too?" Tallie asked

"That was Isobel and Edward. Isobel has carted it all off, now, and the whole house feels lighter."

"I know that feeling," Janet said. "When we moved here, I let go of so many things. Teresa was worried, though, when we met with her. She thought that some of the clutter was too valuable to just give away."

"I kept plenty that was more valuable," Violet said. "More than I should have. People didn't take everything I hoped they would, either. 'Things' are burdens. So are Teresa's constant reminders that I'm old, getting older, and someday won't be able to make my own decisions." Violet put a hand over her mouth then took it away. "Please overlook my outburst."

"No apology needed," Janet said. "My brother badgered my mother the same way. It sent her into a tailspin of depression. To him, that just confirmed the point."

"As if she didn't know what was happening to her," Violet said. Then she grabbed Christine's hand. "Never do that to Helen. Never. Do you hear me?"

"Never," Christine assured her.

"Then I'm glad you came to your senses and came back home to Inversgail. Now, come with me. I do know when I need help, and I have something you lassies might enjoy doing for me. We'll go up to the first floor."

Christine waved Tallie and Summer after Violet, but held Janet back. "She looks delicate, but she has a claw and the grip of a corbie who's not sharing the roadkill."

"Good Lord."

"I hope mine's as strong when I'm that age. Come on."

Violet took them up a grand staircase and down a wide hallway, where they passed two closed doors on either side. The hall came to an end in front of another door. "The real library," Violet said, and opened the door. The room spanned the width of the house and was again as deep. The wall in front of them, as they walked in, was lined with windows looking across the hills. The other walls held floor to ceiling bookshelves.

"Gorgeous," Janet said.

"I'd have let people help themselves to these, too, if I hadn't finally let Teresa have some say. Now I want someone in to value the books and I'll sell them. Donate the money to charity. The library, the school. More to the museum. You have book experience, book knowledge. Can you do it for me?"

All four of them were shaking their heads before she finished asking. "You need someone with more expertise than we have," Janet said.

"You can tell just standing there? You haven't looked at them."

"I don't really need to," Janet said. "The bindings alone—all that leather and gilt—tell me we'd be out of our league."

"Is this Humbug's library?" Christine asked. "Is this where Ian Atkinson has been doing his research?"

"Is that what he's up to? It's hard to know."

"He didn't tell you?" Tallie asked. "Did he tell you about a scrapbook he found?"

"That, yes. He didn't say much about it. But if it was on the top shelf, like he said, it was out of my reach, even with Humbug's ladder. It's a shame it's gone, if he needed it for his research. Then again, if he needed it, maybe he took it himself. He's a secretive sort."

"He is," Janet said.

On their way back down the stairs Tallie asked if anyone had found the missing Rodine. Violet said they hadn't, but no one seemed to mind anymore, so she didn't either. She sounded tired and Janet thought they'd probably disappointed her about the books, too.

"The Rodine's just another thing," Violet said, "and things have a way of going missing, don't they?"

"They do," Tallie said. "Has Isobel told you about the stockings missing from the museum?"

"No, she hasn't. Stockings? Whatever for?" Violet shook her head. "Since the worry over the Rodine, I went to see if I could put my hands on the wee bitty bit of arsenic I used to see in the garden shed. Now that's something you don't want getting into the wrong hands. But I can't find that either."

"Huh," Tallie said. "Maybe someone got rid of it?"

"We must have. I don't mind seeing it anytime recently. Not for yonks."

"How long is a yonk?" Summer asked."

"Quite a while. Do you think I should tell Norman?"

"Yes."

"Then I shall."

"How did you know about our cases and calling ourselves SCONES?" Tallie asked.

"Maida. She bragged about you when she saw Norman looking high and low for the Rodine. She said you'd do a better job. Are you sure about the books?"

"We'll see if we can find someone for you," Janet said.

They thanked her but before they'd finished saying goodbye, Violet had closed the door. On the drive back to town, Summer asked Janet if she had doubted Maida when she told them she hadn't helped Teresa organize the clutter.

"Maida? Never. I wondered about something Teresa said at the decluttering. Violet complimented her on the organization, and Teresa said *under your eye. Always under your eye.* But Maida and Violet say otherwise."

"You find one lie and you start looking for more," Tallie said. "Do we believe Violet about the scrapbook? Or the arsenic? *Arsenic.* Who mentions missing arsenic so casually? *I* sure don't know her well enough to be sure."

"None of us do," Christine said, "and Mum might only remember Violet the girl."

"I really do like the idea of the decluttering," Summer said. "You're right, Janet, we did that before moving here. Once a decade sounds like a plan, to me."

"Teresa thought and still thinks it was nutty," Christine said.

"She would. And it is out of the norm," Summer said. "But is it also out of Violet's norm? What if someone talked her into it as a way to stage a murder?"

"That sounds like a complicated way to stage a murder," Janet said.

"It does," Summer said. "But what if someone knew about the decluttering, knew Fairy Flax Hall, and took advantage of that setup? I'll put that in the 'Theories' document."

"Your complicated theory, too," Janet said. "So, we've heard that Teresa, Edward, and Isobel each took what they wanted. And the museum got its donation and can look forward to a big chunk of change from Violet's will. But I wonder who gets the house?"

"The house could be a motive for murder," Tallie said. "Suppose someone wants it and knows they're not getting it? Or is getting it but doesn't want to wait? Too bad that isn't the kind of thing you can go around and ask."

"Or get an honest answer if you do," Christine said.

"It was nice to have an unsupervised visit with her, though," Tallie said.

"Didn't it seem like Violet was lighter in spirit, too, without Teresa and Edward there?" Janet asked. "It made me worry about her, especially when she said Teresa badgers her. I wonder if we can ask Isobel if Violet's being bullied?"

"There's another difference between this visit and our last," Christine said. "A problem's been solved, if it was a problem. Euan Markwell is dead. Whose mind is resting easier because of that?"

20

Arsenic diary, day eight

Someone has stuck me with a pin. I slump in a corner of the sofa barely able to hold my pen. The only part of me that has not deflated is my sense of melodrama. That author, the one so taken with himself, knows about the scrapbook. He's acting as though he discovered its very existence. As if that gives him ownership. Now he's running up and down the High Street telling anyone who'll listen that it's missing, and people are talking about it. A woman in line ahead of me at the bank told it to the one ahead of her. The women in the bookshop can barely contain themselves, wondering what evil is loose in the world until the scrapbook is found. My words, not theirs. They're actually a fairly level-headed lot. But the point is, all this talk, all this exposure dilutes the pleasure of the scrapbook. The way you feel when you hear people gushing over a novel you feel viscerally connected to, privately so. That public gushing by others pricks a hole. It lets the magic out. Diminishing. Diluting. Deflating.

Deteriorating—if that author chappie had his hands on the scrapbook before I rescued it, did he mistreat it? Did brittle glue unbind? Did fragile clippings slip unheeded into his messenger bag? Perhaps enquiring minds should find out.

Perhaps I might also start my own collection of clippings. Shall I? Hide them away, piece by piece, like a canny, scrapbooking *squirrel? I look around at the books on my shelves. Several of them might be improved with scissors, glue, and the addition of more interesting material. And pictures! Are my creative juices flowing? No, not my style. Instead, I pour a glass and raise it in admiration of other people's energy. I put my feet up and admire the scrapbook again—the dear old girl.*

∞

The women had no particular business information to share at their meeting the next morning. Janet sent a text to Constable Hobbs. Summer set out an extra cup and a plate with two extra freshly baked fig scones. Christine poured tea. Bait laid, they waited. Not for long. Hobbs knocked at the bookshop door, and Tallie went to let him in.

"Good morning, Norman," Janet said. "Is this visit because of my most recent text, or are you attending to the backlog that must be threatening to bury you?"

Hobbs, reaching for the plate of scones Tallie held out to him, pulled his hand back and took out his notebook. Janet immediately felt bad, but also pleased that her carefully worded and timed text had done the trick. *Arsenic at Fairy Flax—urgent*, sent when he'd know that tea and scones were being consumed.

"Eat your scones, Norman," Janet said. "The arsenic news won't take long. Or take them with you, if you want, but at least drink your tea."

"She's right," Christine said. "A hooked fish still gets the worm."

"A delightful invitation, Mrs. Robertson," Hobbs said. He took the plate of scones from Tallie and a cup of tea from Summer. Not a nibbler by nature, he finished the scones quickly and appreciatively, drank his tea, and brought the notebook out again, flipping its iridescent pink cover open.

"Your great-niece has superlative taste in notebooks," Janet said.

"I'll tell her you said so. The arsenic?"

"Is like the Rodine," Janet said. "Violet might or might not have a stash of it. Possibly in the garden shed. She went looking for it, didn't find it, and can't remember when she last saw it. She told us about it yesterday."

"Alarmingly offhand about it," Tallie said.

"But she said she'd tell you." Janet watched him taking his meticulous, crabbed notes. "She hasn't, though—or you wouldn't be taking notes."

Hobbs thanked them, without answering her, and put his notebook away.

"Any information to share?" Janet asked. "Our other texts in your queue asked about the scrapbook and Euan Markwell's supposed suicide." She looked at the others. "Anything else?"

Christine raised her hand. "If you were already there at Fairy Flax Hall Friday night, why did it take you so long to respond?"

Hobbs scratched his eyebrow. Janet couldn't tell if that was contemplative or just an itch. Perhaps it helped with his decision to not answer the question. He thanked them for the tea and scones then nodded toward the tearoom door. Summer let him out.

"Well, he is supposed to be off the case," Tallie said.

"Mm-hm." Christine gathered teacups, teapot, and plates and stalked back to the tearoom kitchen.

Janet agreed with that and stalked to the bookshop sales counter. Not long after they'd opened their doors to the public, the bell above Yon Bonnie's door jingled, and Inspector Reddick walked in.

"Good morning, Mrs. Marsh, Ms. Marsh. If this is not an inopportune time, may we speak in your wee office? Though I don't like to exclude any of you—"

"I'll go get Christine," Tallie said. She came back with Christine and Summer.

"Rab's got the tearoom," Summer said. "Ranger's got the inglenook."

Tallie put Rab's sign asking customers to pay in the tearoom on the counter, then squeezed into the narrow space they used for their office, taking a seat with the other women. Reddick went to the far end of the room, away from the door and remained standing.

"Did you pass our constable friend on your way here?" Christine asked.

Reddick scratched his eyebrow much the way Hobbs had. "That might have been him I caught sight of. I've two updates for you. Information that's to go no further. Understood?"

They nodded agreement.

"Arsenic has been confirmed as the cause of death in both victims." He leaned so heavily on the word *arsenic*, Janet felt she needed a deep breath.

"So then," Reddick said, "I believe you already know that a suicide note was found at the scene of Mr. Markwell's death. However, and this is the second update, we do not believe that he took his own life."

"Why isn't that information being released?" Summer asked.

"It will be in time. Now, if you'll indulge me in one of my hobbies for a moment. I'm a history buff. History of forensics, which probably won't surprise you, and I've a question for the Marsh women. Are you aware that James Marsh of Edinburgh developed the first reliable test for detecting small amounts of arsenic in food and human remains? In one of the earliest developments of a chemical test for investigative purposes—1836. He isn't, by chance, a relation, is he?"

"To my ex-husband, if at all, but his family came from France and Alsace." Janet thought Reddick might have been starstruck if she'd said yes.

"Cool guy," Tallie said, looking at her phone. "But weird hair. He combed it forward at his temples, like Napoleon." She pocketed the phone and disappeared through the door.

"Thank you for trusting us with this information, Inspector," Christine said. "All of it. We will continue to keep our eyes and ears open. We've identified a possible source for the arsenic. But is there more we can do? Search for other sources? Keep tabs on suspects? Tail them? Collect handwriting samples for comparison with the supposed suicide note? I think we might be very good at that last."

"A generous offer, Mrs. Robertson. Your listening skills are most important at this point. I'd rather you not put yourselves in danger with searches and tailing. As for the rest, I shall get my team organized and then get back to you. Keeping in mind that I don't want to keep you from your primary business."

Tallie reappeared and handed Reddick a white bakery bag. "It's not fair the other Norman got some and you didn't. We owe you a cup of tea, though."

"Ta. I look forward to it, and I'll be in touch."

"I think he knew I wasn't being serious," Christine said when he'd left.

"You weren't?" Summer asked. "And did he?"

"Of course he did," Janet said.

"For the most part, anyway" Christine said, and went back to the tearoom.

"I'll make an 'Arsenic' document," Summer said. "Will it be useful to include poisons with similar symptoms to arsenic?"

"It seems unnecessary with arsenic confirmed." Janet looked at Tallie who nodded in agreement.

"Good." Summer pointed after Christine. "I'll keep an eye on that one, too."

Later that morning, between customers, Janet opened the new "Arsenic" document. Even with a busy morning in the tearoom, Summer had found time to assemble an impressive amount of distressing information and send a copy to Hobbs.

∽

It was Hobbs, not Reddick, who got back to them. He stopped in the tearoom first, to thank Summer for the arsenic information she'd sent. He'd found it very informative. "Mindboggling as well." Christine followed him into the bookshop. Hobbs browsed until the sales counter was free of customers, then approached.

"Inspector Reddick wonders if you would speak to Elaine Markwell," he said, looking more at Janet than Christine. "He and his men have questioned her, but she will no doubt react differently to you."

"Does she know that the police don't believe her son committed suicide?" Janet asked. "It would be cruel not to tell her."

"She does. She won't know that you do, and she's been asked not to say anything."

"Also cruel, Norman," Christine said. "What do you hope we'll learn under these circumstances?"

"Although, perhaps not all four of you should go." Hobbs gave Christine a sidelong glance. "Perhaps not—"

"Of course not, Norman," Christine said. "No need to worry. We'll not do that. Rest easy."

"In that case." He touched the brim of his cap somewhat uneasily and left.

"What aren't we doing?" Janet asked.

"We aren't telling *me* to whom I'd best not speak. I'm a fully-trained, board-certified, experienced social worker. If I don't know how to approach a newly bereaved mother, who might be a murderer, *and* approach her with the utmost empathy and kindness, I'd like to know who does. Now, what's the next step?"

"We just told Norman we'd talk to Elaine Markwell."

"That's his idea of a next step. And not bad for starters. What's ours?"

"Organize our thinking. You know how we do this."

"How we do this is we go to Nev's and have several rounds of Selkie's Tears."

"Perfect timing," Tallie said. "It's Monday."

"I'll call Danny and ask what's on for supper."

∽

Helen and David were also regulars at Nev's on Monday nights. They'd missed the last Monday, but came along this time, with David hoping their old routine might disrupt the new one of nightmares. Christine settled them in at a table with old friends then stopped at the bar to order Monday night specials and half pints of Selkie's Tears for her parents and herself. Janet, Tallie, and Summer already waited for her at their usual table.

"A person should be free of bullies during the night," Christine said. "But that's what nightmares are. Maybe with a solution and an arrest that sticks they'll go away."

"That brings up my question about Violet being bullied," Janet said. "I worry about her. Have we wondered before if Wendy was the intended victim? I think we have."

"If she wasn't, that would sure make it harder to figure out a motive," Tallie said.

"Now I remember. When Christine and I were waiting in line at the food truck we wondered about that." Janet took out her phone and added those thoughts to the appropriate documents. Across the table, like a mirror image, Tallie had just finished tapping at her phone.

Christine and Summer mirrored each other too—each lost in thought. Christine kept glancing toward her parents' table. It was easy to guess her worries. Summer's mood was easy to guess, too. Her impatience surfaced at the beginning of every investigation, along with slips into annoyance and snapping at people because she couldn't get hold of facts fast enough. Janet thought she'd probably been like that when she started important or tricky newspaper assignments, too. She'd learned to appreciate Summer's problem-solving skills, but still felt personally snapped at sometimes. She also knew better than to mention that or to mother Summer. Sometimes she mothered anyway.

Christine's mood brightened when Danny brought their suppers. They'd all opted for the special—Scotch Eggs, chips, and beans—from the new menu. Danny sat for a moment while they took first bites.

"Fabulous," Christine pronounced. "With food this good, you're courting danger. It might lure tourists."

"I'm ready for them with limp salads and surly comments, which might deter them, but if not, who am I to judge?"

"Are you mellowing?" Tallie asked.

"I want to replace the cooker and a few more customers will help that along. It's a 'soft open' version of attracting new custom, mind. Nothing as blatant as advertising."

"What about the old sign?" Janet asked. "Or is that a myth?"

"Shrouded in myth and dust in a far corner of the cellar," Danny said. "I thought about re-hanging it. Maybe dusting it off, possibly not. I ran it by James and reckon his idea holds water. Hang the sign, and folk might come to see it. Talk up the mystique surrounding the *absent* sign, and they'll go a step farther and come inside. That saves the work of dusting and hanging it, too." He started back to the bar calling, "Let me know when you're ready for your other halves."

"Myth and mystique sounds like a new scent for bath products," Christine said.

"One of the poets at the slam had a refrain that included 'myth and mystique,'" Summer said. "That reminds me of something I've been trying to tease from the back of my mind. About a connection between the decluttering and the slam. The poetry slam was scheduled weeks in advance, just like the knitting in our inglenook. But knitting at the slam was a late addition to the museum's competition programming."

"But the poetry and knitting happened at the same time as the decluttering, with miles between the pub and Violet's house," Janet said. "What's the connection between them and Wendy's death?"

"Tenuous, tenuous." Summer's eyes and face screwed up with the effort to bring the connection, or the opposite wall, into focus.

"Tenuous is fine," Janet said.

Summer's gaze shifted from the wall to the empty glass in front of her. "There might not be a connection to the murder." She tapped the side of the glass. "Anyone else ready?"

"I'm good," Tallie said. The others murmured the same.

"I'm not." Summer snatched up her glass and went to wait her turn at the bar.

"Maybe the connection is the last-minute timing," Tallie said.

"Maybe you should wait for Ms. Prickles so she can agree or jump down your throat," Christine said.

"I'll repeat it for her," Tallie said. "Isobel's program schedule was so meticulous that I had scheduling envy. But she's obviously open to additions and changes. So then, what if the change gave someone an alibi?"

"How?" Janet asked. "Don't answer yet. Think about it until Summer's back."

"And eat your supper before someone else does," Tallie said. "What'll we do if Danny attracts so many new customers that we can't get our usual table?"

A horrified look came over Christine's face. She gestured for the other two to lean in and whispered, "Start a rumor about food poisoning. Was all this—the rumors, Wendy, Euan's faked suicide—someone being clever and overcomplicated about killing him?"

Summer sat back down and pushed her fresh glass aside. "What if the last-minute addition of knitting to the slam gave someone an alibi?"

Janet decided déjà vu didn't hurt. "How?"

"Someone goes to both. Pretends they only went to the slam. We've already wondered about someone using the decluttering for cover." Summer pulled her plate over and started eating. "Whoa, this is great. What'll we do if Danny starts attracting too much business?" Janet's déjà vu returned full force. Summer took a swallow of ale and went back to eating.

"We should find out the how, why, and who of the knitting being added to the slam," Tallie said, making a note to do that.

"Like Bethia's venue in the tearoom," said Christine.

"That was Rab fixing the difficulty with Kyle," Tallie said. "So did the knitting at the slam fix a problem, too?"

"The more I think it through, the more I think it's rubbish." Summer slumped in her chair, taking her momentary recovery from her dudgeon with her.

"Kyle did show up at both events," Janet said.

"He's a bit of a bumbler," Tallie said.

Summer sat up straighter. "What was that you put in a document last night about bumblers, Janet?"

"What do you call a bumbling, amateur killer?"

"I wonder if we call him Kyle?" Summer bounced out of her chair and grabbed her glass. "Game, Tallie? Best of three."

Tallie groaned and trailed after her.

Janet and Christine noticed another change in Nev's that evening. People dropped by their table more than usual. They sat, shared critiques of the weather, gave news of family members Christine might remember, dropped a crumb of gossip, then bid them goodnight. And then someone else came along.

"Might have a spate of sunshine the morn," one said. "Shame about Wendy. A good fundraiser. A sad loss for the museum."

"Nice to see your mum and dad in tonight," another said. "Nice to have you back in Inversgail, as well. Like when Edward MacAskill came home from Edinburgh after his wife died. Cancer's a scourge."

"What do youse think of Danny's new menu?" From a man carrying two full pints in each hand. He leaned closer, threatening to spill on Christine. "Have you heard about the book of poison recipes that's gone missing? Find that, find some answers, aye?"

And an old friend of Helen's who sat down with them and looked wistfully toward the bar. Christine said it was their round and bought her a shandy. "Ta, Christine. You're so like your lovely mum, and like Violet, too. There's no 'lady of the manor' about her. Joins right in for the hard work when it comes to a church fete. She's a doer, not dour. Edward says that. A great one with a story. So like Violet."

When they were alone again, Christine said, "This has nothing to do with the new menu. What's going on?"

"They might not know the name SCONES," Janet said, "but I think they've heard about us, and they're bringing us tidbits they think might be helpful."

"Most of it isn't. They're bringing us innocuous *clishmaclaver* or warm, fuzzy blather."

"Yeah, phooey on innocuous and warm and fuzzy," Janet said. "We're into cold-blooded and nocuous clishmahaver."

"Claver not haver, though much of it's been havering, too."

"We've heard *some* snark. That couple drinking Newcastle Brown thinks Wendy was jealous of Isobel."

"Jealous of her family, fortune, and grace," Christine said. "Made me think they're jealous, too."

"Maida's better with useful information. She's like a crow bringing us shiny things that usually turn out to be valuable. Don't ever tell her I said she's like a crow."

"I could. It looks like her Pub Scrawl meeting is breaking up. How does this sound? She's like a faithful retriever bringing your newspaper."

"That's better. Don't ever tell her I said that, either."

Maida nodded as she walked past on her way out.

"Goodnight, Maida." Janet said as someone else arrived at their table. "Hello, James. Summer's playing darts."

"Ta, Janet. You've had a lot of traffic this evening. Have you set up a new office? FYI, in case you have, Maida was not impressed by the caliber of your informants. I, on the other hand, am always happy to hear what *you've* been hearing. Anything good?"

"Sorry, James. Maida's right," Christine said.

He flapped a hand and went into the darts room. Christine turned back to Janet. "I hate to say it, but I'm not impressed with our caliber of anything on this case so far."

"Neither am I. We need to do something. Be proactive."

"We've been to Fairy Flax Hall twice and we're going to see Elaine Markwell," Christine said. "We've talked to and been berated by Teresa."

"Then we need to be *more* proactive."

Tallie, on her way from the darts room to the bar, overheard her mother. "Did you just use a buzzword? You hate buzzwords."

"Your mother isn't thinking as clearly as she usually does," Christine said. "Snap out of it, Janet. We count on you for your clear thinking."

"I've had more Selkie's than I usually do."

Rab and Ranger nodded on their way from Maida's meeting to the darts room. The women nodded back.

"Is it my imagination or has Rab been working more hours lately?" Janet asked.

"He's canny that way," Christine said.

"Good, then if the rest of you are amenable, and he is, too, I thought I might volunteer for a few hours a couple of times a week at the museum, if Isobel will have me. It'll be a chance to—"

"Snoop?" Tallie asked.

"Help with dusting or filing. Or something."

"Only if you're careful," Christine said.

"Only if you're legal," Tallie said. "What do you hope to find?"

"No idea. I'll be on a fishing expedition, but I'll try not to get hung up trying to crack Edward's fishy secret sock code."

"Why is it fishy?" Tallie asked. "There really were knitted codes, weren't there?"

"The code *is* fish. So he says. If you want to try working it out, I'll take pictures."

"Don't waste your time on it, Tallie," Christine said. "I can tell you what kind of fish they are and exactly what Edward's coded message means." She had their full attention. "Have you heard of the herring lasses? They followed their fishermen, the ones they knitted the ganseys for, round the coast. That makes Edward's fish herrings. Red herrings. And that's herrings spelt h-a-v-e-r-s."

"I think she's right," Janet said. "The code's in a pair of stockings not a gansey, but that hardly matters. Christine says havers. I say hooey. Knitted codes existed but, in this case, I think Edward made the whole thing up."

"If you do find something that really is fishy at the museum, don't remove it," Tallie said. "Try not to touch it."

"I might not find anything at all. I'm not really expecting to. If I do, I'll take pictures. And don't worry. My number one priority is running our business, not running after criminals."

"That's the clear-thinking Mom I've come to know and love. I'm going to stay for a few more games."

"I'll see she gets home," Christine said. She waited until Tallie was at the bar, then said, "If you find anything the least bit fishy, call me."

21

Janet jerked awake when the cats growled. Had they growled? She'd been reading one of the arsenic articles Summer found, with the cats snuggled beside her on the sofa . . . where were they? She closed the laptop. Stood up. "Smirr? Butter?" She heard the growls again, low in the cats' throats, coming from the dining room. "Have you found something?" She cringed, not really wanting to know, imagining gnashing incisors and a long, hairless tail. Then she heard a shout—yelling—*Tallie!* Janet was out the door running through the dark following her daughter's voice.

They found each other at the bottom of the garden, Tallie breathing hard; Janet wondering if she'd ever breathe again.

"He got away," Tallie said. "If I'd been faster—what am I *saying*? Oh my god, what was I doing chasing that—"

"Did he hurt you?" Janet asked. She held Tallie's face in her hands, looked into her eyes, wrapped her in a hug. "What happened? You're shaking, sweetheart. Are you hurt? Come back to the house. What did he do? Come inside."

"We have to call Norman." Tallie shook Janet off and fumbled for her phone, starting for the house as she pressed 9-9-9. "I'm not hurt," she told her mother, phone to her ear, waiting for the dispatcher to answer. "I promise. And no one was after *me*. Hello, yes, I'm reporting a prowler. I'm pretty sure I just interrupted a break in." Tallie stopped walking as the dispatcher asked questions. "No, not my house. The neighbor's. Ian Atkinson. Fourth house along on the west side of Argyll Terrace. No, I yelled and he took off. Thank you. Yes, we'll meet the constable out front."

"You ran after a prowler in the dark?" Janet asked. "Do you have any idea what my daughter would say if *I* did that?"

"You did, actually. You came to my rescue with no idea what was going on. Like a mother lion. And now I'm going to cry because I scared the beetroot out of myself."

"You have a good cry, darling. I might, too. But first I'm going to shake my fist at Ian who's standing up there in his window with a cup of tea, watching."

Tallie stood with her mouth open for a moment, then snapped it shut. "Okey doke. That worked. I don't feel like crying at all now. Let's go wait for Norman. And if he's going to talk to Ian, I want to be there, too. Norman should let us both be there."

Hobbs arrived faster than he'd responded to Teresa's call at Fairy Flax Hall during the decluttering. Janet barely had time to put a coat on and let the cats know they were heroes with growls of glory, before Hobbs braked to a halt in their driveway, leapt from the car with a large flashlight, and trotted over. He asked Tallie to describe what had happened, then asked if Ian was home.

"He is, but we haven't spoken to him," Tallie said.

"We didn't want to add that element to an already fraught situation," Janet said.

"Very wise."

"He does know something's up, though," Janet added, "because he's been watching from his window."

"Thank you for the warning. Now, if you'll wait here, I'll have a look round the scene. Make sure the prowler's well away and not waiting for a second chance." He walked purposefully around the house, shining the bright light on doors and windows and in the shrubbery. He made a careful search of Ian's backyard, flashed the light over Ian's house, including the window in Ian's writing room where he'd been watching. He repeated the search in the Marsh backyard. After flicking the light one more time at Ian's window, he made his way back to where Janet and Tallie waited.

"Any signs of him?" Tallie asked.

"Mr. Atkinson is no longer in his window, no."

"I meant the prowler."

"Also no longer in evidence."

"Do you think he *will* come back?" Janet asked.

"Why don't we knock on Mr. Atkinson's door and include him in this conversation. He must be curious, and by now he's had plenty of time to put the kettle on."

Ian's kitchen door stood directly below the window in his writing room. Hobbs knocked and appeared to be counting how many seconds went by before Ian opened it. Janet was glad that Ian didn't try to feign surprise. Even though he hadn't come outside to see what was going on, his concern probably wasn't feigned, either. His hospitality was. Though he invited them into the kitchen, and to sit at the table, he didn't offer them anything, despite the steaming kettle on the stove and a package of biscuits on the counter. But he did get in the first words.

"It was all over so fast. By the time the sounds registered as shouts, and the shouts as possible distress, it was quiet again. Then I saw you two. Then Constable Hobbs, and at that point it didn't seem prudent to rush outside and add one more person to whatever confusion there might be. So first, is everyone all right, and then, what happened?"

Tallie let her mouth hang open again, but only for a second this time. "He's right. *I* knew what was going on, and Mom found out because she's Mom and she came running, but if he was up there writing, listening to music, snoozing, standing there with a cup of tea as he so often does, he would hardly notice. It *was* over fast. I'm fine, Ian. We're fine. Thank you for asking. Your house is fine, too. I scared the guy off."

"*What?*"

Hobbs, who so far had only been observing, filled Ian in.

"But *who*?" Ian asked.

"Likely someone local," Hobbs said. "Ran down through the garden, away from the streetlights. Either familiar with the neighborhood or checked it out ahead of time."

Tallie apologized for being such a poor witness. "I think a man. But dark clothes, nothing distinctive about height, weight, or how he ran. He never said a word."

"Any idea why someone would choose your house, Mr. Atkinson?"

"The scrapbook. Why else? I have been trying to tell you and Inspector Reddick that the scrapbook is important to this case. Is this what it takes for you to believe me? Either or both of these women could have been hurt tonight. Why, if the scrapbook has no bearing on the case, has someone tried to get it from me twice?"

"Whilst you've done your messages, visited in and out of the shops, have you told people about the scrapbook?" Hobbs asked.

"Only in an attempt to recover it. You aren't suggesting that I've brought this on myself, are you?"

"Not at all Mr. Atkinson. I just wondered why someone would come looking for something here that you've been telling people you don't have."

"That's for you to figure out." Ian was beginning to sound like an irritated, petulant child.

Janet took pity on him. He often played games, but tonight he'd shown concern for them, and he'd had a shock, too. She changed the subject slightly, shifting the focus. "I hope the scrapbook turns up, Ian. I think Humbug would be happy knowing it's safe and sound again. How did you happen to think of doing research at Fairy Flax Hall?"

"Teresa invited me. We were a bit of an item for a time. She isn't always so buttoned down, you know. She came up with her own cocktail while we were together. Shortly before we split, actually. She calls it the Cheerful Brush-off."

After a wince, Tallie said, "Not to pursue a sore subject, but have you been spreading rumors about secret codes in the scrapbook?"

"I am insulted. I have not distorted the description of the scrapbook in any way. I reported its disappearance and, since then, the theft of my messenger bag. Tonight, someone tried to get into my house. If there is nothing else you need from me, Constable Hobbs, then it is late. My last word on the subject is simply this. Something poisonous is going on."

Hobbs walked Janet and Tallie to their door and thanked them for their community involvement. "Though, in future, I would advise a phone call rather than the additional involvement of a steeplechase after unknown perpetrators. Or known."

"We'll take that to heart, Norman," Janet said. "But what's your take on this. The prowler and Ian insisting the scrapbook is vital to the case?"

"It's late, Mrs. Marsh, and my last word on the subject is simply this." Hobbs pointed his thumb back over his shoulder toward Ian's house. "Master of understatement."

✍

The next morning's spate of sunshine warmed Janet and Christine on their way to see Elaine Markwell. They'd worried about how to explain a request from two strangers to drop by and pry into her tragic loss. They'd decided on the truth—they were friends of Isobel, they'd enjoyed eating at Mr. Potato Chef, and they'd been asked by Violet MacAskill to look for answers about Wendy Erskine's death.

"This might sound odd and self-congratulatory," Christine had told her over the phone, "but we've become quite good at solving—"

"I'll answer your questions. But not for long." Elaine had sounded beaten down. "And aye, Isobel told me about you."

The Markwells lived in a modern detached house on a street not far from where Christine and her parents lived. Janet and Christine saw Elaine watching for them in the large front window. They parked in the driveway behind the food truck and a pickup. Janet nudged Christine when she saw the pickup.

Elaine came out to meet them and said they'd sit in the garden. She led them around to the backyard where a wide, paved path ran from the house to a small wooden summerhouse. Windows on all four sides of the summerhouse looked out on the walled garden. They sat inside.

"Euan built this for his dad," Elaine said. "Pete's not well."

"Isobel told us," Christine said.

"This is killing him." Elaine stared at the back of the house as though her sight penetrated the walls to the man grieving inside.

"I saw you at Violet's decluttering," Janet said. "I envied that watering can, but I'm not the gardener you obviously are."

"The garden's a family effort. It's been good for Euan." Elaine glanced at them. "If you're good at looking for answers, you ken he got mixed up with drugs. He stopped that when Pete had his accident. He was turning into a real entrepreneur with the truck and a new business just getting started. Well, not quite started. We lent him the money for it. We're gey proud of him." Tears streamed down her face. "Ask your questions before I can't answer at all."

"My main question sounds inconsequential at this point," Janet said. "Why didn't you knock on the door in the sunroom when you heard the commotion?"

"It didn't sound desperate. Just not quite right. When I couldn't find Teresa quickly, I told Euan. He came along to the decluttering to help carry. He said he'd just seen Teresa and her mother. It was easier for him to go tell her himself than tell me where to find her. We were in a hurry by then to get home. I don't like to leave Pete for too long."

"How do you know Teresa?" Christine asked.

"By sight. By reputation. Isobel and Euan were at school together."

"We've run into her reputation, too." Janet smiled at the quirk that came and went from a corner of Elaine's lips. "Does she ever eat at Mr. Potato Chef?"

"I've no idea. I only helped out on the truck occasionally."

"What was Euan's new business?" Christine asked.

"A place where people can work out their stress. Sounds a bit mad, now. We bought an old bothy from the writer, Ian Atkinson. Euan thought it was perfect. That's all I can manage. I need to get back inside."

Janet and Christine left, feeling bowed down by the weight of the tragedy.

"I meant to bring scones," Christine said. "What a useless gesture."

"Her grief is absolutely raw."

"But is it grief because someone killed her son, or because she killed him?"

"How can you say that?"

"You thought of it first," Christine said.

"But you saw her. You heard it in her voice. Do you believe she could have done that?"

"No. But I think this is why Reddick wanted us to come see her. I wonder what he believes?"

⁜

Throughout that day, between selling books and brewing pots of tea, the women added entries to their most neglected document—"Suspects." Half an hour into their additions, Janet alphabetized the list by last name. An hour after that, Tallie changed the document's title to "Suspects and Motives."

Early in the afternoon, Tallie learned of two controversial additions to the document when she heard a surprised *what* from her mother and then a resigned *if Isobel's there, they should be, too.* Then a depressed *pfft.* The additions were Kyle, Bethia, and Norman Hobbs. Ian Atkinson was on the list because they included him on every suspect list.

"It's petty," Tallie said. "But not always without reason."

"Satisfying, too. He's always at the top of the list," Janet said "because we've never had a name that comes before Atkinson. He sold his bothy, by the way. To Elaine Markwell and her husband. Euan planned to put a business there."

"Huh."

"Christine has added 'opportunity' under every name. Have we heard from either Norman when they think Wendy swallowed the poison?"

"No, and from what I've read in the "Arsenic" document, it could have been hours before the decluttering."

"So Ian might have opportunity. Hard to see what his motive would be."

"Research purposes," Tallie said. "He can take a tax deduction on the arsenic. No, I've got it. He's framing Teresa for dumping him. I almost feel sorry for him and almost feel better about her."

Christine added a general note about motive to the document that spurred a blatter of additional entries.

CR: People who feel they have no control over a situation might try to impose control where they can. That doesn't necessarily solve the bigger problem, but it helps them cope. Needing control might give them a motive.

TM: What problem did killing Wendy solve? Short term? Long term? Tangential?

JM: Who among our suspects likes to find ways to take control?

SJ: Ian does. That's one of the reasons he's irritating and a suspect.

CR: Is he trying to control things or is he adding elements to situations and watching to see what happens?

JM: Adding elements. They aren't controlled experiments, though, and that's why they tend to blow up in his face.

SJ: Edward.

CR: Again, does he actually try to control?

JM: He watches other people control. He let Teresa take over when we went to look for the Rodine.

TM: Isobel, if you can judge by her scheduling and programming prowess.

SJ: Her attention to detail in preparing exhibits. Her arsenic research.

SJ: Teresa. The ultimate control freak.

TM: This isn't helping us narrow the list.

CR: Look at it from the other side. Who feels out of control?

JM: Violet? Remember her outburst about Teresa haranguing her? It made me think she was afraid. Bethia said she was a recipe that's missing an ingredient. Is control the missing ingredient?

TM: Kyle. He got his way with a new knitting venue.

JM: He got a tailcoat that wasn't part of the clutter.

CR: Norman is controlling what we hear about the case. He still hasn't said why it took him so long to respond to Teresa at the decluttering.

JM: You can't be serious about Norman.

CR: I am always fair and impartial during our investigations.

"Is Christine joking or is she serious about being fair and impartial?" Tallie asked as they closed out the register for the day.

"It would take a better detective than I am to figure that out."

22

Arsenic diary, day nine

The museum's public display of affection for arsenic is annoying. Who would have thought? I blame the museum exhibit. It's the museum's fault for drawing attention to poison and creating this hue and cry.

I was thrilled to discover that my scrapbook has a clipping of the original _London Times_ article quoted in part at the start of the Shocking Stocking exhibit at the museum. What the museum did not include is much more interesting.

"There are so many forms of accidental poisoning already known to be lying in ambush on all sides of us—in our dishes, on our walls, in the dresses, and scandal whispers, even on the blooming cheeks of ball-room beauties—that the discovery of a new social poison is of little interest to any but those whom it immediately concerns."

Oh, the insouciance!

For those of us in the know, and still in possession of a certain scrapbook, the world is our poisonous oyster. Where to start? At the beginning. The source. The arsenic. Regulations put the stuff out of reach for the uninformed. But arsenic cannot be destroyed, so if *one knows where it has been, there is a good chance it still will be there. That leads to a brilliant question: Is one of the threads of the investigation dyed with Scheel's green?*

Two more questions: What if I find the arsenic before anyone else? Will I tell? Oh, the humdrum moral conundrum of it all.

∽

"Bottom line," Summer said at their meeting Wednesday morning, "it wouldn't be that hard to get your hands on a lethal dose of arsenic. You just have to be creative."

Tallie finished her tea then looked askance at the dregs. "Finding the source is something the police can do better than we can."

"Unless we stumble across it," Janet said.

"Let's leave it for the police," Tallie said.

"We do stumble across bodies, or murders in general, more often than you'd think," Christine said.

"Seemingly out of the blue," Janet agreed. "But yes. We'll leave the arsenic to the police."

Tallie smiled. "Good."

"But we'll keep our eyes open," Christine said. "For tripping hazards."

"Speaking of which, I'm tripping along to the museum for my first volunteer session this morning." Janet handed her teacup to Tallie and waved goodbye.

∽

"First day is orientation," Isobel said. "We ask volunteers to read through their information folder and tour the staff areas. Lets you dip your toes before jumping in." With a wicked smile, she handed a thick packet to Janet. "You didn't know what you were in for, did you? Dinnae fash. We don't usually give the whole lot to all the volunteers, but I thought the tour notes might interest you. I don't expect we'll press you into duty as a tour guide, though. The tourists come for the accent as well as the history."

"We get a few disappointed customers in the bookshop," Janet said, "so I understand." *What I don't understand*, she thought, *is how you can't see past my accent, but Edward's stories are hunky dory. Maybe not quite the same thing, though, and I'm not the beloved uncle.*

"You've already seen the staff area on the first floor. Another time I'll show you round the ground floor. I can't take time now. I'm pulling together material for a special meeting of the board. They've decisions to make."

"Wendy's job?"

"Aye."

"Would you be interested if they offer it to you?"

"No use pretending. It's my dream job."

"Then I hope your dream comes true. Shall I sit in the gallery to read this?"

"You aren't paid, but you are staff now, so the staff area's fine." Isobel opened the panel door behind the reception desk for her. "Uncle Edward's bound to wander in, so you're not likely to get lonely. I'll be working out here if you need me. Coat closet is to your left. Worktable's disappeared under Gran's donations."

The donations on the worktable made a stack taller than Janet. No great feat, but more boxes were stowed under the table and on most of the chairs. The total mass of them was exciting. Janet hung her coat up then walked around the table imagining the wonders Violet had bestowed on the museum.

But the orientation folder called. She found an empty chair on the far side of the donation mountain, opened the folder, and ran her eyes down the table of contents. When she got to the bottom of the page, her eyes shifted back to the mountain of donations. Wendy died in the suite with the donations. Because of them? Or because she was alone in the suite, and that's where the killer caught up with her? Or that was where the arsenic caught up with her? But not because Euan gave her that arsenic. And poor Euan, who'd just been getting his feet back under him.

When she heard a pleasant tenor voice singing about a sailor, she momentarily forgot where she was. Then she wondered how long she'd been staring at the boxes. The singing stopped and Edward looked around a corner of the donations at her.

"Hello, Janet, Isobel told me I might find you here. How nice to see you."

"Nice to see you, too, Edward. I've just been marveling over this mound of donations from your mother. Isobel must be pleased. I'm sure Wendy would've been, too."

"You knew her?" Edward asked.

"Um, no."

"I didn't think so. She was never quite satisfied."

"Oh."

"Well, perfectionists rarely are. That's all I meant. She knew what she wanted for the museum and how to go after it. An admirable quality in a leader." Edward moved the boxes from one chair to the precarious stack on another and sat. "She was a completist, as well. I am one myself, but not with collections of things. With the stories in our history. They're fascinating. I love completing a picture. I am rooted in my love of customs, habits, manners, traditions, trappings, and stories. They made me who I am, nurtured me through good times and bad."

Oh dear, Janet thought. *Trapped.*

"Wendy was a completist in her professional life, making it a blessing and a pain in the *bahookie*. She wanted museum collections to be as complete as possible. She wanted exhibits to give complete information, sometimes to the detriment of the exhibit. You might wonder what an old duffer like me knows about it. I'm a career ad man. I know how to catch the public's attention and how to get the necessary information across in as few words as possible. Wendy always wanted more. More information.

Denser labels. When Isobel could wrench the bone of completism from Wendy's teeth, they made a good team."

"Was Wendy unhappy with the donations?" Janet asked. "Teresa had said Wendy was unhappy about the decluttering."

"I wonder what Teresa knows about Wendy and what made her happy. Bad rhymes in poor taste did, for instance. Wendy wouldn't have minded about what I said the night she died. The woman had her faults. We all do. But not being able to take a joke at her own expense wasn't one of them."

"That was sweet, Uncle Edward," Isobel's voice came from the other side of the mountain of boxes. Janet wondered how long she'd been there or if she'd just come in. "A bit backhanded and unfair to Mother, but Wendy would have liked that, too. Janet, I'm leaving a stack of board packets on my desk. I've run out of staples out front. May I interrupt your orientation reading and ask you to staple them for me?"

"Of course. Quick question, before you go, though. The knitting at the poetry slam was such a hit. Was that a late addition to your schedule?"

"Not officially. We have a few rogue knitters in the competition taking matters into their own hands. I wish I *had* thought of it. If you don't find me before you leave, just leave a note or text me when you'll next be in."

"Will do."

"I'm very fond of Isobel and happy to help her and the museum do this important work," Edward said when she'd gone. "Wendy, on the other hand, did not suffer fools."

"I don't blame her," Janet said.

"Nor do I, except that I'm the fool in question. She liked my jokes and rhymes, but she objected when I strayed from the tour notes with material from my own research. On more than one occasion she tried to get rid of me. I'm like the bad taste in some of my rhymes and jokes, though. I linger."

"On that note, I'd better not linger any longer," Janet said. "I want to make a good impression on my first day and I have a date with the stapler."

The stapling took less than two minutes. Janet suspected that Isobel had perfected the art of disrupting Edward. He wandered off as soon as he no longer had an audience. Janet opened her orientation folder again, but decided she'd rather be nosy and flipped through the board packet instead. Budgets, projections, annual reports, programming numbers, five-year plan, etc. Mundane and impressive at the same time. The last two pages, though, were a surprise—floor plans for the ground floor and first floor of Fairy Flax Hall with notations indicating exhibit, storage, and programming space. Janet pulled out her phone and took pictures of the two pages.

After plowing through five pages of the orientation, it was time to go. On her way out Janet looked for Isobel but didn't find her. She did find a group of knitters sitting near the windows overlooking the harbor, though. She didn't see Bethia among them. But Kyle was just coming around the corner. She raised her hand to wave. His shoulders rose, but he didn't turn and flee. And although he shuffled his knitting bag and carrier bags from hand to hand, he didn't drop any of them. Janet decided that was close enough to a pleasant greeting.

"Nice to see you again, Kyle."

An amiable nod accompanied a noncommittal smile.

"I never got the chance to ask how you enjoyed the decluttering Friday night."

Eye contact ceased and the noncommittal smile shifted leftward.

"Oh dear. Under the circumstances that probably isn't the right question, is it?"

"It doesn't matter," Kyle said.

"Still, I—"

"I didn't know her," he said, "so I don't really have any right to feel sorrow at her passing."

"But now you won't have a chance to know her. You might have liked her."

"I might have, but I might not have. Odds were fifty-fifty, I reckon. Or, because I like this museum, I could give her the benefit of the doubt and call it sixty-forty. But most of the people in the world fall into the category of 'do not know, never will.' That makes it difficult to be sentimental."

"I see your point," Janet said.

The noncommittal smile looked less amiable, more automatic.

"Anyway," Janet said, "that was a lovely tailcoat you had on Friday night. Did you see that at the decluttering and snap it up?"

"Snap it up." Eye contact resumed, thoughtful. "I rarely snap up anything."

"Probably best. Have you seen Isobel?"

"No."

Janet didn't see her, either. She sent Isobel a text on her way back to the bookshop.

⸎

Janet stepped into Yon Bonnie Books and felt the calming influence of books and good company wash over her. Tallie and Rab, busy with customers, glanced over with pleasant smiles to see who'd come in. "In the Fen Country" by Vaughan Williams floated down from the sound system. Knitters worked in the inglenook, and though she couldn't hear their needles, she imagined their soothing clicks and Ranger's soft snores. The murmur of voices and soft laughter from the tearoom were real enough and added to the feeling of home. She put her coat and purse in the office, took a moment to send the floor plan photographs to the others, and then went out into the shop to pull her weight. She took the orientation folder with her.

On a quick visit from the tearoom, Christine congratulated Janet for having the presence of mind to take pictures of the Fairy Flax Hall floor plan. Then she told her she should have photographed the entire board packet or brought one home with her. Summer zipped in and left with the orientation folder when she saw that Isobel had included research notes for the exhibits in addition to scripts for tour guides.

Tallie awarded her mother a gold star for good behavior in *not* bringing home a board packet.

"She probably made exactly as many copies as she needed, anyway," Janet said. "She'd either know I took one or she'd blame it on Edward. That hardly seems fair."

"But why the interest in the floor plan?" Tallie asked.

"I don't suppose we need one, but now we have one. Plus, it looks like someone has dreams of moving the museum again. Or had them. Darn. I really should've taken pictures of the whole packet. Maybe the floor plan is explained on another page, with the idea pooh-poohed or attributed to whoever thought it up. I almost sent the pictures to Norman. I'm glad I didn't. Once again, we don't have enough information."

"We did wonder if Fairy Flax Hall had ever been a tour stop with day-trippers falling all over themselves to get pictures. Ask Rab."

Rab said not that he'd ever heard. They agreed he would have.

"So that could be part of the dream." Tallie had her phone out. "There are plenty of companies offering tours of Scots Baronial architecture. And no shortage of balustraded, turreted, bartizaned, corbeled, gargoyled, bay windowed, mullioned, gothic-flourished examples out there. Lots of them bigger, grander, more accessible, and already open to the public."

"In our neck of the woods?"

"Nope. And none with a name as beguiling as Fairy Flax Hall. It'd be a nice draw for the area."

"But if it's only the museum's dream, and not a done deal, and it came to a vote whether or not to pursue it, then a simple vote of 'no' from the board would do," Janet said. "Because arsenic," she whispered, "is overkill. We are suggesting that someone poisoned Wendy to stop it, right?"

"Sure sounds like it. Arsenic would be overkill to start the move, too." At a look from her mother, Tallie explained. "If it was Isobel's idea and Wendy was in the way. The plans were in the board packet, right? Doesn't that make it Isobel's idea?"

"A horrible thought," Janet said. "But all our thoughts are. So, I wonder who *does* get the house in the will and who wants it?"

"Or *did* want it."

Janet added notes from her morning at the museum to their documents as time allowed. She recapped Edward's comments about Wendy and his take on how she and Isobel worked together. She entered a question about Edward,

JM: Would he kill Wendy to give Isobel her dream job?

She added to their discussion of control as a motive,

JM: Edward controls by being obstinate. He said Wendy tried to "fire" him from giving tours at the museum. But he didn't quit.

About Kyle, she wrote,

JM: Kyle claims he didn't know Wendy, but as one of the competition knitters, wouldn't he have met her? Does that fit with that first morning kerfuffle over where he belonged?

And under Isobel's name, she noted,

JM: Isobel says she didn't know about knitting at the poetry slam.
JM: Is that credible?

Then Janet summarized her discussion with Tallie about the floor plan and Violet's will. Not long after making that entry, she got a text from Summer: *Ask James about the floor plan. He's on the museum board. It says so in your orientation material.*

"And that," Janet said to herself, "is why reading is so important." She told Tallie she was going to make a quick call and ducked into the office. Before dialing James's number, she logged into the office laptop and opened their documents so she could make notes.

"Hello, Janet," James said. "How goes the investigation?"

"Progressing. Maybe not in the right direction. If you have a few minutes, can you answer some questions as a member of the museum board?"

"Not as an authorized spokesman, but that sort of nicety rarely stops me."

"Are there or have there ever been plans to move the museum?"

"I mind the current location being discussed in terms of temporary or permanent. There were a number of options discussed. Most didn't get out of the preliminary phase."

"Was Fairy Flax Hall among them?"

"It's possible. Sorry, I miss half the meetings."

"You don't read meeting minutes?"

"You caught me. No. And I feel like a waste of space when I do attend, but Wendy liked having me on the board for the publicity I gave her. She didn't require attention-to-detail from me. Or decisions. She'll be missed. She was far more capable than most of the board members. She was an efficient one-woman show. That includes her canny, as well as excellent decision to hire Isobel."

"If she was canny and efficient, why did she let Edward continue giving fiction-riddled tours?

"*Because* of Isobel, a bit of tiptoeing so as not to offend her by booting her favorite uncle, but mostly because of Violet. She wrote the museum into her will, and Wendy didn't want to offend her either. Did I score a hit with that? Am I the first to tell you about the will?"

Janet laughed. "Sorry. Violet told us about it. But not about who gets the house. Do you know?"

"I do not. But it'll be grand when you find out and tell me."

Janet laughed again, thanked him, and disconnected. Almost immediately he called back.

"Talk to Ian. He was on the board."

"He is?"

"Past tense. *Tense* often goes with Ian, aye? He was there for the name value."

"Thanks, James."

After closing out their registers at the end of the day, Summer returned Janet's museum orientation folder.

"Anything stellar in there that I should rush home and read tonight?" Janet asked.

"It's interesting to see how often Edward strays from the script," Summer said. "If he can provide authoritative sources for his additions and variations then it's not a problem."

"Or stop worrying about it and call his tours 'The Myth and Mystique of Inversgail,'" Christine said.

"There you go," Summer said. "Here's what I'm worried about. Isobel did a lot of fascinating research on arsenic and arsenical products of the nineteenth century. Way more than she needed, because that's what researchers do, and of course you don't throw it all into an article or exhibit or whatever. But she has some tangential stuff, too. Like research into which poisons have similar symptoms to arsenic."

"We've heard that before, about symptoms," Tallie said.

"Because I asked that question," Summer said, "and we decided we didn't need to know. So now my question is, why did Isobel need to know?"

23

Arsenic diary, day nine and a half

I wade, I flounder in the sea of options the old girl shows me were once available. I drown in the drama and pathos of arsenic everywhere.

In children's clothing!

In candles!

In a letter to the <u>Scotsman</u> of 15 March 1882, where an Edinburgh resident details the deleterious effects upon his health from the green and gold flocked wallpaper in his dining room.

In Glasgow in reports of people poisoned by green cake icing.

In the move toward consumer safety requiring the addition of soot and indigo to white arsenic so there'd be no mistaking it for sugar when kept on a shelf in the kitchen. Mind, they still sold farmers staggering amounts of the pure white arsenic for agricultural purposes, no soot or indigo in sight. So, if a neighbor slipped in to borrow a teacupful the farmer likely did not notice.

In turning a blind eye to the 1851 Sale of Arsenic Regulation Act and selling a small amount without recording it, because it's that nice Mrs. Whatsit who needs only a penny-worth or two for her wee rat problem. Ah, the frequently used rat excuse.

I turn the page, twirling imaginary whiskers, and find another clipping about the Bradford peppermint lozenge case. This one

matter of fact. No heartstrings attached. In the <u>Dover Telegraph</u>
<u>and Cinque Ports General Advertiser</u> of 13 November 1858,
poisonings by peppermint lozenges "in the making of which arsenic
had been used in a regrettable but honest mistake in place of
plaster of Paris." The honest and regretting confectioner <u>meant</u> to
add plaster of Paris to his sweeties. It saved him money. White
sugar being dear, he and his confectioner colleagues were wont
to mix white sugar with cheaper white substances, called "daft,"
such as powdered limestone and plaster of Paris.

Ah, the white lie.

Am I daft in holding onto my old girl,
amid the hue and cry?

∞

Janet looked at Tallie over her teacup after supper that evening. "Fair warning, dear. I might be going daft. I'm going to invite Ian over. This evening. I want to ask him what he knows about any museum plans concerning Fairy Flax Hall. The fair warning is for daftness but also in case you want to vacate the premises or hide."

"Two attractive options." Tallie stacked dishes in the sink and started running water. "Here's a third. I won't abandon you in your emerging daftness, but let's take a page out of the playbook Christine thinks the Normans are using. We'll use a clever ruse. If we invite him here, he'll overstay his welcome. Instead, we'll go there. We'll say we're doing a progress report on the scrapbook. There hasn't been any progress, or not much, so that won't take long. We thank him, say goodnight, and then we pull a Columbo. At the door, ask your real question, like it's an afterthought."

"Brilliant."

"Probably dating ourselves by calling it a Columbo, though."

"Classics and iconic TV roles are never out of date. We'll be home in time for a revivifying sherry."

Ian surprised them by inviting them into his living room and offering jam roly-poly. "So fresh, I haven't had a taste yet myself. I'm slowly working my way through my mother's recipes, and if I eat the whole thing, then *I'll* be the roly-poly. So, you're doing me a neighborly favor, just as you are by taking me seriously about the scrapbook."

"Thank you, Ian." Janet took an appreciative sniff of the dessert. "Huh. What kind of jam?"

"Something or other I had in the cupboard. Mother didn't specify."

Janet took a bite and regretted it.

"Do you have any other clues about the scrapbook for us to go on?" Tallie asked.

He shook his head.

Janet saw him watching Tallie take her first bite. She thought it best to distract him as Tallie attempted to swallow hers. "Have you heard anything new at all about the scrapbook? Oh, hey, do you think Wendy took it for the museum exhibit?"

"Ahead of you there," Ian said. "Isobel hasn't seen it. But I do see your faces. How is the roly-poly? Inedible?"

"Well . . . not quite what I expected," Janet said.

"But yeah, inedible," Tallie said. "Sorry, Ian."

"Win some, lose some. So many of the recipes Mother came up with *are* inedible, but it's hard to know which ones until you try them. Don't feel obliged to finish." He took their plates and his own, and they followed him to the kitchen. "I did wonder about her addition of Marmite." He cleared the plates into the garbage disposal. The rest of the roly-poly went down, too.

They told him they'd let him know if they heard anything about the scrapbook. At the door, Janet turned around. "Speaking of the museum, do you remember talk of moving it to Fairy Flax Hall while you were on the board?"

"Good Lord, yes. That was a nonstarter. The amount of money it would take to buy the place! Wendy knew how to raise funds, but we'd be talking about a scale of fundraising you might find in Edinburgh or in London, not Inversgail. One or two were all for trying. I was one, of course. I wanted to show Wendy that I supported her."

"Of course. Who was the other?"

Ian scratched his ear. "I was actually the only one. Christine's father voted 'no.' He was right; the harbor location is far and away better."

They said their goodbyes and Ian closed the door. Tallie started to say something, and Janet shushed her.

"Wheesht until we're home. If he's watching, we don't want him to know we have any urgent need to discuss."

The door opened again and Ian called, "I say, I've remembered something."

Janet and Tallie went the few steps back.

"When Teresa and I were together she liked to hear blow-by-blow descriptions of board meetings. I told her she could come along with me anytime she liked, but I think she rather enjoyed my dramatizations. I reached my pinnacle with the last meeting I attended before rotating off the board. I called it 'Where There's a Will, There's a Way.' Sadly, we broke up soon after."

"When was that?" Tallie asked.

"Last month." With a bereft sigh, he closed the door.

Janet knocked.

"Sorry to disturb you again, Ian, and sorry about the breakup, but did you have a reason for telling us that?"

"Do you know, I don't know. Something in your question about the museum and Fairy Flax Hall brought it to mind, I suppose. Or just the chance to unburden a sorrow. Not many people I know would have bothered to ask. You're good neighbors. Thank you."

Janet and Tallie said their goodnights again. When they let themselves in their own back door Tallie locked it. "In case Ian follows us like a lost puppy."

"I'd be tempted to let him in. That was incredibly sad."

"Mean of Teresa, too," Tallie said. "Using him and then tossing him aside as soon as he's off the board. We use him, but we don't toss him aside."

"I wonder if she'll suck up to someone else on the board now?"

"Did you know David was involved with the museum?"

"No, and that was the urgent piece of information we need to discuss. Helen said something at the decluttering about David recognizing the body as Wendy's right off. We didn't think anything of it. I didn't, anyway. I doubt Christine did either. David wasn't there and it sounded like one of Helen's conversations with the fairies. Hold on, I'll ask Christine." Janet's thumbs played over her phone and she hit send. While she hung up her jacket, her phone buzzed. "Christine says she didn't know David had any ties to the museum. He's gone to bed, so she'll ask him about it in the morning."

"Now that I've managed to digest Ian's mother's roly-poly, do you think he actually pulled a reverse Columbo on us by waiting until we'd gone out the door to call us back and tell us about Teresa's interest in board meetings?"

"A double reverse," Janet said. "Because then he made us knock to find out why he'd told us. And you *know* he waited for us to try the revolting roly-poly first. He waited to see our reactions, and then didn't take a single bite."

"Sneaky devil."

∽

Thursday morning's meeting started on a dreich note, with Christine calling it their meeting between the discards and the dregs. When Janet protested, Christine said she meant to pay tribute to library terms and loose tea.

"Your mum must still be having nightmares," Janet said.

"Aye. Dad's knackered and so am I. I couldn't get a clear answer about the museum, and he looked so peely-wally I didn't want to press."

"Would it help if you take time off?" Summer asked.

"No. Thank you. It'll work itself out."

Tallie told them about their visit with Ian that prompted the question to David. She cautioned Christine and Summer against sampling his mother's recipes. "He should rename the one he tried to kill us with last night peely-wally roly-poly."

"*Did* he try to kill you?" Summer asked. "Is that why it tasted so bad? How are you feeling this morning?"

"He had no way of knowing we were coming over last night," Janet said.

"Summer has a point," Christine said. "He's a suspect, and his behavior is always suspect. Though usually he's just a git and not really dangerous."

"Let's maybe not accept food or drink from our suspects until this is over," Tallie said.

"Roly-poly is only one name for that pudding," Christine said. "It's also called dead man's arm and dead man's leg."

"Good to know," Janet said. "It tasted like both."

∽

The morning passed quietly. Shoppers shopping. Knitters knitting. Kyle wasn't among them, so Bethia worked in the inglenook for a change. Edward wandered in out of the dreary cold and spent time chatting with the knitters and taking pictures. Janet and Tallie were both busy when he queued up behind Janet's customer. At his turn, he set a birthday card on the counter.

"Mother asked me to pick it up for Helen."

"That's so thoughtful. She'll love it." Janet rang it up. "Would you like a bag?"

"Not necessary. Isobel wonders when you'll be coming to the Museum again."

"I sent her a text," Janet said.

"Very good. That's fine, then."

Anxious to end the conversation, Janet stood on her tiptoes and called over his shoulder, "Be right with you." To Edward she said, "I should go help out. Nice to see you. Haste ye back."

"Nice dodge," Tallie said. "Good thing he didn't turn around and see nobody. Are you sure he isn't wondering when *he'll* see you at the museum again? He wasn't waiting for me to ring up the card."

"If that's the case, I won't be volunteering there much longer." Janet's phone buzzed with a text from Christine: *Ian's here. Saw Edward at your counter. Said "we are formed by little scraps of wisdom." Looked at me and said "echo." Wouldn't explain. Sneaking your way now. Up to something.*

Janet passed her phone to Tallie. Tallie read the text then wiggled her eyebrows, put the phone to her ear, and carried on a pretend conversation. "Yes, we do have copies of Ian Atkinson's books. They're very popular. . . . A full set? Cool. . . . Oh, I'm sure Mr. Atkinson will be happy to sign them. . . . Next time I see him I'll let him know."

Out of the corner of her eye, Janet saw the tip of Ian's nose emerging from an aisle of books as he crept closer to listen. She signaled "cut" to Tallie.

"Thanks for calling. Bye."

Ian emerged fully, looked longingly toward them, longingly toward the door, and back at them.

"Someone wants all your books," Tallie said, normally a sure way to lure him from anywhere.

"One must grab every scrap of happiness while one can," he said, choosing the door over them. "I'll be in touch." And he was gone.

"Definitely up to something. Look to see which way he goes," Janet said. She zapped a text to Christine: *My car in back. ASAP.*

"Tailing a rat?" Tallie called from her post at the window. "Hurry. A lorry's jamming traffic. Ian's waiting to back out of a spot in the harbor lot. Should take a few."

Janet grabbed her coat and purse and dashed for the back door. Christine held it for her, and they dashed together for the car. In, buckled, car started, they turned right out of the narrow street behind their shops, and as they turned right again into the High Street, the lorry driver was climbing back into his truck.

"There goes Ian," Christine said. "Follow that twit."

Janet did, and because it was Inversgail, and the lorry probably created the worst traffic the town would see for a week, tailing him was easy. Harder was staying far enough back so that he wouldn't notice them, particularly when he ended up on a quiet tree-lined street. Ian slowed as though looking for a house or a place to park. Janet pulled to the curb, ready to pull out again if he accelerated.

"Plenty of parking along here," Christine said. "He must be looking for an address. There. He's pulling up on the right. Wrong side of the street, twit."

"Binoculars in the glove box," Janet said.

Christine looked askance, then pleased as she focused the binoculars. "He's getting comfortable. Waiting. What do you get up to with these?"

"Bird watching. Seal watching. Suspect watching. See if you can read an address. I'll do a reverse look up."

Christine read the house number out. "What is 'echo' supposed to mean?"

"That's Teresa's house. Tallie's just texted about echo. She says: 'What Ian said about little scraps of wisdom—it's something Umberto Eco said.'"

"That makes Ian more irritating."

"Now he's twice as irritating. He said something about scraps on his way out the door, too. Tallie says it was a misquote of a Noel Coward line. This has to be about the scrapbook. Maybe Teresa has it."

Christine suddenly slid down in her seat. "Vauxhall."

"What? Yours? Where?"

"Wheesht, Janet. We're on stakeout. Dad's just driven past."

"He probably doesn't know my car or the back of my head."

"Can you see him?"

"Ahead of us, not as far along as Ian." Janet took the binoculars. "Also settling in. Why is he here? Oh, oh, oh. Look, look, look." Janet slid down in her seat, too. "Teresa just arrived home."

"Keep watching!" Christine said, eyes closed.

"Ian and your Dad are taking off. Teresa's gone inside. Show's over and we should scuttle in case Teresa's a suspicious beetroot and has binoculars, too."

∞

Christine gave her father time to get home and herself time to calm down before she called him. She made the call from the office in case she hadn't given herself enough time and brought Janet as an extra precaution.

"Hello, Dad. Janet and I saw you in the car this morning, waiting in front of Teresa's house, and wondered what you were doing."

Janet gave her a thumbs-up.

"In front of *Teresa's*? My goodness," said David. "Och, well. The car's been having issues. Overheats. So, I pull over and let it cool down. Is that all then? Cheery-bye."

"I'm proud of him," Christine said when she'd disconnected. "Not a single lie passed his lips."

"So you believe him?" Janet asked.

"Not a bit. I know crafty when I hear it."

"You should; you inherited it."

Tallie had come to the office door. "Why doesn't your dad like Violet?"

"I've no idea. Mum asked him that when the invitation arrived. They had a tiff over it. Rare for them. He refused to go to the party and then, even more rare, he put his foot down and refused to discuss it any further. He said he doesn't spend his evenings parsing people with whom he'd rather not spend time."

"Wow. Will he parse if we press?" Tallie asked.

"Afternoon instead of evening," Janet said, "if that'll make a difference?"

"Possibly, if given the proper incentive," Christine said.

"Proper as in legal and ethical, or proper as in something he can't resist," Tallie asked.

"Proper as in something along the lines of a pilsner, porter, or pale ale."

"Perfect. Let us know when. In the meantime, I've kept Norman waiting out here for you."

"Kept the constable waiting? Atrocious manners," Christine said. "Keep him waiting another minute or two then send him in."

Hobbs told Janet and Christine that the police had not identified the source of arsenic.

"Why not?" Christine asked. "Is this an example of sloppy policework?"

"Arsenic is not all that hard to come by," Hobbs said.

"*That* sounds sloppy," Christine said. "It isn't legal. You can't hop down to the shops and buy a scoop."

"People have it in old barns and sheds, attics and basements. If you had some of that arsenical wallpaper, I read about in the articles Summer sent, you could scrape it and have yourself a tidy wee bit of arsenical dust. Maybe get it in the wash water from a green, arsenical frock. Ian had a bottle of liquid arsenic in his bothy."

"That sounds sloppy and potentially horrific," Janet said. "Imagine if he poured it out somewhere children or animals could get into it."

"It was there when he bought the place, along with instructions for dipping sheep. He brought it to the station yesterday, turned it in."

"Good," both women said.

"You needn't actually go looking for it at all," Hobbs said. "You can buy it online."

"But if you're not out scouring the town for arsenic," Janet said. "Or the web for sales—Norman, isn't the source important?"

"It could have been bought years ago," he said.

"So now the killer can sit pretty, feeling safe as well as murderous," Christine said.

Hobbs wished them good day and left.

"That wasn't really fair, was it." Christine sighed. "Ah, well. That seems to be his lot in life. Did Isobel say if the stockings missing from the museum are poison-dyed?

"No. But even if they are, they didn't disappear until after Wendy and Euan died."

"So she said."

"Yeesh. Have we told Norman about them?" Janet asked. "I don't remember. I'll do it now."

"Why?" Christine asked.

"Professional courtesy. At this point in our career we deserve to call ourselves professional amateur sleuths. Also, I want to rub in the theory that source matters."

"I echo that."

24

Arsenic diary, day ten

I cannot bear the thought of returning the scrapbook. Why should I? To avoid peril? Arsenic cannot be destroyed, but I could destroy the scrapbook. No! How could I? And leave the world without a gem such as this from the <u>Edinburgh Evening News</u> of Tuesday, 26 August 1924.

"WILLIAM LAURIE KING, FORCED TO BECOME
CHARTERED ACCOUNTANT BY HIS PARENTS.
A MOTHER'S DEATH
SON'S STATEMENT

"The trial of William Laurie King, aged 22, on a charge of causing the death of his mother, was resumed in Edinburgh to-day.

The police gave evidence in regard to finding large quantities of arsenic in possession of accused, which he had obtained by a forged order.

Professor Littlejohn gave evidence that he was satisfied none of the food in the house had contained poison.

Accused gave evidence that he was interested in chemistry, and used arsenic in experiments. A packet of arsenic was removed from his pockets by his mother. This he found in the pantry the day after her death. A corner of the packet was opened, and the arsenic spilt on the shelves. Accused denied administering poison.

The court then adjourned."

Poor sod. Forced to become a chartered accountant and then brought up on charges of murder because he had a healthy interest in chemistry and arsenic. So clearly a victim of circumstances. The parallel is not lost on me. I shall have to return the scrapbook before circumstances overtake me.

But how can I give it back without giving myself away? One would think leaving something behind would be easier than removing it in the first place. Don't bet on it. Eyes watch me like the eyes of bloodthirsty stoats. I am the wee, sleekit, timorous beastie waiting to be slaughtered. And with a misstep, likely to be.

Are there statues whose eyes follow viewers, like the eyes in some painted portraits do? I stop beside Stevenson. A steady friend. He does not sneer or look down his nose. His eyes never follow me with steely derision. Together we admire the harbor and lighthouse view. I wonder, did Stevenson run into Buddhism during his travels? Is he reflecting on waves and water, enlightenment and loss?

I have no plans to study Buddhism, but I quite enjoy reading the memes online. Have you heard the one about how collecting things to make yourself happy makes as much sense as strapping sandwiches to your body when you're hungry? I paraphrase. But after reflecting on possessions and sandwiches, and because of the stoat eyes sizing up the back of my neck, I know I will give up the scrapbook. Also, that I want my lunch.

∽

Bethia stopped at the counter on her way to lunch in the tearoom. "I haven't solved your crimes yet, but I find that I nod off less often now that I listen more closely to the conversations around me."

"Is anyone knitting secret codes into their stockings like Edward hoped?" Tallie asked.

"Not that anyone's admitted," Bethia said, "and there are two or three who would if they were. They say they're rule breakers and proud of it, proud of changing the pattern we're all meant to follow, and yet they're all making the same changes. Breaking the rules by following a different set of rules. And all so cheerfully earnest. I never nod off when I listen to them."

"I wonder if they're the ones who organized the knitting at the poetry slam," Janet said. "Do you know their names? Or can you find out?"

"They might be suspects?" Bethia asked. "I'll get the names for you."

"Isobel called them rogue knitters."

"Sock-knitting rogues," Bethia said. "We might need more of them in the world."

After the lunch hour, with no more knitting groups to oversee or listen to, Bethia nodded off. Ranger did, too, though knitters chatting rarely kept him from his appointed rounds of naps. Rab moved between the bookshop and the tearoom. Janet and Tallie stayed busy going to and from the counter with customers. At one point Janet returned to the counter alone and found Kyle Byrne behind the counter standing at their office door.

"That's our office, Kyle. Is there something I can help you with?" She knew her voice was loud and harsh, but he'd startled her and she wanted him to know that she was there, she saw him, and that now everyone else in the shop knew it, too.

"Looking for the loo," he mumbled. "Sorry." He flinched as he passed her and then Tallie and Rab. They watched him leave through the tearoom.

Janet checked the office and found everything as it should be. Rab pointed out small things behind the counter—stacks of bags askew, a drawer slightly open.

"Might have been him," Rab said.

"You're being kind or careful," Janet said. "I think it's clear he snooped around back here."

"I think Rab's right," Tallie said. "Let's be careful about being sure he snooped. On the other hand, I'm sure we should consider him dangerous."

"I'm not sure he's even dangerous with knitting needles," Janet said. "But his normal behavior is guilty behavior."

"Just don't judge him by his looks," Tallie said.

"Ranger's a good judge of character and he's edgy around Kyle. What do you know about him, Rab?"

"Arrested for shoplifting at sixteen. He confessed, received a warning, and it didn't go on a criminal record. That was ten years ago."

"Is that why you've adjusted your schedule?" Tallie asked.

"He was arrested for the one incident. He just wasn't caught for the rest. Some of the shopkeepers remember. And the others accused in his place."

"Euan?" Janet asked.

"Aye."

∞

Shortly before the end of the day, Bethia put a copy of *Kailyard and Scottish Literature* on the counter. "For Maida," she said. "I'll leave it for her on the bed when I go home, so I don't embarrass her. I might read it first myself, very carefully."

"That's thoughtful," Janet said.

Bethia plopped her handbag and knitting bag on the counter. Beside them she thumped the bag of knitting books she carried to share with the competitors. She dug in her handbag for her wallet then tutted while looking through her knitting bag and then the book bag. "Och, what's this old thing? I wondered why my bag had grown so heavy. Someone mistook my bag for their own I suppose." She pulled a book from the bag and held it out to show Janet—a thick book with marbled covers and leather binding.

Janet moved Bethia's bags aside. "Set it down here. We probably shouldn't touch it."

"Och, but I did," Bethia said, eyes wide with alarm.

"Dinnae fash. Just set it down. It probably doesn't matter, anyway, but I think this is the scrapbook missing from Fairy Flax Hall."

Tallie and Rab came to see, Tallie pulling her phone out. "I'll call Norman."

"Not just yet," Janet said. "Someone else first. To verify identification."

Tallie thought a moment. "You're right. Ian first." She made the call, brief and to the point on her end, and after disconnecting reported Ian's gasp, stutters, and shout that he'd be right over.

"Aye, we heard the last bit," Rab said.

While they waited, Bethia found her wallet, paid for her purchase, and when Rab invited her, she trundled behind the counter to sit on the stool. He gave her a bit of a hand to get there. "I've never found long lost treasure before," she said. "I hope no one accuses me of plundering it in the first place."

"You didn't, did you?" Janet asked.

"Norman would never forgive me or himself for having such a wicked nana."

"Besides," Tallie said, "if Violet isn't tall enough to reach that top shelf, even with the ladder, neither is Bethia."

Ian blew through the door spilling exclamations and questions before the bell stopped jingling. "This is an important affirmation of everything I've been saying about the book's significance. But now that it's safe, more work begins. We need answers. Why has it reappeared? Why bring it back? Why now? And why not take it back where it came from? *Oh*, maybe that wasn't possible. He'd be afraid he'd be identified, afraid he'll be accused, but also afraid or certain something in the book is important to the case. Aaaah, but won't his fingerprints be all over it?"

Disregarding his own question, and possibly no longer aware of anything but the scrapbook, Ian opened it and flipped through the pages. "A few blank spaces, but still delightful despite the butchering of the original book. Cared for well, I'd say. Perhaps he wore gloves to protect it. Or in case there were traces of arsenic amongst the pages?" He wiped his fingertips on a handkerchief. "Perhaps he brought it back because he no longer needed it. Or she. Well, not exactly back. He left it somewhere it would be found. In the constable's grandmother's knitting bag, you say? The constable's grandmother's knitting bag," he said, as though savoring each word. "I wonder if that would make a good title."

"Shouldn't think so," Rab said.

"Blank spaces, Ian?" Tallie asked. "Were scraps removed?"

"Or fell out," he said. "The paste or glue Humbug would've used is ancient by now. Hard to know if anything's missing, really, unless you find a residue of paste."

"And did you find residue? Do you *know* if scraps are missing?" Janet asked.

"And what's on them?" Tallie said. "I'm wondering about how-to instructions for poisoner wannabes."

"It would help if I did, wouldn't it," Ian said. "Sorry. No idea. Here's an idea, though. Could that be what my prowler and thief were after? Missing scraps?"

"Did you ever take the scrapbook home?" Janet asked.

"No, but the person who took it wouldn't know that. And if the scraps were already missing, remembering ancient and brittle stickum, he might have wondered and wanted to make the scrapbook whole again. Shall I take it with me and get it back to Fairy Flax Hall?"

"No." Janet took the book from him. "We'll contact the authorities. But thanks so much for coming in to identify it. Cheery-bye."

Ian left, and as there'd been no other customers since he'd arrived, they decided it wouldn't hurt to close a few minutes early.

"You're usually friendlier than that, Mom," Tallie said, after locking the door. "When you said cheery-bye to Ian, you didn't add *haste ye back*."

"There are different ways of being friendly, dear. I didn't say good riddance and at the time, that felt friendly to the point of being fond."

Rab started closing out the register. "You can be friendly with someone without trusting them. Same as you can trust someone to act a certain way and dislike them immensely."

"I wonder if that describes our villain," Bethia said. "A charmer and disarmer and a devil."

"It describes Ian," Tallie said.

"Does it describe Kyle?" Janet asked. "Is that what he was doing sneaking around? Not taking something, but planting it? Took it earlier, got rid of it now that people are aware it's been missing? Like a hot potato from Mr. Potato Chef. He was visibly agitated when I stopped him at the office door."

"More like a deer in the headlights," Rab said.

"Definitely a suspect, though," Tallie said. "But someday I want to find Ian guilty of something."

"I'd best be going," Bethia said. "Norman will be waiting round the back."

"You're fine, Bethia," Janet said. "He's stopping in for you this evening." She'd just sent him a text saying: *If you want your nana, Constable, come and get her.*

Hobbs knocked on their door moments later. He listened to Bethia's excited retelling of her part in the recovery of the missing scrapbook, and then the more matter-of-fact details from Janet, all the while making notes in his pink pearlescent notebook. Janet slipped the scrapbook into a paper bag. With Bethia on one arm, her pocketbook, knitting bag, book bag, and the scrapbook in the other, he thanked them, said he'd be in touch, and left.

"Very professional, our Constable Hobbs," Janet said. "But his eyebrows were as excited as Bethia."

∞

The women celebrated the recovery of the scrapbook with an evening at Nev's. Helen and David joined them as a pre-birthday treat. James Haviland ambled in from the *Inversgail Guardian* office next door and joined them when he heard about the scrapbook. In an unexpected pleasure, Reddick arrived with Bethia and his smooth collie, Quantum. The enlarged group pulled another table over so they could all sit together, Quantum between Bethia and Helen.

David made a toast. "To the birthday girl and the finder of lost scrapbooks."

"A shame Norman couldn't make it," Janet said quietly to Christine.

"A shame he's avoiding us," Christine said, not as quietly.

"What do you think, Inspector," James asked. "Is the scrapbook part of all this?"

"I'm enjoying a rare evening off," Reddick said.

"As am I," James said. "Evening off . . . the record."

"I'll probably still disappoint you." Reddick shook his head. "It's hard to see where it fits into the pattern of the crimes, but we've not ruled it out."

"Maida and I had an interesting discussion the other night about patterns in dust," Bethia said. "She can tell when someone's no longer reading the book on their bedside table, for instance, by the dust."

"That's very astute of Maida," Reddick said.

"Aye, she's an expert on dust," Bethia said.

"I never thought I'd see so many poems about the philosophical nuances of dust," James said. "She's a one-woman factory for odes to dust at our Pub Scrawl meetings."

"Usage patterns as clues. I'd never thought of that," Tallie said. "But we see them all the time—a favorite teacup migrates to another place in the cupboard, to a different shelf or a different place on the same shelf. So then you know a different person is putting away the dishes or using the cup."

"Or straightening or reorganizing," Summer said. "It might be a clue, but it might not be."

"Story of my life," Reddick said. "But the more you know about the patterns involved, and how consistent the people are, the better."

"Like the ganseys at the museum," Bethia said. "What Edward tells people are pattern variations meant to identify drowned sailors are much more likely a way to identify the knitters. Not exactly the same as you were telling us, Inspector, but my consistency is in thinking about knitting patterns."

"Sitting patterns?" Helen said. "Aye, my mum kent sitting patterns. Whose bahookie's been sitting in my best chair she'd ask and point to the telltale signs pressed into the cushion."

Laughter and another round followed, and smaller conversations started up at each end of their double table.

"Do you think Edward believes his stories, Bethia?" Summer asked.

Bethia nodded toward Reddick listening to David and Helen's rhapsodies on the Argyle Trout and their annual lunch there. "I'll borrow his phrase and say I've not ruled it out."

"You've spent a lot of time with Kyle during the competition, haven't you, Bethia?" Tallie asked.

"I've also not ruled out the truth of *his* story," Bethia said. "He told me he's in the competition continuing a tradition of male knitters in his family. I wonder what sort of knitters they were. I seem to be teaching him as he goes."

Janet caught Bethia's smile before she hid it with a sip of her shandy. "Do you know Kyle Byrne, James?"

"Of him."

Janet motioned for him to lean closer. The others at their end of the table did, too. "What do you know about his history of shoplifting?"

"What do you know?" James countered.

"He's a bumbler, and not good at his current job, according to Maida."

"She'd certainly know."

"So how is it he was so good at shoplifting?" Tallie asked.

James took a drink of ale before answering.

"Scrolling through the newsreels of his mind," Summer told the others.

"No reports of running afoul of the law since, that I recall. Could be his technique has improved. If we're talking patterns, could be he does a better job learning the shopkeeper's patterns to determine the best time for nicking."

"He was good enough the first time around, even as a kid," Tallie said. "Other people were accused, right?"

"Before he got nabbed, aye. A one lad crime wave."

"Nabbed by Norman or a furious shopkeeper?" Janet asked.

"By Rab."

"Who else did people accuse?"

"Rab."

∽

"Nice to have two of our storytellers in this morning," Janet said. "Kyle and Edward are quite a pair."

"The same but different," Christine agreed. "The charmer and the sneakthief." She moved the stool to the end of the counter nearest the door and sat. "So we're less likely to be overheard."

The knitters and napping dog in the inglenook were busy. The bookshop and tearoom were not. Yet. The barrage of weekend tour coaches out of Fort William would start arriving mid-morning, and the women were taking advantage of the quiet. Christine had come for a chat with Janet. Tallie had gone to keep Summer company. Rab puttered in the mysterious way of Rab.

"Bethia's not here," Christine said. "I hope Maida doesn't think we kept her out too late last night and is keeping her in today as punishment."

"Don't be silly. We all left by nine. It wasn't us, anyway. I doubt Maida would question anything Reddick does. Helen and David were cute as buttons."

"They've invited you and me to go with them for Mum's birthday lunch."

"Fun! Tell them I accept. Your comment about Bethia—it's just occurred to me that the knitters are rotating between the venues, as they should, including Bethia, but not Kyle. Or not as often."

"Something else to make note of," Christine said. "And Dad's odd behavior, as well."

"No."

"Until we have answers, we have to. You know that. Personal biases can't be allowed to influence the investigation. Dad's been sly and crafty for days, starting with his attic decluttering. We can't dismiss the fact that whatever he's been up to might be related to the murders. We don't know enough about anyone or anything to rule out any possibilities. We don't know their secrets, what they want, and what they want to avoid. We don't know enough of the victims' stories to understand what happened. We don't know enough of the villain's story to understand why he or she did it."

"Do we need to understand why?"

Rab came from dusting the fireplace mantle. "A wee bit softer," he said as he started in straightening the counter.

"Thank you, Rab," Janet said, lowering her voice. "The problem is we don't know who the killer is, so we don't know their story. And we don't know their story, so we can't know who the killer is. I've been thinking it's a tangle of yarn, but I was wrong. It's a circle, an eddy."

"It's the Corryvreckan," Rab said.

"Sorry?" Janet said.

"Great whirlpool between Jura and Scarba. Dangerous for the unaware."

"But for those who are wary there are clues," Christine said. "That's true with the Corryvreckan and killers. So, we make our way carefully and we keep asking questions. And the one thing we do know: the villain is poison."

Janet thought Christine was being a bit melodramatic. Her voice had risen again, too. As though Queen Elizabeth craved an audience. Speaking of people who craved audiences, movement in the nearest aisle of books coalesced into a familiar sneaky shape. "Hello, Ian."

25

Arsenic diary, day eleven

The villain is poison. Such unexpected words to overhear in a cozy bookshop.

So judgmental. So harsh.

And why did I not think of running the bloody thing through a copier? There I go blaming the old girl, again.

Lost and heartbroken.

∽

Tallie had gone home mid-afternoon—comp time, Janet told her, that only made up in a small way for all the times Janet had left her to hold down the fort lately. Christine offered Janet a ride home at the end of the day. After closing up, they let themselves out the back door into the narrow street where they parked most often. The Vauxhall was nowhere in sight.

"You must have walked this morning," Janet said. She watched Christine look up and down the street again. "Did you park someplace else?"

"No."

"Then unless you parked behind the rubbish bins, or your car's been stolen, you must have walked. It was a beautiful morning, and it's not a bad evening, either. Dark, but not arctic."

248

"What day is this?" Christine demanded.

"Friday."

"I drove." Christine had her phone to her ear. "Norman? I wish to report a stolen car . . . I did not. You are not amusing. . . . We will be waiting for you in the tearoom. . . . Of course I mean our tearoom. When did you stop being stodgy and halfway intelligent and start thinking of yourself as a stand-up comedian? Don't be an *eejit*." She dropped her phone into her purse.

"If your car's been stolen—"

"My car's been stolen."

Janet unlocked the back door and held it for the fuming Christine. "Then my car is yours until yours is found or the situation is resolved in whatever way that happens."

"I want a cup of tea."

"I'll pour."

Hobbs knocked on the tearoom door as Christine finished her second cup. Janet unlocked it for him. He came in, removed his cap smartly, and apologized to Christine.

"You reached me at the library. I gave Nana Bethia a ride there for one of the evening knitting sessions and stayed to listen to her. *She* could have been a stand-up comedian."

Christine, feeling better for her tea, accepted his apology.

"Now, Mrs. Robertson, since you've had a chance to calm down, have you also had a chance to mind that you left your car in the library car park earlier today?"

"I did no such thing."

"She didn't, I feel sure," Janet said.

"Could it be that your father came here, took the car, and drove there?"

"Is he at the library now?" Christine asked.

"He is not. When I phoned, he said he's been home all day."

"And you doubted him, so you asked me? How dare—no. Never mind. These days I might have doubted him myself. But I have the keys right here and we've only the one set. How did the thieves get it open and started?"

"Opening and driving off is a car thief's expertise."

"Is it damaged at all?"

"I'll take you there," Hobbs said. "We'll have a look."

The Vauxhall sat alone in a corner of the library car park. Janet and Hobbs followed as Christine stalked around the car twice, looking at doors, windows, paint, and tires before pronouncing the exterior provisionally undamaged. "But the interior, Norman."

"As the doors were not locked when I found the car, I took the liberty of performing a quick, preliminary search."

"Is *that* how you conduct a search, Norman? It's a mess!"

"I did not rearrange anything," Hobbs said with a barely concealed sniff. "I assumed your family isn't particular about how you keep the inside of your car. I also did not know any of you drink Irn-Bru."

"We don't. Those are not our bottles. And we don't keep much of anything in the car, but everything we do is now spread from one end to the other. Was the thief looking for something? Did he *find* something?"

"A crime of this sort is rarely solved," Hobbs said.

"Does that say something about crimes of this sort or a constable of your sort? Will you dust for fingerprints?"

"We call them marks."

Janet pointed out traces of powder clinging to the steering wheel, doorhandles, seats, and dash.

"Och, I thought I'd tidied better," Hobbs said. "There were no marks in the obvious places, in any case. I assume you do not wipe the surfaces regularly?"

Christine's answer was a barely concealed growl.

"The doorknob at Fairy Flax Hall was wiped, too," Janet said. "Is this more serious than a short-term car theft?"

"A thief with an interesting ethic," Hobbs said. "Marks wiped from handles, seatbelts, and wheel. Leaving the rest in a *boorach*. I wish I could give you a definitive answer." Hobbs took out a handkerchief and swiped at some of the remaining fingerprint powder. Then he put the empty Irn-Bru bottles in an evidence bag. "Would you like to start the car? See if they nicked the engine?"

Christine groaned. "I didn't think to look under the hood."

"It's all right. I did," said Hobbs. "But give it a start to be sure."

Christine got in, started it up, checked the instruments, and shut it off. "Norman, with all your searching and dusting, you didn't have time to take it anywhere, did you?"

"No. On empty, is it? I'm not surprised."

"The opposite," Christine said. "This morning the tank *was* near empty. Now it's full."

"Are you certain your father—"

"One set of keys, Norman, and he'd no more know how to open doors and drive off without keys than I."

"All four of you, the SCONES," Hobbs said, "be careful, aye?"

"We will," Christine said. "Thank you, Norman. As much as I like to keep you on your toes and remind you that I babysat you and changed your nappies, I do appreciate you. Tell me, though, were you avoiding us last night? If the inspector can go down the pub for a pint with the constable's own Nana Bethia, so can the constable."

Hobbs held up a finger and went to his car. He came back with a package the size of two or three reams of paper. "This took more of the evening than I expected." He handed the package to Christine. "Copies of the scrapbook pages. One for each SCONE."

"Oh, Norman," Janet said. "Wow. Truly."

"On the police dime?" Christine asked.

"On the police copier. The cream-colored paper is my contribution. To make the copies a bit more like the original."

On the way to Janet's, Christine's shoulders rose, subsided, and rose again. "It's just a car," she said, "but with someone prowling through it, I feel invaded. I'd rather not tell Mum and add fuel to her nightmares.

And as sure as I am about Dad not knowing how to jimmy a door and hotwire a car, I'm suddenly not at all sure that he doesn't know someone who does."

"You don't believe that."

"I don't. In my heart. But it's time we find out what he's been up to and what's going on in his dear old head."

Janet texted an invitation to Tallie and Summer: *Up for pressing David this evening? If so, we'll pick you up and explain on the way.* She received an *Absolutely* and a *You bet.* "Should we warn your mum and dad?"

"Not of the full scope of our invasion. I'll tell them I'm bringing carryout from Basant's. We'll stop for that, and a variety of potables, and they'll be thrilled."

∞

Christine knew her parents well. She'd added cake to their shopping list and when the four women arrived, they sang "Happy Birthday" to Helen. After they'd eaten—Basant's tarkari and flat bread followed by a moist pistachio cake with chocolate ganache—and sung one more round to Helen, Christine sat next to her father, looked him in the eye, and said they wanted his story.

"A true tale, Dad. This is serious."

David scratched the back of his neck. "Aye, well. Where does it start?"

"When were you on the museum board?" Janet asked. "How about starting there?"

"Och, I wasn't much use there. Wendy liked me on the board for status. Retired head teacher. She liked glitz. This was some years back, before Wendy hired Isobel. If you want exact dates, I kept my copies of meeting minutes. They're in a box in the attic."

"Status and glitz fits with what James said about being on the board," Janet said.

"It could account for Ian being on the board, too," Tallie said.

Useful or not, David had enjoyed having that to do, until Violet came into the picture, because of Isobel, and then Edward. He'd waited a polite amount of time, enough that he knew he was making the right decision, and then resigned. He liked Isobel, and thought she was good for the museum, but she was hired to cement the MacAskill connection. He was fine with that but not with the onset of her relatives.

"David," Janet said, "may I ask, what is it about Isobel's relatives that you don't like?"

"It started a long while back. When Teresa and Edward were at school and I was head teacher. Violet was one of those parents always battling for her children's advantage."

"A helicopter parent?" Tallie asked.

"A midge parent. Violet's not big enough to be a helicopter. Teresa inherited the midge DNA." David looked at Helen. "I am sorry, though. I know you love Violet like a sister."

"But to you she's always been the midge up your nose," Helen chortled. "And I'm the lucky one, because I love you both."

"Edward is harmless enough," David continued. "Except to my mental health. Possibly to the mental health of his former advertising colleagues. His claim to fame is an award-winning series of ads for gin with a continuing storyline. People loved them for tugging at the heartstrings. They sold loads of gin."

"He does know how to spin a tale," Janet said.

"Yet he took early retirement soon after," David said. "Might be coincidence."

David's dislike of Edward tied in with his spurt of decluttering in the attic. He hadn't stopped because Helen and Christine asked him to. He'd stopped because he'd found what he was looking for.

"I didn't want it found after I'm gone and couldn't explain." He leaned over, fished under the sofa skirt, and brought out a yellowed paper ream box. He handed it to Christine.

"What am I going to find here, Dad? Tarnish on my image of you?"

"Not at all. Take a look." He turned to Janet. "A small bit of tarnish wouldn't hurt, mind? It's been a long, hard life living up to Helen and Chrissie's ideal of husband and father."

"When in your long, hard life did you perfect the twinkle in your eye?" Tallie asked.

"Sorry, but that's proprietary knowledge for ideal husbands and fathers only." He covered a burp and accepted a refill from Summer.

"It's a manuscript," Christine said. "With your name on it. How did I not know about this? Is it any good? Have you read it, Mum?"

"Your dad has a pretty way with words. It's a lovely romance. Tugs at the heartstrings."

"No—are you kidding me?" Summer's angry outburst surprised the others.

"Not at all," David said. "Despite how I felt about him, I showed the manuscript to Edward. I'd heard he had publishing connections in Edinburgh. He kept it for himself. Used the storyline in his gin commercials. When I confronted him, he laughed and said he had more money and bigger lawyers than I'd ever have or could imagine. He'd bury me. Ruin my education career, as well. I backed down. Told myself it wasn't that important. I could write something else if I wanted. Apparently, I didn't. In the end, my happy, quiet life with Helen in Inversgail is all I need."

"But?" Janet said.

"Aye, but. I saw Wendy at the library a month or more back. Around the time Violet's invitation arrived. Wendy had just been chatting with Ian Atkinson. Or, more accurately, Ian had just been blethering at Wendy. I asked her how things were at the museum. She was in a hurry by then. She made an offhand remark about annoying myth mongers and their bloody fictions. I assumed she meant Ian. Didn't ask. Later, it popped into my head that she'd said mongers, plural, and that she had to deal with Edward havering at the museum, as well. That's when my agile, ancient brain added decluttering and annoying myth mongers together, and came up with clearing an annoying bit of clutter from my own life. I went to the attic. For my own peace of mind, I decided to clear the air with Edward. I'm twenty-five years closer to the grave than he is, but we're both old men. I hoped he'd changed."

"I hope he apologized," Summer said.

"We're both wrong, then. I lied about having a dentist appointment that morning before Violet's party. I phoned Edward and asked to see him. He sounded friendly enough. Said he'd save me the drive to Fairy Flax Hall and meet me at Teresa's. I took the manuscript with me." David stopped and sipped whisky.

"And?" Tallie asked.

"He laughed. And laughed some more, and asked what did I plan to do, beat him over the head with it? Make him die the death of a thousand paper cuts?"

"What did you do?" Christine asked. "I might have gone for both."

"Came home. Shoved it under the sofa."

"Okay, so what were you really doing outside Teresa's house the other morning?" Janet asked.

"I'd heard something from Wendy about Edward having money issues. That he'd fallen on hard times and was actually living with Teresa." David shrugged. "I wanted to see proof of that."

"Karma?" Summer asked.

"Just petty satisfaction. I'm not proud of that, but he and I have never liked each other. Not in any grand way. At least not until the rather grand way of plagiarizing my story, which now that I remember, he told me I should take as a compliment. But never rammies in Tesco's produce aisle. He's just always let me know that he looks down on me. I let all that get in the way of any wee bit of usefulness I might have had on the museum board."

"That's all right, Dad. I look down on *him* these days," Christine said. "On his freckled scalp, anyway. He has a marked stoop."

David, whose own posture was excellent, kissed Christine on the top of her head before refilling her glass. "I didn't connect Wendy's comment with her murder. Who would? Or with arsenic? Again, who would? Who thinks that way?"

"Jane does," Helen said. "*She's* a knitter. Is she one of your knitters in the shop, Chrissie?"

"Jane?" David turned a blank look to Christine and shook his head.

"Do you mean your cousin Jane, Mum?" Christine asked.

"Not at all," said Helen. "She's been dead for years. Did you not know?"

"I thought it might have slipped your mind, is all," Christine said. "Jane who, then?"

"Not a local woman. English," Helen said. "You might not know her and so it's just as well that I've forgot the rest of her name."

"On the subject of forgetting," David said, "it seems your mum managed to slip something into her coat pocket at Violet's party after all. A wee watercolor of fairy flax. The flower, not the MacAskill's bit of rubble. She doesn't remember taking it."

"Because I did not."

"You didn't, Mum," Christine said. "Edward took our coats at the door, and when we went to the loo, you left your pocketbook in the sitting room. No doubt someone mistook your coat for their own and were disappointed when they got home without the picture."

"That settles that, then," Helen said. "I kent I wasn't that daft. And now I ken Jane's surname. She's Jane Marple."

"That's wonderful, Mum. I do know Jane Marple. Neither one of you is daft."

"What's your book called, David?" Summer asked.

"Och, I'm rubbish at titles and never got round to that."

"And you really don't write anymore?" Tallie asked.

"Not fiction. A journal. Christine will have it when I'm gone."

"If you don't have any pressing need for that box of museum minutes," Janet said, "may we take it with us?"

With David's directions through the clutter in the attic, Tallie and Summer found the box. They loaded it into the Vauxhall and Christine drove them home.

"There's a lot of meeting minutes to unpack from that box," Summer said.

"There's a lot to unpack from Dad's story."

"Details, thoughts, and questions go into our documents," Janet said. "The minutes were my idea, so I'll tackle them."

"We can share them," Summer said.

"Oh, *thank* you," Janet said. "I wasn't really looking forward to that, and I'm not a pleasant martyr. Christine, do you believe that's how the picture got into your mum's coat pocket?"

"Simplest is best." Christine sounded thoughtful. Or tired.

"Does David's story move Edward to number one suspect?" Tallie asked.

"Do we want to be that focused on one person?" Janet asked.

"I do," Summer said. "Kindly old duffer my bahookie."

"Dad's still a suspect," Christine said.

"What? No," Janet said. "His story makes sense and accounts for all your questions. Why on earth would he kill Wendy?"

"He wouldn't. But Bethia is a suspect, and she wasn't making sneaky trips and holding back information."

"Gosh," Janet said. "Who does that remind me of? You have your dad's height, too. Don't you dare go down that dark path thinking he's guilty, Christine."

Christine didn't answer.

"Christine. Look at me. *No*, don't look at me. You're driving. Not down that path. Not for one second. Aye or nae?"

"Aye."

"Thank you. You get in these moods, and I have to say, you end up with *yer bum oot the windae.*" Janet sneaked a sidelong glance at Christine and saw her trying not to smile. "Next question. Did Helen mean Elaine Markwell? Elaine, Jane. Markwell, Marple."

"Are we sure Helen didn't watch a Miss Marple episode on TV recently?" Summer asked. "Why would she think Elaine knows something about arsenic?"

"It wouldn't hurt to talk to Elaine again, anyway," Janet said. "Check in with her. See how she's doing."

"Christine's car thief left a usage pattern behind," Tallie said. "Who drinks Irn-Bru?"

"Half of Scotland and most of the tourists," Christine said. "At least a sip."

26

Arsenic diary, day twelve

I type, I click, et voilà, another helpful hint appears: Do not take arsenic supplements as they are LIKELY UNSAFE. The caps are the website's, not mine. I ask you, who? Who <u>are</u> these people with barm for brains who need that warning?

Another hint from online research now that I'm cut off from my old girl: You won't want to eat mutton from Ronaldsay in the Orkneys. They found arsenic in sheep urine there. Presumably from eating seaweed. Avoid the seaweed, too, I suppose.

And a question you might have: If one boils water containing arsenic, will the boiling remove the arsenic? Answer: Au contraire. Because water evaporates when you boil it, the arsenic concentration will actually increase. Food or drink for thought? LIKELY UNSAFE. Caps mine.

Last hint, perhaps most helpful of all: Beware leftover lumber from your old DIY projects. If it bears a greenish tint, that green likely came from treating the wood with copper chrome arsenic. It's been outlawed, and no longer sold, but if you find a few pieces in your shed or if it's what was used for that decking you're tearing out, best not to burn it. Mind that arsenic is with us forever. One tablespoon of ash from CCA-treated wood is enough to kill an adult. The other byproduct is toxic as well—smoke.

"I'm just saying." Janet's jaw began to ache from clenching her teeth. *When did I develop that bad habit?* she wondered. *Oh, yes, five minutes ago when Norman developed his bad habit of being a stubborn—*

Hobbs had knocked on the door during their morning meeting. He'd read the summary of David's revelations that Christine had sent the night before. He agreed with their conclusion that David's story revealed Edward as unscrupulous, willing to take what wasn't his, and a bully when threatened. But he would not tell them if David was a suspect—now, still, or confirmed. Christine was silent. Possibly catatonic, Janet thought. With guilt for sending the summary? Angry at Hobbs? Janet didn't know but wasn't going to let this pass.

"I'm just saying, Norman, that David's story has nothing to do with the murders." Janet tilted her head back to give him her furious mother look. So what if it gave him a look up her nostrils, too. Served him right. "True, David looked fishy, but we landed that fish and gutted it."

Tallie and Summer applauded. Christine remained mute and staring. Hobbs took his leave.

"Right," Janet said. "I'm going to the museum for a volunteer stint, but first I'm going after him to straighten him out."

Tallie unlocked the door for her. "You go, Mom!"

Janet saw Hobbs ahead, walking in the direction she meant to go. She caught up with him by running the short distance between them. She had a suspicion she looked like a militarized puffin stalking along with her nose red from cold and him towering beside her in his uniform.

"I'm just *saying*, Norman, that where there's *smoke* there's *fire*. And thank you. Thank you, *very* much, because now you've reduced me to spouting *clichés* when all I'm *trying* to do is get *you* to take our question *seriously*. Honest to petrified penguin patooties."

"I beg your pardon?"

"Nope," Janet said with an angry chop of her hand. "You can't have it both ways, Norman. You can't ignore the question of David's status in this investigation and then turn around and beg my pardon because you're affronted or suddenly interested in my randomly associated alliterations. It's all or nothing. And that's strike two against you for making me use another cliché. Phooey. And I spell phooey with a *ph*, so you can add *that* to your putrified penguins."

"I believe you described them as petrified the first time. Putrified sounds much less pleasant. Would you like to stop for a cup of tea, Mrs. Marsh?"

"We just left the best tearoom in Inversgail."

"A lemonade? Or to catch your breath?"

Janet crossed her arms and glared at a seagull perched on a bollard. "What are *you* looking at?" she snarled at it. The gull turned its back on her.

"An ice cream?" Hobbs asked.

"Don't patronize me."

"Never." Hobbs looked at his phone. "It's just gone half ten. Bit early for a pint."

"Oh for heaven's sake. Take your pint and put it with your penguins."

"Your *p*assion for *p*ursuing the *p*oisoner is *p*raiseworthy," Hobbs said.

"And your insistence on sticking to legalities so that we don't jeopardize the investigation or cost you your career is completely irritating." Janet shook her arms out, resettled her shoulders. "But it's understandable." Janet suddenly stopped walking. Unaware, Hobbs kept going. *Typical lack of attention to detail*, Janet thought, then wondered if she should feel bad for sounding so much like Christine.

"Norman," she called. By the time she did, he'd noticed her absence and started back. "Why are you continuing to walk with me if you have no intention of answering the question? Why not avoid the question and my harangue and beetle off somewhere else? You aren't hoping to get *more* information out of me about David, are you? I can be just as tight-lipped as you—if I try." She glanced at him to make sure she didn't see a smile. He probably knew better.

"I could just as well ask why you're continuing to walk with me if you're getting no satisfaction beyond denigrating penguins, a bird of which I am rather fond."

"I was denigrating policemen, too, in case you hadn't noticed."

"I'm on my way to the museum to follow up on Isobel's report of a pair of missing stockings. My trip seems to have coincided with one of your own."

"You're only now following up on that?"

"She just made the report yesterday."

"*I* told you about the stockings two days ago, and they've been missing far longer."

"An interesting gap, don't you think?" Hobbs said.

"Huh. I'm on my way to the museum, too. I've been volunteering for a few hours here and there, helping out since Isobel lost Wendy. She's getting frazzled doing two jobs."

"A commendable response in a time of need," Hobbs said. "Any thoughts on undercover surveillance while you're there?" He didn't *sound* as though he was poking fun.

"Of course," Janet said, deciding to get in the first poke herself. "Self-appointed. Janet Marsh: museum dogsbody and spy."

"I'll make a note of that in the official case record."

"Very droll. As long as you're making it official, though, why don't I sit in on Isobel's report on the missing stockings? Any objection?"

"Only if she has any. But why don't we be on our way before we both turn into penguins."

As they passed the Stevenson statue, Janet saw that someone had crocheted coverings for his shoes—orange, and they looked like penguin feet.

"I don't often find the time to visit the museum." Hobbs held the door for Janet. "Nana Bethia is keen for me to see the gansey exhibit."

"Elevator or stairs?" Janet asked.

"Lift."

No one greeted them when they reached the reception desk, but the handbell and the sign inviting visitors to ring it stood on the desk's corner.

"A bell like this was stolen from St. Finan's Isle," he said. "I saw it once. Took a kayak trip up Loch Shiel as a teen and landed on St. Finan's. Not many made the trip back then." He looked at the bell suspiciously.

"It's a reproduction, Norman. You can't think Isobel would let people ring the original."

"I rang the original. I can only describe the experience as holy." He lifted the bell, gave it several swings, listening to the *bong, bong.* "It sounds nothing like the original. You cannae feel it resonate in your chest," he said, replacing it. "Medieval craftsman had secrets we can only guess at."

The panel door behind the desk opened and Edward appeared. "Hello! A lovely surprise. Isobel is just finishing up a tour." He looked back through the door. "Ah, here she comes." He stepped aside, making room for Isobel. "Isobel, my dear, this is me away."

"Oh? See you later, then."

"You wish to make a report about missing stockings?" Hobbs asked.

"Sounds silly, doesn't it? Walk with me. I'll check on the knitters whilst we talk."

"Do you mind if I come along?" Janet asked.

"Not at all. I think you know I give volunteers special privileges." She smiled toward the elevator where Edward had gone. As they walked down the gallery, she recounted her process of looking for the stockings and Edward's idea that one of the knitters had "borrowed" them.

"Have you asked the knitters?" Hobbs asked.

"Yes. No joy. Uncle Edward has been going round the knitting venues, chatting them up, taking a wee *keek* into knitting bags. No joy there, either."

The knitters sat in a pool of sunlight, looking to Janet as though they sat in their own warm, yellow harbor. Bethia was among them, and Kyle. Bethia waved her needles in answer to a discreet nod from Hobbs. Kyle watched his own needles intently, seemingly unaware that one of his balls of yarn had rolled under Bethia's chair.

"All going well?" Isobel asked. The knitters held up their lengthening stockings. Isobel made admiring comments and thanked them for all their work. She nodded her head back toward the desk, and the three started back. "I feel awful. So guilty. I shouldn't have left them unattended. Shouldn't have even taken them out of safekeeping."

Hobbs took his notebook out. "Monetary value?"

"We don't do that," she said. "They're like the St. Finan's bell. Not replaceable, and not a commodity for the museum."

"Are they some of the arsenical stockings?" Janet asked.

Isobel grimaced. "That's the other problem, and why I don't believe Uncle Edward's theory. I've told all the knitters about the stockings, about the arsenic. They saw how I wore gloves when touching them. The stockings are kept in a bag, and that's missing as well, but what if someone were to mishandle them? I asked that they be brought back or left anonymously. No questions asked. They've not been returned. That's why I called you."

"Thank you, Ms. Ritchie," Hobbs said. "We'll hope for the best, aye? I'll be in touch."

"I'll be back in a minute, Isobel," Janet said. "I want to be sure Constable Hobbs sees how beautiful it is to look up toward the windows from the bottom of the stairs." She did, too, but she also wanted to ask him if the stockings could be the source of the arsenic.

"If you come down the stairs," Janet said, as they walked down them, "and you stand in just the right place," she guided him there, "and you look up, it's not the experience of ringing the bell on St. Finan's Isle, but with the angles, the windows, the wall, the light—"

"I see exactly what you mean. It brings a sense of awe. Thank you, Janet."

"You're welcome. Now, these stockings."

As Hobbs brought out his notebook again, Janet heard a noise above them. She looked up and saw the handbell sitting on the balcony. *That* didn't look safe. She started to point it out to Hobbs, saw the bell move, and with no time to shout, grabbed his arm and yanked him backward. The bell crashed to the floor, just missing Hobbs, and landing with a tremendous and sickening thud. It left an impression an inch deep in the wood floor.

Hobbs looked at the bell, then at Janet. "Saved from the bell. Thank you."

As soon as the initial shock passed, Janet let go of his arm and started for the stairs, intent on running up them to see what idiot—Hobbs stopped her, pulling her back so they couldn't be seen from the balcony. He put a finger to his lips. Pointed to his ear and then up.

Janet didn't hear the sounds of anyone reacting above them. Was it an accident? Kids? Possibly. If so, they crept away with no sounds of parents in the background. Hadn't anyone heard the crash? Had it been on purpose? Janet was glad Hobbs still held her arm. She felt wobbly. When he let go to take pictures with his phone, she was glad not to topple. The longer the silence continued above them, the more likely it seemed someone had tried to kill one or both of them.

Then Isobel peered over the balcony. She didn't scream, but her face shifted from disbelief to horror and she pelted down the stairs shouting, "What *happened*?"

"If you've a bag of some sort, I'll take the bell away with me and see if I can find out," Hobbs said. "Is there another entrance besides the front door?"

"Of course."

"Security cameras?"

"Aye."

"I'll want to see them."

When Isobel returned with a bag, she looked sick. "The system was turned off."

"How would that happen?" Hobbs asked. "Would it be hard to do?"

"We have all the mod cons, but some of them are not much better than nothing."

Hobbs nodded. "I'll be up directly."

Janet waited until Isobel climbed the stairs again, then said, "So anyone could have come and gone."

"Looks like."

27

Arsenic diary, day twelve and a half
  <u>The slings and arrows of outrageous fortune.</u> What are these awful things that are not my fault? <u>That is the question.</u> I oppose them and would end this sea of troubles. My mind suffers from slings and arrows.
  S&A.
  Stockings and arsenic.
  I feel rather cheered.

Janet's brush with death and her heroism in saving Constable Hobbs revived and energized Christine. A text from her father helped. He'd spent several hours with Inspector Reddick, that morning, telling him much of what he'd told them the evening before. Reddick had asked to read his novel.

"Dad has an alibi for the bell incident with which Norman cannot begin to quibble," Christine said. "If he does, I'll say *dong, dong, dong* and watch him quail. But Janet, you missed a chance by not staying for your volunteer stint. You could've given us a valuable firsthand account of Norman's investigation into the incident and kept tabs on some of our suspects at the same time."

Janet was relieved to have Christine back and ebullient but told her she couldn't possibly have stayed at the museum. Tallie agreed with her mother. Rab brought Janet a cup of tea.

The women didn't keep their photocopies of the scrapbook a secret or under wraps. Rab made no secret of finding the scrapbook fascinating. He forewent his usual puttering, dusting, and waiting on book and tea customers, in favor of reading it in the inglenook, next to a napping Ranger. Tallie sat on the stool at one end of the counter reading her share of the museum board minutes, which they'd also decided not to hide.

Janet, still feeling a shiver of adrenaline from the crashing handbell, said she'd take care of customers. She wanted the healing contact with books.

In the tearoom, Christine and Summer dipped into the minutes and scrapbook as time allowed.

"Wendy ramped up going after specific and residuary legacy gifts a few years ago," Tallie said after waiting for Janet's latest customers to pay and start for the door. "That might be when Violet put the museum in her will."

"Anything unusual about that?" Janet asked.

"No. Wendy was a smart fundraiser. It takes a lot of currying to develop those kinds of donors, but from what we've heard, she had a knack for it."

"Interesting that Violet went along with that but felt so pressured by Teresa over the decluttering."

"Wendy might've had a softer touch. You'd better go see why Christine is waving a white napkin at you." Tallie pointed toward the far end of a book aisle where Christine fluttered a serviette in their direction.

"Oh dear. Be right back." Janet trotted down the aisle. "I almost hate to ask. What's happened now?"

"Nothing beyond questions fizzing up in my brain and a room full of tea swillers, so I've no real time to talk. Here's the big fizz of the moment: If Violet is lonely, why does Edward stay with Teresa? He and Violet seem to dote on each other and he says Teresa is better suited to living alone. And for heaven's sake, why does Teresa let him stay? They obviously grate on each other. So, what's he up to? Torturing both of them? That's all. I wanted to get those thoughts out of my head before it exploded. Let me know if you come up with any answers."

Twirling her serviette, Christine returned to the tearoom, leaving Janet feeling like a teapot mistakenly filled with soda water. She went back, folded her hands on the counter, and waited quietly for the next customer.

"All right there?" Tallie asked.

Janet fluttered a wave and refolded her hands.

"I'm happy to help if I can," Tallie said.

Janet turned and pointed at her. "Happy. That's the answer." She pulled out her phone and punched in a number. When Christine answered, Janet said, "Teresa lets him stay because she's loyal to family, even though she seems to be the only one who doesn't know how to create a convincing story of happy families. She's missing that gene." She disconnected and looked at Tallie again. "Something she asked about."

"I don't know what the question was, but the answer sounded good," Tallie said. "Try this one. What if Wendy wanted Fairy Flax Hall in addition to the generous chunk of money Violet promised, but met some resistance?"

Janet thought for a moment. "Edward called Wendy a completist. The Hall, in addition to the money, would complete the museum's solvency for decades to come if not longer."

"Sounds great," Tallie said. "What if Wendy pushed Violet to give the house to the museum and also wanted the money sooner rather than later? Sort of a pre-legacy legacy."

"Violet could say no."

"That sounds simple enough."

"Unless . . ." Janet said. "Unless Wendy wanted the money sooner and Violet said no, so she tried to kill Violet when there were a bunch of people wandering all over the house, giving her the cover of confusion, but her aim was catastrophically off. High-powered fundraising gone horribly wrong."

Tallie looked at the woman who'd just made that suggestion—her mild, now slightly out of breath, retired librarian mother. "So how do we account for Euan's death?"

"Same scenario—greed, poor aim, wrong victim—maybe Wendy had a partner. Someone else poured the poison and then used Euan as misdirection while making a better plan to get rid of Violet later when the heat is off. Which means she's still in danger. Or maybe Euan saw or heard something at the party that he shouldn't have, and here come customers so let's put this discussion on hold."

"Better yet, I'll put it in a document."

"Put in whatever it was I said to Christine, too." Janet smiled.

"Looks like she already did."

Tallie's and Christine's document entries inspired a series of group texts between bookshop and tearoom. Janet started the string with: *Do Edward, Teresa, or Isobel want more than Violet is willing to give? The house? Money? Clutter going out the door?*

While Janet rang up one of Ian's books for a customer, Tallie read Summer's response aloud. "Violet said they had their chance to take what they wanted."

The customer raised her eyebrows. "I don't know who Violet is, but do 'they' think they really had a chance?"

"Good question," Janet said.

"Your Violet might be more greedy than generous," the customer said. "On the other hand, one of 'them' might regret not taking more. Sounds like a good plot for one of Ian Atkinson's books. Cheers."

Janet called thanks as the customer went out the door.

"Minus the reference to Ian, those were good points," Tallie said. "I'll get them into a text."

"You could keep reading texts out loud," Janet said. "Change the names and identifiable locations. Take advantage of armchair detectives out shopping."

"For now, let's just be more careful."

"Good advice, dear. That's why we like having a lawyer on the payroll."

Their phones buzzed with a text from Christine: *Isobel. She'd want everything Wendy wanted for the museum and more.*

Janet countered with: *Oh, come on!*

From Summer: *We can't play favorites.*

Tallie sent: *Edward* is *the favorite.* Then turned to Janet. "We should try to eliminate the other suspects, though."

"Poor word choice, but you're right. Hang on." Janet sent: *Let's agree Bethia, David, and Norman are not suspects.* And received three thumbs-up emojis in return.

Summer wrote: *I'd like a chance to question Kyle.*

"Safety-conscious lawyer hat on," Tallie said in an aside to Janet, then sent: *Not alone. Too dangerous. Mom was lucky this morning. The bell might have been for her. Time to initiate our traveling in pairs safety protocol.*

Summer wrote: *Aye-aye, coming over to consult.*

"Here she comes," Tallie said, "in full Summer action mode. Like there's a stopwatch ticking in her brainstem."

"And in perfect choreography, there goes Rab to the tearoom," Janet said. "Hello, Summer."

"Christine said I need to make a case for interviewing Kyle." Summer laid her palms flat on the counter and looked back and forth between Janet and Tallie. "She called it confronting him, but I think that's the wrong approach."

"Interview is better," Janet agreed. "You can just tell us without the case, if you want."

Summer's hands rose to their fingertips. "But this is good. Listen. Why Kyle? The scrapbook. His history. He might know how to hotwire a car. He could've pushed the bell. He might've had history with Wendy. Conjecture on the last two."

"We do a lot of that," Tallie said.

"Right. So. We meet him at Nev's—it's safe, we'll be surrounded by people. We order a plate of Danny's new Burns club sandwiches for the table. Byrne, Burns, get it? It'll sound friendly. We sit near the door, with him closest to it, so he can leave easily at anytime and won't feel cornered."

"And fight like a rat to get out," Janet said. "Why do you think he'll agree to meet us?"

"Christine found the note to look for ripe opportunities for clever ruses in her pocket, so we've devised one. You'll see it in action tonight. Sound good?"

"Sounds super," Tallie said.

Summer waved over her shoulder and was gone.

"Do we want to make a case for interviewing anyone or devising a clever ruse?" Tallie asked.

"No, I'm good. Do you want lunch first or second?"

"Second's fine."

"Okey doke. I'll be in here." Janet went into the office to eat the sandwich she'd brought from home. The adrenaline had cleared her system but left behind an uneasy *what if.* What if the bell had hit her or Hobbs? She shoved the sandwich aside, logged onto the office laptop, and opened a blank document. She named it "What If" and started typing.

What if Wendy convinced Violet to leave a generous amount of money *and* Fairy Flax Hall to the museum? What if Edward knows how much effort went into that and how much Wendy counted on it? What if Edward knows that Violet has second thoughts about her will? What if Edward heard Wendy's reaction to the possibility of losing all that, including some regrettable comments? What if Edward thought Wendy would kill Violet to get the museum's inheritance before she changed her will? What if Edward struck first? What if he killed Euan to shift blame?

Janet's unease became a lowering dark cloud. She let the others know about the document, ate a few bites of her sandwich, then went back to the comfort of books.

∽

The women arrived at Nev's half an hour before the time Kyle had agreed to meet them. Janet and Tallie expressed surprise and delight when Bethia and Maida joined them at the table closest to the door. Mostly surprise.

"In the dark?" Maida said. "The mark of a good ruse. You should explain, mind," she told Summer. "So Janet and Tallie don't give us away."

Kyle, Summer told them, had won the "Supper with a Knitting Superstar" prize, awarded for exceptional participation in public knitting, and sponsored by Yon Bonnie Books, Cakes and Tales Tearoom, and Maida's company. She and Christine had told him when he came to knit that afternoon in the tearoom. Taken aback, because he hadn't heard of the prize, he'd nonetheless agreed to meet them at Nev's.

"I'm the superstar," Bethia said.

"I'm here to make it look official," said Maida.

Kyle arrived with only one carrier bag and only slightly late. He took the last chair at the table—nearest the door. They all congratulated him, and Bethia presented him with a copy of *Knit Fix: Problem Solving for Knitters* and one of her own knitted creations, a bright-green Loch Ness monster. Christine went to the bar for a round of drinks and came back with a tray piled with sandwiches.

"This is nice," Summer said. "Do you know, I was so jealous when I heard you found a tailcoat at the decluttering. I asked Janet to look for a *Downton Abbey*-ish evening gown."

"I thought I might find one," Janet said. "Especially after seeing you in the tailcoat. And then Isobel told me there *weren't* any clothes in the clutter." She tried to mix disappointed and flummoxed on her face. Perhaps not very well.

"Fine," Kyle snapped. "It was a cast-off, all right? Edward gave it to me."

"Cool. That's how I've gotten some of my favorite things," Tallie said. "Have a sandwich. They're new on the menu. Called Burns clubs. She pushed the plate toward him.

Kyle ignored it. "You thought I took the coat."

"Who would blame you? Janet said it looked elegant on you," Christine said. "I heard that you clean for Maida at Fairy Flax Hall. That can't pay much. Sorry, Maida, nothing personal and no harm meant. But you'd know where to find the coat."

"Do you think I took the scrapbook, too?"

"What scrapbook?" Janet asked.

"Don't try that one on. Ian Atkinson's blethered about the scrapbook everywhere. How do you think I would have found it? There's a vast number of bookcases in that house. With all the dusting I do, am I supposed to have spare time to look for books worth nicking, too?"

"You might have seen Ian with it," Summer said, "and noticed where he took it from or put it back.

"Your stories are almost as good as Edward MacAskill's."

"He does have some doozies." Janet said.

"So, no. I didn't take the minging scrapbook. But when I found it in my knitting bag, I knew I'd be blamed, so I passed it off as fast as I could."

"Like a hot potato from Mr. Potato Chef," Christine said. "We wondered how it ended up in Bethia's bag."

"Didn't want to *burn* my fingers. I hope it didn't cause you any trouble, Bethia. I reckoned you'd get it where it needed to go."

"I did, and you've won the award, so no need to worry at all. The sandwiches are delicious. Is that—"

"Aye, haggis and pickle." Maida helped herself to another sandwich and passed the plate. "Do you have any idea who put the scrapbook in your bag or when it could have happened?"

"No."

"Sorry if we come across like inquisitors," Tallie said. "I'm a lapsed lawyer who's having trouble shaking the habit."

"Is that all?" Kyle put the book and stuffed monster in his carrier bag.

"Oh, stay for supper," Summer said. "One Burns club?"

"Too close to my own name. I don't want to turn cannibal."

"Can I get you an Irn-Bru before you go?" Christine asked. "Och, I guess not. Out the door. He made more eye contact with Nessie than any of us."

"His humor needs work," Maida said. "His work needs work as well."

Janet took another sandwich. "So do his lies."

"We'll be off, too," Maida said. "Let you make your report to Norman."

Christine thanked them for their help. She ate the last sandwich, then asked the others, "What are we putting in this report to Norman besides a summary of tonight?"

Janet had her phone out, checking their texts and documents for anything to add. She found two additions to "What If."

What if Edward killed Wendy to give Isobel her dream job?
What if, instead of protecting Violet, Edward tried to kill her to
stop her from giving away more of the money and the house?

"We'll tell him Edward is the prime suspect and why. Any objections?" Tallie and Christine shook their heads.

"Everything fits," Summer said. "Go for it. I'll go for another round."

Janet would rather have composed the email to Hobbs on her laptop but felt the pressure of the lowering cloud. She gave him a summary of Kyle's answers, their opinion that he likely lied, corroborated by the lack of consistent eye contact. She told him their consensus that Edward was the prime suspect and shared the "What If" document with him. She copied the others and hit send. "Check your email, you'll see what I sent." While they did, she took a good swallow of Selkie's Tears and wished she had another Burns club.

Their phones pinged and chirped with a response from Hobbs. "Edward has an alibi, confirmed by Reddick."

"If you ask me, that proves he's guilty," Christine said.

Tallie fired back to Hobbs asking what Edward's alibi was.

Another round of pings and chirps delivered the message, "I am not at liberty to say."

"Well, rats," Summer said. "I thought we'd found our bad guy."

"But we didn't." Janet said. "And maybe this time we won't."

28

Arsenic diary, day thirteen
   I am not cut out to be a detective.
   Or a criminal.

"We really might not figure it out, though," Janet said the next morning.

The four women had agreed to an early breakfast in the inglenook to see where their investigation could go from the shambles of the night before. Janet and Tallie walked down the hill toward the harbor on their way there.

"And do you know what? We should be alright with that," Tallie said. "We're booksellers, not supersleuths. But we'll go over everything again this morning. See what emerges. Then you and Christine will go have lunch with Helen and David at the Argyle Trout. If it's fabulous, you can take me there for *my* birthday. Deal?"

The clouds hanging over the harbor matched the one hanging over Janet. Not entirely, though, she realized. Hers had congealed overnight into a uniform, dismal gray. The harbor clouds moved, drifted, shifted from dark gray through to a light gray before finally settling on something almost like mother of pearl.

"Mom? Deal?

"Look at the clouds. They're like Smirr's belly."

"That cheers you up?"

"I think it does. Cats and clouds are mysteries. They're never the same thing twice and there's always something new to look at. The same with our suspects, I guess. Let's look again."

Summer had gotten up early, made quiche, and started the kettle. Janet, who was suddenly starved, felt like kissing her, so she did.

At Tallie's suggestion, they began by reading through their documents and text strings while they ate. "Then we can talk about each of them, opportunity, possible motives, and whatever else might be relevant. Can I make a request, though? Can we avoid prefacing everything with 'Well, if it isn't Edward?'"

"If we did, it would be more like a jolly game," Christine said. "After Norman's bombshell last night, some of us might need that. Your mother, for instance."

"I'm better this morning," Janet said. "Maybe not jolly, but ready to jump back in. Let's do Kyle first. Opportunity? Yes, including scrapbook and bell. Motive? Unknown, but I like the idea that it was personal between him and Wendy. He said he didn't know her, but he's another storyteller and he spends time at the museum."

"Maybe an actor, too," Tallie said. "He came into the shop, that first day, like he battled a wind or a current. Very much like a pantomime or pratfall artist. Like Danny Kaye in an old movie. Plus, his shoplifting expertise."

"Euan might have seen or heard something," Summer said. "Holes in the theory? We have no evidence of any kind of relationship between him and Wendy. Or the museum. He claims he didn't know her, but suspects lie. Euan might have figured it out."

"Violet," Christine said. "Opportunity for Wendy. Iffy for Euan and the bell. Opportunity for scrapbook, but really? She already owned it;

why stage its theft? Motive is a possible dislike of Wendy's continuing strong arm tactics."

"And to that," Summer said, "*I* say really? All she had to do was get Teresa, Edward, Isobel, or her lawyer to tell Wendy to lay off."

"People make illogical decisions when they're under pressure," Tallie sad. "There are loads of criminals behind bars who could have done something legal instead of what they did. We don't really need to come up with ironclad motives for these guys. We're puzzling something out and giving the results to the Normans."

"You don't want to plug information holes?" Janet asked.

"We can't plug them all," Tallie reasoned. "That's what the police are for. Move on to Isobel?"

"We are blinded by her charm," Christine said. "So let's lay into her."

"Opportunity for Wendy, Euan, scrapbook, and the bell," Janet said.

"She had a perfectly good reason for her arsenic research," Summer said. "The amount of detail she went into is a bit much, but she might be a research junkie and compulsive note-taker."

"Motive—to get her dream job," Tallie paused. "Um, why haven't we looked at her seriously before?"

"Blinded by Edward," Janet said. "That might be my fault. He said that Isobel always finds a way to get things done and implied that she and Wendy didn't always get along."

"Alternate motive," Christine said. "Isobel loves the museum and the building it's in. What if she also loves Fairy Flax Hall and wants it for herself. Best of both worlds and both her own?"

"Feeling sick," Janet said, "but also like we might be getting somewhere. Teresa. Same opportunities as Isobel. Motive?"

"Wants Fairy Flax Hall?" Summer said. "Or like Edward, to protect Violet? Has she ever lied to us?

"She lied about bringing Mr. Potato Chef to Wendy at the museum," Janet said.

"Unless that was someone else's clever ruse," Christine said. "I wish Edward wasn't in the clear, but Kyle or Isobel could have given the name Teresa when they ordered. If you ask me, too many clever clogs ruin the business of ruses."

"Back to Teresa," Summer said. "She doesn't seem to be as good at creating narratives as other MacAskills. She's just there. Like the numbers she works with. I don't think poison would pop into her head as a solution to a problem."

"We haven't covered Elaine," Tallie said.

"Our mystery Jane Marple." Christine looked at the time. "We might consider wrapping up soon, it's almost time for us to head out for lunch. Elaine had opportunity for everything except maybe the scrapbook. She had access to arsenic, too, in Ian's bothy. Motive, a sad one. To end Euan's downward spiral, which included killing Wendy. Hmm. I vote for scratching Elaine off. I can't bear the thought she killed her son."

"She might have other motives," Summer said.

"Then we'll let the police find them," said Janet. "But guess who else might know about the arsenic in Ian's bothy—Teresa. They were an item, and you know how he likes to show women his bothy."

"Yes, I do," Summer said. "Some of us are just better at thwarting him."

"I wonder how often Teresa thwarts Violet," Janet said. "She didn't like the idea of the decluttering, but she organized it anyway. And even though Maida said Teresa did the work, do you remember what Teresa said that night?"

"'Under your eye, Mother. Always under your eye.' Very good, Janet," Christine said.

They were silent for a moment, staring at the space in front of Christine, as though the words hung there. Then all their words fell on top of each other.

"What's their motive if Teresa and Violet are in it together?"

"They mesh. Where one didn't have opportunity, the other did."

"If Violet couldn't lift the bell, Teresa could."

"If Violet wanted something done, Teresa might do it."

"If Violet did something, Teresa might cover it up."

"But doesn't Teresa browbeat Violet?"

"But maybe she won't let anyone else do the same."

"Reality check," Tallie said over them. "Are we serious about this? We were serious about Edward."

"And made a good case," Janet said.

"And we're pretty serious about Isobel now, too," Tallie said.

"Is the whole family rotten?" Summer asked.

"We're just taking the clues they're giving us and building their stories," Christine said. "Like any good detectives. The police have oodles of resources at their disposal, and *they* haven't solved this yet. So, we'll do our bit, give them our new first, second, and third place suspects, and then we'll go enjoy the rest of our Sunday. Is everybody agreed that Kyle is good for third place? Excellent. Who do we like for second and first?"

They settled on Isobel for second place and the team of Violet and Teresa for first. Christine sent the report to both Normans. She and Janet went to pick up Helen and David. And the four of them set out on the winding way to the Argyle Trout for Helen's birthday lunch.

Several miles along, as the narrow road climbed and dipped and took unexpected curves, David spoke up from the back seat beside Janet. "We might be going a wee bit too fast on the downhills. I only mention it because we're coming to a series of steep curves."

"We might be having trouble with the brakes," Christine said. She readjusted the wonky rearview mirror and saw a pickup come into view behind them. When she glanced in the mirror, again, the truck was closer. As they started into the downhill curves, the truck put on a burst of speed.

29

"Oh, good Lord," Christine said. "Hold on."

The Vauxhall lurched forward, hit from behind by the pickup.

"Bloody hel—bloody cheek," David said.

"What's happening? Who did that?" Helen asked.

"Bloody Edward." Christine strained to hold the speeding car steady, stomping on the brake. "Alibi my foot."

"He's trying to come alongside," Janet said, then, "Oh, good Lord," as the pickup sideswiped them.

As Christine fought to keep the car on the road, the truck veered into the opposite lane, missing the next curve, and flying down the hillside, smashing and crumpling into a stone wall at the bottom.

"Oh, *dear* Lord," Janet said. "We should stop, Christine. Go back."

"Render aid, Chrissie," David said.

"Believe me, I'd like nothing better," Christine said. "The brakes are gone. Dad, that dodgy curve above Glen Sgail, how far is it? A mile?"

"At most."

"We won't make it round the curve. We'll go over. What do I do?"

"You won't panic, Chrissie," Helen said. "You won't because you never do."

"And pray," David said.

"Not panicking," Christine said, "and the rest of you pray. Shall I turn off the ignition?"

"I'm looking it up." Janet tapped furiously at her phone.

"I'm going to turn it off," Christine said.

"Don't!" Janet said. "Sorry, didn't mean to shout, but they say no, don't turn it off. Here's what you do. Ready? Take your foot off the gas. Put your hazard lights on. Pump the brake pedal hard and fast."

"Pumping," Christine said. "Hard and fast, hard and fast, hard and fast. That's not noticeably helping. There must be something else."

"*Cautiously* apply the hand brake. Don't yank it. And steer to safety."

"We're speeding down a bloody hill toward a deep, bloody glen. Safety is what's missing at this moment."

"Och, but look at the dear sheep on the brae," Helen said.

"Mum, you're brilliant. Hold on, all of you. Big bumps ahead." Christine broke through a wire fence into a field full of sheep. "Run for your lives, sheep!"

"We're still too fast," David said. "Our old bones won't like bailing out at this speed."

"No bailing at any speed," Christine said. "But now what?"

"Runaway truck ramp," Janet said. "Head *up* the hill. The steepest one. It'll slow us."

"Going up," Christine said. "We're slowing! We're slower, slower. We're stopped." She yanked on the hand brake, and sat with her forehead on the steering wheel while Janet called 9-9-9. Then they all climbed out.

"It's a chilly day for a ramble," Helen said. "But there's a bothy."

While Christine and Janet debated getting the two old people safely down the hill, the Vauxhall's handbrake popped out and the car started to roll.

"I might be able to catch it," David said.

"No." Christine held him firmly by the arm, and they all watched as the Vauxhall gained speed before smashing into a shed at the back of the bothy.

"What were the odds," Janet said. "Isn't that Ian's bothy?"

When the four of them, holding onto each other and watching their footing, had picked their way down the hill to the bothy, Ian pulled up in front.

"Hello there," he said getting out of his car. Then he turned in a complete circle and looked at them again. "How on earth did you arrive here?"

They took him around back to show him the damage. The car had destroyed the backwall of the shed and been stopped by the solid granite of the bothy. Ian pronounced the bothy intact and the Vauxhall almost certainly totaled. "But how on earth did the Vauxhall arrive in the shed?"

"We were run off the road," Janet said. "It's a long story."

"I love long stories," he said.

"So do I," said Helen.

"Then let's get you inside to warm up, and you can tell me over tea."

"Shouldn't we take Ian's car and go back to see what we can do for bloody Edward? I'm sorry, Helen," David said. "MacAskill or no, the man's a bloody menace."

"MacAskill?" Ian asked. "Why, what's happened? He and I were just chatting in Basant's before I came here. I offered him a ride home with his shopping trolley, but he said he likes the exercise."

"How long ago?" Janet asked.

"The meat pie I bought for lunch is still warm."

"Then who was driving the pickup?" Christine said.

Constable Hobbs arrived in a scatter of gravel as Ian's electric kettle whistled. Following Janet's 9-9-9 call, he told them, police had found Teresa MacAskill seriously injured behind the wheel of the pickup with Violet in the passenger seat. Police also found a shotgun. Violet had suffered life-threatening injuries in the accident. "It might be several days before either of them can answer questions," he said. "And may I ask what your part in this is, Mr. Atkinson?"

"Incidental tea maker. Elaine Markwell's meeting me here. She and her husband entered into an agreement to buy the bothy for Euan's new business. Under the circumstances, I'm giving them the opportunity to back out."

Elaine arrived in the middle of Hobbs taking a report from Christine and her passengers. She greeted Helen warmly, then went with Hobbs, Christine, and Janet to see the Vauxhall. It made her laugh almost to tears. "Euan would have laughed, too, she said. "This was going to be a place where you could come and work out your stress by smashing things. With sledgehammers, golf clubs, shinty bats. He'd been collecting old monitors, keyboards, televisions—driving around in the Mr. Potato Chef truck and picking them up. He shouldn't have used the food truck, I expect. If people saw him, that might be how the food poisoning rumors started."

She looked at the newly opened end of the shed. "He'd plans for a sitooterie as well. People like a nice place to sit outside that's a bit sheltered from the weather." She pulled a board loose and tossed it aside. "I reckon the car taking down the wall makes a good start on the sitooterie, too. But the *car*—" Elaine started laughing again, then wiped her eyes. "He named the business Smashing 'S Math Sin, which sounds like the same word twice. But the second word is Gaelic. It sounds virtually the same, but it's not spelt the same and means great, terrific, brilliant."

"Will you go ahead with the business, then?" Janet asked.

"For my boy. Aye."

"Any idea why my mother thought you'd know something about arsenic?" Christine asked.

"Is Helen your mother? A district nurse, aye? I worked for the chemist on the High Street straight out of school. Your mum used to call me Agatha because she'd see me reading Miss Marple and Poirot. She said Agatha Christie worked as a pharmacy assistant once upon a time, too."

"I believe the facts as you've told me, Mrs. Robertson and Mrs. Marsh," Hobbs said. "But the coincidence of you being on this road and Teresa and Violet coming upon you and hatching such a plan is much more difficult to believe."

"Helen's birthday lunch," Janet said.

"She's right," Christine said. "Mum and Dad have lunch at the Argyle Trout at quarter past twelve every year on her birthday. Violet knew that. She verified it at the decluttering."

"Do you think the brakes were tampered with?" Hobbs asked.

"That's a horrifying idea," Janet said.

"It's certainly possible, but the car is ancient," Christine said. "It's been having issues for some time."

"Mrs. MacAskill knows her way around cars," Hobbs said. "She trained as a mechanic during the Second World War. Like the queen."

Janet never wanted to hear Violet compared to the queen again.

∾

Three days after the road attack, Reddick stopped by the bookshop at closing time. "I've come to say goodbye and thank you. And to let you know what Teresa has been saying now that she's able to speak to us. I've come to believe Teresa was equal partners with her mother in whatever plan they had. We have more work to do, but your theory that Wendy pushed for a bigger donation, and Violet resisted and changed her mind may be right."

"Why didn't they just tell Wendy the deal was off?" Tallie asked.

"The threat of bad press. Apparently, Wendy said she would make sure that happened, and they felt it was easier to be rid of Wendy. Euan, poor chap, was an attempt to shift the blame once they realized Teresa was the main suspect. Teresa claims her mother killed Wendy and Euan, and that she knew nothing about it until afterward. However, her story has been inconsistent. She has also said that Euan walked in on her and Violet arguing at the decluttering and Violet then killed him in case he'd heard something he shouldn't have. Teresa was short on details, though. She stumbled when asked *where* Euan walked in on them and what exactly she and her mother were arguing about. She does not appear to be a practiced liar."

"Teresa's good with numbers," Janet said, "but not making up stories."

"She's trying to do it on the fly. Not a good strategy if you want to be a successful murderer," Reddick said.

"She might be blaming Violet because she doesn't think she'll survive to tell the truth herself," Christine said.

"Edward would have told a better story," Summer said. "Did he take the scrapbook?"

"He says no, and none of the partial fingerprints we found were his," Reddick said. "Hobbs says you deserve to know what Edward's unshakable alibi is."

"We do," said Christine.

"Regular fishing dates with the Chief Constable. They're both mad about salmon fishing. Every year, before 15 January, they spend hours together tying flies. The season starts on 15 January and after that they spend hours together scaring the salmon. And now it's my sad duty to tell you that Violet MacAskill died this afternoon due to her injuries. She never regained consciousness."

∽

The women heard from Maida that Isobel and Edward were in shock. They hadn't gone to Fairy Flax Hall since Teresa's arrest and Violet's death. The museum was closed for the time being.

The Vauxhall's frame was irreparably bent. David and Helen hadn't agreed on a new vehicle yet. Style wasn't the problem, it was color. Helen wanted a bright red or yellow, and David wasn't sure he could say no, although he wanted to. Christine stayed out of the discussion.

Ian dropped by to say that he'd remembered something about the last museum board meeting he dramatized for Teresa. "It included a discussion of Violet's will. No wonder I gave my performance that title. Do you think that had anything to do with Wendy's death? And the scrapbook was a red herring after all. I thought it might be. See ya!"

Janet left her copy of the scrapbook on the counter one afternoon and it disappeared. She was pretty sure Kyle was in the shop at the time.

Bethia assured the knitting competitors and the venues that the knitting competition would carry on. When she came to tell the women at the bookshop and tearoom, she also told them a story she'd been telling the knitters that they'd found amusing. On the night of the decluttering, when she'd been staying at Fairy Flax Hall, she'd asked Norman to try on the lilac jumper she was knitting for his sister. "How he managed it, I'll never know, but he got himself stuck half in and half out. He wiggled and he jigged. He turned in circles and I thought he might try a bit of a Highland fling, and in the middle of all that his phone rang. Och, I thought he'd be the death of me. I couldn't help him at all for laughing. But eventually we got the jumper all the way on, and it looked lovely."

Some weeks later, Edward stopped into the tearoom and told Christine he needed to follow up on something to bring closure to the night that started his current nightmare. Violet had given him a tiny watercolor with a note and asked him to give them to Helen for her birthday. But after the commotion of finding Wendy, he'd slipped the picture and the note into Helen's pocket instead. "I just wanted to be sure she found them."

Helen found the note when Christine called home to tell them. Helen's own nightmares had gradually faded away.

Rab found a buyer for the Mr. Potato Chef truck—a cousin in Orkney.

"Is it worth it?" Janet asked. "Getting it all the way there?"

"Price is right."

On a Monday evening at Nev's, James Haviland stopped by the women's table and told them that Maida was working on an entry for the McGonagall contest. "She's writing in the combined styles of McGonagall and John Gay, and if she can maintain the quality, she'll be the one to beat. She has the first two lines of it. She's calling it 'Dust Finds a Way.'"

30

Edward MacAskill carried his briefcase into Teresa's house. He'd told her he would take care of it for her while she was gone. If indeed she ever returned. He didn't think taking care of it meant he had to live there, though. He didn't quite think he could bear it. Certainly not Fairy Flax Hall either. After his mother's estate was settled, he planned to find something small of his own. All the rest should go to Isobel. Not that money could replace her mother or grandmother.

Edward sat at the partners desk in Teresa's study and set the briefcase on top. He opened the brass clasps and raised the lid. *Nice of Norman Hobbs to return it*, he thought, *and from the looks of it such ado over nothing much.* Still, one never knew where a good story might come from. He settled back comfortably and opened the scrapbook.

✎

Kyle Byrne sat at the scarred table in his bedsit. He took his knitted Loch Ness monster from a carrier bag and set it on the corner of the table. From another bag, he took a sheaf of A4 copier paper, set it on the table, and smoothed the top sheet. The cream color was an unexpected and thoughtful touch. He slid the table's drawer open, admired the lovely pair of Inversgail stockings the museum missed but surely didn't need, and took out a pen and leather journal. He slipped the elastic from around the journal and opened it to the ribbon bookmark. He put a hand on the sheaf of papers, imagined the warmth of a beating heart, and then with a flourish, clicked the pen open and wrote.

Arsenic diary, a fresh start
Hello, old girl.

ACKNOWLEDGMENTS

While writing this book, I've had so many adventures. First, I retired from my job in the children's department at the public library. What a fabulous job it was—because of the collections, the patrons, and the building, but most of all because of the staff. Every one of you works to give free access to information and to share the joy of books. Thank you for always taking an interest in *my* books and cheering me on.

Next, for two months, I took on the adventure of being Granny Nanny for our first grade and preschool grandsons during virtual schooling. What a blast! Michael and Emmanuel, you are the delight in my heart.

Then there was the adventure of having and getting over COVID-19 before vaccinations were widely available. It slowed me down for a few months, but I recovered fully, and feel very lucky. Thanks for everyone's good wishes during that time, and special thanks to Laura and Gordon for getting me back on my feet and back to the keyboard.

Lots more people helped this book along the way. James Haviland continues to let me use his name for a character of whom I've grown very fond. I hope you like the typewriters you scored at the decluttering,

James. Caroline Wickham-Jones and Guillermo Lopez gave me the perfect name for the food truck. Jennie and Bill Brockie weren't a gansey knitter and a fisherman, but in the mid-'70s, as chaplain, Bill welcomed students to Edinburgh University's Anglican Chaplaincy as warmly as Jennie welcomed students into their family. I have wonderful memories of Sunday tea at their house, playing ping-pong with their seven-year-old who beat me every time, and spending Christmas with them. Val and Mike Rogalla dreamed up a cocktail called the Cheerful Brush-off on their trip down the Seine a few years back, and they've let me borrow it. Linda Wessels sent the word sitooterie to me, knowing I would love it. Janice N. Harrington and Betsy Hearne, as good friends and first readers, make every piece of writing better. Becky Allen always offers the encouraging words, "Don't blow it!" Thank you, Becky. So far, so good.

This book wouldn't have gotten anywhere at all, though, without my agent, Cynthia Manson, or Claiborne Hancock and everyone else at Pegasus Crime. Especially not without Victoria Wenzel, the kind of editor every writer dreams of, and that I'm lucky enough to have.

Thanks, Ross, for general kitchen wizardry, and Cecily, for French toast. And, as always and forever, thanks to my Mike for everything.